U0005185

附英文原詩

米爾頓 John Milton——原著
劉怡君 改寫 陳彬彬——圖片解說

失樂園

新裝珍藏版

PARADISE LOST
BY JOHN MILTON

西方三大史詩之一
神、撒旦、亞當、夏娃、伊甸園的故事
通俗易讀的改寫&180張全彩名畫

好讀出版

CONTENTS

約翰・米爾頓簡介 4

關於本書 5

Chapter 1 > 撒旦的叛變 6

Chapter 2 > 地獄群魔會 39

Chapter 3 > 上帝的預言 71

Chapter 4 > 初探伊甸園 96

Chapter 5 > 天使的警示 128

Chapter 6 > 天庭的戰爭 153

Chapter 7 > 創造新世界 180

Chapter 8 > 人類的誕生 199

Chapter 9 > 人類的原罪 215

Chapter 10 > 上帝的懲罰 243

Chapter 11 > 人類的懺悔 271

Chapter 12 > 逐出伊甸園 295

約翰‧米爾頓簡介

約翰‧米爾頓（John Milton，1608—1674年）。出生於英國，因家庭富裕，故米爾頓從小接受一流的教育，他畢業於英國聖保羅學校和劍橋大學。六十多年的生涯中，以遊歷義大利、擔任政府秘書期間和晚年的失明對他影響最大。米爾頓的時代，正是保皇、和共和兩派爭鬥最嚴重的時代，他是個堅定的共和派，所以參加克倫威爾政府，與保皇派論戰，辯倒了當時歐洲最有聲望的大學者沙爾馬修，令世人震驚。

著名的作品有《寇瑪斯》（Comus，1634）、《失樂園》（Paradise Lost，1667）、《復樂園》（Paradise Regained，1671）、《參孫力士》（Samson Agonistes，1671）等等。

如果米爾頓沒有在二十幾年後寫出《失樂園》的話，或許他會被以克倫威爾政府的拉丁秘書和支持推翻君主建立軍事獨裁的辯護者的身份，在當時歷史時期佔一席之地。雖然後來米爾頓雙眼失明、政治失利，但依舊口述創作出《失樂園》、《復樂園》、《參孫力士》三部偉大的史詩。尤其是《失樂園》的成功使米爾頓成為史詩詩人中的巨人，並公認為是任何語言文學中最為宏偉的史詩。

關於本書

　　《失樂園》是十七世紀英國詩人米爾頓晚期三大詩作之一。內容敘述魔鬼撒旦發動天國叛變，被基督打落地獄；他為了要達成復仇的心願，無懼於艱險的路程，長途跋涉來到上帝創造的新世界，並潛入伊甸園中，誘惑人類的始祖亞當和夏娃犯下偷吃禁果的罪行。之後，人類被趕出伊甸園，除了要自行謀生，且必須以死亡和堅貞的信仰來求得救贖；而撒旦與其黨羽，不但報不了仇，且沉淪在更黑暗的深淵裡。

　　原書為十二卷、一萬多行的長篇敘事詩。但為引起讀者的閱讀興趣，本書改以小說的體裁表現，且為突顯故事張力、展現故事內容的緊湊，故省略了原詩部分華麗的詞藻、頌讚之辭和比喻。為了方便讀者閱讀，多將文中引自希臘羅馬神話故事和《聖經》的典故直接安排在故事中，減少以註解的方式呈現。

　　本書並於每頁附上《失樂園》原版英文全文，方便讀者在閱讀之際，可以一同領略原詩沉鬱頓挫之美。

撒旦的叛變

　　這是位於天界外，荒冥的混沌地帶，魔鬼撒旦與他的部眾們群集於此；原本尊貴的天使身分，因一次叛變而喪失。現在，他們已成爲罪與惡的化身，在撒旦的領導下，於烈焰沖天的地獄建立起惡魔之殿 —— 潘地曼尼南。

天界外的混沌之地,烈焰沖天,硫磺氣味瀰漫在灰濛濛的空氣中,悶熱的旋風夾帶濃重的燥熱與不安,席捲著這座宛若巨大熔爐的地獄;觸目所見,除了嶙峋的岩石與四處蔓延的火苗之外,一無他物。

< 撒旦與叛亂天使往地獄墜落
杜雷 版畫 1866年

撒旦率領八等天使撒拉弗大軍反叛上帝,卻不敵天使長米迦勒率領的天神大軍,從此被逐出天國,墜落到地獄的深淵。原本光明聖潔的天使,如今狼狽地墜落,身體互相堆疊,一個個躺在火湖之中。

Of Mans First Disobedience, and the Fruit
Of that Forbidden Tree, whose mortal tast
Brought Death into the World, and all our woe,
With loss of Eden, till one greater Man
Restore us, and regain the blissful Seat, [5]
Sing Heav'nly Muse,that on the secret top
Of Oreb, or of Sinai, didst inspire
That Shepherd, who first taught the chosen Seed,
In the Beginning how the Heav'ns and Earth
Rose out of Chaos: Or if Sion Hill [10]
Delight thee more, and Siloa's Brook that flow'd
Fast by the Oracle of God; I thence
Invoke thy aid to my adventrous Song,

∨ 叛亂天使的墜落
老布勒爾哲 油畫 1562年

這場天使之間的大戰原出自新約聖經的《啟世錄》,透過米爾頓在《失樂園》中的描述,讓整個故事更完整生動了。

這是正義的全能之神為反叛者準備的牢籠，要讓他們的不死之身，被金鋼鎖鏈銬在永不熄滅的刑火中九天九夜，做為叛變的懲罰。

一陣巨痛，撒旦從浩渺無涯的火海中醒來。黯紅似血的天幕與四周可怕的景象，一遍遍衝擊著他高傲的自尊，

「這地方和靜穆光明的天庭是多麼的不同啊！」悲憤的情緒籠罩著他，讓他忘卻身體的痛苦和戰爭的挫敗。「我要報仇！我一定要報仇！」撒旦心中不斷地吶喊著。

他以一雙傲然的復仇之眼環視四周。看見他最親密的部屬 —— 鬼王別西卜正躺臥在附近。

「別西卜，」撒旦以豪壯的聲音喚醒夥伴，「快起來吧！別再沉溺於懊惱的深淵，復仇的大業正等著我們去完成呢！」

撒旦接著說道：

「我倆曾經住在光明的淨土，那兒

That with no middle flight intends to soar
Above th' Aonian Mount, while it pursues [15]
Things unattempted yet in Prose or Rhime.
And chiefly Thou O Spirit, that dost prefer
Before all Temples th' upright heart and pure,
Instruct me, for Thou know'st; Thou from the first
Wast present, and with mighty wings outspread [20]
Dove-like satst brooding on the vast Abyss
And mad'st it pregnant: What in me is dark
Illumin, what is low raise and support;
That to the highth of this great Argument
I may assert Eternal Providence, [25]
And justifie the wayes of God to men.

Say first, for Heav'n hides nothing from thy view
Nor the deep Tract of Hell, say first what cause
Mov'd our Grand Parents in that happy State,
Favour'd of Heav'n so highly, to fall off [30]
From thir Creator, and transgress his Will
For one restraint, Lords of the World besides?
Who first seduc'd them to that foul revolt?
Th' infernal Serpent; he it was, whose guile
Stird up with Envy and Revenge, deceiv'd [35]
The Mother of Mankind, what time his Pride
Had cast him out from Heav'n, with all his Host
Of Rebel Angels, by whose aid aspiring
To set himself in Glory above his Peers,
He trusted to have equal'd the most High, [40]
If he oppos'd; and with ambitious aim
Against the Throne and Monarchy of God
Rais'd impious War in Heav'n and Battel proud
With vain attempt. Him the Almighty Power
Hurld headlong flaming from th' Ethereal Skie [45]
With hideous ruine and combustion down
To bottomless perdition, there to dwell
In Adamantine Chains and penal Fire,
Who durst defie th' Omnipotent to Arms.
Nine times the Space that measures Day and Night [50]
To mortal men, he with his horrid crew
Lay vanquisht, rowling in the fiery Gulfe
Confounded though immortal: But his doom
Reserv'd him to more wrath; for now the thought

燦爛如星，光芒四射。你我結成同盟共赴劫難，懷著同樣的希望欲成就偉大事業，共享榮光。

「如今，卻從高高的天庭墜入悲慘的深淵。天神施以威力凶狠的雷霆，對我們展現祂的強大；但這威嚇嚇不了我，也不能讓我改變初衷。

▽ 路西法
希土克 油畫 1890年

　　路西法原意是「光之使者」，是眾天使最美麗的一位，卻因為過度驕傲自負，發起戰爭想和上帝較量高低，不料戰敗被逐出天庭，經過九個晨昏的墜落，最後落入地獄而變成魔鬼撒旦。

Both of lost happiness and lasting pain [55]
Torments him; round he throws his baleful eyes
That witness'd huge affliction and dismay
Mixt with obdurate pride and stedfast hate:
At once as far as Angels kenn he views
The dismal Situation waste and wilde, [60]
A Dungeon horrible, on all sides round
As one great Furnace flam'd, yet from those flames
No light, but rather darkness visible
Serv'd onely to discover sights of woe,
Regions of sorrow, doleful shades, where peace [65]
And rest can never dwell, hope never comes
That comes to all; but torture without end
Still urges, and a fiery Deluge, fed
With ever-burning Sulphur unconsum'd:
Such place Eternal Justice had prepar'd [70]
For those rebellious, here thir Prison ordain'd
In utter darkness, and thir portion set
As far remov'd from God and light of Heav'n
As from the Center thrice to th' utmost Pole.
O how unlike the place from whence they fell! [75]
There the companions of his fall, o'rewhelm'd
With Floods and Whirlwinds of tempestuous fire,
He soon discerns, and weltring by his side
One next himself in power, and next in crime,
Long after known in Palestine, and nam'd [80]
Beelzebub. To whom th' Arch-Enemy,
And thence in Heav'n call'd Satan, with bold words
Breaking the horrid silence thus began.

If thou beest he; But O how fall'n! how chang'd
From him, who in the happy Realms of Light [85]
Cloth'd with transcendent brightness didst out-shine
Myriads though bright: If he Whom mutual league,
United thoughts and counsels, equal hope
And hazard in the Glorious Enterprize,
Joynd with me once, now misery hath joynd [90]
In equal ruin: into what Pit thou seest
From what highth fall'n, so much the stronger prov'd
He with his Thunder: and till then who knew
The force of those dire Arms? yet not for those,
Nor what the Potent Victor in his rage [95]

「我的外表雖被雷霆擊傷，已無昔日的光彩，但意志卻更加堅強，絕不彎腰屈膝，乞求祂的憐憫。我要再次號召大軍，準備威力更強的武器，以不滅的復仇之心與祂力拼。瞧！祂現在正得意洋洋，於天庭誇耀勝利呢！」

別西卜聽見撒旦的呼喚，用力扯著盤繞在身上的金鋼鎖鏈，掙扎著想從火燄中爬起，沒想到鎖鍊卻越纏越緊。他絕望地對撒旦說：

「啊！大王，掌管權勢的首領呀，英勇的八等天使撒拉弗（Seraphim）大軍[1]，在您的指揮下與天神大軍作戰。

「這令天庭震驚的偉大行動，原是要使天上至尊陷於危難，但卻反而遭到懲罰。在祂的神力下，全數大軍盡皆覆滅，墜入無底的深淵。這證明了祂至高無上的地位，是無人可以取代的。

「我們原本的光輝已經喪失，天使

Can else inflict, do I repent or change,
Though chang'd in outward lustre; that fixt mind
And high disdain, from sence of injur'd merit,
That with the mightiest rais'd me to contend,
And to the fierce contention brought along [100]
Innumerable force of Spirits arm'd
That durst dislike his reign, and me preferring,
His utmost power with adverse power oppos'd
In dubious Battel on the Plains of Heav'n,
And shook his throne. What though the field be lost? [105]
All is not lost; the unconquerable Will,
And study of revenge, immortal hate,
And courage never to submit or yield:
And what is else not to be overcome?
That Glory never shall his wrath or might [110]
Extort from me. To bow and sue for grace
With suppliant knee, and deifie his power,
Who from the terrour of this Arm so late
Doubted his Empire, that were low indeed,
That were an ignominy and shame beneath [115]
This downfall; since by Fate the strength of Gods
And this Empyreal substance cannot fail,
Since through experience of this great event
In Arms not worse, in foresight much advanc't,
We may with more successful hope resolve [120]
To wage by force or guile eternal Warr
Irreconcileable, to our grand Foe,
Who now triumphs, and in th' excess of joy
Sole reigning holds the Tyranny of Heav'n.

註1：羅馬教皇格雷高里一世（Gregory I）將天上的天使分成九種等級：一、天使（Angels），二、天使長（Archangels），三、德性（Virtues），四、權勢（Powers），五、王國（Principalities），六、治權（Dominations），七、寶座（Thrones），八、撒拉弗（Seraphim），九、基路伯（Cherubim）。

身分也被剝奪，再也無法回到天堂享受快樂與榮光；現在伴隨我們身邊的，只剩下深沉的悲哀。

「天上的征服者讓我們保有生命，只不過是為了讓我們的軀體在這蠻荒陰暗的地府，一遍遍遭受無情烈焰的折磨罷了。」

「真是可悲呀！別西卜，」撒旦喝斥一聲，雙眼斜睨著別西卜說道，「示弱是可悲的，無論做任何事或遭受何種苦難皆然。我們之所以違抗天神的意旨，乃是因為我們擁有邪惡的本質，行善絕非我們的本分，做惡才能為我們帶來快樂；天神企圖引導我們往善的路上行去，我們就應該違背祂的意志，於路途中偏離，尋求惡的途徑才是。」

撒旦伸手揮向別西卜，幫他扯去身上的鎖鍊，接著說道：

「你看，憤怒的勝利者已經把復仇使者召回天門，暴風雨般猛烈擊打我們的硫磺霰彈趨於平緩，雷霆不再發

⋀ 撒旦遊說別西卜
杜雷 版畫 1866年

　　別西卜的地位僅次於撒旦，堪稱地獄王國的宰相。由於他有統領眾鬼的權力，所以又稱為「鬼王」。

So spake th' Apostate Angel, though in pain, [125]
Vaunting aloud, but rackt with deep despare:
And him thus answer'd soon his bold Compeer.

O Prince, O Chief of many Throned Powers,
That led th' imbattelld Seraphim to Warr
Under thy conduct, and in dreadful deeds [130]
Fearless, endanger'd Heav'ns perpetual King;
And put to proof his high Supremacy,
Whether upheld by strength, or Chance, or Fate,
Too well I see and rue the dire event,
That with sad overthrow and foul defeat [135]

射，火燄的波濤也平靜不少。這表示
什麼呢？

「或許是仇敵輕蔑我們，抑或放鬆
了警戒；不管如何，這正宣告著我們
機會的到來。

「快點站起來，跟隨我離開這炎熱
的火湖，往前方那片杳無人跡的荒原
上去，在那裡休息一下，想想未來該
如何。

「希望能獲得外來的援助，若不
行，我們自己也該設法振作起來，想
辦法解決眼前的困境才是。」

撒旦說著此話的同時，他的頭已從
火湖中抬起，躍出洪濤烈燄；他的雙
眼散發著炯炯光芒，巨大的軀體浮臥
在火浪上面，宛如神話中的巨人泰坦
族（Titans）²、又像百手怪物布里
亞洛斯（Briarios）³或百頭巨蛇泰風
（Typhon）⁴；或者，用海怪列未坦
（Leiviathan）來形容會更加貼切。列
未坦居住在深海中，體形似鯨魚，皮
膚有鱗片，是海洋中最龐大的怪獸；

Hath lost us Heav'n, and all this mighty Host
In horrible destruction laid thus low,
As far as Gods and Heav'nly Essences
Can perish: for the mind and spirit remains
Invincible, and vigour soon returns, [140]
Though all our Glory extinct, and happy state
Here swallow'd up in endless misery.
But what if he our Conquerour, (whom I now
Of force believe Almighty, since no less
Then such could hav orepow'rd such force as ours) [145]
Have left us this our spirit and strength intire
Strongly to suffer and support our pains,
That we may so suffice his vengeful ire,
Or do him mightier service as his thralls
By right of Warr, what e're his business be [150]
Here in the heart of Hell to work in Fire,
Or do his Errands in the gloomy Deep;
What can it then avail though yet we feel
Strength undiminisht, or eternal being
To undergo eternal punishment? [155]
Whereto with speedy words th' Arch-fiend reply'd.

Fall'n Cherube, to be weak is miserable
Doing or Suffering: but of this be sure,
To do ought good never will be our task,
But ever to do ill our sole delight, [160]
As being the contrary to his high will
Whom we resist. If then his Providence
Out of our evil seek to bring forth good,
Our labour must be to pervert that end,
And out of good still to find means of evil; [165]
Which oft times may succeed, so as perhaps

註2：泰坦族（Titans），希臘羅馬神話中的
　　　巨人族，天和地的兒女；體型碩大，
　　　力量奇大無比。
註3：布里亞洛斯（Briarios），希臘羅馬神
　　　話中，幫助宙斯與泰坦族作戰的百手
　　　怪物，有一百隻手和五十個頭。
註4：泰風（Typhon），嘴巴會噴火的百頭
　　　怪物，為地母所生之泰坦族後裔。

常有迷途的小舟於挪威海面遇見牠，由於牠體形巨大又靜止不動，所以船員們誤以為牠是海中島嶼，便把船錨拋擲在牠的鱗片上停泊，靜待黎明的到來。

　　一會兒，撒旦撐起碩大的身軀，從火湖中站立起來；他揮手拂去身上的火苗，並擺動身體掙脫束縛；在他身旁的火燄往四面濺散，瞬間捲成兩條巨浪，形成一個中空的溪谷。

　　撒旦張開翅膀，腳尖一蹬，瞬間凌上高空，往陸地的方向飛去；地府凝濁的空氣，彷彿更加沉重了。他一直飛到乾燥的陸地才停下來，降落到地面上。

　　這片乾燥的陸地，同樣受著烈火的燻烤，焦黑的顏色，如同西西里島東北角被旋風狂刮掉一座山峰的皮洛盧斯山；或像艾特那火山被雷電擊成鋸齒狀的斜坡，從火山底噴發出來的熔岩，隨著風勢，所到之處盡成一片焦土，瀰漫著惡臭和火燄。

Shall grieve him, if I fail not, and disturb
His inmost counsels from thir destind aim.
But see the angry Victor hath recall'd
His Ministers of vengeance and pursuit [170]
Back to the Gates of Heav'n: The Sulphurous Hail
Shot after us in storm, oreblown hath laid
The fiery Surge, that from the Precipice
Of Heav'n receiv'd us falling, and the Thunder,
Wing'd with red Lightning and impetuous rage, [175]
Perhaps hath spent his shafts, and ceases now
To bellow through the vast and boundless Deep.
Let us not slip th' occasion, whether scorn,
Or satiate fury yield it from our Foe.
Seest thou yon dreary Plain, forlorn and wilde, [180]
The seat of desolation, voyd of light,
Save what the glimmering of these livid flames

∧　撒旦
佛雪 青銅雕像 1834年

撒旦與隨後而來的別西卜停歇的陸
地，正像熔岩燒灼過的焦土。

撒旦得意洋洋，轉頭對別西卜說：

「你瞧！我們這不是逃離了地獄的
火燄嗎？這證明我倆的本領高強，氣
力也已經恢復如先前一般。

「只可惜，我們耗盡心力，以光明
幸福的天堂換來的地方，竟如此悽慘
幽暗、令人沮喪。

「罷了，就讓自鳴得意的勝利者去
統治天庭吧！誰叫我們雖有跟祂相當
的智慧，能力卻輸給祂呢？我相信，
只要保持一顆堅定不屈的心，地獄也
就如同天堂。況且，成為地獄的主
宰，遠勝淪為天堂的奴隸。

「目前首要之務，是前去喚醒蜷伏
在火湖中的伙伴們，安定他們驚慌恐
懼的心，與我們共享冥府的歡樂；並
靜待機會的來臨再度興兵作亂，試試
天庭有多少東西可以收復。」

別西卜答道：

「戰士們被全能上帝的雷霆轟擊，

Casts pale and dreadful? Thither let us tend
From off the tossing of these fiery waves,
There rest, if any rest can harbour there, [185]
And reassembling our afflicted Powers,
Consult how we may henceforth most offend
Our Enemy, our own loss how repair,
How overcome this dire Calamity,
What reinforcement we may gain from Hope, [190]
If not what resolution from despare.

Thus Satan talking to his neerest Mate
With Head up-lift above the wave, and Eyes
That sparkling blaz'd, his other Parts besides
Prone on the Flood, extended long and large [195]
Lay floating many a rood, in bulk as huge
As whom the Fables name of monstrous size,
Titanian, or Earth-born, that warr'd on Jove,
Briareos or Typhon, whom the Den
By ancient Tarsus held, or that Sea-beast [200]
Leviathan, which God of all his works
Created hugest that swim th' Ocean stream:
Him haply slumbring on the Norway foam
The Pilot of some small night-founder'd Skiff,
Deeming some Island, oft, as Sea-men tell, [205]
With fixed Anchor in his skaly rind
Moors by his side under the Lee, while Night
Invests the Sea, and wished Morn delayes:
So stretcht out huge in length the Arch-fiend lay
Chain'd on the burning Lake, nor ever thence [210]
Had ris'n or heav'd his head, but that the will
And high permission of all-ruling Heaven
Left him at large to his own dark designs,
That with reiterated crimes he might
Heap on himself damnation, while he sought [215]
Evil to others, and enrag'd might see
How all his malice serv'd but to bring forth
Infinite goodness, grace and mercy shewn
On Man by him seduc't, but on himself
Treble confusion, wrath and vengeance pour'd. [220]
Forthwith upright he rears from off the Pool
His mighty Stature; on each hand the flames
Drivn backward slope thir pointing spires, and rowld

從高聳的天庭摔落地府，現在，他們四處橫陳，全身埋臥於火湖中，遭受烈燄的燒灼，內心滿佈著深層的恐懼。

「此刻，唯有您可以讓他們鼓起勇氣、恢復信心，因為您曾經英勇地在戰場上領導他們，與天神大軍展開激戰；因此，他們一聽見您的聲音，定能振奮精神，重新振作起來。」

別西卜的話才剛說完，魔鬼撒旦便朝著火湖走去；他背著那頂在天庭鑄造的圓形盾牌，龐大、厚重，如同十七世紀義大利科學家伽俐略（Galileo）用自己創造的望遠鏡，於黃昏時分，在飛索爾山頂（Fiesole）或瓦達諾山谷（Vadarno）探視到的天空裡新的星球 —— 月亮。撒旦披掛在身邊的盾牌，正如將一輪明月掛在身上。

從盛產松樹的挪威山群，砍伐其中最高的一棵松木，其長度已經可以用作軍鑑桅杆，但拿來跟撒旦手中的長

In billows, leave i'th' midst a horrid Vale.
Then with expanded wings he stears his flight [225]
Aloft, incumbent on the dusky Air
That felt unusual weight, till on dry Land
He lights, if it were Land that ever burn'd
With solid, as the Lake with liquid fire;
And such appear'd in hue, as when the force [230]
Of subterranean wind transports a Hill
Torn from Pelorus, or the shatter'd side
Of thundring Ætna, whose combustible
And fewel'd entrals thence conceiving Fire,
Sublim'd with Mineral fury, aid the Winds, [235]
And leave a singed bottom all involv'd
With stench and smoak: Such resting found the sole
Of unblest feet.   Him followed his next Mate,
Both glorying to have scap't the Stygian flood
As Gods, and by thir own recover'd strength, [240]
Not by the sufferance of supernal Power.

Is this the Region, this the Soil, the Clime,
Said then the lost Arch-Angel, this the seat
That we must change for Heav'n, this mournful gloom
For that celestial light? Be it so, since he [245]
Who now is Sovran can dispose and bid
What shall be right: fardest from him is best
Whom reason hath equald, force hath made supream
Above his equals. Farewel happy Fields
Where Joy for ever dwells: Hail horrours, hail [250]
Infernal world, and thou profoundest Hell
Receive thy new Possessor: One who brings
A mind not to be chang'd by Place or Time.
The mind is its own place, and in it self
Can make a Heav'n of Hell, a Hell of Heav'n. [255]
What matter where, if I be still the same,
And what I should be, all but less then he
Whom Thunder hath made greater? Here at least
We shall be free; th' Almighty hath not built
Here for his envy, will not drive us hence: [260]
Here we may reign secure, and in my choyce
To reign is worth ambition though in Hell:
Better to reign in Hell, then serve in Heav'n.
But wherefore let we then our faithful friends,

矛一比，就變得像一根小棍子了。撒
旦把長矛充作拐杖，忍受著地面焦土
的灼熱，一步步邁開沉重的步伐來到
火湖岸邊。

　　如何來描述這群潰敗的撒旦大軍
呢？他們的身體互相堆疊，一個個躺
臥在火湖中；稠密得像義大利佛羅倫
斯伐隆布洛紗山谷（Valombrosa）裡
秋天的落葉，綿綿密密地鋪滿溪邊的
石子，那溪谷的兩岸，古木參天、林
蔭茂密。

　　他們隨火浪漂浮的模樣，又像紅

Th' associates and copartners of our loss [265]
Lye thus astonisht on th' oblivious Pool,
And call them not to share with us their part
In this unhappy Mansion, or once more
With rallied Arms to try what may be yet
Regaind in Heav'n, or what more lost in Hell? [270]

So Satan spake, and him Beelzebub
Thus answer'd. Leader of those Armies bright,
Which but th' Omnipotent none could have foyld,
If once they hear that voyce, thir liveliest pledge
Of hope in fears and dangers, heard so oft [275]
In worst extreams, and on the perilous edge
Of battel when it rag'd, in all assaults
Thir surest signal, they will soon resume
New courage and revive, though now they lye
Groveling and prostrate on yon Lake of Fire, [280]
As we erewhile, astounded and amaz'd,
No wonder, fall'n such a pernicious highth.

He scarce had ceas't when the superiour Fiend
Was moving toward the shoar; his ponderous shield
Ethereal temper, massy, large and round, [285]
Behind him cast; the broad circumference
Hung on his shoulders like the Moon, whose Orb
Through Optic Glass the Tuscan Artist views
At Ev'ning from the top of Fesole,
Or in Valdarno, to descry new Lands, [290]
Rivers or Mountains in her spotty Globe.

≺ 路西法
威廉葛夫 大理石雕像 1848年
比利時列日 聖保羅大教堂
　　此尊白色大理石雕像是比利時雕塑家
威廉葛夫的作品。原先教堂擺放的是弟弟
約瑟夫的作品，卻因為那個撒旦雕像太過
「崇高美麗」，因此被教堂撤掉，改由哥
哥另外製作了這尊雕像。威廉加了很多細
節，例如沉重的腳鐐、咬了一口的蘋果和
斷裂的權杖，突顯雕像確實是惡魔撒旦，
不會再讓人混淆了。

»» 撒旦喚醒他的部屬
杜雷 版畫 1866年

惨敗的撒旦大軍原本委頓在地，經過撒旦的「精神喊話」，終於振翅飛離火湖，追隨撒旦而去。

海巨浪上的藻類，受到奧利安星宿（Orion）所帶來暴風的影響，遭受猛烈襲擊、隨海浪拍打著海岸。

或者，《舊約・出埃及記》[5]更能清楚的描繪他們此刻的樣子。食言的法老王率領埃及大軍前去追趕以色列人，士兵們在越過紅海時，全部被席捲而下的海浪高牆淹沒，漂浮在海面的埃及大軍屍體和殘破的馬車車輪，就跟眼前的撒旦軍一模一樣。

撒旦見到眼前的慘況，不禁黯然神傷。他停步在火湖岸邊，發出低沉而憤怒的吼聲，其怒嚎迴盪於陰鬱炎熱的地府，驚醒浮臥於火浪中的戰士們。

「你們是怎麼啦？只因為一次挫

註5：《舊約・出埃及記》中記載，耶和華指示摩西將以色列人領出埃及，並顯現「使杖變作蛇」、「水變血之災」、「蛙災」、「虱災」、「蠅災」、「畜疫之災」、「瘡災」、「雹災」、「蝗災」、「黑暗之災」等眾多神蹟，來讓埃及法老知道耶和華的存在。最後，在耶和華把埃及地上所有的長子及一切頭胎牲畜，盡都殺了之後，法老才答應讓摩西帶走以色列人。但事後法老後悔了，率兵追趕至紅海邊。摩西向海伸杖，水便分開，成為乾地。以色列人下海中走乾地，水在他們的左右作了牆垣。埃及人追趕他們，所有的馬匹、車輛和埃及士兵下到海中時，摩西又伸杖讓海水合了起來，使追兵的車輛和兵馬，全部淹沒在海水中。

敗，就讓原本的天國精英一蹶不振，頹唐地傾倒在火湖中？天庭本是屬於我們的，只要稍事休息，等恢復力量之後，咱們即可重整旗鼓，奪回天庭。

「但現在，你們卻像鬥敗的公雞一樣，垂頭喪氣、向敵人屈服；你們以為謙恭地向敵人豎起白旗，他們就會放過我們嗎？快別天真了，你瞧，他們正在天上疾馳，遙遙的監視我們，準備隨時再降下雷電，把我們擊打至

His Spear, to equal which the tallest Pine
Hewn on Norwegian hills, to be the Mast
Of some great Ammiral, were but a wand,
He walkt with to support uneasie steps [295]
Over the burning Marle, not like those steps
On Heavens Azure, and the torrid Clime
Smote on him sore besides, vaulted with Fire;
Nathless he so endur'd, till on the Beach
Of that inflamed Sea, he stood and call'd [300]
His Legions, Angel Forms, who lay intrans't
Thick as Autumnal Leaves that strow the Brooks
In Vallombrosa, where th' Etrurian shades
High overarch't imbowr; or scatterd sedge
Afloat, when with fierce Winds Orion arm'd [305]
Hath vext the Red-Sea Coast, whose waves orethrew
Busiris and his Memphian Chivalry,
While with perfidious hatred they pursu'd
The Sojourners of Goshen, who beheld
From the safe shore thir floating Carkases [310]
And broken Chariot Wheels, so thick bestrown
Abject and lost lay these, covering the Flood,
Under amazement of thir hideous change.
He call'd so loud, that all the hollow Deep
Of Hell resounded. Princes, Potentates, [315]
Warriers, the Flowr of Heav'n, once yours, now lost,
If such astonishment as this can sieze
Eternal spirits; or have ye chos'n this place
After the toyl of Battel to repose
Your wearied vertue, for the ease you find [320]
To slumber here, as in the Vales of Heav'n?
Or in this abject posture have ye sworn
To adore the Conquerour? who now beholds
Cherube and Seraph rowling in the Flood

≪ 墜落天使
貝維 青銅雕像 1877年
西班牙馬德里 麗池公園

　　這座雕像是西班牙雕塑家貝維最著名的作品，他從米爾頓的《失樂園》得到啟發，完成這座充滿戲劇張力的雕像，呈現天使自天堂墜落後的痛苦與懊悔。

>> 撒旦喚醒他的部屬
布雷克 水彩 1807年

　　英國畫家布雷克相當喜愛米爾頓的詩作，向來不喜歡油畫的他，曾經以水彩和蛋彩繪製一系列的《失樂園》畫作。布雷克本身也是浪漫派詩人，他的畫作自然多了一些詩意的想像。圖中的撒旦宛如《失樂園》裡真正的英雄，當撒旦登高一呼，墜落的天使紛紛仰頭，露出敬畏的神情。

地獄的最深淵。

　　「英勇的戰士們，快快振作起來，否則便會永遠地沉淪了。」

　　四處橫陳的叛軍們聽見撒旦嚴厲的呼喚，全都感到萬分羞愧；如同站崗時打盹被長官抓到的士兵，猛然從睡意朦朧中驚醒。他們振起羽翅、紛紛飛離火湖，緊緊地跟隨在撒旦後頭；人數之多，宛如一道黑幕，密密麻麻地遮蔽了地獄的上空。

　　那壯觀的景象，有如摩西受耶和華指示，在埃及降下蝗災[6]；摩西向埃及地伸杖，那一晝一夜，耶和華使東風颳在埃及地上。到了早晨，蝗蟲被東風颳來了，落在埃及四境，傾刻

註6：出自《舊約‧出埃及記》，請參照註5。

With scatter'd Arms and Ensigns, till anon [325]
His swift pursuers from Heav'n Gates discern
Th' advantage, and descending tread us down
Thus drooping, or with linked Thunderbolts
Transfix us to the bottom of this Gulfe.
Awake, arise, or be for ever fall'n. [330]

They heard, and were abasht, and up they sprung
Upon the wing, as when men wont to watch
On duty, sleeping found by whom they dread,
Rouse and bestir themselves ere well awake.
Nor did they not perceave the evil plight [335]
In which they were, or the fierce pains not feel;
Yet to thir Generals Voyce they soon obeyd
Innumerable. As when the potent Rod
Of Amrams Son in Egypts evill day
Wav'd round the Coast, up call'd a pitchy cloud [340]
Of Locusts, warping on the Eastern Wind,
That ore the Realm of impious Pharaoh hung
Like Night, and darken'd all the Land of Nile:
So numberless were those bad Angels seen
Hovering on wing under the Cope of Hell [345]
'Twixt upper, nether, and surrounding Fires;
Till, as a signal giv'n, th' uplifted Spear

>> **撒旦引領叛軍飛離火湖**
杜雷 版畫 1866年

數不清的墜落天使飛離火湖，密密麻麻遮蔽了地獄的上空，如此聲勢驚人的撒旦大軍，宛如可怕的蝗災。

間，尼羅河流域宛若惡夜降臨；牠們佈滿地面，吃地上的一切菜蔬和樹上的果子。埃及遍地，連一點綠色的植物都沒留下來。

此時，數量眾多的撒旦軍就如同遍佈埃及地面的蝗蟲一般。他們在火湖的上方盤旋飛舞，於火燄之頂左右跳躍；隨即，於撒旦長矛的指揮下，身手矯健地降落於狹窄的硫磺焦地上，一時間，地面便顯得擁擠不堪。

他們擠滿每一寸焦土，就連西元五世紀時，像洪水一般入侵羅馬的蠻族汪達爾人（Vandals）軍隊[7]，也比不上這群魔鬼大軍稠密。

軍隊的各路指揮，從隸屬於自己的行伍中走出來，急急地奔向他們的大

Of thir great Sultan waving to direct
Thir course, in even ballance down they light
On the firm brimstone, and fill all the Plain; [350]
A multitude, like which the populous North
Pour'd never from her frozen loyns, to pass
Rhene or the Danaw, when her barbarous Sons
Came like a Deluge on the South, and spread
Beneath Gibralter to the Lybian sands. [355]
Forthwith from every Squadron and each Band
The Heads and Leaders thither hast where stood

註7：汪達爾人，曾經入侵羅馬的北方蠻夷部落。於西元五世紀前葉進攻高盧、西班牙、非洲北部等地方。

首領撒旦；他們一個個英姿煥發，氣宇軒昂，原本都是天庭裡佔有一席之地的天使，如今卻因參與叛變，被上帝從生命冊中永遠的除名，扔進火湖裡[8]。

直到天神為了試探人心，默許諸魔到人間遊蕩；他們便趁此機會脫離地獄苦海。從此，撒旦的黨羽們遍佈世界各地，他們使出各種詭計，用荒謬的言語欺騙世人，使他們背棄上帝，且化成各種獸類形象，裝飾得金碧輝煌，接受世人的膜拜。

這其中，最早出現的偽神是亞捫人崇拜的火神摩洛（Moloch）。亞捫人用黃銅鑄成牛頭人身的火神像，舉行火神祭典時，做為祭品的小孩被放在神像的手中，接著亞捫人開始用力擊鼓，試圖以振耳欲聾的鼓聲來掩蓋小孩和親人的哭泣聲；最後，帶著眼淚的小孩們被摔落於神像下方的火盆中燒死，當做對神的獻祭。[9]

摩洛不僅在亞捫人的京城拉巴

Thir great Commander; Godlike shapes and forms
Excelling human, Princely Dignities,
And Powers that earst in Heaven sat on Thrones; [360]
Though of thir Names in heav'nly Records now
Be no memorial blotted out and ras'd
By thir Rebellion, from the Books of Life.
Nor had they yet among the Sons of Eve
Got them new Names, till wandring ore the Earth, [365]
Through Gods high sufferance for the tryal of man,
By falsities and lyes the greatest part
Of Mankind they corrupted to forsake
God thir Creator, and th' invisible
Glory of him that made them, to transform [370]
Oft to the Image of a Brute, adorn'd
With gay Religions full of Pomp and Gold,
And Devils to adore for Deities:
Then were they known to men by various Names,
And various Idols through the Heathen World. [375]
Say, Muse, thir Names then known, who first, who last,
Rous'd from the slumber, on that fiery Couch,
At thir great Emperors call, as next in worth
Came singly where he stood on the bare strand,
While the promiscuous croud stood yet aloof? [380]
The chief were those who from the Pit of Hell
Roaming to seek thir prey on earth, durst fix
Thir Seats long after next the Seat of God,
Thir Altars by his Altar, Gods ador'd
Among the Nations round, and durst abide [385]
Jehovah thundring out of Sion, thron'd

註8：出自《新約·啟示錄》，「……案卷展開了，並且另有一卷展開，就是生命冊。死了的人都憑著這些案卷所記載的，照他們所行的受審判。……死亡和陰間也被扔在火湖裡，這火湖就是第二次的死。若有人名字沒記在生命冊上，他就被扔在火湖裡。」

註9：《舊約·申命記》，「……因為他們向他們的神行了耶和華所憎嫌所恨惡的一切事，甚至將自己的兒女用火焚燒，獻與他們的神。」

（Rabba）接受血的供奉，其影響力也遠及約旦河東邊的亞珥歌伯（Argob）和巴珊（Basan），甚至到達亞押南端的亞嫩河流域（Arnon）。

就連以色列人的第三任王──所羅門，也曾經供奉過火神。天神賜與所羅門王極大的智慧、聰明和寬廣的心，使他的名聲傳揚於四周列國；他曾作箴言三千句、詩歌一千零五首，並能向人講論草木、飛禽走獸、昆蟲魚蟹等知識。

所羅門王的智慧勝過萬人，但卻在晚年的時候受到嬪妃的誘惑，於耶路撒冷對面的山上建築摩洛的神廟，褻瀆了真神的聖殿[10]。他又把耶路撒冷西南方的欣嫩子山谷（Hinnom）封鎖起來，做為摩洛的聖山[11]；祭祀火神時必需擊鼓，因此，當地日後便有了陀斐特（Topher）和格痕拿（Gehenna）的名稱。陀斐特有「鼓」的意思，而格痕拿則是「黑暗

Between the Cherubim; yea, often plac'd
Within his Sanctuary it self thir Shrines,
Abominations; and with cursed things
His holy Rites, and solemn Feasts profan'd, [390]
And with thir darkness durst affront his light.
First Moloch, horrid King besmear'd with blood
Of human sacrifice, and parents tears,
Though for the noyse of Drums and Timbrels loud
Thir childrens cries unheard, that past through fire [395]
To his grim Idol. Him the Ammonite
Worshipt in Rabba and her watry Plain,
In Argob and in Basan, to the stream
Of utmost Arnon. Nor content with such
Audacious neighbourhood, the wisest heart [400]
Of Solomon he led by fraud to build
His Temple right against the Temple of God
On that opprobrious Hill, and made his Grove
The pleasant Vally of Hinnom, Tophet thence
And black Gehenna call'd, the Type of Hell. [405]
Next Chemos, th' obscene dread of Moabs Sons,
From Aroar to Nebo, and the wild
Of Southmost Abarim; in Hesebon
And Horonaim, Seons Realm, beyond
The flowry Dale of Sibma clad with Vines, [410]
And Eleale to th' Asphaltick Pool.
Peor his other Name, when he entic'd
Israel in Sittim on thir march from Nile
To do him wanton rites, which cost them woe.

註10：《舊約·列王記上》，「所羅門王年老的時候，他的嬪妃誘惑他的心去隨從別神，……所羅門隨從西頓人的女神亞斯他錄和亞押人可憎的神米勒公。……為摩押可憎的神基抹和亞押人可憎的神摩洛，在耶路撒冷對面的山上建築邱壇。」

註11：《舊約·列王記下》，「但是邱壇的祭司不登耶路撒冷耶和華的壇，只在他們弟兄中間吃無酵餅。又污穢欣嫩子谷的陀斐特，不許人在那裡把兒女經火獻給摩洛；……」

∧ 所羅門祭拜維納斯神像
巴爾東 油畫 1520年

　　智慧過人的所羅門王，晚年迎娶各國公主當嬪妃，自然也接納了她們的信仰，為了討美人歡心，甚至還幫她們建造自己的小神廟，這或許表示所羅門王思想開放，能兼容不同的信仰，但是以基督教的觀點來看，崇拜偶像簡直是褻瀆上帝，是邪魔歪道的異教分子。

的地獄」之意。

　　第 二 個 出 現 的 偽 神 叫 基 抹（Chemos），乃 亞 嫩 河 南 方 的摩 押 人（Moabs）所 崇 拜 的 日神；他 的 影 響 範 圍 遍 及 亞 嫩 河 流域，從 阿 洛 埃（Aroer）到 尼 波（Nebo），且 一 直 延 伸 到 死 海 東岸 的 荒 原 亞 巴 林（Abarim）。另外，希 實 本（Hesebon）、何 羅念（Horonaim）、亞 摩 力 王 西 宏（Seon）的 領 土、綴 滿 葡 萄 藤 與 花 朵繽 紛 的 西 比 瑪（Sibma）山 谷 和 以 利亞 利 城，直 到 水 面 漂 浮 著 瀝 青 的 死 海（Asphaltick Pool），都 在 基 抹 的 影 響範 圍。

　　基 抹 另 一 個 名 字 叫 做 毘 珥（Peor），當 以 色 列 人 從 埃 及 逃 出 來之 後，曾 經 住 在 約 旦 河 東 邊 的 什 亭（Sittim），他 們 在 此 地 受 到 摩 押 女 子的 蠱 惑，一 同 向 她 們 的 神 毘 珥 頂 禮 膜拜，並 為 他 建 立 淫 祠。這 種 行 為 讓 上帝 非 常 生 氣，祂 降 下 瘟 疫，殺 死 了 二

Yet thence his lustful Orgies he enlarg'd [415]
Even to that Hill of scandal, by the Grove
Of Moloch homicide, lust hard by hate;
Till good Josiah drove them thence to Hell.
With these came they, who from the bordring flood
Of old Euphrates to the Brook that parts [420]
Egypt from Syrian ground, had general Names
Of Baalim and Ashtaroth, those male,
These Feminine. For Spirits when they please
Can either Sex assume, or both; so soft
And uncompounded is thir Essence pure, [425]
Not ti'd or manacl'd with joynt or limb,
Nor founded on the brittle strength of bones,
Like cumbrous flesh; but in what shape they choose
Dilated or condens't, bright or obscure,
Can execute thir aerie purposes, [430]
And works of love or enmity fulfill.
For those the Race of Israel oft forsook
Thir living strength, and unfrequented left
His righteous Altar, bowing lowly down
To bestial Gods; for which thir heads as low [435]
Bow'd down in Battel, sunk before the Spear
Of despicable foes. With these in troop
Came Astoreth, whom the Phoenicians call'd
Astarte, Queen of Heav'n, with crescent Horns;
To whose bright Image nightly by the Moon [440]
Sidonian Virgins paid thir Vows and Songs,
In Sion also not unsung, where stood
Her Temple on th' offensive Mountain, built
By that uxorious King, whose heart though large,
Beguil'd by fair Idolatresses, fell [445]
To Idols foul. Thammuz came next behind,
Whose annual wound in Lebanon allur'd
The Syrian Damsels to lament his fate
In amorous dittyes all a Summers day,
While smooth Adonis from his native Rock [450]
Ran purple to the Sea, suppos'd with blood
Of Thammuz yearly wounded: the Love-tale
Infected Sions daughters with like heat,
Whose wanton passions in the sacred Porch
Ezekiel saw, when by the Vision led [455]
His eye survay'd the dark Idolatries

萬四千個以色列人。[12] 毘珥還將其淫祠擴展到摩洛的山林，讓淫邪和兇惡相鄰；一直到約西亞王登基，才將他們統統趕回了地獄。[13]

年代淵遠流長的古幼發拉底河流域，與流經埃及、敘利亞的分界河地帶，是古代敘利亞人的神祇巴力（Baal）和阿斯他錄（Ashtaroth）的領域，巴力為男性太陽神，阿斯他錄則是女性月神。

但真正的天使是沒有性別之分的，他們可自由幻化成男性或女性，也可兼具兩種性別；因為他們的本質既柔軟而純粹，不需依靠肢體骨骼來撐托，所以可以隨著自己的心意與身分任意變形，於天空中自由自在地飛翔。

由於妖魔到處肆虐鼓惑以色列人，讓他們遺忘了賜予人們生命的真神，不但冷落真神的聖殿，且熱切地去膜拜披著獸類外形的偽神。因此，他們得在戰場上犧牲生命，用頭顱來做出

Of alienated Judah. Next came one
Who mourn'd in earnest, when the Captive Ark
Maim'd his brute Image, head and hands lopt off
In his own Temple, on the grunsel edge, [460]
Where he fell flat, and sham'd his Worshipers:
Dagon his Name, Sea Monster, upward Man
And downward Fish: yet had his Temple high
Rear'd in Azotus, dreaded through the Coast
Of Palestine, in Gath and Ascalon [465]
And Accaron and Gaza's frontier bounds.
Him follow'd Rimmon, whose delightful Seat
Was fair Damascus, on the fertil Banks
Of Abbana and Pharphar, lucid streams.
He also against the house of God was bold: [470]
A Leper once he lost and gain'd a King,
Ahaz his sottish Conquerour, whom he drew
Gods Altar to disparage and displace
For one of Syrian mode, whereon to burn
His odious off'rings, and adore the Gods [475]
Whom he had vanquisht. After these appear'd
A crew who under Names of old Renown,
Osiris, Isis, Orus and their Train
With monstrous shapes and sorceries abus'd
Fanatic Egypt and her Priests, to seek [480]
Thir wandring Gods disguis'd in brutish forms
Rather then human. Nor did Israel scape
Th' infection when thir borrow'd Gold compos'd

註12：《舊約‧民數記》，「以色列人住在什亭，百姓與摩押女子行起淫亂。因為這女子叫百姓來，一同給他們的神獻祭，百姓就吃他們的祭物、跪拜她們的神。以色列人與巴力毘珥連合，耶和華的怒氣就向以色列人發作。……那時遭瘟疫死的，有二萬四千人。」

註13：《舊約‧歷代志下》，「約西亞登基的時候年八歲，在耶路撒冷作王三十一年。……潔淨猶大和耶路撒冷，除掉邱壇、木偶、雕刻的像和鑄造的像。」

獻祭。

　　這其中有個妖魔叫阿斯托勒（Astoreth），是腓尼基人所祭拜的月亮女神，為太陽神的王后，他們稱呼她為阿斯塔蒂（Astarte）。她的頭上有著一對宛如新月的彎角，每當月圓之夜，西頓城的腓尼基處女們便齊聲唱著優美的歌來頌揚她的美麗；所羅門王因著嬌艷嬪妃的唆使，也曾在耶路撒冷的山上為阿斯托勒建過廟宇。

　　敘利亞人崇拜偽神搭模斯（Thammuz），他原本是一位英俊的王子，有一天在黎巴嫩的山林狩獵時，被野豬給咬死了；他的血沿著山麓流下來，染紅了山下的河水。相傳，他每年都會復活一次，然後再死去。敘利亞境內有一條河叫阿多尼斯河（Adonis），每年到了夏天的時

The Calf in Oreb: and the Rebel King
Doubl'd that sin in Bethel and in Dan, [485]
Lik'ning his Maker to the Grazed Ox,
Jehovah, who in one Night when he pass'd
From Egypt marching, equal'd with one stroke
Both her first born and all her bleating Gods.
Belial came last, then whom a Spirit more lewd [490]
Fell not from Heaven, or more gross to love
Vice for it self: To him no Temple stood
Or Altar smoak'd; yet who more oft then hee
In Temples and at Altars, when the Priest
Turns Atheist, as did Ely's Sons, who fill'd [495]
With lust and violence the house of God.
In Courts and Palaces he also Reigns

>> 阿斯塔蒂
羅塞提 油畫 1877年

　　腓尼基人所崇拜的月亮女神，象徵豐饒和愛。她的代表物是獅子、馬、斯芬克斯和鴿子。

候，河水就會變成紅色；人們相信，這是搭模斯的血。因此，每年到了這個季節，敘利亞人即為他舉行祭典；祭祀開始的時候，女人們首先哭泣著哀悼他的死亡，而後，再以淫辭豔語來慶賀他的重生。耶路撒冷的女孩們也深受搭模斯的影響，同樣為著他的悲慘遭遇而落下淚來——而這就是猶太先知以西結曾經在夢中所看見的，猶太人背棄真神、膜拜偶像的醜陋景象。[14]

大袞（Dagon）是上半身人形、下半身魚形的海妖；非利士人奉他為國神，於都城亞實突為他建廟。有天，非利士人從以色列人那兒搶來裝著真神法版的約櫃（the ark）[15]，他們把約櫃搬到大袞廟中，放在大袞獸像的旁邊。第二天早上，以利亞人來到廟中，發現大袞臉朝下、仆倒在約櫃前面，他們趕緊把他扶起，放回原處。第三天清晨，獸像又被人發現倒臥在約櫃前方，他的雙手和頭顱折斷在廟

And in luxurious Cities, where the noyse
Of riot ascends above thir loftiest Towrs,
And injury and outrage: And when Night [500]
Darkens the Streets, then wander forth the Sons
Of Belial, flown with insolence and wine.
Witness the Streets of Sodom, and that night
In Gibeah, when the hospitable door
Expos'd a Matron to avoid worse rape. [505]
These were the prime in order and in might;
The rest were long to tell, though far renown'd,
Th' Ionian Gods, of Javans Issue held
Gods, yet confest later then Heav'n and Earth
Thir boasted Parents; Titan Heav'ns first born [510]
With his enormous brood, and birthright seis'd
By younger Saturn, he from mightier Jove
His own and Rhea's Son like measure found;
So Jove usurping reign'd: these first in Creet
And Ida known, thence on the Snowy top [515]
Of cold Olympus rul'd the middle Air
Thir highest Heav'n; or on the Delphian Cliff,
Or in Dodona, and through all the bounds
Of Doric Land; or who with Saturn old

註14：《舊約‧以西結書》，「他領我到耶和華殿外院朝北的門口。誰知，在那裡有婦女坐著，為搭模斯哭泣。他對我說：『人子啊，你看見了嗎？你還要看見比這更可憎的事。』」

註15：《舊約‧出埃及記》，「耶和華曉諭摩西說：『你告訴以色列人當為我送禮物來，……又當為我造聖所，使我可以住在他們中間。製造帳幕和其中的一切器具，都要照我所指示你的樣式。』約櫃的做法『要用皂莢木做一櫃，長二肘半，寬一肘半，高一肘半。要裡外包上精金，四圍鑲上金牙邊。……必將我所要賜給你的法版放在櫃裡。』」

宇門檻上，面目悽慘，他的信徒們皆為此景象感到羞愧[16]。

巴勒斯坦人也都很敬畏大袞，巴勒斯坦境內五大名城 —— 亞瑣都、迦特、亞實基倫、以革倫、迦薩，都有他的信奉者，亞瑣都城中更有一座金碧輝煌的大袞廟。 敘利亞人信奉偽神臨門（Rimmon），他是掌管暴雨之神；美麗的大馬士革有他的廟宇坐落，在清澈肥沃的亞罷拿和法珥法兩條河流沿岸，他的信奉者竟敢與上帝的教堂相抗衡。

敘利亞將軍乃縵在以色列先知以利沙的幫助下，治好了身上的大痲瘋，改而信奉真神[17]；臨門雖然失去一位大痲瘋將軍，但日後換來了猶大王亞哈斯的崇奉。亞哈斯征服大馬士革時，為臨門宏偉輝煌的廟宇所吸引，於是仿照其樣式在國內蓋了一座新壇，且用敘利亞人的儀式來進行獻祭，成為臨門的信徒。[18]

埃 及 人 是 農 業 之 神 奧 西 利 斯

Fled over Adria to th' Hesperian Fields, [520]
And ore the Celtic roam'd the utmost Isles.
All these and more came flocking; but with looks
Down cast and damp, yet such wherein appear'd
Obscure some glimps of joy, to have found thir chief
Not in despair, to have found themselves not lost [525]
In loss it self; which on his count'nance cast
Like doubtful hue: but he his wonted pride
Soon recollecting, with high words, that bore
Semblance of worth, not substance, gently rais'd
Thir fainting courage, and dispel'd thir fears. [530]
Then strait commands that at the warlike sound
Of Trumpets loud and Clarions be upreard
His mighty Standard; that proud honour claim'd

註16：《舊約・撒母耳記上》，「非利士人將神的約櫃從以便以謝抬到亞實突。非利士人將神的約櫃抬進大袞廟，放在大袞的旁邊。次日清早，亞實突人起來，見大袞仆倒在耶和華的約櫃前，臉伏於地，就把大袞仍立在原處。又次日清早起來，見大袞仆倒在耶和華的約櫃前，臉伏於地，並且大袞的頭和兩手都在門檻上折斷，只剩下大袞的殘體。」

註17：《舊約・列王記下》，「以利沙打發一個使者對乃縵說：『你去在約旦河中沐浴七回，你的肉就必復原，而得潔淨。』……於是乃縵下去，照神人的話，在約旦河沐浴七回，他的肉復原，好像小孩子的肉，他就潔淨了。……乃縵說：『……從今以後，僕人必不再將燔祭或平安祭獻與別神，只獻給耶和華。』」

註18：《舊約・列王記下》，「亞哈斯王上大馬士革去迎接亞述王提革拉毗列色，在大馬士革看見一座壇，就照壇的規模樣式做法畫了圖樣，送到祭司烏利亞那裡。……建築一座壇。」

（Osiris）、頭上有半月形牛角的土
地之神埃西斯（Isis）與鷹頭人身奧
魯斯（Orus）的忠實信徒。奧西利斯
為他的弟弟所殺害，屍體被切成一塊
一塊地丟進尼羅河中；他的妻子埃西
斯偷偷地把屍塊撿起來，藏在筐中，
讓他復活。奧魯斯是他們兩人的兒
子，為埃及的日神。由於他們的外表
怪異，有動物的長相，形成埃及人祭
拜遊蕩之神的風俗，如果某隻動物身
上具備了上述三偽神的特徵，如：一
隻牛額頭上有著半月形毛皮，他們就
會把牠當做神的分身，加以膜拜。

　　以色列人也無法避免偽神的引誘。
摩西的哥哥亞倫，就曾經鑄造了一隻
金牛犢，讓駐紮在西奈曠野的以色列
人膜拜[19]；此外，耶羅波安背叛所羅
門王的兒子羅波安，自己登上王位，
他鑄造了兩個金牛犢，要百姓前來
朝拜。這兩個人都褻瀆了真神，因為
他們把造物主的形象，塑造成吃草的
牛。[20]

Azazel as his right, a Cherube tall:
Who forthwith from the glittering Staff unfurld [535]
Th' Imperial Ensign, which full high advanc't
Shon like a Meteor streaming to the Wind
With Gemms and Golden lustre rich imblaz'd,
Seraphic arms and Trophies: all the while
Sonorous mettal blowing Martial sounds: [540]
At which the universal Host upsent
A shout that tore Hells Concave, and beyond
Frighted the Reign of Chaos and old Night.
All in a moment through the gloom were seen
Ten thousand Banners rise into the Air [545]
With Orient Colours waving: with them rose
A Forest huge of Spears: and thronging Helms
Appear'd, and serried shields in thick array
Of depth immeasurable: Anon they move
In perfect Phalanx to the Dorian mood [550]
Of Flutes and soft Recorders; such as rais'd
To hight of noblest temper Hero's old
Arming to Battel, and in stead of rage
Deliberate valour breath'd, firm and unmov'd
With dread of death to flight or foul retreat, [555]
Nor wanting power to mitigate and swage
With solemn touches, troubl'd thoughts, and chase

註19：《舊約‧出埃及記》，「亞倫對他
　　　們說：『你們去摘下你們妻子、兒
　　　女耳上的金環，拿來給我。』百姓
　　　就都摘下他們耳上的金環，拿來給
　　　亞倫。亞倫從他們手裡接過來，鑄
　　　了一隻牛犢，用雕刻的器具做成。
　　　他們就說：『以色列啊，這是領你
　　　出埃及地的神！』」
註20：《舊約‧列王記上》，「耶羅波安
　　　王就籌劃定妥，鑄造了兩個金牛
　　　犢，對眾民說：『以色列人哪，你
　　　們上耶路撒冷去實在是難，這就是
　　　領你們出埃及地的神。』他就把牛
　　　犢一隻安在伯特利，一隻安在但。
　　　這事叫百姓陷在罪裡，因為他們往
　　　但去拜那牛犢。」

　　彼列（Belial）是眾墮落天使中最荒
淫、邪惡的偽神，雖然沒有人為他建
廟立祠，也沒有祭壇為了燒祭品給他
而煙霧繚繞；但他的黑暗勢力卻直達
上帝的聖殿，像猶太祭司以利的兩個
兒子那樣，奪取前來殿堂獻祭者的祭
物，把上帝的祭壇弄得烏煙障氣[21]。
彼列的影響力還遍及宮廷與繁華的城
市，當夜幕低垂，他淫邪的信眾們便

Anguish and doubt and fear and sorrow and pain
From mortal or immortal minds. Thus they
Breathing united force with fixed thought [560]
Mov'd on in silence to soft Pipes that charm'd
Thir painful steps o're the burnt soyle; and now
Advanc't in view, they stand, a horrid Front
Of dreadful length and dazling Arms, in guise
Of Warriers old with order'd Spear and Shield, [565]

註21：《舊約‧撒母耳記上》，「以利的
　　　兩個兒子是惡人，不認識耶和華。
　　　這二祭司待百姓是這樣的規矩：凡
　　　有人獻祭，……祭司都取了去。如
　　　此，這二少年人的罪在耶和華面前
　　　甚重了，因為他們使人厭棄給耶和
　　　華獻祭。」

來到街道遊蕩，四處做惡，犯下罪行；所多瑪城（Sodom）和基比亞城（Gibeah）發生的兩件姦污異鄉旅客婦女的醜事，就是他的信徒做的。[22]

以上所說的這些偽神，算是地位較高、本領較大的一群；另外還有許多散佈各地、數量多到不勝枚舉的邪魔。其中，希臘人的祖先——以色列人後裔雅完（Javan）的子孫，他們所尊崇的愛奧尼諸神（Ionian），即一般人所知道的希臘諸神，雖然名聞遐邇，擁有極為顯赫的名聲，且自稱是希臘人的祖先，但其實開天闢地的真神比他們出現的時間更要早的多呢![23]

泰坦神族是天和地的兒女，為體型碩大、力氣驚人的巨人族。其中，最為有名的是克羅納斯（Kronos），或叫撒頓（Saturn）；他奪去哥哥泰坦（Titan）的統治地位，取得權力。後

◄ 金牛膜拜
普桑 油畫 1660年

　　膜拜金牛自然是褻瀆真神的行為，這等於把造物主的形象，變成了吃草的牲畜。

Awaiting what command thir mighty Chief
Had to impose: He through the armed Files
Darts his experienc't eye, and soon traverse
The whole Battalion views, thir order due,
Thir visages and stature as of Gods, [570]
Thir number last he summs. And now his heart
Distends with pride, and hardning in his strength
Glories: For never since created man,
Met such imbodied force, as nam'd with these
Could merit more then that small infantry [575]
Warr'd on by Cranes: though all the Giant brood
Of Phlegra with th' Heroic Race were joyn'd
That fought at Theb's and Ilium, on each side
Mixt with auxiliar Gods; and what resounds

註22：《舊約·創世紀》，「那兩個天使晚上到了所多瑪。羅得正坐在所多瑪城門口，看見他們，就起來迎接，臉伏於地下拜，說：『我主啊，請你們到僕人家裡洗洗腳，住一夜，清早起來再走。』……他們還沒有躺下，所多瑪城裡各處的人，連老帶少，都來圍住那房子，呼叫羅得說：『今日晚上到你這裡來的人在哪裡呢？把他們帶出來，任我們所為。』」《舊約·士師記》，「那利未人，就是被害之婦人的丈夫回答說：『我和我的妾到了便雅憫的基比亞住宿。基比亞人夜間起來，圍了我住的房子，想要殺我，又將我的妾強姦至死。』」

註23：《舊約·創世紀》，「挪亞的兒子閃、含、雅弗的後代記在下面。洪水以後，他們都生了兒子。雅弗的兒子是歌篾、瑪各、瑪代、雅完、土巴、米設、提拉。雅完的兒子是以利沙、他施、基提、多單。這些人的後裔將各國的地土、海島分開居住，各隨各的方言、宗族立國。」

來，他也被自己的兒子宙斯（Zeus）推翻，逃到義大利去，為當地帶來輝煌的「黃金時代」。[24]

這些神最初在克里特島（Crete）的伊達山（Ida）受人尊崇，相傳此處為宙斯的出生地；後來，又在奧林帕斯山上（Olympus）掌管人間事，自稱天神。這其中，太陽神阿波羅曾在特爾斐（Delphi）的山岩顯靈，而天神宙斯則於多陀那（Dodona）顯靈過，希臘諸神的足蹟遍及希臘各地；有些神祇則跟著撒頓飛越亞得里亞海，來到義大利；或橫越法蘭西，於愛爾蘭、英格蘭等地彰顯勢力。

這些日後化成偽神的將領，原本是一群從天庭墜落地獄的反叛天使；現

⋀　克羅納斯吞噬其子
哥雅 油畫 1819~1823年

克羅納斯是宙斯的父親，因為知道將來兒子會推翻自己，所以太太瑞亞一生下小孩，他就將小孩吃掉以絕後患。

註24：泰坦族是《希臘羅馬神話故事》中所出現的巨人族，他們是天和地的兒女，而希臘眾神則為他們的子孫。克羅納斯（Kronos）的拉丁文叫做撒頓（Saturn），是泰坦族中地位較高的，他和自己的妹妹莉亞（Rhea）生了六個孩子，前面五個都被他給吞進肚子，莉亞生下第六個孩子 — 宙斯（Zeus）後，把他偷偷地藏到克里特島去扶養，宙斯長大後推翻自己的父親，奪得統治地位成為希臘首神。

In Fable or Romance of Uthers Son [580]
Begirt with British and Armoric Knights;
And all who since, Baptiz'd or Infidel
Jousted in Aspramont or Montalban,
Damasco, or Marocco, or Trebisond,
Or whom Biserta sent from Afric shore [585]
When Charlemain with all his Peerage fell
By Fontarabbia. Thus far these beyond
Compare of mortal prowess, yet observ'd
Thir dread commander: he above the rest

在，他們集聚撒旦面前，原本憂傷沮喪的面容，在見到大首領炯炯有神的目光之後，重新拾回勇氣，內心恐懼霎時如冰雪消融，臉上漸漸展露出喜悅的神情。

「就讓我來執掌軍旗吧！」

一個洪亮的聲音從群眾中響起，這是個名叫阿撒塞勒（Azazel）的高大天使，他舉起了金光燦爛的軍旗，向四方揮舞；那閃爍著寶石般光彩的旗子在空中飛揚，宛若一顆流星劃過天際。

一時間，號聲響起，聲振蒼穹，士兵們吶喊著從四面八方湧向前來；旗海飄揚，長矛森森，無數的盔甲、盾牌相互簇擁著，發出刺眼的光芒，相信任何軍隊皆無法與它抗衡。

撒旦站在陣前，那出眾的儀表如旭日初升，在晦暗的雲霧中隱現，正等候著白日的降臨，準備射出耀眼的光輝。

士兵們排成半月形包圍著他，那被

In shape and gesture proudly eminent [590]
Stood like a Towr; his form had yet not lost
All her Original brightness, nor appear'd
Less then Arch Angel ruind, and th' excess
Of Glory obscur'd: As when the Sun new ris'n
Looks through the Horizontal misty Air [595]
Shorn of his Beams, or from behind the Moon
In dim Eclips disastrous twilight sheds
On half the Nations, and with fear of change
Perplexes Monarchs. Dark'n'd so, yet shon
Above them all th' Arch Angel: but his face [600]
Deep scars of Thunder had intrencht, and care
Sat on his faded cheek, but under Browes
Of dauntless courage, and considerate Pride
Waiting revenge: cruel his eye, but cast
Signs of remorse and passion to behold [605]
The fellows of his crime, the followers rather
(Far other once beheld in bliss) condemn'd
For ever now to have thir lot in pain,
Millions of Spirits for his fault amerc't
Of Heav'n, and from Eternal Splendors flung [610]
For his revolt, yet faithfull how they stood,
Thir Glory witherd. As when Heavens Fire
Hath scath'd the Forrest Oaks, or Mountain Pines,
With singed top thir stately growth though bare
Stands on the blasted Heath. He now prepar'd [615]
To speak; whereat thir doubl'd Ranks they bend
From wing to wing, and half enclose him round
With all his Peers: attention held them mute.
Thrice he assayd, and thrice in spight of scorn,
Tears such as Angels weep, burst forth: at last [620]
Words interwove with sighs found out thir way.

O Myriads of immortal Spirits, O Powers
Matchless, but with th' Almighty, and that strife
Was not inglorious, though th' event was dire,
As this place testifies, and this dire change [625]
Hateful to utter: but what power of mind
Foreseeing or presaging, from the Depth
Of knowledge past or present, could have fear'd
How such united force of Gods, how such
As stood like these, could ever know repulse? [630]

烈火殛傷的臉龐雖然佈滿塵埃，但他們凝視撒旦時的眼神卻充滿著期盼與希望。

「英勇的戰士們啊！因為我的輕疏，害大家從天國墜落到這個悲慘的境地，我的內心充滿了無限的愧疚；天上的至尊存心陷害我們，祂早就預知我們的行動，所以創造了黑暗陰森的地獄等著我們沉淪。目的不言可喻，乃是為了鞏固他的神子 —— 基督在天界的地位。

「祂憑恃著高強本領達到目的，使我們喪失了天使的尊榮；祂這種自私又無情的舉動應該受到討伐，我們的力量雖然比不上祂，但我們可動動腦筋，採用智取的方式來與祂對抗，現在我們首先要做的事，就是建造一座新的基地，坐下來好好思考如何反敗為勝。」

撒旦說完，奮力朝天高舉起盾牌。

嘹亮的號聲再度響起，軍士們戰敗的悲傷情緒得到紓解，發出一陣又一

For who can yet beleeve, though after loss,
That all these puissant Legions, whose exile
Hath emptied Heav'n, shall fail to re-ascend
Self-rais'd, and repossess thir native seat?
For mee be witness all the Host of Heav'n, [635]
If counsels different, or danger shun'd
By me, have lost our hopes. But he who reigns
Monarch in Heav'n, till then as one secure
Sat on his Throne, upheld by old repute,
Consent or custome, and his Regal State [640]
Put forth at full, but still his strength conceal'd,
Which tempted our attempt, and wrought our fall.
Henceforth his might we know, and know our own
So as not either to provoke, or dread
New warr, provok't; our better part remains [645]
To work in close design, by fraud or guile
What force effected not: that he no less
At length from us may find, who overcomes
By force, hath overcome but half his foe.
Space may produce new Worlds; whereof so rife [650]
There went a fame in Heav'n that he ere long
Intended to create, and therein plant
A generation, whom his choice regard
Should favour equal to the Sons of Heaven:
Thither, if but to pry, shall be perhaps
Our first eruption, thither or elsewhere: [655]
For this Infernal Pit shall never hold
Cælestial Spirits in Bondage, nor th' Abyss
Long under darkness cover. But these thoughts
Full Counsel must mature: Peace is despaird, [660]
For who can think Submission? Warr then, Warr
Open or understood must be resolv'd.

He spake: and to confirm his words, out-flew
Millions of flaming swords, drawn from the thighs
Of mighty Cherubim; the sudden blaze [665]
Far round illumin'd hell: highly they rag'd
Against the Highest, and fierce with grasped arms
Clash'd on thir sounding Shields the din of war,
Hurling defiance toward the vault of Heav'n.

There stood a Hill not far whose griesly top [670]

陣高昂尖銳的怒吼聲，那呼聲有如暴風狂掃、激起沖天巨浪，一波波地在陰暗的地府湧動著。

瑪門（Mommon）從隊伍中走出來，向群聚高聲呼喊：

「大家跟著我來，我知道那裡有建造宮殿的材料。」

說完，隨即領著士兵們朝附近一座

Belch'd fire and rowling smoak; the rest entire
Shon with a glossie scurff, undoubted sign
That in his womb was hid metallic Ore,
The work of Sulphur. Thither wing'd with speed
A numerous Brigad hasten'd. As when Bands [675]
Of Pioners with Spade and Pickax arm'd
Forerun the Royal Camp, to trench a Field,
Or cast a Rampart. Mammon led them on,
Mammon, the least erected Spirit that fell
From heav'n, for ev'n in heav'n his looks and thoughts [680]
Were always downward bent, admiring more
The riches of Heav'ns pavement, trod'n Gold,
Then aught divine or holy else enjoy'd
In vision beatific: by him first
Men also, and by his suggestion taught, [685]
Ransack'd the Center, and with impious hands
Rifl'd the bowels of thir mother Earth
For Treasures better hid. Soon had his crew
Op'nd into the Hill a spacious wound
And dig'd out ribs of Gold. Let none admire [690]
That riches grow in Hell; that soyle may best
Deserve the precious bane. And here let those
Who boast in mortal things, and wond'ring tell
Of Babel, and the works of Memphian Kings
Learn how thir greatest Monuments of Fame, [695]
And Strength and Art are easily out-done
By Spirits reprobate, and in an hour
What in an age they with incessant toyle
And hands innumerable scarce perform.
Nigh on the Plain in many cells prepar'd, [700]
That underneath had veins of liquid fire
Sluc'd from the Lake, a second multitude
With wondrous Art found out the massie Ore,
Severing each kind, and scum'd the Bullion dross:
A third as soon had form'd within the ground [705]

≪ 撒旦發表演說，重振軍心
杜雷版畫 1866年

　　撒旦的號角響起，在他慷慨激昂的演說後，反叛天使集結歸隊，振奮戰敗的悲傷情緒，尋求反敗為勝的機會。

冒著煙霧的山丘走去。

　　瑪門在天國的地位並不高，但他非常喜愛財寶，所以能探知那兒的地底下埋藏了黃金[25]，日後，他成為貪婪之神，專門激發人類深層的慾望，引誘他們追求財富；人類之所以喜歡去挖取地底下的寶石，破壞大自然的生態，全都是仿傚瑪門而來。

　　果然，在瑪門所指示的山丘裡，眾人挖掘到大量的黃金；他們把黃金搬運到廣闊的平原上，以烈燄熔解，然後灌入地面上一個個由其他士兵預先雕琢好的模型洞窟裡，待其風乾成型，再由另一批戰士扛去搭建城堡。

　　瑪門在天國時，也負責權貴天使們所居住的宮庭的承建工作，因此在他熟練的指揮下，一座巍峨的宮殿從烈燄中逐漸升騰，在漆黑的地獄中，宛如一團金色火球，向四方閃現耀眼光芒。

　　宮殿的城牆外頭，矗立著一根根方形壁柱和多利亞式圓柱石，柱石上端

A various mould, and from the boyling cells
By strange conveyance fill'd each hollow nook,
As in an Organ from one blast of wind
To many a row of Pipes the sound-board breaths.
Anon out of the earth a Fabrick huge [710]
Rose like an Exhalation, with the sound
Of Dulcet Symphonies and voices sweet,
Built like a Temple, where Pilasters round
Were set, and Doric pillars overlaid
With Golden Architrave; nor did there want [715]
Cornice or Freeze, with bossy Sculptures grav'n,
The Roof was fretted Gold. Not Babilon,
Nor great Alcairo such magnificence
Equal'd in all thir glories, to inshrine
Belus or Serapis thir Gods, or seat [720]
Thir Kings, when Ægypt with Assyria strove
In wealth and luxurie. Th' ascending pile
Stood fixt her stately highth, and strait the dores
Op'ning thir brazen foulds discover wide
Within, her ample spaces, o're the smooth [725]
And level pavement: from the arched roof
Pendant by suttle Magic many a row
Of Starry Lamps and blazing Cressets fed
With Naphtha and Asphaltus yeilded light
As from a sky. The hasty multitude [730]
Admiring enter'd, and the work some praise
And some the Architect: his hand was known
In Heav'n by many a Towred structure high,
Where Scepter'd Angels held thir residence,
And sat as Princes, whom the supreme King [735]
Exalted to such power, and gave to rule,
Each in his Hierarchie, the Orders bright.
Nor was his name unheard or unador'd
In ancient Greece; and in Ausonian land
Men call'd him Mulciber; and how he fell [740]

註25：《新約·馬太福音》，「一個人不能事奉兩個主。不是惡這個愛那個，就是重這個輕那個。你們不能又事奉神，又事奉瑪門（註：「瑪門」是「財利」的意思）。」

頂著金黃色的橫樑；屋簷和牆壁刻鏤著精緻的浮雕，房頂鑲著黃澄澄的金子；懸掛在大廳天花板上的超大華麗水晶燈，照射出有如星星般燦爛的亮光；寬大的地板更是平滑光亮的如凝結的冬季湖面。

士兵們像黃蜂出巢般湧向新宮殿，他們跨過高聳的大門階梯，往那深邃而寬廣的走廊前進，不一會即來到撒旦面前。

「哇！咦！」

「嘖嘖……」

目睹了宮殿的富麗堂皇之後，士兵們不由地發出一陣陣讚嘆，讚美聲迴盪在大廳中，宛如蜜蜂的嗡嗡鳴聲。

「為了讓我們所有的叛軍，都能參與即將舉行的會議，我必須暫時先把各位占據的空間縮小。」

說完，撒旦舉手往下一揮，原先擠得水洩不通的大廳，立刻空出許多空間，原來，士兵們巨大無比的身體都被縮成如小矮人一般的尺寸；也因為

From Heav'n, they fabl'd, thrown by angry Jove
Sheer o're the Chrystal Battlements: from Morn
To Noon he fell, from Noon to dewy Eve,
A Summers day; and with the setting Sun
Dropt from the Zenith like a falling Star, [745]
On Lemnos th' Ægean Ile: thus they relate,
Erring; for he with this rebellious rout
Fell long before; nor aught avail'd him now
To have built in Heav'n high Towrs; nor did he scape
By all his Engins, but was headlong sent [750]
With his industrious crew to build in hell.
Mean while the winged Haralds by command
Of Sovran power, with awful Ceremony
And Trumpets sound throughout the Host proclaim
A solemn Councel forthwith to be held [755]
At Pandæmonium, the high Capital
Of Satan and his Peers: thir summons call'd
From every Band and squared Regiment
By place or choice the worthiest; they anon
With hunders and with thousands trooping came [760]
Attended: all access was throng'd, the Gates
And Porches wide, but chief the spacious Hall
(Though like a cover'd field, where Champions bold
Wont ride in arm'd, and at the Soldans chair
Defi'd the best of Paynim chivalry [765]
To mortal combat or carreer with Lance)
Thick swarm'd, both on the ground and in the air,
Brusht with the hiss of russling wings. As Bees
In spring time, when the Sun with Taurus rides,
Pour forth thir populous youth about the Hive [770]
In clusters; they among fresh dews and flowers
Flie to and fro, or on the smoothed Plank,
The suburb of thir Straw-built Cittadel,
New rub'd with Baum, expatiate and confer
Thir State affairs. So thick the aerie crowd [775]
Swarm'd and were straitn'd; till the Signal giv'n.
Behold a wonder! they but now who seemd
In bigness to surpass Earths Giant Sons
Now less then smallest Dwarfs, in narrow room
Throng numberless, like that Pigmean Race [780]
Beyond the Indian Mount, or Faerie Elves,
Whose midnight Revels, by a Forrest side

如此，更多的墜落天使才能如潮水一般，紛紛擠進大廳來，準備參加群魔大會。

是的，這些原本高貴良善的天使，至此境地已徹底轉變成惡魔了。一場改變人類命運的會議，即將在此惡魔之殿 —— 潘地曼尼南展開。

Or Fountain some belated Peasant sees,
Or dreams he sees, while over-head the Moon
Sits Arbitress, and neerer to the Earth [785]
Wheels her pale course, they on thir mirth and dance
Intent, with jocond Music charm his ear;
At once with joy and fear his heart rebounds.
Thus incorporeal Spirits to smallest forms
Reduc'd thir shapes immense, and were at large, [790]
Though without number still amidst the Hall
Of that infernal Court. But far within
And in thir own dimensions like themselves
The great Seraphic Lords and Cherubim
In close recess and secret conclave sat [795]
A thousand Demy-Gods on golden seats,
Frequent and full. After short silence then
And summons read, the great consult began.

> 潘地曼尼南
約翰馬丁 油畫 1841年

　　米爾頓將這個惡魔之殿命名為「潘地曼尼南」，原意為「小惡魔」，為了讓所有叛軍都能參加即將舉行的群魔會，撒旦特地把墜落天使的身體縮小，以便全員都能進入這所轟立在烈焰中的華麗宮殿。

地獄群魔會

撒旦與他的部眾們因為發動天國叛變,被萬能的天神以威力強大的雷霆驅趕至烈焰沖天的陰暗地獄;他們從善良的天使轉化成邪惡的魔鬼,並用剩餘的法力在地獄建築了惡魔之殿。此刻,魔鬼們群集於宮殿大廳,商量反攻的計策,並遴選出一位前去探訪預言中「新天地」的人選 —— 魔鬼撒旦。

∧ **群魔大會於惡魔殿召開**
杜雷 版畫 1866年

　　撒旦高居寶座,處在奢華如奧木斯的大殿,又被滿堂部眾簇擁著,撒旦很快恢復王者風範,開始構思他的反攻計劃。

寬敞如競技場的惡魔殿大廳中群魔集結，撒旦威風凜凜地坐在裝飾著無數珠玉鑽石的寶座上頭，它的奢華遠勝於東方珠寶集散地奧木斯（Ormus）和印度地方的富麗堂皇[1]；在魔鬼大軍的簇擁下，撒旦重新拾回信心，渾身散發著王者的傲氣，趾高氣昂的對底下的魔鬼軍發表聲明。

「親愛的部眾們！今天，我得以坐擁最高權力地位，乃是經由大家一致的推舉；我的領導權是合理且站得住腳的，應該不會有人懷疑才對。請仔細想一想，地獄之王的名銜並不像天國的王位那般擁有許多好處，反而危險多多，是上帝雷擊的第一目標；因此，相信沒有人會蠢到來嫉妒我，覬覦這個寶座吧？」

撒旦以充滿威嚇的目光向群眾掃射一遍，接著說道：「現在請大家商量一下，看是要重整大軍攻返天庭，還是施用權謀，以智力取回天使地位？有意見的請直接發言。」

High on a Throne of Royal State, which far
Outshon the wealth of Ormus and of Ind,
Or where the gorgeous East with richest hand
Showrs on her Kings Barbaric Pearl and Gold,
Satan exalted sat, by merit rais'd [5]
To that bad eminence; and from despair
Thus high uplifted beyond hope, aspires
Beyond thus high, insatiate to pursue
Vain Warr with Heav'n, and by success untaught
His proud imaginations thus displaid. [10]

Powers and Dominions, Deities of Heav'n,
For since no deep within her gulf can hold
Immortal vigor, though opprest and fall'n,
I give not Heav'n for lost. From this descent
Celestial vertues rising, will appear [15]
More glorious and more dread then from no fall,
And trust themselves to fear no second fate:
Mee though just right, and the fixt Laws of Heav'n
Did first create your Leader, next free choice,
With what besides, in Counsel or in Fight, [20]
Hath bin achievd of merit, yet this loss
Thus farr at least recover'd, hath much more
Establisht in a safe unenvied Throne
Yielded with full consent. The happier state
In Heav'n, which follows dignity, might draw [25]
Envy from each inferior; but who here
Will envy whom the highest place exposes
Formost to stand against the Thunderers aim
Your bulwark, and condemns to greatest share
Of endless pain? where there is then no good [30]
For which to strive, no strife can grow up there
From Faction; for none sure will claim in Hell
Precedence, none, whose portion is so small

註1：奧木斯（Ormus）為波斯灣古城，位在波斯灣入口附近的一個小島上，是十三世紀至十七世紀時東方珍珠、寶石、瑪瑙等高價珠寶的集散地，與當時的印度一樣富麗堂皇。這裡用來突顯撒旦新寶座的華麗。

「這還用討論嗎？當然是發動戰爭，攻打回去。」摩洛雙眉緊蹙，聲如洪鐘地大喊。他曾是戰場上衝鋒陷陣、最驍勇善戰的英雄，若要他像老鼠一般地躲在漆黑的地獄，還不如拚死一搏保住尊嚴。

「我們的外表雖然因為受到雷擊而變得襤褸不堪，但我們的實力並未消減，仍有足夠的力量反攻天庭；再說，就算不幸又打了敗戰，那又有什麼關係呢？死亡並不能摧毀我們的本質，況且再也沒有比現在更艱惡的處所了。你們應該知道，地獄中那一大片火湖的名字叫做忘湖，飲了它的湖水會遺忘所有的記憶；趁著咱們記憶未失，快領著地獄的火燄和雷電，振翅飛回天上去焚燒天庭、電擊天國軍，如此必能點燃上帝心頭的怒火，讓祂無法安安穩穩地坐在寶座上頭享樂，這也算報了一箭之仇呢！」摩洛說完，帶著復仇的神色退向一邊，讓其他人發言。

Of present pain, that with ambitious mind
Will covet more. With this advantage then [35]
To union, and firm Faith, and firm accord,
More then can be in Heav'n, we now return
To claim our just inheritance of old,
Surer to prosper then prosperity
Could have assur'd us; and by what best way, [40]
Whether of open Warr or covert guile,
We now debate; who can advise, may speak.

He ceas'd, and next him Moloc, Scepter'd King
Stood up, the strongest and the fiercest Spirit
That fought in Heav'n; now fiercer by despair: [45]
His trust was with th' Eternal to be deem'd
Equal in strength, and rather then be less
Care'd not to be at all; with that care lost
Went all his fear: of God, or Hell, or worse
He reck'd not, and these words thereafter spake. [50]

My sentence is for open Warr: Of Wiles,
More unexpert, I boast not: them let those
Contrive who need, or when they need, not now.
For while they sit contriving, shall the rest,
Millions that stand in Arms, and longing wait [55]
The Signal to ascend, sit lingring here
Heav'ns fugitives, and for thir dwelling place
Accept this dark opprobrious Den of shame,
The Prison of his Tyranny who Reigns
By our delay? no, let us rather choose [60]
Arm'd with Hell flames and fury all at once
O're Heav'ns high Towrs to force resistless way,
Turning our Tortures into horrid Arms
Against the Torturer; when to meet the noise
Of his Almighty Engin he shall hear [65]
Infernal Thunder, and for Lightning see
Black fire and horror shot with equal rage
Among his Angels; and his Throne it self
Mixt with Tartarean Sulphur, and strange fire,
His own invented Torments. But perhaps [70]
The way seems difficult and steep to scale
With upright wing against a higher foe.
Let such bethink them, if the sleepy drench

「我反對！」

彼列爾（Belial）緩緩地站起來，嘴角帶著一抹微笑，不懷好意地對摩洛說：「摩洛兄，尚未開戰哪！你就先懷有不幸戰敗的心理準備，這表示你對魔鬼軍並無信心，那又何苦要大夥兒陪你去逞一時之勇呢？何況，真正聰明的作法應該是保存實力，用智謀去贏回尊嚴；而不是像你這樣莽莽撞撞，枉送性命。」

語畢，彼列爾轉頭面向群眾，以婉轉悅耳的聲音說道：「大家都知道，天庭四周本來就有軍隊在負責巡邏，經過一次叛變的衝擊之後，更是警備森嚴；此刻無論天庭內外、白晝或黑夜，到處佈滿了警哨，選擇這個時候發動戰爭，無異於以卵擊石、自取滅亡。況且若再次激怒上帝，祂勢必斬草除根，徹底消滅我們，屆時，我們將永無翻身的機會。所以依我個人的看法，暫時按兵不動是比較安全的選擇。」

Of that forgetful Lake benumm not still,
That in our proper motion we ascend [75]
Up to our native seat: descent and fall
To us is adverse. Who but felt of late
When the fierce Foe hung on our brok'n Rear
Insulting, and pursu'd us through the Deep,
With what compulsion and laborious flight [80]
We sunk thus low? Th' ascent is easie then;
Th' event is fear'd; should we again provoke
Our stronger, some worse way his wrath may find
To our destruction: if there be in Hell
Fear to be worse destroy'd: what can be worse [85]
Then to dwell here, driv'n out from bliss, condemn'd
In this abhorred deep to utter woe;
Where pain of unextinguishable fire
Must exercise us without hope of end
The Vassals of his anger, when the Scourge [90]
Inexorably, and the torturing hour
Calls us to Penance? More destroy'd then thus
We should be quite abolisht and expire.
What fear we then? what doubt we to incense
His utmost ire? which to the highth enrag'd, [95]
Will either quite consume us, and reduce
To nothing this essential, happier farr
Then miserable to have eternal being:
Or if our substance be indeed Divine,
And cannot cease to be, we are at worst [100]
On this side nothing; and by proof we feel
Our power sufficient to disturb his Heav'n,
And with perpetual inrodes to Allarme,
Though inaccessible, his fatal Throne:
Which if not Victory is yet Revenge. [105]

He ended frowning, and his look denounc'd
Desperate revenge, and Battel dangerous
To less then Gods. On th' other side up rose
Belial, in act more graceful and humane;
A fairer person lost not Heav'n; he seemd [110]
For dignity compos'd and high exploit:
But all was false and hollow; though his Tongue
Dropt Manna, and could make the worse appear
The better reason, to perplex and dash

接著，瑪門站起來發言：「無論發動戰爭或求和都不是我們的本意，與其去追求難以獲得的地位或委身為僕，倒不如安居此地，努力消除環境中的惡質元素，求得一片新天地。這兒雖然陰暗恐怖，遠遠比不上天庭的美好；但在烈焰熊熊的地底，卻埋藏了挖掘不盡的黃金，我們可以用它來建造一座座宮殿，我保證，絕對會比天上的宮殿來得富麗堂皇。

「或許有人會說，地獄中炎熱的

Maturest Counsels: for his thoughts were low; [115]
To vice industrious, but to Nobler deeds
Timorous and slothful: yet he pleas'd the ear,
And with perswasive accent thus began.

I should be much for open Warr, O Peers,
As not behind in hate; if what was urg'd [120]
Main reason to persuade immediate Warr,
Did not disswade me most, and seem to cast
Ominous conjecture on the whole success:
When he who most excels in fact of Arms,
In what he counsels and in what excels [125]
Mistrustful, grounds his courage on despair

⌄ 撒旦主持群魔會
約翰馬丁 版畫 1824年

撒旦聆聽他的部眾慷慨發言，有的主戰，有的主張苟且偷安，但撒旦早有定見，他示意親信別西卜主張尋找新樂園，果然獲得眾人支持，這一切都在撒旦的運籌帷幄中。

火燄讓人難以忍受；須知，只要我們把它視作生活的一部分，時間久了，自然就能夠習慣它、將灼熱化成溫暖了。」

瑪門的建議正好切中兵士們恐懼重回戰場的心理，所以立即獲得眾人熱烈的掌聲。

最後，副首領別西卜在撒旦的授意下，撐起如扛天巨人阿特拉斯（Atlas）的碩大身軀[2]，威風凜凜地說道：

「瑪門的建議固然好，但就算我們在地獄建造了金碧輝煌的堡壘，卻也只不過是陷入另一個牢籠罷了；事實上，我們仍處在上帝的股掌之中，地獄原是由祂所創造，我們在此地的一舉一動，完全逃不過祂的眼睛。我們在此地安身，也只能是暫時的選擇，

註2：阿特拉斯（Atlas）是希臘羅馬神話中的擎天巨神，因與天神宙斯爭戰失敗，被懲罰以雙肩永遠地扛負著沉重的世界和天空；曾經幫大英雄海克力斯取得金蘋果，讓他完成第十一件贖罪任務。

And utter dissolution, as the scope
Of all his aim, after some dire revenge.
First, what Revenge? the Towrs of Heav'n are fill'd
With Armed watch, that render all access [130]
Impregnable; oft on the bordering Deep
Encamp thir Legions, or with obscure wing
Scout farr and wide into the Realm of night,
Scorning surprize. Or could we break our way
By force, and at our heels all Hell should rise [135]
With blackest Insurrection, to confound
Heav'ns purest Light, yet our great Enemy
All incorruptible would on his Throne
Sit unpolluted, and th' Ethereal mould
Incapable of stain would soon expel [140]
Her mischief, and purge off the baser fire
Victorious. Thus repuls'd, our final hope
Is flat despair; we must exasperate
Th' Almighty Victor to spend all his rage,
And that must end us, that must be our cure, [145]
To be no more; sad cure; for who would loose,
Though full of pain, this intellectual being,
Those thoughts that wander through Eternity,
To perish rather, swallowd up and lost
In the wide womb of uncreated night, [150]
Devoid of sense and motion? and who knows,
Let this be good, whether our angry Foe
Can give it, or will ever? how he can
Is doubtful; that he never will is sure.
Will he, so wise, let loose at once his ire, [155]
Belike through impotence, or unaware,
To give his Enemies thir wish, and end
Them in his anger, whom his anger saves
To punish endless? wherefore cease we then?
Say they who counsel Warr, we are decreed, [160]
Reserv'd and destin'd to Eternal woe;
Whatever doing, what can we suffer more,
What can we suffer worse? is this then worst,
Thus sitting, thus consulting, thus in Arms?
What when we fled amain, pursu'd and strook [165]
With Heav'ns afflicting Thunder, and besought
The Deep to shelter us? this Hell then seem'd
A refuge from those wounds: or when we lay

當今之計，唯有派出一個機智過人、心思縝密的戰士，前去探查預言中的新樂園。據說，在天堂和地獄之外，有一個美麗的新世界正在形成，生活在其中的新種族叫做『人類』；他們承受上帝的特別恩寵，在新樂園快樂無憂地生活著。

「如果真有這樣一個地方，我們大可取代人類，遷移到那兒生活，就如同上帝驅趕我們一般；或者，用陰謀詭計引誘人類，讓他們加入我們的陣營，一起反對上帝，這樣更能叫上帝忿怒痛苦，有什麼比被自己深愛的人背叛更痛苦的呢？同時祂必得忍痛摧毀自己親手創造的新種族，這樣的復仇方式豈不更加痛快？」

別西卜額頭上思慮的刻痕，因發表了這番激動的演說，而愈發閃現出智慧的光華。

「好啊！真是妙計。」

「對呀！就這麼辦。」

眾人紛紛附和別西卜的建議，吵雜

Chain'd on the burning Lake? that sure was worse.
What if the breath that kindl'd those grim fires [170]
Awak'd should blow them into sevenfold rage
And plunge us in the flames? or from above
Should intermitted vengeance arm again
His red right hand to plague us? what if all
Her stores were open'd, and this Firmament [175]
Of Hell should spout her Cataracts of Fire,
Impendent horrors, threatning hideous fall
One day upon our heads; while we perhaps
Designing or exhorting glorious warr,
Caught in a fierie Tempest shall be hurl'd [180]
Each on his rock transfixt, the sport and prey
Of racking whirlwinds, or for ever sunk
Under yon boyling Ocean, wrapt in Chains;
There to converse with everlasting groans,
Unrespited, unpitied, unreprevd, [185]
Ages of hopeless end; this would be worse.
Warr therefore, open or conceal'd, alike
My voice disswades; for what can force or guile
With him, or who deceive his mind, whose eye
Views all things at one view? he from heav'ns highth [190]
All these our motions vain, sees and derides;
Not more Almighty to resist our might
Then wise to frustrate all our plots and wiles.
Shall we then live thus vile, the race of Heav'n
Thus trampl'd, thus expell'd to suffer here [195]
Chains and these Torments? better these then worse
By my advice; since fate inevitable
Subdues us, and Omnipotent Decree
The Victors will. To suffer, as to doe,
Our strength is equal, nor the Law unjust [200]
That so ordains: this was at first resolv'd,
If we were wise, against so great a foe
Contending, and so doubtful what might fall.
I laugh, when those who at the Spear are bold
And vent'rous, if that fail them, shrink and fear [205]
What yet they know must follow, to endure
Exile, or ignominy, or bonds, or pain,
The sentence of thir Conquerour: This is now
Our doom; which if we can sustain and bear,
Our Supream Foe in time may much remit [210]

的喧囂如山谷迴音，在寬廣的惡魔殿
大廳嗡嗡地迴響著。

「那麼，有誰願意前去尋找新樂園
的所在地？」別西卜問道。

沒有人敢冒險承擔這個重責大任，
大家面面相覷，聲浪漸漸變小了，如
同狂風暫歇，海浪輕輕拍打岸邊岩石
的節奏，囈語般的茫然。

「我去。」

撒旦從寶座上一躍而起，以無比威
嚴的聲調向群魔宣布：

「身為領袖，如果連這點擔當都沒
有，怎有臉面繼續領導各位。」

語氣中無一絲恐懼，而且神情泰然
自若；眾人聽聞，一時皆羞愧於己身
的膽小懦弱，並對撒旦生出一股崇敬
之情，他們不由地抬起頭來，以無比
尊敬的目光望著大首領，聆聽他接著
發表的言論。

「首先，這旅途的艱險是無庸置疑
的。就說這地獄吧！本身就有九層深
淵，處處佈滿著炙熱的烈火；一面堅

His anger, and perhaps thus farr remov'd
Not mind us not offending, satisfi'd
With what is punish't; whence these raging fires
Will slack'n, if his breath stir not thir flames.
Our purer essence then will overcome [215]
Thir noxious vapour, or enur'd not feel,
Or chang'd at length, and to the place conformd
In temper and in nature, will receive
Familiar the fierce heat, and void of pain;
This horror will grow milde, this darkness light, [220]
Besides what hope the never-ending flight
Of future dayes may bring, what chance, what change
Worth waiting, since our present lot appeers
For happy though but ill, for ill not worst,
If we procure not to our selves more woe. [225]

Thus Belial with words cloath'd in reasons garb
Counsell'd ignoble ease, and peaceful sloath,
Not peace: and after him thus Mammon spake.

Either to disinthrone the King of Heav'n
We warr, if Warr be best, or to regain [230]
Our own right lost: him to unthrone we then
May hope when everlasting Fate shall yeild
To fickle Chance, and Chaos judge the strife:
The former vain to hope argues as vain
The latter: for what place can be for us [235]
Within Heav'ns bound, unless Heav'ns Lord supream
We overpower? Suppose he should relent
And publish Grace to all, on promise made
Of new Subjection; with what eyes could we
Stand in his presence humble, and receive [240]
Strict Laws impos'd, to celebrate his Throne
With warbl'd Hymns, and to his Godhead sing
Forc't Halleluiah's; while he Lordly sits
Our envied Sovran, and his Altar breathes
Ambrosial Odours and Ambrosial Flowers, [245]
Our servile offerings. This must be our task
In Heav'n, this our delight; how wearisom
Eternity so spent in worship paid
To whom we hate. Let us not then pursue
By force impossible, by leave obtain'd [250]

硬的金剛石大門阻絕了出路，得另覓
蹊徑才能離開。但在地獄外頭的『黑
夜』，早已張開血盆大口，虎視眈眈
地等著旅人自投羅網。如果幸運的躲
開黑夜的魔掌，誰又能知曉未知的新
世界是個什麼樣子？會不會佈滿更多
的險惡。

「我這番獨自冒險，完全是出於
想為各位尋得美好生活環境的熱切心
理，希望各位耐心些，暫時把地獄當
作居所，等我帶好消息回來。」

說畢，撒旦隨即宣布解散，不讓部
眾有反對的機會，藉此來堅定自己的
決心，並對士兵們彰顯己身非凡的氣
魄。

對於首領充滿自信的決定，將士們
除了暗自佩服之外，並無其他異議；
解散之後，從惡魔殿湧出的人潮，如
高山上的瀑布向下傾洩，白花花的水
珠濺向四方，兵士們也分散開來，在
地獄中尋找各自的樂趣。

有的在平野上狂奔比快，或在天

Unacceptable, though in Heav'n, our state
Of splendid vassalage, but rather seek
Our own good from our selves, and from our own
Live to our selves, though in this vast recess,
Free, and to none accountable, preferring [255]
Hard liberty before the easie yoke
Of servile Pomp. Our greatness will appeer
Then most conspicuous, when great things of small,
Useful of hurtful, prosperous of adverse
We can create, and in what place so e're [260]
Thrive under evil, and work ease out of pain
Through labour and indurance. This deep world
Of darkness do we dread? How oft amidst
Thick clouds and dark doth Heav'ns all-ruling Sire
Choose to reside, his Glory unobscur'd, [265]
And with the Majesty of darkness round
Covers his Throne; from whence deep thunders roar
Must'ring thir rage, and Heav'n resembles Hell?
As he our darkness, cannot we his Light
Imitate when we please? This Desart soile [270]
Wants not her hidden lustre, Gemms and Gold;
Nor want we skill or Art, from whence to raise
Magnificence; and what can Heav'n shew more?
Our torments also may in length of time
Become our Elements, these piercing Fires [275]
As soft as now severe, our temper chang'd
Into their temper; which must needs remove
The sensible of pain. All things invite
To peaceful Counsels, and the settl'd State
Of order, how in safety best we may [280]
Compose our present evils, with regard
Of what we are and were, dismissing quite
All thoughts of warr: ye have what I advise.

He scarce had finisht, when such murmur filld
Th' Assembly, as when hollow Rocks retain [285]
The sound of blustring winds, which all night long
Had rous'd the Sea, now with hoarse cadence lull
Sea-faring men orewatcht, whose Bark by chance
Or Pinnace anchors in a craggy Bay
After the Tempest: Such applause was heard [290]
As Mammon ended, and his Sentence pleas'd,

際翱翔爭勝，如奧林匹克競技場上爭
相競逐的選手，喧嚷紛紜；有的編排
成伍，如上戰場般地向前衝鋒；更有
人以怒吼來宣洩情緒，發出泰坦巨人
般狂暴的叫聲，似山岩崩塌，轟隆隆
地響徹地府，讓人聯想起希臘神話中
的大力士海克力斯（Hercules）悲慘
的遭遇。當時海克力斯背叛妻子愛上
了其他女人，被妻子以毒袍焚身，劇
痛難當之際，以顫抖的雙手連根拔起
數棵巨松，並舉起無辜的妻子拋向大
海，剎時激起一陣巨浪，發出海浪拍
擊的狂嘯聲。[3]

　　個性較為溫和的一群則漫步到山
谷，閒散地坐臥於岩石，一邊撫琴彈
奏出柔和優美的樂章，那和諧美妙的

註3：海克力斯（Hercules）是希臘神話中的大英
　　雄，為世間最強壯的人，但他處理事情經常是
　　有勇無謀，曾經得罪過天后赫拉（Hera）；
　　海克力斯的妻子黛安妮拉（Deianira）深深愛
　　著他，無法忍受他的變心，於是當他帶著利底
　　亞的公主回家來時，她便拿出沾著人頭馬鮮血
　　的長袍騙丈夫穿上，原本想讓丈夫回心轉意，
　　不料卻反而中了人頭馬的詭計，毒死心愛的
　　人；最後，自己也落得死亡的下場。

Advising peace: for such another Field
They dreaded worse then Hell: so much the fear
Of Thunder and the Sword of Michael
Wrought still within them; and no less desire [295]
To found this nether Empire, which might rise
By pollicy, and long process of time,
In emulation opposite to Heav'n.
Which when Beelzebub perceiv'd, then whom,
Satan except, none higher sat, with grave [300]
Aspect he rose, and in his rising seem'd
A Pillar of State; deep on his Front engraven
Deliberation sat and public care;
And Princely counsel in his face yet shon,
Majestic though in ruin: sage he stood [305]
With Atlantean shoulders fit to bear
The weight of mightiest Monarchies; his look
Drew audience and attention still as Night
Or Summers Noon-tide air, while thus he spake.

Thrones and Imperial Powers, off-spring of heav'n [310]
Ethereal Vertues; or these Titles now
Must we renounce, and changing stile be call'd
Princes of Hell? for so the popular vote
Inclines, here to continue, and build up here
A growing Empire; doubtless; while we dream, [315]
And know not that the King of Heav'n hath doom'd
This place our dungeon, not our safe retreat
Beyond his Potent arm, to live exempt
From Heav'ns high jurisdiction, in new League
Banded against his Throne, but to remaine [320]
In strictest bondage, though thus far remov'd,
Under th' inevitable curb, reserv'd
His captive multitude: For he, be sure
In heighth or depth, still first and last will Reign
Sole King, and of his Kingdom loose no part [325]
By our revolt, but over Hell extend
His Empire, and with Iron Scepter rule
Us here, as with his Golden those in Heav'n.
What sit we then projecting peace and Warr?
Warr hath determin'd us, and foild with loss [330]
Irreparable; tearms of peace yet none
Voutsaf't or sought; for what peace will be giv'n

歌聲吸引了許多聽眾，齊來聆賞宛若天籟般悅耳的音樂。還有些喜愛思考的，他們聚在一塊兒，討論著理性、命運與自由意志等高深的學問，談的雖多，卻無明確的結論，猶似墜入茫茫雲霧，虛空而無益。

另外一些具有冒險性格的則展開探勘行動，他們沿著四條注入火湖的河流向前邁進。這四條地獄之河的名稱為恨河、怨河、嘆河與火河，分別有憎恨、愁怨、悲嘆、炎燄的意涵；另外，離它們稍遠處尚有一條忘河，

To us enslav'd, but custody severe,
And stripes, and arbitrary punishment
Inflicted? and what peace can we return, [335]
But to our power hostility and hate,
Untam'd reluctance, and revenge though slow,
Yet ever plotting how the Conqueror least
May reap his conquest, and may least rejoice
In doing what we most in suffering feel? [340]
Nor will occasion want, nor shall we need

▽ **橫渡冥河**
帕德尼耶 油畫 1510年

　　冥河泛指在地獄間流動的河流，主要有四大河，包括恨河（守誓河）、怨河（苦惱河）、悲河（悲歎）、火河。要進入地獄會先經過怨河，想過河的死者必須支付船資給擺渡人卡龍，否則會被趕下船。悲河則是由地獄亡靈的眼淚集結而成。恨河的水據說能讓天神失去神性，所以成為天神發誓的場所。火河則是熊熊炙焰，用來區隔地獄的各個區域。

若飲了忘河的河水，不但會遺忘所有
過往的記憶，而且連喜悅、憤怒、哀
傷、快樂等情緒也會一併喪失。[4]

　忘河流經一片廣闊的冰原，終年
冰天雪地，不斷遭受颶風和冰雹的襲
擊；冰雹無法消融，經年累月堆疊成
一座座冰山，像是廢棄古城裡的斷壁
殘垣，無比荒涼。冰原的外圍環繞著
一道無底深淵，有如埃及的撒卜尼斯
湖（Serbonis），四周佈滿沙漠，當大
風一吹，瞬間飛沙走石、遮雲蔽日，
讓一整隊的埃及大軍淹沒其中；深淵
異常乾燥，且冷風陣陣刺人肌骨；復
仇三女神把世間的罪犯抓來此地，先
丟進烈火裡焚燒一段時日，再命令他
們渡過忘河來到深淵受冰凍之苦，一
遍又一遍，犯人的肉體得反覆遭受極
熱與極冷的痛楚[5]。

註4：希臘神話中的地獄之河有四條：一、恨
　　　河，希臘文「Styx」；二、怨河，希
　　　臘文「Acheron」；三、嘆河，希臘
　　　文「Cocytus」；四、火河，希臘文
　　　「Phlegethon」。另有一條較小的河流叫忘
　　　河，希臘文「Lethe」。

With dangerous expedition to invade
Heav'n, whose high walls fear no assault or Siege,
Or ambush from the Deep. What if we find
Some easier enterprize? There is a place [345]
(If ancient and prophetic fame in Heav'n
Err not) another World, the happy seat
Of some new Race call'd Man, about this time
To be created like to us, though less
In power and excellence, but favour'd more [350]
Of him who rules above; so was his will
Pronounc'd among the Gods, and by an Oath,
That shook Heav'ns whol circumference, confirm'd.
Thither let us bend all our thoughts, to learn
What creatures there inhabit, of what mould, [355]
Or substance, how endu'd, and what thir Power,
And where thir weakness, how attempted best,
By force or suttlety: Though Heav'n be shut,
And Heav'ns high Arbitrator sit secure
In his own strength, this place may lye expos'd [360]
The utmost border of his Kingdom, left
To their defence who hold it: here perhaps
Som advantagious act may be achiev'd
By sudden onset, either with Hell fire
To waste his whole Creation, or possess [365]
All as our own, and drive as we were driven,
The punie habitants, or if not drive,
Seduce them to our Party, that thir God
May prove thir foe, and with repenting hand
Abolish his own works. This would surpass [370]
Common revenge, and interrupt his joy
In our Confusion, and our Joy upraise
In his disturbance; when his darling Sons
Hurl'd headlong to partake with us, shall curse
Thir frail Original, and faded bliss, [375]
Faded so soon. Advise if this be worth
Attempting, or to sit in darkness here
Hatching vain Empires. Thus Beelzebub
Pleaded his devilish Counsel, first devis'd
By Satan, and in part propos'd: for whence, [380]
But from the Author of all ill could Spring
So deep a malice, to confound the race
Of mankind in one root, and Earth with Hell

當這些犯罪者搭船來回接受冷熱的懲罰時，他們渴望能夠掬飲一口忘河中的河水，那怕是一小口也好，就能忘卻身體所遭受的痛苦；但女妖美杜莎（Medusa）把守在渡口，頭上蛇髮磐結，寸步不移地以兇惡的目光監視著他們，不讓他們有彎腰的機會[6]；況且，這河水本身也是被施以詛咒的，只要有人張口接近，它便飛快遠離，如神話中的坦特勒斯（Tantalus），因褻瀆神祇被其父親宙斯懲罰，全身除了頭顱之外都浸泡在地獄的水池中，每當他張嘴想飲水時，水便立即退去，讓他陷在極度饑渴之中。[7]

這個佈滿重重險阻與無底深淵的黑暗牢籠，是上帝親手創造的「惡」境，這兒只有死亡與痛苦，生者入則死，死者入則生，生命反其道而行，於是繁衍出許多猙獰邪惡的怪物，那外貌醜陋的程度，更甚於神話裡的蛇髮女妖、九頭蛟龍海德拉（Hydra）

To mingle and involve, done all to spite
The great Creatour? But thir spite still serves [385]
His glory to augment. The bold design
Pleas'd highly those infernal States, and joy
Sparkl'd in all thir eyes; with full assent
They vote: whereat his speech he thus renews.

Well have ye judg'd, well ended long debate, [390]
Synod of Gods, and like to what ye are,
Great things resolv'd; which from the lowest deep
Will once more lift us up, in spight of Fate,
Neerer our ancient Seat; perhaps in view
Of those bright confines, whence with neighbouring Arms [395]
And opportune excursion we may chance

註5：復仇三女神為希臘羅馬神話中的神祇，有「黑暗行者」之稱，她們的雙眼佈滿紅色血絲，以公正不阿的態度在世間追捕犯罪者，把他們抓到陰間接受懲罰。

註6：美杜莎（Medusa）為希臘羅馬神話中的蛇髮三女妖之一，她有著一對巨大的翅膀，全身滿佈金色鱗片，頭髮是一團不斷扭動的毒蛇，誰若看了她一眼，立刻便化成石頭。除了美杜莎外，其他兩個女妖都能夠長生不死。

註7：坦特勒斯（Tantalus）是希臘神話中天神宙斯於凡間所生的眾子女之一，宙斯最為寵愛他，但他生性驕傲自大，甚至兇殘地殺死自己的兒子，分屍切割烹煮給神祇們吃，想藉此顯出祂們的愚蠢；但其詭計被眾神識破，宙斯憤怒地把他禁錮在黑暗地獄的水池中，當其口渴，彎腰想喝水時，池水便退至池底，不讓他喝到；池子旁邊滿是垂掛著累累果實的果樹，當他饑餓，伸手欲採摘果子時，一陣狂風就會吹來，把樹枝吹向高處不讓他搆著，讓他承受饑渴的無盡煎熬，以此懲戒他輕視神祇和傲慢殘忍的行為。

與噴火怪獸基抹拉（Ohimaera）。[8]

　　這支極具冒險性的探勘隊伍，在親眼目睹了地獄中的可怕景象之後，內心頓時茫然起來，對未來更是喪失了信心；他們走累了，卻找不到一處可以休息的地方，只好繼續前進，一邊忍受沿途反覆交錯的炎熱火燄與嚴寒冰雪，一邊從嘴裡發出喃喃的嘆息

Re-enter Heav'n; or else in some milde Zone
Dwell not unvisited of Heav'ns fair Light
Secure, and at the brightning Orient beam
Purge off this gloom; the soft delicious Air, [400]
To heal the scarr of these corrosive Fires
Shall breath her balme. But first whom shall we send
In search of this new world, whom shall we find
Sufficient? who shall tempt with wandring feet
The dark unbottom'd infinite Abyss [405]
And through the palpable obscure find out
His uncouth way, or spread his aerie flight
Upborn with indefatigable wings
Over the vast abrupt, ere he arrive
The happy Ile; what strength, what art can then [410]
Suffice, or what evasion bear him safe
Through the strict Senteries and Stations thick
Of Angels watching round? Here he had need
All circumspection, and we now no less
Choice in our suffrage; for on whom we send, [415]
The weight of all and our last hope relies.

This said, he sat; and expectation held
His look suspence, awaiting who appeer'd
To second, or oppose, or undertake

註8：九頭蚊龍海德拉（Hydra）為希臘羅馬神話中的怪物，住在沼澤地區，九頭中有一顆頭顱是長生不死的，因此要是砍錯其他八顆頭，反而會加倍長出新的頭顱，後來被海克力斯殺死。噴火怪獸基抹拉（Ohimaera）則是由獅子、山羊、蛇等外形所構成的可怕怪物。

◁ 地獄裡悲慘可怕的景象
杜雷 版畫 1866年

　　根據米爾頓的描述，地獄是個反其道而行的可怕惡境，所以繁衍出各種醜陋猙獰的怪物。撒旦的部眾探險至此，好不容易重新鼓舞的精神，恐怕又涼了一大半。

∧ 地獄之門
羅丹 青銅雕塑 1880~1917年

　　地獄之門厚厚九重，三重鐵鑄、三重銅造、三重金剛岩，確保地獄的亡魂惡靈無法破門而出。法國雕塑家羅丹從但丁《神曲》的地獄篇得到靈感，花了三十多年完成一件群雕門飾，將地獄的貪嗔癡欲通通集結在門上。

The perilous attempt; but all sat mute, [420]
Pondering the danger with deep thoughts; and each
In others count'nance read his own dismay
Astonisht: none among the choice and prime
Of those Heav'n-warring Champions could be found
So hardie as to proffer or accept [425]
Alone the dreadful voyage; till at last
Satan, whom now transcendent glory rais'd
Above his fellows, with Monarchal pride
Conscious of highest worth, unmov'd thus spake.

O Progeny of Heav'n, Empyreal Thrones, [430]
With reason hath deep silence and demurr
Seis'd us, though undismaid: long is the way
And hard, that out of Hell leads up to light;
Our prison strong, this huge convex of Fire,
Outrageous to devour, immures us round [435]
Ninefold, and gates of burning Adamant
Barr'd over us prohibit all egress.
These past, if any pass, the void profound
Of unessential Night receives him next
Wide gaping, and with utter loss of being [440]
Threatens him, plung'd in that abortive gulf.
If thence he scape into whatever world,
Or unknown Region, what remains him less
Then unknown dangers and as hard escape.
But I should ill become this Throne, O Peers, [445]
And this Imperial Sov'ranty, adorn'd
With splendor, arm'd with power, if aught propos'd
And judg'd of public moment, in the shape
Of difficulty or danger could deterr
Mee from attempting. Wherefore do I assume [450]
These Royalties, and not refuse to Reign,
Refusing to accept as great a share
Of hazard as of honour, due alike
To him who Reigns, and so much to him due
Of hazard more, as he above the rest [455]
High honourd sits? Go therefore mighty Powers,
Terror of Heav'n, though fall'n; intend at home,
While here shall be our home, what best may ease
The present misery, and render Hell
More tollerable; if there be cure or charm [460]

聲，哀泣自己可悲的命運。

　　另一方面，撒旦已飛離潘地曼尼南，獨自邁向未知的旅程。他展開巨大的雙翼，貼伏著湖面忽上忽下地飛掠，一會偏向左方、一會偏向右方，

宛如遙遙望見的遠方舟影，飄忽隱現；終於，他抵達了地獄大門。

地獄之門總共有厚厚九重，三重鐵鑄、三重銅造、另三重則是由金剛岩所煉成；門的四周有熊熊大火燃燒，兩旁的門柱底下各坐著一個看守人。

右邊是一個人頭蛇身的女人，她有著一頭及肩長髮，上半身婀娜多姿，相當美麗，但下半身卻是一條覆滿鱗片的巨大毒蛇尾巴；最恐怖的是，在她蜷曲的腹部，竟有一大堆長著三顆腦袋的猛犬圍繞，正齜牙咧嘴地朝撒旦狂吠[9]。這個景象，就像遇見了盤踞在義大利海域中的吃人怪物希拉，原本她是一個非常美麗迷人的仙女，但賽西施用法術把她的下半身變成一群不斷狂吠著的狗，使她成了一個六頭十二足的恐怖怪物。[10]

左邊則是一個模糊不清的兇惡物體，為什麼稱它作「物體」呢？因為實在無法看清楚它實際的面目，它像是一團影子，但卻又並非虛幻無形，

To respite or deceive, or slack the pain
Of this ill Mansion: intermit no watch
Against a wakeful Foe, while I abroad
Through all the Coasts of dark destruction seek
Deliverance for us all: this enterprize [465]
None shall partake with me. Thus saying rose
The Monarch, and prevented all reply,
Prudent, least from his resolution rais'd
Others among the chief might offer now
(Certain to be refus'd) what erst they fear'd; [470]
And so refus'd might in opinion stand
His Rivals, winning cheap the high repute
Which he through hazard huge must earn. But they
Dreaded not more th' adventure then his voice
Forbidding; and at once with him they rose; [475]
Thir rising all at once was as the sound
Of Thunder heard remote. Towards him they bend
With awful reverence prone; and as a God
Extoll him equal to the highest in Heav'n:
Nor fail'd they to express how much they prais'd, [480]
That for the general safety he despis'd
His own: for neither do the Spirits damn'd
Loose all thir vertue; least bad men should boast
Thir specious deeds on earth, which glory excites,
Or clos ambition varnisht o're with zeal. [485]
Thus they thir doubtful consultations dark
Ended rejoycing in thir matchless Chief:
As when from mountain tops the dusky clouds
Ascending, while the North wind sleeps, O'respread
Heav'ns chearful face, the lowring Element [490]
Scowls ore the dark'nd lantskip Snow, or showre;
If chance the radiant Sun with farewell sweet
Extend his ev'ning beam, the fields revive,
The birds thir notes renew, and bleating herds
Attest thir joy, that hill and valley rings. [495]

註9：出自希臘羅馬神話中的地獄犬，牠有三顆頭、一條龍尾，坐在地獄大門邊負責守衛，讓所有的陰魂進入，不讓任何人出來。

註10：出自荷馬《奧德賽》第十二卷。

^ 撒旦來到地獄之門
杜雷 版畫 1866年

　　地獄大門的兩旁各有可怕的怪物看守，撒旦為了離開地獄去尋找新樂園，毅然上前挑戰守門人，沒想這兩個醜陋的怪物，一個是女兒兼愛人的「罪惡」，一個是他的兒子「死亡」。

它正揮舞著尖銳的長矛，張牙舞爪地朝撒旦怒吼。

「滾開！醜陋的東西，別擋住我的去路。」

撒旦毫不畏懼地朝它大喊。

「哼！你就是那個膽敢發動天庭叛變的傢伙？還真是猖狂啊！不好好待在火湖接受應得的懲罰，竟然膽敢跑來我的地盤放肆。快點飛回火湖去，否則休怪我動手，以蠍尾鞭毒打你，或者，你想嚐嚐被長矛刺穿的滋味？」

那物體開口說道，凶惡的外貌又比先前更顯猙獰了。

「笑話！我可是尊貴的大天使，怎麼會怕你這個窩在地獄裡的無名小子？」

撒旦忿怒地回答，怒火如燃燒的慧星，又像天空中燃燒的北極星劃過長空。

空氣中隱隱流動著一股殺氣，他倆面對面站著，怒目相視，彷彿兩朵滿

O shame to men! Devil with Devil damn'd
Firm concord holds, men onely disagree
Of Creatures rational, though under hope
Of heavenly Grace; and God proclaiming peace,
Yet live in hatred, enmity, and strife [500]
Among themselves, and levie cruel warres,
Wasting the Earth, each other to destroy:
As if (which might induce us to accord)
Man had not hellish foes anow besides,
That day and night for his destruction waite. [505]

The Stygian Counsel thus dissolv'd; and forth
In order came the grand infernal Peers:
Midst came thir mighty Paramount, and seemd
Alone th' Antagonist of Heav'n, nor less
Than Hells dread Emperour with pomp Supream, [510]
And God-like imitated State; him round
A Globe of fierie Seraphim inclos'd
With bright imblazonrie, and horrent Arms.
Then of thir Session ended they bid cry
With Trumpets regal sound the great result: [515]
Toward the four winds four speedy Cherubim
Put to thir mouths the sounding Alchymie
By Haralds voice explain'd: the hollow Abyss
Heard farr and wide, and all the host of Hell
With deafning shout, return'd them loud acclaim. [520]
Thence more at ease thir minds and somwhat rais'd
By false presumptuous hope, the ranged powers
Disband, and wandring, each his several way
Pursues, as inclination or sad choice
Leads him perplext, where he may likeliest find [525]
Truce to his restless thoughts, and entertain
The irksom hours, till his great Chief return.
Part on the Plain, or in the Air sublime
Upon the wing, or in swift Race contend,
As at th' Olympian Games or Pythian fields; [530]
Part curb thir fierie Steeds, or shun the Goal
With rapid wheels, or fronted Brigads form.
As when to warn proud Cities warr appears
Wag'd in the troubl'd Skie, and Armies rush
To Battel in the Clouds, before each Van [535]
Prick forth the Aerie Knights, and couch thir Spears

載雷電的烏雲，在裡海上空發出轟隆隆的巨響，陰沉的地獄即將爆發一場惡鬥。

「快住手！」

蛇尾女妖衝到兩人中間，一臉驚慌，她先對撒旦說：

「啊！親愛的父親，你怎麼忍心殺死自己的兒子？」

接著，她又對那物體說：

「兒子，快放下手中的長矛，站在

Till thickest Legions close; with feats of Arms
From either end of Heav'n the welkin burns.
Others with vast Typhœan rage more fell
Rend up both Rocks and Hills, and ride the Air [540]
In whirlwind; Hell scarce holds the wilde uproar.
As when Alcides from Oechalia Crown'd
With conquest, felt th' envenom'd robe, and tore
Through pain up by the roots Thessalian Pines,
And Lichas from the top of Oeta threw [545]
Into th' Euboic Sea. Others more milde,
Retreated in a silent valley, sing
With notes Angelical to many a Harp
Thir own Heroic deeds and hapless fall
By doom of Battel; and complain that Fate [550]
Free Vertue should enthrall to Force or Chance.
Thir Song was partial, but the harmony
(What could it less when Spirits immortal sing?)
Suspended Hell, and took with ravishment
The thronging audience. In discourse more sweet [555]

∧ 撒旦、罪惡與死亡（左圖）、撒旦來到地獄門前（右圖）
布雷克 水彩畫 1807年、1808年
　　眼見父子就要殘殺起來，「罪惡」急得擋在兩人中間，真是戲劇性十足的衝突場面。

你眼前的，可是你的親生父親呀！如
果你殺了他，就中了上帝的詭計；此
刻，也許祂正得意洋洋地坐在高高的
寶座上，等待觀賞這場好戲呢！」

　　「什麼！我怎麼會是你的父親？
況且，我也不曾有個那麼醜陋的兒
子。」

　　撒旦冷冷地說著，一臉鄙夷。

　　「還記得那時你英俊挺拔的模樣，
和眾天使齊聚北方城堡商議叛變計
畫；你意氣風發地發表計策，突然一
陣劇痛，火燄從你的腦門迸射出來，
我就是從你頭顱左邊的裂口生出來
的。[11]

　　「當時的我是多麼美麗呀！宛若天
仙，姿態容貌就跟你一個樣，你視我
如己身，對我萬般寵愛，我倆在天庭
中過了一段如膠似漆的美好日子，難

註11：「罪惡」從撒旦的頭腦中生出，類似於希臘
　　　羅馬神話中雅典娜（Athena）出生的故事。
　　　雅典娜身著戰袍，直接從天神宙斯的腦袋中
　　　跳出來，成為凶狠無情的戰爭女神，並沒有
　　　母親。

(For Eloquence the Soul, Song charms the Sense,)
Others apart sat on a Hill retir'd,
In thoughts more elevate, and reason'd high
Of Providence, Foreknowledge, Will and Fate,
Fixt Fate, free will, foreknowledg absolute, [560]
And found no end, in wandring mazes lost.
Of good and evil much they argu'd then,
Of happiness and final misery,
Passion and Apathie, and glory and shame,
Vain wisdom all, and false Philosophie: [565]
Yet with a pleasing sorcerie could charm
Pain for a while or anguish, and excite
Fallacious hope, or arm th' obdured brest
With stubborn patience as with triple steel.
Another part in Squadrons and gross Bands, [570]
On bold adventure to discover wide
That dismal world, if any Clime perhaps
Might yield them easier habitation, bend
Four ways thir flying March, along the Banks
Of four infernal Rivers that disgorge [575]
Into the burning Lake thir baleful streams;
Abhorred Styx the flood of deadly hate,
Sad Acheron of sorrow, black and deep;
Cocytus, nam'd of lamentation loud
Heard on the ruful stream; fierce Phlegeton [580]
Whose waves of torrent fire inflame with rage.
Farr off from these a slow and silent stream,
Lethe the River of Oblivion roules
Her watrie Labyrinth, whereof who drinks,
Forthwith his former state and being forgets, [585]
Forgets both joy and grief, pleasure and pain.
Beyond this flood a frozen Continent
Lies dark and wilde, beat with perpetual storms
Of Whirlwind and dire Hail, which on firm land
Thaws not, but gathers heap, and ruin seems [590]
Of ancient pile; all else deep snow and ice,
A gulf profound as that Serbonian Bog
Betwixt Damiata and Mount Casius old,
Where Armies whole have sunk: the parching Air
Burns frore, and cold performs th' effect of Fire. [595]
Thither by harpy-footed Furies hail'd,
At certain revolutions all the damn'd

道你都忘記了嗎？直到戰爭開始，我跟著大家從天上墜落，墮入這個陰森可怕的地獄，並被賦予看管地獄之門的責任，成為『罪惡』。」

蛇尾女妖紅了眼眶，眼淚簌簌地滑下臉頰。

「唉！我可憐的女兒和愛人呀，沒想到你竟有如此悲慘的境遇，我並不曾忘記你，只是無法把眼前的你，與昔日那嬌艷美麗的女人聯想在一塊兒。」

撒旦恍然大悟，彷彿想起什麼似的，語氣轉趨和緩。

「是呀！也難怪你認不出我來。那日，從天庭掉落當時我已經懷孕，你口中所說的醜陋怪物，叫做『死亡』，正是你的兒子；他在我的肚子裡劇烈蠕動，使我承受極大的痛苦，最後，終於撕裂我的腸子鑽了出來。我的下半身就在那個時候變成這副恐怖的模樣。

「可是，這個孽種竟然毫不感激我

Are brought: and feel by turns the bitter change
Of fierce extreams, extreams by change more fierce,
From Beds of raging Fire to starve in Ice [600]
Thir soft Ethereal warmth, and there to pine
Immovable, infixt, and frozen round,
Periods of time, thence hurried back to fire.
They ferry over this Lethean Sound
Both to and fro, thir sorrow to augment, [605]
And wish and struggle, as they pass, to reach
The tempting stream, with one small drop to loose
In sweet forgetfulness all pain and woe,
All in one moment, and so neer the brink;
But fate withstands, and to oppose th' attempt [610]
Medusa with Gorgonian terror guards
The Ford, and of it self the water flies
All taste of living wight, as once it fled
The lip of Tantalus. Thus roving on
In confus'd march forlorn, th' adventrous Bands [615]
With shuddring horror pale, and eyes agast
View'd first thir lamentable lot, and found
No rest: through many a dark and drearie Vaile
They pass'd, and many a Region dolorous,
O'er many a Frozen, many a fierie Alpe, [620]
Rocks, Caves, Lakes, Fens, Bogs, Dens, and shades of death,
A Universe of death, which God by curse
Created evil, for evil only good,
Where all life dies, death lives, and Nature breeds,
Perverse, all monstrous, all prodigious things, [625]
Abominable, inutterable, and worse
Then Fables yet have feign'd, or fear conceiv'd,
Gorgons and Hydra's, and Chimera's dire.

Mean while the Adversary of God and Man,
Satan with thoughts inflam'd of highest design, [630]
Puts on swift wings, and towards the Gates of Hell
Explores his solitary flight; som times
He scours the right hand coast, som times the left,
Now shaves with level wing the Deep, then soares
Up to the fiery Concave touring high. [635]
As when farr off at Sea a Fleet descri'd
Hangs in the Clouds, by Æquinoctial Winds
Close sailing from Bengala, or the Iles

給予他生命，落地那一刻便視我為敵人，揮舞著長矛要殺我；我在地獄中奔逃，一邊驚呼著『死亡』，那聲音傳遍地獄，發出陣陣嘆息。最後，我被他抓住了，並被凌辱，生下這群不斷狂吠的怪物；它們隨意進出我的肚子，啃嚙我的腸子，讓我沉淪在無盡的痛苦與驚嚇中。

「沒想到還能夠見到你，我真是太高興了；你千萬不可輕忽『死亡』手

▽ 撒旦、罪惡與死亡
霍爾加 油畫 1735~1740年

　　原先劍拔弩張的場面，卻變成骨肉相逢的認親大會，撒旦也在死亡和罪惡的幫助下，順利逃離地獄的封鎖。

Of Ternate and Tidore, whence Merchants bring
Thir spicie Drugs: they on the Trading Flood [640]
Through the wide Ethiopian to the Cape
Ply stemming nightly toward the Pole. So seem'd
Farr off the flying Fiend: at last appeer
Hell bounds high reaching to the horrid Roof,
And thrice threefold the Gates; three folds were Brass, [645]
Three Iron, three of Adamantine Rock,
Impenetrable, impal'd with circling fire,
Yet unconsum'd. Before the Gates there sat
On either side a formidable shape;
The one seem'd Woman to the waste, and fair, [650]
But ended foul in many a scaly fould
Voluminous and vast, a Serpent arm'd
With mortal sting: about her middle round
A cry of Hell Hounds never ceasing bark'd
With wide Cerberian mouths full loud, and rung [655]
A hideous Peal: yet, when they list, would creep,
If aught disturb'd thir noyse, into her woomb,
And kennel there, yet there still bark'd and howl'd
Within unseen. Farr less abhorrd than these
Vex'd Scylla bathing in the Sea that parts [660]
Calabria from the hoarse Trinacrian shore:
Nor uglier follow the Night-Hag, when call'd
In secret, riding through the Air she comes
Lur'd with the smell of infant blood, to dance
With Lapland Witches, while the labouring Moon [665]
Eclipses at thir charms. The other shape,
If shape it might be call'd that shape had none
Distinguishable in member, joynt, or limb,
Or substance might be call'd that shadow seem'd,
For each seem'd either; black it stood as Night, [670]
Fierce as ten Furies, terrible as Hell,
And shook a dreadful Dart; what seem'd his head
The likeness of a Kingly Crown had on.
Satan was now at hand, and from his seat
The Monster moving onward came as fast [675]
With horrid strides, Hell trembled as he strode.
Th' undaunted Fiend what this might be admir'd,
Admir'd, not fear'd; God and his Son except,
Created thing naught valu'd he nor shun'd
And with disdainful look thus first began. [680]

中的長矛，它的威力強大，就連天上的統治者都要讓它三分哩！」

說完，「罪惡」用手抹去眼角泊泊湧出的淚水。

「放心！既然知道『死亡』是我的兒子，我便不會再與他為敵。而且，我還要讓你們擺脫這個陰暗可怕的牢籠，到一個美麗、富足的新天地；此刻，我就是要前去探勘傳言中的新世界，只要找到它的方位，我必定會回來，領著你們母子倆一塊去過幸福的生活。」撒旦說道。

「是嗎，真有這樣一個地方？」

「死亡」用狐疑的目光望著撒旦，手中高舉的長矛已緩緩放下。

「當然，天庭早就有這個預言在流傳著，而且上帝也曾經示意天使們不可以去打擾那個即將形成的新天地。」撒旦露出自信的笑容，一邊說著。

「那好，你就把鑰匙給他吧！」

「死亡」轉頭對「罪惡」說。

Whence and what art thou, execrable shape,
That dar'st, though grim and terrible, advance
Thy miscreated Front athwart my way
To yonder Gates? through them I mean to pass,
That be assured, without leave askt of thee: [685]
Retire, or taste thy folly, and learn by proof,
Hell-born, not to contend with Spirits of Heav'n.

To whom the Goblin full of wrauth reply'd,
Art thou that Traitor Angel, art thou hee,
Who first broke peace in Heav'n and Faith, till then [690]
Unbrok'n, and in proud rebellious Arms
Drew after him the third part of Heav'ns Sons
Conjur'd against the highest, for which both Thou
And they outcast from God, are here condemn'd
To waste Eternal dayes in woe and pain? [695]
And reck'n'st thou thy self with Spirits of Heav'n,
Hell-doom'd, and breath'st defiance here and scorn
Where I reign King, and to enrage thee more,
Thy King and Lord? Back to thy punishment,
False fugitive, and to thy speed add wings, [700]
Least with a whip of Scorpions I pursue
Thy lingring, or with one stroke of this Dart
Strange horror seise thee, and pangs unfelt before.

So spake the grieslie terror, and in shape,
So speaking and so threatning, grew tenfold [705]
More dreadful and deform: on th' other side
Incenst with indignation Satan stood
Unterrifi'd, and like a Comet burn'd,
That fires the length of Ophiucus huge
In th' Artick Sky, and from his horrid hair [710]
Shakes Pestilence and Warr. Each at the Head
Level'd his deadly aime; thir fatall hands
No second stroke intend, and such a frown
Each cast at th' other, as when two black Clouds
With Heav'ns Artillery fraught, come rattling on [715]
Over the Caspian, then stand front to front
Hov'ring a space, till Winds the signal blow
To join thir dark Encounter in mid air:
So frownd the mighty Combatants, that Hell
Grew darker at thir frown, so matcht they stood; [720]

「不！除了我自己，沒有人能夠打開地獄之門，這是上帝授予我的權力，我將親手為父親打開這一道道大門。」

說完，「罪惡」猛力揮動蛇尾，拔去大門上的門閂；接著，她取出鑰匙圖片鎖孔，一旋轉，「喀嚓！」地獄之門應聲而開。

「再見！我深愛的父親與愛人，請你務必遵守諾言，回來領我母子倆到

▽ 撒旦、罪惡與死亡
吉爾雷 插畫 1792年

吉爾雷曾經以《失樂園》這幕「撒旦、罪惡與死亡」來諷刺當時英國政局的角力。死神暗指當時的總理大臣彼特，撒旦暗指大法官特勞，夾在兩人中間的正是當時的皇后夏洛特。

For never but once more was either like
To meet so great a foe: and now great deeds
Had been achiev'd, whereof all Hell had rung,
Had not the Snakie Sorceress that sat
Fast by Hell Gate, and kept the fatal Key, [725]
Ris'n, and with hideous outcry rush'd between.

O Father, what intends thy hand, she cry'd,
Against thy only Son? What fury O Son,
Possesses thee to bend that mortal Dart
Against thy Fathers head? and know'st for whom; [730]
For him who sits above and laughs the while
At thee ordain'd his drudge, to execute
What e're his wrath, which he calls Justice, bids,
His wrath which one day will destroy ye both.

She spake, and at her words the hellish Pest [735]
Forbore, then these to her Satan return'd:

So strange thy outcry, and thy words so strange
Thou interposest, that my sudden hand
Prevented spares to tell thee yet by deeds
What it intends; till first I know of thee, [740]
What thing thou art, thus double-form'd, and why
In this infernal Vaile first met thou call'st
Me Father, and that Fantasm call'st my Son?
I know thee not, nor ever saw till now
Sight more detestable then him and thee. [745]

T' whom thus the Portress of Hell Gate reply'd;
Hast thou forgot me then, and do I seem
Now in thine eye so foul, once deemd so fair
In Heav'n, when at th' Assembly, and in sight
Of all the Seraphim with thee combin'd [750]
In bold conspiracy against Heav'ns King,
All on a sudden miserable pain
Surprisd thee, dim thine eyes, and dizzie swumm
In darkness, while thy head flames thick and fast
Threw forth, till on the left side op'ning wide, [755]
Likest to thee in shape and count'nance bright,
Then shining Heav'nly fair, a Goddess arm'd
Out of thy head I sprung; amazement seis'd

新世界去享樂，我不願繼續過著這種可怕的生活。我將守在這兒，等你帶回來好消息。」

　　撒旦走出地獄大門，眼前一片黑壓壓，待他適應了黑暗，才看清在他前方的是漫無邊際的汪洋，分辨不出高度、廣度與長度，時間和空間也在這裡消失了。

　　「自然」的始祖 ── 「夜」與「渾沌」，從遙遠的太古時期便統治著這個地方；「冷」、「熱」、「燥」、「濕」四個凶悍戰士終日爭戰，屬於他們四者的原子胚胎群，也揮動著各自專屬的旗幟，浩浩蕩蕩地加入戰局，像非洲北部巴卡（Barca）地方的沙漠，燥熱的砂子被捲入風裡，增加了風的重量，使它更為狂暴。

　　「渾沌」是他們的仲裁者，但他並不阻止戰爭，反而以無理的判決擴大事端，讓他們爭鬥得更加厲害；藉由製造混亂，來鞏固自己的統治地位；「機會」則是更高一級的仲裁者。

All th' Host of Heav'n back they recoild affraid
At first, and call'd me Sin, and for a Sign [760]
Portentous held me; but familiar grown,
I pleas'd, and with attractive graces won
The most averse, thee chiefly, who full oft
Thy self in me thy perfect image viewing
Becam'st enamour'd, and such joy thou took'st [765]
With me in secret, that my womb conceiv'd
A growing burden. Mean while Warr arose,
And fields were fought in Heav'n; wherein remain
(For what could else) to our Almighty Foe
Cleer Victory, to our part loss and rout [770]
Through all the Empyrean: down they fell
Driv'n headlong from the Pitch of Heaven, down
Into this Deep, and in the general fall
I also; at which time this powerful Key
Into my hand was giv'n, with charge to keep [755]
These Gates for ever shut, which none can pass
Without my op'ning. Pensive here I sat
Alone, but long I sat not, till my womb
Pregnant by thee, and now excessive grown
Prodigious motion felt and rueful throes. [780]
At last this odious offspring whom thou seest
Thine own begotten, breaking violent way
Tore through my entrails, that with fear and pain
Distorted, all my nether shape thus grew
Transform'd: but he my inbred enemie [785]
Forth issu'd, brandishing his fatal Dart
Made to destroy: I fled, and cry'd out Death;
Hell trembl'd at the hideous Name, and sigh'd
From all her Caves, and back resounded Death.
I fled, but he pursu'd (though more, it seems, [790]
Inflam'd with lust then rage) and swifter far,
Mee overtook his mother all dismaid,
And in embraces forcible and foule
Ingendring with me, of that rape begot
These yelling Monsters that with ceasless cry [795]
Surround me, as thou sawst, hourly conceiv'd
And hourly born, with sorrow infinite
To me, for when they list into the womb
That bred them they return, and howle and gnaw
My Bowels, thir repast; then bursting forth [800]

這個昏暗紛亂的地方是「自然」的起源，或者，也可以說是它的墳墓；它並非海、地、風、火的產物，但卻是由它們交相混融而成，中間歷經了不斷紛爭的過程，直等著那萬能的造物主來把它們重新捏塑，築成一個新的世界。

　　撒旦站在黑暗狂亂的深淵旁邊，思考著該如何渡過這個境地往前行，一陣陣轟雷聲響徹耳際，彷彿是神話中的女戰神貝洛娜（Bellona），正在揮動手中的武器攻打城池，發出猛烈的撞擊聲；又像支撐天庭的柱石傾倒，大地崩塌傳來的巨響。

　　終於，他張開巨大如船帆的雙翼往上飛去，穿梭在雲層裡；不久，突遇真空之境，一不小心失去重心，往萬丈深淵墜落，眼看就要掉回地獄了；還好，一團亂雲接住他，藉著硫磺火燄的幫助，帶他回到原來的高度，繼續往上飛升。

　　後來，他失足踏入一片低窪潮溼的

A fresh with conscious terrours vex me round,
That rest or intermission none I find.
Before mine eyes in opposition sits
Grim Death my Son and foe, who sets them on,
And me his Parent would full soon devour [805]
For want of other prey, but that he knows
His end with mine involvd; and knows that I
Should prove a bitter Morsel, and his bane,
Whenever that shall be; so Fate pronounc'd.
But thou O Father, I forewarn thee, shun [810]
His deadly arrow; neither vainly hope
To be invulnerable in those bright Arms,
Though temper'd heav'nly, for that mortal dint,
Save he who reigns above, none can resist.

She finish'd, and the suttle Fiend his lore [815]
Soon learnd, now milder, and thus answerd smooth.
Dear Daughter, since thou claim'st me for thy Sire,
And my fair Son here showst me, the dear pledge
Of dalliance had with thee in Heav'n, and joys
Then sweet, now sad to mention, through dire change [820]
Befalln us unforeseen, unthought of, know
I come no enemie, but to set free
From out this dark and dismal house of pain,
Both him and thee, and all the heav'nly Host
Of Spirits that in our just pretenses arm'd [825]
Fell with us from on high: from them I go
This uncouth errand sole, and one for all
Myself expose, with lonely steps to tread
Th' unfounded deep, and through the void immense
To search with wandring quest a place foretold [830]
Should be, and, by concurring signs, ere now
Created vast and round, a place of bliss
In the Purlieues of Heav'n, and therein plac't
A race of upstart Creatures, to supply
Perhaps our vacant room, though more remov'd, [835]
Least Heav'n surcharg'd with potent multitude
Might hap to move new broiles: Be this or aught
Then this more secret now design'd, I haste
To know, and this once known, shall soon return,
And bring ye to the place where Thou and Death [840]
Shall dwell at ease, and up and down unseen

沼澤，腳跟都陷在泥淖裡，差點就被流沙攫住，往下沉沒；他奮力抬起雙足，使盡全身的力氣，半跑半飛地往前狂奔，極欲擺脫這片既非陸地、也

▽ 撒旦艱苦的旅程
杜雷 版畫 1866年

　　離開地獄大門的撒旦，進入一片混沌未明的境地，沿途盡是凶險，除了狂風暴雨，還有萬丈深淵和沼澤流沙需要一一克服，在米爾頓筆下，要成為萬惡之王的撒旦，也有自己的一段艱苦旅程。

Wing silently the buxom Air, imbalm'd
With odours; there ye shall be fed and fill'd
Immeasurably, all things shall be your prey.
He ceas'd, for both seem'd highly pleasd, and Death [845]
Grindd horrible a gastly smile, to hear
His famine should be fill'd, and blest his mawe
Destin'd to that good hour: no less rejoyc'd
His mother bad, and thus bespake her Sire.

The key of this infernal Pit by due, [850]
And by command of Heav'ns all-powerful King
I keep, by him forbidden to unlock
These Adamantine Gates; against all force
Death ready stands to interpose his dart,
Fearless to be o'rmatcht by living might. [855]
But what ow I to his commands above
Who hates me, and hath hither thrust me down
Into this gloom of Tartarus profound,
To sit in hateful Office here confin'd,
Inhabitant of Heav'n, and heav'nlie-born, [860]
Here in perpetual agonie and pain,
With terrors and with clamors compasst round
Of mine own brood, that on my bowels feed:
Thou art my Father, thou my Author, thou
My being gav'st me; whom should I obey [865]
But thee, whom follow? thou wilt bring me soon
To that new world of light and bliss, among
The Gods who live at ease, where I shall Reign
At thy right hand voluptuous, as beseems
Thy daughter and thy darling, without end. [870]

Thus saying, from her side the fatal Key,
Sad instrument of all our woe, she took;
And towards the Gate rouling her bestial train,
Forthwith the huge Porcullis high up drew,
Which but her self not all the Stygian powers [875]
Could once have mov'd; then in the key-hole turns
Th' intricate wards, and every Bolt and Bar
Of massie Iron or sollid Rock with ease
Unfast'ns: on a sudden op'n flie
With impetuous recoile and jarring sound [880]
Th' infernal dores, and on thir hinges grate

非海的地方。就像半獅半鷹的怪獸格
里芬（Gryphon），急速地往前追趕
那盜取黃金的獨眼龍，越過山谷和沼
澤，直追到荒蕪的曠野。

　　在經過不停地展翅、疾馳，或飛、
或潛、或涉水，頭、手、翼、足交相
使用之後，撒旦忽被黑暗所籠罩，周
遭一片漆黑，只耳邊傳來震耳欲聲的
喧嘩聲；他並不感到害怕，心中反而
有一絲喜悅，他往噪音的方向走去，
希望找到一個能夠指引光明路徑的下
界精靈。

　　等他走近，看見「混沌」和他的妻
子「夜」正坐在寶座上頭，他們的背
後是陰霾廣袤的天幕與巨浪衝天的大
海；站在旁邊的則是冥界之神奧克斯
（Orcus）、阿得斯（Ades）與可怕的
命運之神德摩高根（Demogorgon）。
另外，「謠言」、「投機」、「喧
擾」、「混亂」與有著千張嘴巴的
「吵鬧」也圍在附近，鬧哄哄地亂成
一團。

Harsh Thunder, that the lowest bottom shook
Of Erebus. She op'nd, but to shut
Excel'd her power; the Gates wide op'n stood,
That with extended wings a Bannerd Host [885]
Under spread Ensigns marching might pass through
With Horse and Chariots rankt in loose array;
So wide they stood, and like a Furnace mouth
Cast forth redounding smoak and ruddy flame.
Before thir eyes in sudden view appear [890]
The secrets of the hoarie deep, a dark
Illimitable Ocean without bound,
Without dimension, where length, breadth, & highth,
And time and place are lost; where eldest Night
And Chaos, Ancestors of Nature, hold [895]
Eternal Anarchie, amidst the noise
Of endless Warrs, and by confusion stand.
For hot, cold, moist, and dry, four Champions fierce
Strive here for Maistrie, and to Battel bring
Thir embryon Atoms; they around the flag [900]
Of each his faction, in thir several Clanns,
Light-arm'd or heavy, sharp, smooth, swift or slow,
Swarm populous, unnumber'd as the Sands
Of Barca or Cyrene's torrid soil,
Levied to side with warring Winds, and poise [905]
Thir lighter wings. To whom these most adhere,
Hee rules a moment; Chaos Umpire sits,
And by decision more imbroiles the fray
By which he Reigns: next him high Arbiter
Chance governs all. Into this wilde Abyss, [910]
The Womb of nature and perhaps her Grave,
Of neither Sea, nor Shore, nor Air, nor Fire,
But all these in thir pregnant causes mixt
Confus'dly, and which thus must ever fight,
Unless th' Almighty Maker them ordain [915]
His dark materials to create more Worlds,
Into this wild Abyss the warie fiend
Stood on the brink of Hell and look'd a while,
Pondering his Voyage: for no narrow frith
He had to cross. Nor was his eare less peal'd [920]
With noises loud and ruinous (to compare
Great things with small) then when Bellona storms,
With all her battering Engines bent to rase

撒旦大膽地走近「混沌」的寶座，對他說道：

「我來此的目的，並不是想探聽貴國的祕密，更非蓄意騷擾；傳聞幽冥與天國的交界處有一個光明的世界，我想到那兒去，不曉得您能否為我指引去路？」

「我知道你是誰，當日以你為首的叛軍從天庭墜落，向地獄奔逃時，曾經過我的領地，天國的千軍萬馬在後追擊的聲音，也轟隆隆地振動了幽冥界；我雖然努力地固守著這片領土，但除去內部的紛紛擾擾不說，那四面八方蜂湧而來的外來勢力，正一步步地蠶食『夜』的主權。

「首先是地獄，從下方拓展疆土，奪取我們廣大的地盤；接著，天和地也來進犯，或許就是你所說的光明的世界，它就位在我的頭頂上方，用一條金鍊與天國相連在一起。快去吧！盡你所能地摧殘、毀壞，阻止它繼續擴張，那便會為我帶來了益處。」

Som Capital City; or less then if this frame
Of Heav'n were falling, and these Elements [925]
In mutinie had from her Axle torn
The stedfast Earth. At last his Sail-broad Vannes
He spreads for flight, and in the surging smoak
Uplifted spurns the ground, thence many a League
As in a cloudy Chair ascending rides [930]
Audacious, but that seat soon failing, meets
A vast vacuitie: all unawares
Fluttring his pennons vain plumb down he drops
Ten thousand fadom deep, and to this hour
Down had been falling, had not by ill chance [935]
The strong rebuff of som tumultuous cloud
Instinct with Fire and Nitre hurried him
As many miles aloft: that furie stay'd,
Quencht in a Boggy Syrtis, neither Sea,
Nor good dry Land: nigh founderd on he fares, [940]
Treading the crude consistence, half on foot,
Half flying; behoves him now both Oare and Saile.
As when a Gryfon through the Wilderness
With winged course ore Hill or moarie Dale,
Pursues the Arimaspian, who by stelth [945]
Had from his wakeful custody purloind
The guarded Gold: So eagerly the fiend
Ore bog or steep, through strait, rough, dense, or rare,
With head, hands, wings, or feet pursues his way,
And swims or sinks, or wades, or creeps, or flyes: [950]
At length a universal hubbub wilde
Of stunning sounds and voices all confus'd
Borne through the hollow dark assaults his eare
With loudest vehemence: thither he plyes,
Undaunted to meet there what ever power [955]
Or Spirit of the nethermost Abyss
Might in that noise reside, of whom to ask
Which way the neerest coast of darkness lyes
Bordering on light; when strait behold the Throne
Of Chaos, and his dark Pavilion spread [960]
Wide on the wasteful Deep; with him Enthron'd
Sat Sable-vested Night, eldest of things,
The Consort of his Reign; and by them stood
Orcus and Ades, and the dreaded name
Of Demogorgon; Rumor next and Chance, [965]

「混沌」略顯不安，以顫抖的語氣回答撒旦。

「謝謝你！等我找到新的天地，必將占領者驅逐出去，將幽冥界的失地歸還，讓『夜』恢復統治權。」撒旦說完，精神大振地往上飛騰而去。路途的艱險，甚於阿爾哥斯號（Argos）航行於凶險的波斯喜魯斯海峽[12]，抑或奧德賽斯為閃躲海中怪物，因而冒險沿著漩渦航行[13]。撒旦正是在如此艱困危險的氛圍中，往前邁進。

只要等到撒旦度過艱難的關口，接著而來的就是人類的墮落。撒旦走過的道路，那通向地獄與人間的橋梁已被高高築起，所有的惡魔將可攀上這

註12：阿爾哥斯號（Argos）為希臘神話中的大船。傑生（Jason）為希臘某國的王子，為取回被篡奪的王位，率領眾英雄搭上阿爾哥斯號，前去尋找金羊毛。曾航行於凶險的波斯喜魯斯海峽，後得仙女赫拉的幫助，躲開怪物與漩渦平安脫險。

註13：奧德賽斯（Odysseus）為特洛伊戰爭中的大英雄，著名的木馬屠城計即是由他所設計，戰爭結束後，他所乘坐的船於歸鄉途中遭遇海難，他幸運未死，但卻在外頭漂泊了十年才回到故鄉。他於迷航途中，曾經為了閃躲海中怪物而冒險沿著漩渦航行。

And Tumult and Confusion all imbroild,
And Discord with a thousand various mouths.

T' whom Satan turning boldly, thus. Ye Powers
And Spirits of this nethermost Abyss,
Chaos and ancient Night, I come no Spy, [970]
With purpose to explore or to disturb
The secrets of your Realm, but by constraint
Wandring this darksome Desart, as my way
Lies through your spacious Empire up to light,
Alone, and without guide, half lost, I seek [975]
What readiest path leads where your gloomie bounds
Confine with Heav'n; or if som other place
From your Dominion won, th' Ethereal King
Possesses lately, thither to arrive
I travel this profound, direct my course; [980]
Directed no mean recompence it brings
To your behoof, if I that Region lost,
All usurpation thence expell'd, reduce
To her original darkness and your sway
(Which is my present journey) and once more [985]
Erect the Standard there of ancient Night;
Yours be th' advantage all, mine the revenge.

Thus Satan; and him thus the Anarch old
With faultring speech and visage incompos'd
Answer'd. I know thee, stranger, who thou art, [990]
That mighty leading Angel, who of late
Made head against Heav'ns King, though overthrown.
I saw and heard, for such a numerous Host
Fled not in silence through the frighted deep
With ruin upon ruin, rout on rout, [995]
Confusion worse confounded; and Heav'n Gates
Pourd out by millions her victorious Bands
Pursuing. I upon my Frontieres here
Keep residence; if all I can will serve,
That little which is left so to defend [1000]
Encroach on still through our intestine broiles
Weakning the Scepter of old Night: first Hell
Your dungeon stretching far and wide beneath;
Now lately Heaven and Earth, another World
Hung ore my Realm, link'd in a golden Chain [1005]

座橋梁，通行無阻地到人間去引誘人類犯罪，除非人類有上帝和天使們的保護，否則將很難擺脫墮落的命運。因為「罪惡」與「死亡」早已跟隨

▽ 天地的創造
波希 油畫 1504年

　　波希筆下的混沌天地是一個圓。天空有陽光穿透雲層，地面有土地植物，天地間蘊藏了無限生機，這就是撒旦在尋找的新世界。

To that side Heav'n from whence your Legions fell:
If that way be your walk, you have not farr;
So much the neerer danger; go and speed;
Havock and spoil and ruin are my gain.

He ceas'd; and Satan staid not to reply, [1010]
But glad that now his Sea should find a shore,
With fresh alacritie and force renew'd
Springs upward like a Pyramid of fire
Into the wilde expanse, and through the shock
Of fighting Elements, on all sides round [1015]
Environ'd wins his way; harder beset
And more endanger'd, then when Argo pass'd
Through Bosporus betwixt the justling Rocks:

在撒旦足跡後頭，前往人類居住的樂
園。

終於，一道亮光出現，從天邊射向
「夜」的底層，「混沌」退守，「自
然」開始劃分界限；宛如歷經狂風巨
浪的小船，船身雖已破破爛爛，卻已
駛回平靜安全的港灣。

撒旦放鬆心情，緩緩地收起羽翼，
目光朝向遠方環繞著淡淡白暈的天
庭，那乳白色的宮殿樓台，曾經是他
的居所；一條金鍊懸掛在天邊，連著
一個小小的宇宙，彷彿月亮旁邊繫著
一個細微的星球。

忿怒的火燄再度燃起，撒旦暗自許
諾，一定要到此地去復仇，於是他奮
力跨步，急急地朝向新世界前進。

Or when Ulysses on the Larbord shunnd
Charybdis, and by th' other whirlpool steard. [1020]
So he with difficulty and labour hard
Mov'd on, with difficulty and labour hee;
But hee once past, soon after when man fell,
Strange alteration! Sin and Death amain
Following his track, such was the will of Heav'n, [1025]
Pav'd after him a broad and beat'n way
Over the dark Abyss, whose boiling Gulf
Tamely endur'd a Bridge of wondrous length
From Hell continu'd reaching th' utmost Orbe
Of this frail World; by which the Spirits perverse [1030]
With easie intercourse pass to and fro
To tempt or punish mortals, except whom
God and good Angels guard by special grace.
But now at last the sacred influence
Of light appears, and from the walls of Heav'n [1035]
Shoots farr into the bosom of dim Night
A glimmering dawn; here Nature first begins
Her fardest verge, and Chaos to retire
As from her outmost works a brok'n foe
With tumult less and with less hostile din, [1040]
That Satan with less toil, and now with ease
Wafts on the calmer wave by dubious light
And like a weather-beaten Vessel holds
Gladly the Port, though Shrouds and Tackle torn;
Or in the emptier waste, resembling Air, [1045]
Weighs his spread wings, at leasure to behold
Farr off th' Empyreal Heav'n, extended wide
In circuit, undetermind square or round,
With Opal Towrs and Battlements adorn'd
Of living Saphire, once his native Seat; [1050]
And fast by hanging in a golden Chain
This pendant world, in bigness as a Starr
Of smallest Magnitude close by the Moon.
Thither full fraught with mischievous revenge,
Accurst, and in a cursed hour he hies. [1055]

上帝的預言

全能的上帝與神子並肩坐在天上的寶座，往下觀看撒旦的一舉一動；上帝且預示人類將會受到撒旦的誘惑而犯罪，而這罪將禍延子孫。另一方面，撒旦歷經萬般險阻，在「混沌」的指引下，即將抵達預言中的新世界；他的內心燃燒著強烈的復仇念頭，準備一找到機會就要引誘人類犯下背叛的罪行。此刻，他正逐漸接近傳說中的新天地——伊甸園。

∧ **上帝預言人類的沉淪**
杜雷版畫 1866年

撒旦歷經重重險阻，就快到達預言的新世界。這一切都看在上帝的眼裡。面對如此頑強、鍥而不捨的魔王，上帝知道人類絕對抵擋不住誘惑，終究步上沉淪的路途。

　　全能的天父高高地坐在天頂的清
虛境地，向下俯視由自己親手創造的
一切。首先看見的，是被安置在幸福
樂園中的人類始祖 —— 亞當和夏娃，
他倆手牽著手，無憂無慮地徜徉在美
麗的新天地，臉上洋溢著戀愛般的甜
美笑容；接著，離他們不遠的地方，
魔鬼撒旦的身影出現了，他正沿著
「夜」國的邊緣，往天國的方向疾馳
而來。

　　神子基督坐在上帝的右手邊，儀表
出眾，身上散發著仁愛的光輝；數量
眾多的天使宛若閃爍群星，侍立在祂
倆身旁，皆因得以親眼見到上帝的姿
容，內心感到無比的幸福美好[1]。

　　「你瞧！」上帝對神子說：

　　「是撒旦，復仇之火竟能讓他變得
如此狂暴，連地獄厚重的九道門栓、

註1：《新約‧希伯來書》：「他是神榮耀所發的光
　　輝，是神本體的真像，常用他權能的命令托住
　　萬有。他洗淨了人的罪，就坐在高天至大者的
　　右邊。他所承受的名，既比天使的名更尊貴，
　　就遠超過天使。」

Hail holy light, ofspring of Heav'n first-born,
Or of th' Eternal Coeternal beam
May I express thee unblam'd? since God is light,
And never but in unapproached light
Dwelt from Eternitie, dwelt then in thee, [5]
Bright effluence of bright essence increate.
Or hear'st thou rather pure Ethereal stream,
Whose Fountain who shall tell? before the Sun,
Before the Heavens thou wert, and at the voice
Of God, as with a Mantle didst invest [10]
The rising world of waters dark and deep,
Won from the void and formless infinite.
Thee I re-visit now with bolder wing,
Escap't the Stygian Pool, though long detain'd
In that obscure sojourn, while in my flight [15]
Through utter and through middle darkness borne
With other notes then to th' Orphean Lyre
I sung of Chaos and Eternal Night,
Taught by the heav'nly Muse to venture down
The dark descent, and up to reascend, [20]
Though hard and rare: thee I revisit safe,
And feel thy sovran vital Lamp; but thou
Revisit'st not these eyes, that rowle in vain
To find thy piercing ray, and find no dawn;
So thick a drop serene hath quencht thir Orbs, [25]
Or dim suffusion veild. Yet not the more
Cease I to wander where the Muses haunt
Cleer Spring, or shadie Grove, or Sunnie Hill,
Smit with the love of sacred Song; but chief
Thee Sion and the flowrie Brooks beneath [30]
That wash thy hallowd feet, and warbling flow,
Nightly I visit: nor somtimes forget
Those other two equal'd with me in Fate,
So were I equal'd with them in renown,
Blind Thamyris and blind Mæonides, [35]
And Tiresias and Phineus Prophets old.
Then feed on thoughts, that voluntarie move
Harmonious numbers; as the wakeful Bird
Sings darkling, and in shadiest Covert hid
Tunes her nocturnal Note. Thus with the Year [40]
Seasons return, but not to me returns
Day, or the sweet approach of Ev'n or Morn,

金鋼鎖鏈的捆縛、與晦暗艱險的深淵都不能阻止他。他掙脫了一切的枷鎖，義無反顧地朝向新天地而去，想毀滅人類，或施用詭計引誘他們墮落，要藉由這種方式來向我報復。

「而人類，我所深愛的子女，將會掉入撒旦所設下的陷阱，產生冒犯天神的思想來。這結果我早已預知，因為我在創造人類時，便賦予了他們自由的意志，讓他們能夠隨著自己的思想去行事，藉此可以看清他們的本心，是忠誠信實？抑或墮落背叛？

「人類選擇了背叛，他們除了要為自己的行為付出代價之外，其罪行也將禍及子孫，世世代代接受『死亡』的懲罰。」

「父親，」神子以無比尊敬的語氣輕呼上帝。

「人類是您所寵愛的幼子，您怎忍心讓他們永遠沉淪？由於您的恩慈，天和地都曾一齊高聲讚頌，優美的樂音也終日繚繞著您的寶座。

Or sight of vernal bloom, or Summers Rose,
Or flocks, or heards, or human face divine;
But cloud in stead, and ever-during dark [45]
Surrounds me, from the chearful wayes of men
Cut off, and for the Book of knowledg fair
Presented with a Universal blanc
Of Nature's works to mee expung'd and ras'd,
And wisdome at one entrance quite shut out. [50]
So much the rather thou Celestial light
Shine inward, and the mind through all her powers
Irradiate, there plant eyes, all mist from thence
Purge and disperse, that I may see and tell
Of things invisible to mortal sight. [55]

Now had the Almighty Father from above,
From the pure Empyrean where he sits
High Thron'd above all highth, bent down his eye,
His own works and their works at once to view:
About him all the Sanctities of Heaven [60]
Stood thick as Starrs, and from his sight receiv'd
Beatitude past utterance; on his right
The radiant image of his Glory sat,
His onely Son; On Earth he first beheld
Our two first Parents, yet the onely two [65]
Of mankind, in the happie Garden plac't,
Reaping immortal fruits of joy and love,
Uninterrupted joy, unrivald love
In blissful solitude; he then survey'd
Hell and the Gulf between, and Satan there [70]
Coasting the wall of Heav'n on this side Night
In the dun Air sublime, and ready now
To stoop with wearied wings, and willing feet
On the bare outside of this World, that seem'd
Firm land imbosom'd without Firmament, [75]
Uncertain which, in Ocean or in Air.
Him God beholding from his prospect high,
Wherein past, present, future he beholds,
Thus to his onely Son foreseeing spake.

Onely begotten Son, seest thou what rage [80]
Transports our adversarie, whom no bounds
Prescrib'd, no barrs of Hell, nor all the chains

「如果，您因為人類的無知而懲罰他們，那不就順了撒旦的意，讓他得意洋洋地凱旋而歸，把人類全帶到地獄去向群魔炫耀。這樣做的話，您慈善的心與讓人尊崇的地位，恐怕就要受到質疑和嘲笑了。」

「我親愛的兒子呀！你真是我心中最大的喜悅，你所道出的正是我所考量的。當然，人類並不會完完全全地墮落，只要他們願意，還是可以得到救贖，因為我並未收回他們的自由意志呀！」上帝露出慈祥的笑容對神子說道。

「而且，我將挑選其中某些人，賜予他們特殊的榮耀，並置他們於眾人之上。至於其他人，我也會在他們犯下罪行之前預先顯示徵兆，讓他們昏晦的心有即時清醒的機會，避免觸怒天神；另外，我會把良知放進他們的心裡，那些能夠及時醒悟、自我反省，且願意聽從我，對我誠心祈禱的人類，就能夠得回光明幸福；但那些

Heapt on him there, nor yet the main Abyss
Wide interrupt can hold; so bent he seems
On desparate reveng, that shall redound [85]
Upon his own rebellious head. And now
Through all restraint broke loose he wings his way
Not farr off Heav'n, in the Precincts of light,
Directly towards the new created World,
And Man there plac't, with purpose to assay [90]
If him by force he can destroy, or worse,
By some false guile pervert; and shall pervert
For man will hear'n to his glozing lyes,
And easily transgress the sole Command,
Sole pledge of his obedience: So will fall, [95]
Hee and his faithless Progenie: whose fault?
Whose but his own? ingrate, he had of mee
All he could have; I made him just and right,
Sufficient to have stood, though free to fall.
Such I created all th' Ethereal Powers [100]
And Spirits, both them who stood and them who faild;
Freely they stood who stood, and fell who fell.
Not free, what proof could they have givn sincere
Of true allegiance, constant Faith or Love,
Where onely what they needs must do, appeard, [105]
Not what they would? what praise could they receive?
What pleasure I from such obedience paid,
When Will and Reason (Reason also is choice)
Useless and vain, of freedom both despoild,
Made passive both, had servd necessitie, [110]
Not mee. They therefore as to right belongd,
So were created, nor can justly accuse
Thir maker, or thir making, or thir Fate,
As if predestination over-rul'd
Thir will, dispos'd by absolute Decree [115]
Or high foreknowledge; they themselves decreed
Thir own revolt, not I: if I foreknew,
Foreknowledge had no influence on their fault,
Which had no less prov'd certain unforeknown.
So without least impulse or shadow of Fate, [120]
Or aught by me immutablie foreseen,
They trespass, Authors to themselves in all
Both what they judge and what they choose; for so
I formd them free, and free they must remain,

頑固地堅持作惡、不知悔改的人類與他們的後代，將世世代代受到毀滅的教訓。

「除非有人願意出面代他們受過，並設法使正義在人間伸張，這樣人類的罪行才能得到完全的赦免。」

說到這，上帝轉頭環視在場的所有天使，問道：

「有誰願意化為凡人，用深厚的愛前去救贖全人類，使他們免受死罪的懲罰；並用己身的正義來解救人類的不義呢？」

上帝話語剛落，神子隨即站起來向祂懇求：

「請讓我來承擔人類即將犯下的罪行吧！我願意捨棄光榮的地位，到人間代人類受過。」

「啊！不愧為我最摯愛的兒子。雖

Till they enthrall themselves: I else must change [125]
Thir nature, and revoke the high Decree
Unchangeable, Eternal, which ordain'd
Thir freedom, they themselves ordain'd thir fall.
The first sort by thir own suggestion fell,
Self-tempted, self-deprav'd: Man falls deceiv'd [130]
By the other first: Man therefore shall find grace,
The other none: in Mercy and Justice both,
Through Heav'n and Earth, so shall my glorie excel,
But Mercy first and last shall brightest shine.

Thus while God spake, ambrosial fragrance fill'd [135]
All Heav'n, and in the blessed Spirits elect
Sense of new joy ineffable diffus'd:
Beyond compare the Son of God was seen
Most glorious, in him all his Father shon
Substantially express'd, and in his face [140]
Divine compassion visibly appeerd,
Love without end, and without measure Grace,
Which uttering thus he to his Father spake.

>> **耶穌請纓去救贖人類**
布雷克　水彩畫 1808年

　　耶穌起身向上帝請求，要用深厚的愛去救贖全人類，到人間代為受過，他張開雙臂，彷彿已經知道日後被釘上十字架的苦刑。

然人類的背叛深深地刺傷了我的心，
但他們必竟是由我所親手創造的，我
對他們仍然有著深厚的情感；你雖說
自願為人類贖罪，但你可知贖罪之路
並不好走，除了必須化作凡人降到人
間之外，還得把人類的本性加在你的
本性上頭，並以『死』來完成救贖，
這樣，你還願意前去為人類謀求和平
嗎？」上帝溫和地問著。

▽ 告知受胎
達文西 油畫 1472年

　　上帝派天使下凡告知少女馬利亞即將孕育上
帝之子，產下即將代人類受苦受難的耶穌基督。

O Father, gracious was that word which clos'd
Thy sovran sentence, that Man should find grace; [145]
For which both Heav'n and Earth shall high extoll
Thy praises, with th' innumerable sound
Of Hymns and sacred Songs, wherewith thy Throne
Encompass'd shall resound thee ever blest.
For should Man finally be lost, should Man [150]
Thy creature late so lov'd, thy youngest Son
Fall circumvented thus by fraud, though joynd
With his own folly? that be from thee farr,
That farr be from thee, Father, who art Judg
Of all things made, and judgest onely right. [155]
Or shall the Adversarie thus obtain
His end, and frustrate thine, shall he fulfill
His malice, and thy goodness bring to naught,
Or proud return though to his heavier doom,
Yet with revenge accomplish't and to Hell [160]
Draw after him the whole Race of mankind,
By him corrupted? or wilt thou thy self
Abolish thy Creation, and unmake,
For him, what for thy glorie thou hast made?
So should thy goodness and thy greatness both [165]
Be questiond and blaspheam'd without defence.

「我願意！無論有多困難，我都願
意。就讓我化作凡身，下降到人間去
吧！屆時，『死』雖然會把怒氣施加
在我身上，使我屈服於它的黑暗統治
之下；但您既然給了我永恆的生命，
當不忍心看我永遠地沉埋在黑暗的
墳墓，必會讓我東山再起，給『死』
致命的一擊，從征服者手中奪回戰利
品。

「當勝利的那一天來到時，我將
俘虜黑暗的統治者，把『死』的屍首
丟進墳墓裡。然後領著已受到救贖的
眾生歸返天國，重回您的懷抱；我相
信，那個時候您臉上的怒容將不再復
見，因它將被無窮的喜悅所取代。」
神子堅定地回答。

「好吧！就讓你暫且離開我的身
邊，前去解救人類；你將由人間的處
女所生，生活在凡人之間。亞當犯
了罪，且禍及子孫，造成全人類的滅
亡；你雖身為亞當的子孫，但由於你
的功德替他們贖了罪，因此你將是人

To whom the great Creatour thus reply'd.
O Son, in whom my Soul hath chief delight,
Son of my bosom, Son who art alone
My word, my wisdom, and effectual might, [170]
All hast thou spok'n as my thoughts are, all
As my Eternal purpose hath decreed:
Man shall not quite be lost, but sav'd who will,
Yet not of will in him, but grace in me
Freely voutsaft; once more I will renew [175]
His lapsed powers, though forfeit and enthrall'd
By sin to foul exorbitant desires;
Upheld by me, yet once more he shall stand
On even ground against his mortal foe,
By me upheld, that he may know how frail [180]
His fall'n condition is, and to me ow
All his deliv'rance, and to none but me.
Some I have chosen of peculiar grace
Elect above the rest; so is my will:
The rest shall hear me call, and oft be warnd [185]
Thir sinful state, and to appease betimes
Th' incensed Deitie while offerd grace
Invites; for I will cleer thir senses dark,
What may suffice, and soft'n stonie hearts
To pray, repent, and bring obedience due. [190]
To Prayer, repentance, and obedience due,
Though but endevord with sincere intent,
Mine ear shall not be slow, mine eye not shut.
And I will place within them as a guide
My Umpire Conscience, whom if they will hear, [195]
Light after light well us'd they shall attain,
And to the end persisting, safe arrive.
This my long sufferance and my day of grace
They who neglect and scorn, shall never taste;
But hard be hard'nd, blind be blinded more, [200]
That they may stumble on, and deeper fall;
And none but such from mercy I exclude.
But yet all is not don; Man disobeying,
Disloyal breaks his fealtie, and sinns
Against the high Supremacie of Heav'n, [205]
Affecting God-head, and so loosing all,
To expiate his Treason hath naught left,
But to destruction sacred and devote,

類的第二個根源，他們將從你的身上
獲得重生的機會。

「你的善心與慈悲是天國最終取得
勝利的主要因素，因為那濃厚的愛戰
勝了地獄的恨；你因愛而死，這偉大
的自我犧牲，讓那些被地獄的憎恨所
輕易俘虜的人得到救贖，但是，仍有
些得到恩惠卻不去接受的人，就讓他
們留在地獄接受摧毀吧！

「你本可以留在天上享受極高的尊
榮，卻為了拯救人類而甘心放棄，從
這裡可以看出你那豐沛的愛心更勝於
光榮的地位，因此，你將同時具備神
性與人性，成為宇宙的君王，統領天
上地下和幽冥地獄等所有的地方。

「屆時，你將在天庭召開大法庭，
傳令的大天使則四處宣告各方生靈，
前來聆聽審訊，並接受判刑；所有的
惡人和墮落天使將無由遁形，全部扔
進地獄受苦，待地獄擠滿了人犯時，
就把地獄之門永遠地關閉起來。到了
那個時候，世界遭到烈火焚燬，新天

He with his whole posteritie must dye,
Dye hee or Justice must; unless for him [210]
Som other able, and as willing, pay
The rigid satisfaction, death for death.
Say Heav'nly Powers, where shall we find such love,
Which of ye will be mortal to redeem
Mans mortal crime, and just th' unjust to save, [215]
Dwels in all Heaven charitie so deare?

He ask'd, but all the Heav'nly Quire stood mute,
And silence was in Heav'n: on mans behalf
Patron or Intercessor none appeerd,
Much less that durst upon his own head draw [220]
The deadly forfeiture, and ransom set.
And now without redemption all mankind
Must have bin lost, adjudg'd to Death and Hell
By doom severe, had not the Son of God,
In whom the fulness dwells of love divine, [225]
His dearest mediation thus renewd.

Father, thy word is past, man shall find grace;
And shall grace not find means, that finds her way,
The speediest of thy winged messengers,
To visit all thy creatures, and to all [230]
Comes unprevented, unimplor'd, unsought,
Happie for man, so coming; he her aide
Can never seek, once dead in sins and lost;
Attonement for himself or offering meet,
Indebted and undon, hath none to bring: [235]
Behold mee then, mee for him, life for life
I offer, on mee let thine anger fall;
Account mee man; I for his sake will leave
Thy bosom, and this glorie next to thee
Freely put off, and for him lastly dye [240]
Well pleas'd, on me let Death wreck all his rage;
Under his gloomie power I shall not long
Lie vanquisht; thou hast givn me to possess
Life in my self for ever, by thee I live,
Though now to Death I yield, and am his due [245]
All that of me can die, yet that debt paid,
Thou wilt not leave me in the loathsom grave
His prey, nor suffer my unspotted Soule

＾ 最後的審判

米開朗基羅 壁畫 1541年

　　《最後的審判》出自新約聖經的《啓示錄》，自古以來就是宗教繪畫的重要主題，時時提醒信徒謹記戒律，遠離魔鬼的誘惑，因為每個人日後都要面臨審判，善人得以上天堂，惡人將無所遁形，全數被打入地獄。

地便由灰燼中重生，居住在那兒的都是正義善良的好人，光明美好的世界來臨。

「那時你就可以把權杖拋棄，因為上帝無所不有，世界不再需要王權。但你仍然能夠得到同我一樣的尊崇，因為你曾經捨身為人類贖罪的緣故。」上帝彷彿宣告預言，滿身榮光，對神子說道。

眾天使初聞上帝與神子的對話，一時間啞口無語，直至上帝顯現榮光，才猛然醒悟；他們把不凋花和冠冕放在寶座前，舉首高聲禮讚，並歡欣鼓舞地唱起滿載著祝福的頌歌[2]。　不凋花是永遠不會凋謝的一種花，只要在它枯萎時給與水分，它便會再度活起來；它原本生長在人間，在生命樹的周圍含苞待放，卻因為人類犯下罪

註2：表示讚頌的意思，出自《新約‧啓示錄》：
　　　「那二十四位長老就俯伏在寶座的面前，敬拜那活到永永遠遠的，又把他們的冠冕放在寶座前，說：『我們的主，我們的神，你是配得榮耀、尊貴、權柄的！因為你創造了萬物，並且萬物是因你的旨意被創造而有的。』」

For ever with corruption there to dwell;
But I shall rise Victorious, and subdue [250]
My Vanquisher, spoild of his vanted spoile;
Death his deaths wound shall then receive, and stoop
Inglorious, of his mortal sting disarm'd.
I through the ample Air in Triumph high
Shall lead Hell Captive maugre Hell, and show [255]
The powers of darkness bound. Thou at the sight
Pleas'd, out of Heaven shalt look down and smile,
While by thee rais'd I ruin all my Foes,
Death last, and with his Carcass glut the Grave:
Then with the multitude of my redeemd [260]
Shall enter Heaven long absent, and returne,
Father, to see thy face, wherein no cloud
Of anger shall remain, but peace assur'd,
And reconcilement; wrauth shall be no more
Thenceforth, but in thy presence Joy entire. [265]

His words here ended, but his meek aspect
Silent yet spake, and breath'd immortal love
To mortal men, above which only shon
Filial obedience: as a sacrifice
Glad to be offer'd, he attends the will [270]
Of his great Father. Admiration seis'd
All Heav'n, what this might mean, and whither tend
Wondring; but soon th' Almighty thus reply'd:

O thou in Heav'n and Earth the only peace
Found out for mankind under wrauth, O thou [275]
My sole complacence! well thou know'st how dear,
To me are all my works, nor Man the least
Though last created, that for him I spare
Thee from my bosom and right hand, to save,
By loosing thee a while, the whole Race lost. [280]
Thou therefore whom thou only canst redeem,
Thir Nature also to thy Nature joyn;
And be thy self Man among men on Earth,
Made flesh, when time shall be, of Virgin seed,
By wondrous birth: Be thou in Adams room [285]
The Head of all mankind, though Adams Son.
As in him perish all men, so in thee
As from a second root shall be restor'd,

惡，被移植到天國，在那裡開出美麗
的花兒。綠蔭庇護著生命之泉，一條
琥珀色的河流從天國中間貫穿而過，
清澈的河水灌溉著鮮花遍野的幸福園
地。

天使們用手輕輕地撩撥黃金豎琴
的琴弦，發出美妙動人的交響樂章，
和著柔美的歌聲，唱出完美的天籟聖
音。他們唱著：

「天父啊！天使們齊聲歌頌您。
您是全能的宇宙主宰、萬物的創造者
與光明的泉源。當您坐在寶座上，全
身籠罩著燦爛的光輝，沒有人能夠看
清楚您的身影；但當您隱去光華，把
雲朵引來寶座四周，您居雲中，猶如
一個聚光點，炫目光彩，讓人無法逼
視，連代表光明的撒拉弗天使也得伸
出翅膀來遮住您眩目的光芒。」

接著，眾天使翱翔在點點星光中繼
續唱頌：

「天父啊！我們齊聲歌頌您。您是
一切創造物的源頭，神子基督是您的

As many as are restor'd, without thee none.
His crime makes guiltie all his Sons, thy merit [290]
Imputed shall absolve them who renounce
Thir own both righteous and unrighteous deeds,
And live in thee transplanted, and from thee
Receive new life. So Man, as is most just,
Shall satisfie for Man, be judg'd and die, [295]
And dying rise, and rising with him raise
His Brethren, ransomd with his own dear life.
So Heav'nly love shall outdoo Hellish hate,
Giving to death, and dying to redeeme,
So dearly to redeem what Hellish hate [300]
So easily destroy'd, and still destroyes
In those who, when they may, accept not grace.
Nor shalt thou by descending to assume
Mans Nature, less'n or degrade thine owne.
Because thou hast, though Thron'd in highest bliss [305]
Equal to God, and equally enjoying
God-like fruition, quitted all to save
A World from utter loss, and hast been found
By Merit more then Birthright Son of God,
Found worthiest to be so by being Good, [310]
Farr more then Great or High; because in thee
Love hath abounded more then Glory abounds,
Therefore thy Humiliation shall exalt
With thee thy Manhood also to this Throne;
Here shalt thou sit incarnate, here shalt Reign [315]
Both God and Man, Son both of God and Man,
Anointed universal King, all Power
I give thee, reign for ever, and assume
Thy Merits; under thee as Head Supream
Thrones, Princedoms, Powers, Dominions I reduce: [320]
All knees to thee shall bow, of them that bide
In Heaven, or Earth, or under Earth in Hell;
When thou attended gloriously from Heav'n
Shalt in the Sky appear, and from thee send
The summoning Arch-Angels to proclaime [325]
Thy dread Tribunal: forthwith from all Windes
The living, and forthwith the cited dead
Of all past Ages to the general Doom
Shall hast'n, such a peal shall rouse thir sleep.
Then all thy Saints assembl'd, thou shalt judge [330]

翻版，他清秀的臉龐，閃耀著光輝，並未被雲影所遮住；他察知您心中對人類的憐愛，不願同懲治叛軍般地處罰他們，於是他挺身而出，願意代替人類受過，以此來換回人類重生的機會。這種情懷，多麼高貴神聖呀！我們將把他做為詩歌的題材，讚美他，如同頌讚您一般。」

　　正當天使們在天上歡唱歌舞的時候，撒旦已來到「夜」的邊界 —— 宇宙的外緣。宇宙遠觀像是一個圓形球體，走近時才發現它是一塊漆黑無涯的黑暗大陸，地球存在於它內部的某個角落；「混沌」不斷地吹起狂烈風暴襲擊它的外圍，只有靠近天國的那一邊，有一絲溫暖的光線照射過來。

　　撒旦收斂翅膀，降落到宇宙的表層，並以急促地腳步在它粗糙的表面上行走，宛若一隻生長在中國西部雪山上的鷹，及目所見只有皚皚白雪和流浪的韃靼人，又振翅飛往放牧牛羊的山巒而去；牠飛越重重山峰，飛向

Bad men and Angels, they arraignd shall sink
Beneath thy Sentence; Hell her numbers full,
Thenceforth shall be for ever shut. Mean while
The World shall burn, and from her ashes spring
New Heav'n and Earth, wherein the just shall dwell [335]
And after all thir tribulations long
See golden days, fruitful of golden deeds,
With Joy and Love triumphing, and fair Truth.
Then thou thy regal Scepter shalt lay by,
For regal Scepter then no more shall need, [340]
God shall be All in All. But all ye Gods,
Adore him, who to compass all this dies,
Adore the Son, and honour him as mee.

No sooner had th' Almighty ceas't, but all
The multitude of Angels with a shout [345]
Loud as from numbers without number, sweet
As from blest voices, uttering joy, Heav'n rung
With Jubilee, and loud Hosanna's filld
Th' eternal Regions: lowly reverent
Towards either Throne they bow, and to the ground [350]
With solemn adoration down they cast
Thir Crowns inwove with Amarant and Gold,
Immortal Amarant, a Flour which once
In Paradise, fast by the Tree of Life
Began to bloom, but soon for mans offence [355]
To Heav'n remov'd where first it grew, there grows,
And flours aloft shading the Fount of Life,
And where the river of Bliss through midst of Heavn
Rowls o're Elisian Flours her Amber stream;
With these that never fade the Spirits elect [360]
Bind thir resplendent locks inwreath'd with beams,
Now in loose Garlands thick thrown off, the bright
Pavement that like a Sea of Jasper shon
Impurpl'd with Celestial Roses smil'd.
Then Crown'd again thir gold'n Harps they took, [365]
Harps ever tun'd, that glittering by thir side
Like Quivers hung, and with Præamble sweet
Of charming symphonie they introduce
Thir sacred Song, and waken raptures high;
No voice exempt, no voice but well could joine [370]
Melodious part, such concord is in Heav'n.

恆河的發源地，途中經過絲綢之野，
撇見中國人在遼闊的平原上，利用風
帆來駕馭藤車。

　　撒旦此刻便如同那隻饑餓的猛禽，
急速地在多風似海洋的大地上尋覓獵
物，那個時期，大地尚未生出其他生
物，所以他只能孤伶伶地獨自徘徊。

　　後來，因人類追求虛無縹緲的名聲
和地位，並把幸福寄託在盲目的迷信
上頭，那些念頭便往上升騰，使這地
方逐漸被罪惡與紛爭填滿。

　　臨近處，在銀色的月球上面，也寄
託著許多人虛幻的夢想；居住著介乎
天使和人類中間的精靈、升天的人、
和遠古時代由上帝的兒子們與人間女
子所生下的巨人族 3。巨人族在古老
的年代頗享盛名，建立許多虛空的功
業。

　　另外，在那灑滿銀色光輝的世界住
著的居民還有挪亞的子孫，他們在示
拿平原住下，本打算建城築塔，但後
來因上帝的阻撓並未建成，所以那未

Thee Father first they sung Omnipotent,
Immutable, Immortal, Infinite,
Eternal King; thee Author of all being,
Fountain of Light, thy self invisible [375]
Amidst the glorious brightness where thou sit'st
Thron'd inaccessible, but when thou shad'st
The full blaze of thy beams, and through a cloud
Drawn round about thee like a radiant Shrine,
Dark with excessive bright thy skirts appeer, [380]
Yet dazle Heav'n, that brightest Seraphim
Approach not, but with both wings veil thir eyes,
Thee next they sang of all Creation first,
Begotten Son, Divine Similitude,
In whose conspicuous count'nance, without cloud [385]
Made visible, th' Almighty Father shines,
Whom else no Creature can behold; on thee
Impresst the effulgence of his Glorie abides,
Transfus'd on thee his ample Spirit rests.
Hee Heav'n of Heavens and all the Powers therein [390]
By thee created, and by thee threw down
Th' Aspiring Dominations: thou that day
Thy Fathers dreadful Thunder didst not spare,
Nor stop thy flaming Chariot wheels, that shook
Heav'ns everlasting Frame, while o're the necks [395]
Thou drov'st of warring Angels disarraid.
Back from pursuit thy Powers with loud acclaime
Thee only extoll'd, Son of thy Fathers might,
To execute fierce vengeance on his foes,
Not so on Man; him through their malice fall'n, [400]
Father of Mercie and Grace, thou didst not doome
So strictly, but much more to pitie encline:
No sooner did thy dear and onely Son
Perceive thee purpos'd not to doom frail Man
So strictly, but much more to pitie enclin'd, [405]
He to appease thy wrauth, and end the strife
Of Mercy and Justice in thy face discern'd,
Regardless of the Bliss wherein hee sat

註3：《舊約‧創世紀》：「後來神的兒子
　　們和人的女子們交合生子，那就是上
　　古英武有名的人。」

建成的城便有了巴別（Babel）之名，乃變亂的意思 [4]。如今，巴別城也不過是一座空幻的城池罷了。

　　還有些居民是獨自前來的，如西元前五世紀的希臘哲學家恩匹多克里斯（Empedocles），為了要證明自己的預言能力超越眾人，於是他告訴人們說：「我跳進火山裡並不會被岩漿燒死，因為神祇會前來引領我。」但是，待他躍入火山之後，一隻從火山口噴發出來的鞋子，毫不留情地揭發了他的謊言。

　　希臘哲學家克隆布洛圖（Cleombrotus）在讀了柏拉圖所著的《斐多篇》之後，竟沉迷於書中所描述的極樂世界，最後以跳海自殺的方式，讓自己能夠早日前往極樂之地。

　　此外還有其他許多人，但若一一描述則顯得過於繁瑣，無非是些未成熟的、愚蠢的，像穿著黑色、白色、灰色三種階級衣服的羅馬教托缽僧，他們手中拿著無用的法寶，口裡總是說著

Second to thee, offerd himself to die
For mans offence. O unexampl'd love, [410]
Love no where to be found less then Divine!
Hail Son of God, Saviour of Men, thy Name
Shall be the copious matter of my Song
Henceforth, and never shall my Harp thy praise
Forget, nor from thy Fathers praise disjoine. [415]

Thus they in Heav'n, above the starry Sphear,
Thir happie hours in joy and hymning spent.
Mean while upon the firm opacous Globe
Of this round World, whose first convex divides
The luminous inferior Orbs, enclos'd [420]
From Chaos and th' inroad of Darkness old,
Satan alighted walks: a Globe farr off
It seem'd, now seems a boundless Continent
Dark, waste, and wild, under the frown of Night
Starless expos'd, and ever-threatning storms [425]
Of Chaos blustring round, inclement skie;
Save on that side which from the wall of Heav'n
Though distant farr some small reflection gaines
Of glimmering air less vext with tempest loud:
Here walk'd the Fiend at large in spacious field. [430]
As when a Vultur on Imaus bred,
Whose snowie ridge the roving Tartar bounds,

註4：《舊約‧創世紀》：「那時，天下人的口音言語都是一樣。他們往東邊遷移的時候，在示拿地遇見一片平原，就住在那裡。他們彼此商量說：『來吧！我們要做磚，把磚燒透了。』他們就拿磚當石頭，又拿石漆當灰泥。他們說：『來吧！我們要建造一座城和一座塔，塔頂通天，為要傳揚我們的名，免得我們分散在全地上。』……於是，耶和華使他們從那裡分散在全地上，他們就停工不造那城了。因為耶和華在那裡變亂天下人的語言，使眾人分散在全地上，所以那城名叫巴別。」

騙人的話語。另一批人則雲遊到耶路撒冷附近，前往各各他（Golgotha）尋找那活在天堂的死人[5]。

上述的這些人都深深地迷戀於找尋幸福的園地，以為只要穿上托缽僧的袈裟，裝扮一下就可前往天國；他們一路通過七星天、……恆星天、水晶天，最後來到原動天，越過此地就

Dislodging from a Region scarce of prey
To gorge the flesh of Lambs or yeanling Kids
On Hills where Flocks are fed, flies toward the Springs [435]
Of Ganges or Hydaspes, Indian streams;
But in his way lights on the barren Plaines
Of Sericana, where Chineses drive
With Sails and Wind thir canie Waggons light:
So on this windie Sea of Land, the Fiend [440]
Walk'd up and down alone bent on his prey,
Alone, for other Creature in this place
Living or liveless to be found was none,
None yet, but store hereafter from the earth
Up hither like Aereal vapours flew [445]
Of all things transitorie and vain, when Sin
With vanity had filld the works of men:
Both all things vain, and all who in vain things
Built thir fond hopes of Glorie or lasting fame,
Or happiness in this or th' other life; [450]

註5：各各他（Golgotha）即骷髏地，位於耶路撒冷附近，是耶穌被釘上十字架的地方；出自《新約‧路加福音》：「到了一個地方，名叫骷髏地，就在那裡把耶穌釘在十字架上，又釘了兩個犯人；一個在左邊，一個在右邊。……那些婦女帶著所預備的香料來到墳墓前，看見石頭已經從墳墓滾開了，她們就進去，只是不見主耶穌的身體。正在猜疑之間，忽然有兩個人站在旁邊，衣服放光。婦女們驚怕，將臉伏地。那兩個人就對她們說：『為甚麼在死人中找活人呢？他不在這裡，已經復活了。』」

≪ **耶穌將鑰匙交給聖彼得**
魯本斯 油畫 1614年
　　彼得原是漁夫，他是最早追隨耶穌的信徒之一。耶穌把天國的鑰匙交給他，認為他將是教會的基石。

是宇宙的外緣了[6]。守門天使聖彼得
（St.Peter）正等在天國大門，準備為
他們開啟天國之門[7]；誰知，那天國
的大門一開，眾人才剛邁出步伐，一
陣漫天漫地的狂風便席捲而來，把他
們從天梯上吹到數萬里遠的空中。只
見他們渾身穿戴的僧袍、僧帽和頭巾
等物品，全都在狂風的撕扯下化成碎
片；無數的聖骨、念珠、贖罪券、特
許證、寬恕證等皆成為風的玩具，被
高高地捲入空中不斷盤旋，一直飛越
過世界背後，落到地獄邊緣的「愚者
的樂園」。這地方是靈魂受審之處，
日後將會變得非常有名[8]。

註6：依據舊天文學的說法，宇宙共由十層天所構
　　成，「七星天」是第一層、「恒星天」、「水
　　晶天」、「原動天」則分屬第八、九、十層。
　　「原動天」之外即為宇宙的外緣。

註7：聖彼得（St.Peter）為耶穌十二門徒之一，掌
　　管天國的鑰匙。《新約・馬太福音》：「耶穌
　　對他說：『西門巴約拿，你是有福的！因為這
　　不是屬血肉的指示你的，乃是我在天上的父指
　　示的。我還告訴你：你是彼得，我要把我的教
　　會建造在這磐石上，陰間的權柄不能勝過他。
　　我要把天國的鑰匙給你，凡你在地上所捆綁
　　的，在天上也要捆綁；凡你在地上所釋放的，
　　在天上也要釋放。』」

All who have thir reward on Earth, the fruits
Of painful Superstition and blind Zeal,
Naught seeking but the praise of men, here find
Fit retribution, emptie as thir deeds;
All th' unaccomplisht works of Natures hand, [455]
Abortive, monstrous, or unkindly mixt,
Dissolvd on earth, fleet hither, and in vain,
Till final dissolution, wander here,
Not in the neighbouring Moon, as some have dreamd;
Those argent Fields more likely habitants, [460]
Translated Saints, or middle Spirits hold
Betwixt th' Angelical and Human kinde:
Hither of ill-joynd Sons and Daughters born
First from the ancient World those Giants came
With many a vain exploit, though then renownd: [465]
The builders next of Babel on the Plain
Of Sennaar, and still with vain designe
New Babels, had they wherewithall, would build:
Others came single; he who to be deem'd
A God, leap'd fondly into Ætna flames [470]
Empedocles, and hee who to enjoy
Plato's Elysium, leap'd into the Sea,
Cleombrotus, and many more too long,
Embryo's and Idiots, Eremits and Friers
White, Black and Grey, with all thir trumperie. [475]
Here Pilgrims roam, that stray'd so farr to seek
In Golgotha him dead, who lives in Heav'n;
And they who to be sure of Paradise
Dying put on the weeds of Dominic,
Or in Franciscan think to pass disguis'd; [480]
They pass the Planets seven, and pass the fixt,
And that Crystalline Sphear whose ballance weighs
The Trepidation talkt, and that first mov'd;
And now Saint Peter at Heav'ns Wicket seems
To wait them with his Keys, and now at foot [485]
Of Heav'ns ascent they lift thir Feet, when loe
A violent cross wind from either Coast
Blows them transverse ten thousand Leagues awry
Into the devious Air; then might ye see
Cowles, Hoods and Habits with thir wearers tost [490]
And flutterd into Raggs, then Reliques, Beads,
Indulgences, Dispenses, Pardons, Bulls,

撒旦走遍整個星球，終於發現一道微弱的光線，便趕緊加快腳步，朝那方向而去；遠遠地，一座富麗堂皇的高樓躍入撒旦眼眸，它的大門裝飾著黃金、金剛石與東方的珠寶，燦爛耀眼，非筆墨所能描繪。它的頂上有一座梯子，從寬廣的階梯拾級而上，可以到達天國；這階梯的樣子就如雅各逃離家鄉時，於旅途中夢見的景象[9]，階梯並非固定的，它時常被收到天

The sport of Winds: all these upwhirld aloft
Fly o're the backside of the World farr off
Into a Limbo large and broad, since calld [495]
The Paradise of Fools, to few unknown
Long after, now unpeopl'd, and untrod;
All this dark Globe the Fiend found as he pass'd,
And long he wanderd, till at last a gleame
Of dawning light turnd thither-ward in haste [500]
His travell'd steps; farr distant he descries
Ascending by degrees magnificent
Up to the wall of Heaven a Structure high,
At top whereof, but farr more rich appeer'd
The work as of a Kingly Palace Gate [505]
With Frontispice of Diamond and Gold
Imbellisht, thick with sparkling orient Gemmes
The Portal shon, inimitable on Earth
By Model, or by shading Pencil drawn.
The Stairs were such as whereon Jacob saw [510]
Angels ascending and descending, bands
Of Guardians bright, when he from Esau fled
To Padan-Aram in the field of Luz,
Dreaming by night under the open Skie,
And waking cri'd, This is the Gate of Heav'n [515]
Each Stair mysteriously was meant, nor stood
There alwayes, but drawn up to Heav'n somtimes
Viewless, and underneath a bright Sea flow'd
Of Jasper, or of liquid Pearle, whereon
Who after came from Earth, sayling arriv'd, [520]
Wafted by Angels, or flew o're the Lake

註8：地獄的邊緣有三個樂園，是靈魂接受
　　　審判之處，分別為「聖者的樂園」、
　　　「嬰兒的樂園」與「愚者的樂園」。

≪ 洪荒之地的幽靈們
杜雷 版畫 1866年

　　並不是穿上僧侶的袈裟，握著念珠、贖罪券等聖物就能進入天堂之門，這些假宗教之名的愚蠢幽靈，被天堂的狂風一掃，頓時跌回洪荒之地中。

庭上，失去了蹤影。

　　高樓的下面是一片晶瑩碧藍的海洋，從地球上來的，必經此海；由天使駕帆引導，或乘坐火馬車奔馳水面。

　　此時，梯子是放下來的，彷彿在向撒旦示意：「進入天堂並不難喔！」或者，是想觸動撒旦無法重回天庭的悲忿心情。大門的對面，即是幸福樂園的上方，有條道路筆直地通向地球，它的寬廣遠勝於通往錫安山頂的大道，也比那條通到上帝珍愛的「應許之地」[10]的道路遼闊。天使們頻頻往返於此路，拜訪那些有福的人，傳達上帝的旨意；從約旦河的發源地潘尼亞斯（Paneas）到別士巴（Beersaba）[11]，這個埃及與阿拉伯相接的區域，經常受到上帝的眷顧，廣被恩澤。大道的出口彷彿無限延伸的海岸堤壩，成為光明與黑暗的分界點。

　　撒旦登上天梯，傾身向下俯視這個

Rapt in a Chariot drawn by fiery Steeds.
The Stairs were then let down, whether to dare
The Fiend by easie ascent, or aggravate
His sad exclusion from the dores of Bliss. [525]
Direct against which opn'd from beneath,
Just o're the blissful seat of Paradise,
A passage down to th' Earth, a passage wide,
Wider by farr then that of after-times
Over Mount Sion, and, though that were large, [530]
Over the Promis'd Land to God so dear,
By which, to visit oft those happy Tribes,
On high behests his Angels to and fro
Pass'd frequent, and his eye with choice regard
From Paneas the fount of Jordans flood [535]
To Beersaba, where the Holy Land
Borders on Ægypt and th' Arabian shoare;
So wide the op'ning seemd, where bounds were set
To darkness, such as bound the Ocean wave.
Satan from hence now on the lower stair [540]
That scal'd by steps of Gold to Heav'n Gate
Looks down with wonder at the sudden view

註9：當時，雅各施用詭計，騙得父親把對長子的祝福給了他，奪去長子以掃所應得的福分，這讓以掃相當忿怒，欲追殺他。雅各逃往哈蘭，打算前去依靠舅舅拉班，途中於某地方做夢，夢見通往天國的梯子，醒來後驚呼：「天的門。」出自《舊約‧創世紀》：「雅各出了別是巴，向哈蘭走去。到了一個地方，因為太陽落了，就在那裡住宿，……夢見一個梯子立在地上，梯子的頭頂著天，有神的使者在梯子上，上去下來。……雅各睡醒了，說：『……這地方何等可畏！這不是別的，乃是神的殿，也是天的門。』」

註10：「應許之地」即為今日的巴勒斯坦。

註11：潘尼亞斯位於約旦河的發源地，是巴勒斯坦北端的城市；別士巴則在巴勒斯坦南端。

新世界，「哇！真是太美了。」就像一個迷途的偵察兵，冒著生命的危險在漆黑的夜晚，摸索著山徑往前走，終於在晨光乍現時來到一處山崖，他感到疲憊不堪，正想找個地方坐下來休息，突然一片燦爛金光炫入眼目，這才發現眼前的異國建築，那美不勝收的亭台樓閣在日出的照射下，閃耀著璀璨光芒。

撒旦極目四望，一顆由羨生妒的

Of all this World at once. As when a Scout
Through dark and desart wayes with peril gone
All night; at last by break of chearful dawne [545]
Obtains the brow of some high-climbing Hill,
Which to his eye discovers unaware
The goodly prospect of some forein land
First-seen, or some renown'd Metropolis
With glistering Spires and Pinnacles adorn'd, [550]
Which now the Rising Sun guilds with his beams.
Such wonder seis'd, though after Heaven seen,

▽ 雅各夜夢天梯
提耶波洛 壁畫 18世紀

舊約《創世紀》提到雅各曾經夢到一座通往天國的梯子。他看到天使和上帝出現在梯子的頂端，答應在他逃難的途中給予幫助。米爾頓在《失樂園》中引用這段記載，描述撒旦就是登上天梯，探問到新樂園的所在地。

心蠢蠢欲動，待他遍覽了整個宇宙之後，隨即張開翅膀朝新世界的第一區飛去。星光點點，一顆顆閃亮的星星與他擦身而過，像是一座座神話中的美麗島嶼，田野、森林清新純淨，百合花開滿了整個山谷。他首先選擇降落在太陽，因為它耀眼的光芒與天庭近似，吸引了他的目光；待他停妥之

The Spirit maligne, but much more envy seis'd
At sight of all this World beheld so faire.
Round he surveys, and well might, where he stood [555]
So high above the circling Canopie
Of Nights extended shade; from Eastern Point
Of Libra to the fleecie Starr that bears
Andromeda farr off Atlantic Seas
Beyond th' Horizon; then from Pole to Pole [560]
He views in bredth, and without longer pause
Down right into the Worlds first Region throws
His flight precipitant, and windes with ease
Through the pure marble Air his oblique way
Amongst innumerable Starrs, that shon [565]
Stars distant, but nigh hand seemd other Worlds,
Or other Worlds they seemd, or happy Iles,
Like those Hesperian Gardens fam'd of old,
Fortunate Fields, and Groves and flourie Vales,
Thrice happy Iles, but who dwelt happy there [570]
He stayd not to enquire: above them all
The golden Sun in splendor likest Heaven
Allur'd his eye: Thither his course he bends
Through the calm Firmament; but up or downe
By center, or eccentric, hard to tell, [575]
Or Longitude, where the great Luminarie
Alooff the vulgar Constellations thick,
That from his Lordly eye keep distance due,
Dispenses Light from farr; they as they move
Thir Starry dance in numbers that compute [580]
Days, months, & years, towards his all-chearing Lamp
Turn swift thir various motions, or are turnd
By his Magnetic beam, that gently warms
The Univers, and to each inward part
With gentle penetration, though unseen, [585]
Shoots invisible vertue even to the deep:

◄ **撒旦飛向太陽**
杜雷 版畫 1866年

　　在浩瀚的宇宙星辰中，撒旦最先注意到耀眼的太陽。它的燦爛光明就像他曾經熟悉的天庭，於是撒旦首先飛向太陽，經過重重波折的艱辛旅程，這是個適合落腳休息的好地方。

後，看見星星們正浸潤在太陽溫暖的光線中，依著規律的週期繞太陽運行，就跟踩著節奏跳舞一樣。

燦亮的太陽表面無任何陰暗處，因此撒旦的眼睛能夠看到很遠的地方，他四下張望，突然，一位光明天使出現在他的視線中 [12]。他背對著撒旦，肅穆地站著，彷彿在思考著什麼重要的事；太陽用光線織就了一頂金冠戴在他頭上，散發著淡淡的黃暈，捲曲的鬢髮則披散在背後翅膀和雙肩上，隨風飛揚宛若翻捲的波浪。

撒旦化身成一個年輕的天使基路伯，眉清目秀，臉頰兩旁的捲髮上下飄盪，洋溢著一股青春的氣息；他振起色彩繽紛的雙翅，輕盈地朝光明天使飛去。光明天使遠遠地便聽到翅膀拍動的聲音，他迅速地轉過頭來，

「喔！原來是尤烈兒（Uriel）。」

撒旦馬上認出光明天使的身分，他是上帝寶座前的七位天使之一，時常代替上帝到四處巡察，掌有很高的權

So wondrously was set his Station bright.
There lands the Fiend, a spot like which perhaps
Astronomer in the Sun's lucent Orbe
Through his glaz'd Optic Tube yet never saw. [590]
The place he found beyond expression bright,
Compar'd with aught on Earth, Medal or Stone;
Not all parts like, but all alike informd
With radiant light, as glowing Iron with fire;
If mettal, part seemd Gold, part Silver cleer; [595]
If stone, Carbuncle most or Chrysolite,
Rubie or Topaz, to the Twelve that shon
In Aarons Brest-plate, and a stone besides
Imagind rather oft then elsewhere seen,
That stone, or like to that which here below [600]
Philosophers in vain so long have sought,
In vain, though by thir powerful Art they binde
Volatil Hermes, and call up unbound
In various shapes old Proteus from the Sea,
Draind through a Limbec to his Native forme. [605]
What wonder then if fields and region here
Breathe forth Elixir pure, and Rivers run
Potable Gold, when with one vertuous touch
Th' Arch-chimic Sun so farr from us remote
Produces with Terrestrial Humor mixt [610]
Here in the dark so many precious things
Of colour glorious and effect so rare?
Here matter new to gaze the Devil met
Undazl'd, farr and wide his eye commands,
For sight no obstacle found here, nor shade, [615]
But all Sun-shine, as when his Beams at Noon
Culminate from th' Æquator, as they now
Shot upward still direct, whence no way round
Shadow from body opaque can fall, and the Aire,

註12：即《新約・啟示錄》中，約翰所說的：「我又看見一位天使站在日頭中，向天空所飛的鳥大聲喊著說：『你們聚集來赴神的大筵席！可以吃君王與將軍的肉，壯士與馬和騎馬者的肉，並一切自主的、為奴的以及大小人民的肉。』」

力[13]。

「你好啊，大天使。又出來巡視啦！真是辛苦呢！」

撒旦擠出滿臉笑容，以崇拜的語氣向尤烈兒打著招呼。

「你好啊！小天使，到這兒來有什麼事嗎？」

尤烈兒以打量的眼神審視著由撒旦化成的年輕天使，一邊嚴肅的問道。

「喔！事情是這樣的，現在天國最熱門的話題就是上帝所創造的新樂園，聽說那兒充滿著幸福和快樂，我想親眼去瞧瞧；並且看一看那些被上帝專寵的人類，到底長得是什麼模樣。

「但我從天梯下來之後便迷失了方向，只好先往光亮的太陽飛來，想到這裡來找個人問路；真高興遇見的是你，你一定知道新樂園的位置吧！能否告訴我它的方位？」撒旦隨口編出一套謊言，並以渴望的眼神望著尤烈兒。

No where so cleer, sharp'nd his visual ray [620]
To objects distant farr, whereby he soon
Saw within kenn a glorious Angel stand,
The same whom John saw also in the Sun:
His back was turnd, but not his brightness hid;
Of beaming sunnie Raies, a golden tiar [625]
Circl'd his Head, nor less his Locks behind
Illustrious on his Shoulders fledge with wings
Lay waving round; on som great charge imploy'd
He seemd, or fixt in cogitation deep.
Glad was the Spirit impure as now in hope [630]
To find who might direct his wandring flight
To Paradise the happie seat of Man,
His journies end and our beginning woe.
But first he casts to change his proper shape,
Which else might work him danger or delay: [635]
And now a stripling Cherube he appeers,
Not of the prime, yet such as in his face
Youth smil'd Celestial, and to every Limb
Sutable grace diffus'd, so well he feign'd;
Under a Coronet his flowing haire [640]
In curles on either cheek plaid, wings he wore
Of many a colour'd plume sprinkl'd with Gold,
His habit fit for speed succinct, and held
Before his decent steps a Silver wand.
He drew not nigh unheard, the Angel bright, [645]
Ere he drew nigh, his radiant visage turnd,
Admonisht by his ear, and strait was known
Th' Arch-Angel Uriel, one of the seav'n
Who in God's presence, neerest to his Throne
Stand ready at command, and are his Eyes [650]
That run through all the Heav'ns, or down to th' Earth
Bear his swift errands over moist and dry,
O're Sea and Land; him Satan thus accostes;

註13：出自《新約‧啓示錄》：「但願從那昔在、今在、以後永在的神和他寶座前的七靈（即七天使），並那誠實作見證的，從死裡首先復活，……我看見那站在神面前的七位天使，有七枝號賜給他們。」

「嗯，的確是有這麼一個地方，不過你到那兒去做什麼呢？」尤烈兒嘴角微微上揚，略帶笑容地問著。

「我想看看上帝親手創造的新世界，尤其是那神奇的創造物 ── 人類，看他們是如何得到上帝的寵愛，藉由萬物的美好來讚揚上帝的賢明，並將自己的祝福給予他們。」撒旦神色自若，毫不猶豫地答覆。

「的確，造物主是非常偉大的，我曾親眼看見新世界的創造過程。太初之時，世界黯淡無光，只有無邊無際的水；『渾沌』服從上帝的指示讓出廣大的空間，畫分出界限來。上帝說：『要有光！』黑暗中射進一道黎明的曙光，稱之『白天』；不久，亮光消逝，便稱之『夜晚』，混亂中逐漸生出秩序來了[14]。

「接著，地、水、風、火四元素各自歸位；而清靈的第五元素『以太』

註14：上帝創造天地的過程出自《舊約·創世記》。請參照本書第七卷，註2。

Uriel, for thou of those seav'n Spirits that stand
In sight of God's high Throne, gloriously bright, [655]
The first art wont his great authentic will
Interpreter through highest Heav'n to bring,
Where all his Sons thy Embassie attend;
And here art likeliest by supream decree
Like honor to obtain, and as his Eye [660]
To visit oft this new Creation round;
Unspeakable desire to see, and know
All these his wondrous works, but chiefly Man,
His chief delight and favour, him for whom
All these his works so wondrous he ordaind, [665]
Hath brought me from the Quires of Cherubim
Alone thus wandring. Brightest Seraph tell
In which of all these shining Orbes hath Man
His fixed seat, or fixed seat hath none,
But all these shining Orbes his choice to dwell; [670]
That I may find him, and with secret gaze,
Or open admiration him behold
On whom the great Creator hath bestowd
Worlds, and on whom hath all these graces powrd;
That both in him and all things, as is meet, [675]
The Universal Maker we may praise;
Who justly hath driv'n out his Rebell Foes
To deepest Hell, and to repair that loss
Created this new happie Race of Men
To serve him better: wise are all his wayes. [680]

So spake the false dissembler unperceivd;
For neither Man nor Angel can discern
Hypocrisie, the onely evil that walks
Invisible, except to God alone,
By his permissive will, through Heav'n and Earth: [685]
And oft though wisdom wake, suspicion sleeps
At wisdoms Gate, and to simplicitie
Resigns her charge, while goodness thinks no ill
Where no ill seems: Which now for once beguil'd
Uriel, though Regent of the Sun, and held [690]
The sharpest sighted Spirit of all in Heav'n;
Who to the fraudulent Impostor foule
In his uprightness answer thus returnd.

則化成各種形象，那旋轉成圓形球體
的升到空中，成了無數閃亮的星辰，
未化作星星的就變做宇宙的城牆，環
繞在周圍。

　　「往下看哪！你要找的新世界就是
底下的那顆星球，受太陽光照射的這

Faire Angel, thy desire which tends to know
The works of God, thereby to glorifie [695]
The great Work-Maister, leads to no excess
That reaches blame, but rather merits praise
The more it seems excess, that led thee hither
From thy Empyreal Mansion thus alone,
To witness with thine eyes what some perhaps [700]
Contented with report hear onely in heav'n:
For wonderful indeed are all his works,
Pleasant to know, and worthiest to be all
Had in remembrance alwayes with delight;

➢ 第一日、第二日
伯恩瓊斯 水彩畫 1870~1876年

　　混沌之初，地球是一片飄
浮在虛無太空中的黑暗世界，
上帝在第一天創造了第一道曙
光，從此有了白天和黑夜。第
二天又創造了天空和大海，讓
風和雲有了去處，新世界在造
物者手中漸漸形成。

片區域是白天，另外那一面則稱之黑夜；在黑夜的那一邊，有一顆小星球面對著它，叫做月亮，每月繞行地球一周，因能否照射到光線而有盈虛圓缺的樣貌。

「快去看看吧！上帝所創造的人類——亞當，就居住在那茂密的林木裡，我無法領你前去，因我須往另一個方向巡視。再見！祝你好運。」說完，尤烈兒即轉身往天上飛去。

撒旦遵循天庭的禮節向尤烈兒深深地鞠了一躬，當大天使離開後，他便滿懷喜悅地往地球的方向飛去，途中，因過度興奮而在空中盤旋了幾圈，然後才筆直地降落到尼法提斯山（Niphates）[15]。

註15：尼法提斯山位於美索不達米亞境內，站在它的頂上可以鳥瞰伊甸園。

But what created mind can comprehend [705]
Thir number, or the wisdom infinite
That brought them forth, but hid thir causes deep.
I saw when at his Word the formless Mass,
This worlds material mould, came to a heap:
Confusion heard his voice, and wilde uproar [710]
Stood rul'd, stood vast infinitude confin'd;
Till at his second bidding darkness fled,
Light shon, and order from disorder sprung:
Swift to thir several Quarters hasted then
The cumbrous Elements, Earth, Flood, Aire, Fire, [715]
And this Ethereal quintessence of Heav'n
Flew upward, spirited with various forms,
That rowld orbicular, and turnd to Starrs
Numberless, as thou seest, and how they move;
Each had his place appointed, each his course, [720]
The rest in circuit walles this Universe.
Look downward on that Globe whose hither side
With light from hence, though but reflected, shines;
That place is Earth the seat of Man, that light
His day, which else as th' other Hemisphere [725]
Night would invade, but there the neighbouring Moon
(So call that opposite fair Starr) her aide
Timely interposes, and her monthly round
Still ending, still renewing through mid Heav'n,
With borrowd light her countenance triform [730]
Hence fills and empties to enlighten th' Earth,
And in her pale dominion checks the night.
That spot to which I point is Paradise,
Adams abode, those loftie shades his Bowre.
Thy way thou canst not miss, me mine requires. [735]

Thus said, he turnd, and Satan bowing low,
As to superior Spirits is wont in Heaven,
Where honour due and reverence none neglects,
Took leave, and toward the coast of Earth beneath,
Down from th' Ecliptic, sped with hop'd success, [740]
Throws his steep flight in many an Aerie wheele,
Nor staid, till on Niphates top he lights.

Chapter

4 > 初探伊甸園

在騙得大天使尤烈兒的指引之後，撒旦終於來到傳說中的
新世界，他降落在傳說中能夠遍覽伊甸樂園的尼法提斯山山頂，
先偷偷地觀察上帝的新子民——人類的動靜，然後再設法想出個
引誘他們的計策來。另一方面，尤烈兒已經發現自己中了撒旦的
詭計，連忙趕往地球，通知管理伊甸園的天使加百列；當夜晚降
臨，亞當和夏娃沉入甜美夢境的同時，加百列正率領著眾多天使
四處搜尋撒旦的蹤跡，終於，他們在夏娃的身旁抓住了他。但
是，魔鬼邪惡的思想，已緩緩滲入夏娃的夢裡。

撒旦站在尼法提斯山的山頂上，傳說這個地方可以鳥瞰伊甸園的全景，他以銳利的目光四下搜尋，欲盡快找到人類，好把自己滿腔的憤懣發洩在他們身上；但另一方面，撒旦的內心卻也充滿著矛盾。

「也許事情還有轉圜的餘地，只要我向上帝認了錯，……但是，我要怎樣跟地獄裡的跟隨者交代呢？」

上帝曾經給予撒旦「自由意志」與「權力地位」，「自由意志」原是要讓天使們選擇「善」的思想，往良善的方向走，可是撒旦卻因「權力地位」而生出了無窮的野心，甚至讓「惡」來主導了自己的「自由意志」，做出叛變的舉動。因此，雖然現在「善」的聲音在他的心靈深處喚

＜ 撒旦內心的掙扎
杜雷 版畫 1866年

　　撒旦在尋找伊甸園的同時，也曾在善惡之間短暫掙扎。然而大錯已經鑄成，現在向上帝認錯恐怕太遲了，他的尊嚴掃地，絕望油然而生，此刻只能抱著萬劫不復的心理，繼續施行他的邪惡計劃。

O for that warning voice, which he who saw
Th' Apocalyps, heard cry in Heaven aloud,
Then when the Dragon, put to second rout,
Came furious down to be reveng'd on men,
Wo to the inhabitants on Earth! that now, [5]
While time was, our first-Parents had bin warnd
The coming of thir secret foe, and scap'd
Haply so scap'd his mortal snare; for now
Satan, now first inflam'd with rage, came down,
The Tempter ere th' Accuser of man-kind, [10]
To wreck on innocent frail man his loss
Of that first Battel, and his flight to Hell:
Yet not rejoycing in his speed, though bold,
Far off and fearless, nor with cause to boast,
Begins his dire attempt, which nigh the birth [15]
Now rowling, boiles in his tumultuous brest,
And like a devillish Engine back recoiles
Upon himself; horror and doubt distract
His troubl'd thoughts, and from the bottom stirr
The Hell within him, for within him Hell [20]
He brings, and round about him, nor from Hell
One step no more then from himself can fly
By change of place: Now conscience wakes despair
That slumberd, wakes the bitter memorie
Of what he was, what is, and what must be [25]
Worse; of worse deeds worse sufferings must ensue.
Sometimes towards Eden which now in his view
Lay pleasant, his grievd look he fixes sad,
Sometimes towards Heav'n and the full-blazing Sun,
Which now sat high in his Meridian Towre: [30]
Then much revolving, thus in sighs began.

O thou that with surpassing Glory crownd,
Look'st from thy sole Dominion like the God
Of this new World; at whose sight all the Starrs
Hide thir diminisht heads; to thee I call, [35]
But with no friendly voice, and add thy name
O Sun, to tell thee how I hate thy beams
That bring to my remembrance from what state
I fell, how glorious once above thy Sphear;
Till Pride and worse Ambition threw me down [40]
Warring in Heav'n against Heav'ns matchless King:

著他，試圖找回他的良心，但在強大野心的驅使下，撒旦的「自由意志」仍然往「地獄」的方向行去了。

　　絕望，能讓人徹底的摒棄自尊，當一個人不在乎自己尊嚴的時候，就不可能喚回他的良知了；撒旦就是如此，明知上帝將會降下更重的懲罰，卻仍抱著萬劫不復的心理，朝著罪惡的方向走去。撒旦抬起頭，對著熾熱的太陽喃喃說道：

　　「太陽呀！為什麼要用耀眼的光芒來喚起我心中痛苦的回憶？曾經，我凌駕在你之上，是天庭中屬一屬二的大天使，掌有至高的權力地位，甚至比起你那讓群星隱去的光芒還要來的光亮；如今我因為無窮的野心而遭受到沉淪的命運，你想，我還有懺悔的機會嗎？

　　「不！不可能。上帝早就徹底地摒棄我們，否則祂不會再造一個新樂園，人類就是用來取代我們的。對，就是這樣，情況很清楚，我們再無回

Ah wherefore! he deservd no such return
From me, whom he created what I was
In that bright eminence, and with his good
Upbraided none; nor was his service hard. [45]
What could be less then to afford him praise,
The easiest recompence, and pay him thanks,
How due! yet all his good prov'd ill in me,
And wrought but malice; lifted up so high
I sdeind subjection, and thought one step higher [50]
Would set me highest, and in a moment quit
The debt immense of endless gratitude,
So burthensome, still paying, still to ow;
Forgetful what from him I still receivd,
And understood not that a grateful mind [55]
By owing owes not, but still pays, at once
Indebted and dischargd; what burden then?
O had his powerful Destiny ordaind
Me some inferiour Angel, I had stood
Then happie; no unbounded hope had rais'd [60]
Ambition. Yet why not? som other Power
As great might have aspir'd, and me though mean
Drawn to his part; but other Powers as great
Fell not, but stand unshak'n, from within
Or from without, to all temptations arm'd. [65]
Hadst thou the same free Will and Power to stand?
Thou hadst: whom hast thou then or what to accuse,
But Heav'ns free Love dealt equally to all?
Be then his Love accurst, since love or hate,
To me alike, it deals eternal woe. [70]
Nay curs'd be thou; since against his thy will
Chose freely what it now so justly rues.
Me miserable! which way shall I flie
Infinite wrauth, and infinite despaire?
Which way I flie is Hell; my self am Hell; [75]
And in the lowest deep a lower deep
Still threatning to devour me opens wide,
To which the Hell I suffer seems a Heav'n.
O then at last relent: is there no place
Left for Repentance, none for Pardon left? [80]
None left but by submission; and that word
Disdain forbids me, and my dread of shame
Among the Spirits beneath, whom I seduc'd

頭的餘地了。」

　　毫無盡頭的絕望讓撒旦鐵了心，他收斂起因嫉妒而不經意顯露的猙獰面孔，以幻化的天使姿態走向伊甸園。

　　就在撒旦偷偷窺視伊甸園的時候，尤烈兒在天上發現了撒旦凶狠的目光和慘綠的面容，

　　「啊！糟糕。原來是撒旦偽裝的。」

　　尤烈兒原本就奉命尋找逃出地獄的叛徒撒旦的下落，卻因單純善良之心，一時給蒙蔽了智慧，做出錯誤的舉動，為魔鬼指出樂園的方向。

　　「不行，我得快點去警告守門天使才行。」

　　說完，尤烈兒疾速地往地球趕去。

　　撒旦來到伊甸（Eden）邊境，從他站著的峭壁往前望去，只見一片綠意盎然的叢林景象，松、杉、樅、柏等蒼翠林木宛如劇院裡的觀眾，把階梯狀的座位密密麻麻地擠得水洩不通。伊甸樂園居於林蔭深處，一道青翠的

With other promises and other vaunts
Then to submit, boasting I could subdue [85]
Th' Omnipotent. Ay me, they little know
How dearly I abide that boast so vaine,
Under what torments inwardly I groane:
While they adore me on the Throne of Hell,
With Diadem and Sceptre high advanc'd [90]
The lower still I fall, onely Supream
In miserie; such joy Ambition findes.
But say I could repent and could obtaine
By Act of Grace my former state; how soon
Would higth recall high thoughts, how soon unsay [95]
What feign'd submission swore: ease would recant
Vows made in pain, as violent and void.
For never can true reconcilement grow
Where wounds of deadly hate have peirc'd so deep:
Which would but lead me to a worse relapse [100]
And heavier fall: so should I purchase deare
Short intermission bought with double smart.
This knows my punisher; therefore as farr
From granting hee, as I from begging peace:
All hope excluded thus, behold in stead [105]
Of us out-cast, exil'd, his new delight,
Mankind created, and for him this World.
So farewel Hope, and with Hope farewel Fear,
Farewel Remorse: all Good to me is lost;
Evil be thou my Good; by thee at least [110]
Divided Empire with Heav'ns King I hold
By thee, and more then half perhaps will reigne;
As Man ere long, and this new World shall know.

Thus while he spake, each passion dimm'd his face
Thrice chang'd with pale, ire, envie and despair, [115]
Which marr'd his borrow'd visage, and betraid
Him counterfet, if any eye beheld.
For heav'nly mindes from such distempers foule
Are ever cleer. Whereof hee soon aware,
Each perturbation smooth'd with outward calme, [120]
Artificer of fraud; and was the first
That practisd falshood under saintly shew,
Deep malice to conceale, couch't with revenge:
Yet not anough had practisd to deceive

▽ 撒旦俯視伊甸園

杜雷 版畫 1866年

　　撒旦從山頂俯視，只見伊甸園一片綠意盎然，其間還點綴著金色花朵和果實，空氣是一陣陣馥郁的芳香，這和熊熊烈火的地獄真是天壤之別。

圍籬環繞著它，隱約可見從裡頭伸展出來的嫩綠枝枒；籬笆裡面長有最美麗的樹木，茂密的枝葉裡，結滿了金色的花朵和果實，在陽光暖暖的照射中，閃爍著燦爛的金光。

　　微風輕輕拂過，帶來一陣芳香的氣味，讓人不禁想起盛產香木的遠方國

Uriel once warnd; whose eye pursu'd him down [125]
The way he went, and on th' Assyrian mount
Saw him disfigur'd, more then could befall
Spirit of happie sort: his gestures fierce
He markd and mad demeanour, then alone,
As he suppos'd all unobserv'd, unseen. [130]
So on he fares, and to the border comes
Of Eden, where delicious Paradise,
Now nearer, Crowns with her enclosure green,
As with a rural mound the champain head
Of a steep wilderness, whose hairie sides [135]
With thicket overgrown, grottesque and wilde,
Access deni'd; and over head up grew
Insuperable highth of loftiest shade,
Cedar, and Pine, and Firr, and branching Palm
A Silvan Scene, and as the ranks ascend [140]
Shade above shade, a woodie Theatre
Of stateliest view. Yet higher then thir tops
The verdurous wall of paradise up sprung:
Which to our general Sire gave prospect large
Into his neather Empire neighbouring round. [145]
And higher then that Wall a circling row
Of goodliest Trees loaden with fairest Fruit,
Blossoms and Fruits at once of golden hue
Appeerd, with gay enameld colours mixt:
On which the Sun more glad impress'd his beams [150]
Then in fair Evening Cloud, or humid Bow,
When God hath showrd the earth; so lovely seemd
That Lantskip: And of pure now purer aire
Meets his approach, and to the heart inspires
Vernal delight and joy, able to drive [155]
All sadness but despair: now gentle gales
Fanning thir odoriferous wings dispense
Native perfumes, and whisper whence they stole
Those balmie spoiles. As when to them who saile
Beyond the Cape of Hope, and now are past [160]
Mozambic, off at Sea North-East windes blow
Sabean Odours from the spicie shoare
Of Arabie the blest, with such delay
Well pleas'd they slack thir course, and many a League
Chear'd with the grateful smell old Ocean smiles. [165]
So entertaind those odorous sweets the Fiend

度 ── 沙巴（Sabean）[1]；那時船隻剛剛經過好望角，正在莫桑比克海峽航行的當兒，從海面飄來一陣陣馥郁的芳香，那是從阿拉伯古國沙巴傳來的香味，船員們聞到這香味，立即感到神清氣爽，長期航海的辛苦，也都一點一點地在香味中融解了。

「好香啊！」

撒旦聞到這股清新的空氣，就如同上述船員們所發生的的情況一般，精神立刻為之一振。他沉醉在這股芳香裡，步履漸趨緩慢，直走到被一叢叢灌木擋住去路才停下來，往四周望望，發現東側有一扇門，

「哼！想阻擋我？我偏偏不從大門進去。」

說完，往上一躍，輕易地便翻過圍籬落入園中。這行徑，就像一隻饑餓

註1：沙巴又叫示巴，為阿拉伯古國，其女王曾經贈送所羅門王香料和寶石。《舊約．列王紀上》：「於是示巴女王將一百二十他連得金子和寶石，與極多的香料，送給所羅門王。」

Who came thir bane, though with them better pleas'd
Then Asmodeus with the fishie fume,
That drove him, though enamourd, from the Spouse
Of Tobits Son, and with a vengeance sent [170]
From Media post to Ægypt, there fast bound.

Now to th' ascent of that steep savage Hill
Satan had journied on, pensive and slow;
But further way found none, so thick entwin'd,
As one continu'd brake, the undergrowth [175]
Of shrubs and tangling bushes had perplext
All path of Man or Beast that past that way:
One Gate there only was, and that look'd East
On th' other side: which when th' arch-fellon saw
Due entrance he disdaind, and in contempt, [180]
At one slight bound high over leap'd all bound
Of Hill or highest Wall, and sheer within
Lights on his feet. As when a prowling Wolfe,
Whom hunger drives to seek new haunt for prey,
Watching where Shepherds pen thir Flocks at eeve [185]
In hurdl'd Cotes amid the field secure,
Leaps o're the fence with ease into the Fould:
Or as a Thief bent to unhoord the cash
Of some rich Burgher, whose substantial dores,
Cross-barrd and bolted fast, fear no assault, [190]
In at the window climbs, or o're the tiles;
So clomb this first grand Thief into Gods Fould:
So since into his Church lewd Hirelings climbe.
Thence up he flew, and on the Tree of Life,
The middle Tree and highest there that grew, [195]
Sat like a Cormorant; yet not true Life
Thereby regaind, but sat devising Death
To them who liv'd; nor on the vertue thought
Of that life-giving Plant, but only us'd
For prospect, what well us'd had bin the pledge [200]
Of immortality. So little knows
Any, but God alone, to value right
The good before him, but perverts best things
To worst abuse, or to thir meanest use.
Beneath him with new wonder now he views [205]
To all delight of human sense expos'd
In narrow room Natures whole wealth, yea more,

的狼，趁著牧羊人把羊群都趕進羊圈
之後，再跳過柵欄進去吃羊；又像小
偷無懼於富人所設的重重門栓，選擇
從窗戶或屋瓦潛入，竊得財物。

　　園裡的景象比外頭更要美上好幾
倍，撒旦飛到園子正中央的生命樹
上，像水鳥鸕鶿[2]一般地蹲伏在枝
幹，生命樹給予人們真實生命中的
「善」，若能善用它的功能，誠心懺
悔，就能得到永生的機會；但撒旦並
不了解，他只不過是把生命樹當做偵
查哨，俯瞰人類所居住的幸福園地。

　　上帝讓人類生活在伊甸東邊的園林
中，伊甸的範圍從約旦河東邊的浩蘭
向東延伸，直到底格里斯河右岸的西
流古（Seleucia）王塔[3]，或至美索不達
米亞南部的提拉撒（Telassar），此地
為古代伊甸子孫們所居住的地方[4]。

註2：鸕鶿，一種水鳥，長嘴、白頸，能夠潛入水中
　　　捕魚；也叫「水老鴉」和「魚鷹子」，常被漁
　　　夫抓去飼養，訓練成捕魚工具。
註3：西流古（Seleucia）王塔為底格里斯河右岸四
　　　大名城之一，相傳為亞歷山大王手下的著名將
　　　領西流古所建。

A Heaven on Earth, for blissful Paradise
Of God the Garden was, by him in the East
Of Eden planted; Eden stretchd her Line [210]
From Auran Eastward to the Royal Towrs
Of Great Seleucia, built by Grecian Kings,
Or where the Sons of Eden long before
Dwelt in Telassar: in this pleasant soile
His farr more pleasant Garden God ordaind; [215]
Out of the fertil ground he caus'd to grow
All Trees of noblest kind for sight, smell, taste;
And all amid them stood the Tree of Life,
High eminent, blooming Ambrosial Fruit
Of vegetable Gold; and next to Life [220]
Our Death the Tree of Knowledge grew fast by,
Knowledge of Good bought dear by knowing ill.
Southward through Eden went a River large,
Nor chang'd his course, but through the shaggie hill
Pass'd underneath ingulft, for God had thrown [225]
That Mountain as his Garden mould high rais'd
Upon the rapid current, which through veins
Of porous Earth with kindly thirst up drawn,
Rose a fresh Fountain, and with many a rill
Waterd the Garden; thence united fell [230]
Down the steep glade, and met the neather Flood,
Which from his darksom passage now appeers,
And now divided into four main Streams,
Runs divers, wandring many a famous Realme
And Country whereof here needs no account, [235]
But rather to tell how, if Art could tell,
How from that Saphire Fount the crisped Brooks,
Rowling on Orient Pearl and sands of Gold,
With mazie error under pendant shades
Ran Nectar, visiting each plant, and fed [240]
Flours worthy of Paradise which not nice Art
In Beds and curious Knots, but Nature boon
Powrd forth profuse on Hill and Dale and Plaine,
Both where the morning Sun first warmly smote
The open field, and where the unpierc't shade [245]
Imbround the noontide Bowrs: Thus was this place,
A happy rural seat of various view;
Groves whose rich Trees wept odorous Gumms and Balme,

生命樹的旁邊有棵知識樹，吃了它的果實便能夠分別善惡[5]，日後，人類就是因為此樹而必須面對死亡的威脅。

亞當與夏娃

魯本斯 油畫 1600年

亞當與夏娃居住的伊甸園的正中央是一棵生命樹，生命的旁邊是知識樹，吃了它的果實就能分辨善惡，但也會招來死亡的厄運。生命與死亡就這樣比鄰而居，各自生生不息。

Others whose fruit burnisht with Golden Rinde
Hung amiable, Hesperian Fables true, [250]
If true, here only, and of delicious taste:
Betwixt them Lawns, or level Downs, and Flocks
Grasing the tender herb, were interpos'd,
Or palmie hilloc, or the flourie lap
Of som irriguous Valley spred her store, [255]
Flours of all hue, and without Thorn the Rose:
Another side, umbrageous Grots and Caves
Of coole recess, o're which the mantling vine
Layes forth her purple Grape, and gently creeps
Luxuriant; mean while murmuring waters fall [260]
Down the slope hills, disperst, or in a Lake,
That to the fringed Bank with Myrtle crownd,
Her chrystal mirror holds, unite thir streams.
The Birds thir quire apply; aires, vernal aires,
Breathing the smell of field and grove, attune [265]
The trembling leaves, while Universal Pan
Knit with the Graces and the Hours in dance
Led on th' Eternal Spring. Not that faire field
Of Enna, where Proserpin gathering flours
Her self a fairer Floure by gloomie Dis [270]
Was gatherd, which cost Ceres all that pain
To seek her through the world; nor that sweet Grove
Of Daphne by Orontes, and th' inspir'd
Castalian Spring, might with this Paradise
Of Eden strive; nor that Nyseian Ile [275]
Girt with the River Triton, where old Cham,
Whom Gentiles Ammon call and Lybian Jove,

註4：提拉撒（Telassar），位於美索不達米亞南部。《舊約‧以賽亞書》：「亞述王一聽見，就打發使者去見希西家，吩咐他們說：『……我列祖所毀滅的，就是歌散、哈蘭、利色和屬提拉撒的伊甸人。』」
註5：知識樹即聖經中所說的「分別善惡的樹」，《舊約‧創世紀》：「耶和華神在東方伊甸立了一個園子，把所造的人安置在那裡。……園子當中又有生命樹和分別善惡的樹。」

一條大河從地底下穿過，形成無數的細流，它們朝地面湧出，為樂園帶來涓涓不盡的清泉，滋潤著茂密的林園；流過伊甸地區之後，此河即劃分成四道，往不同的方向流去[6]。

芳香鮮美的花朵，盛開在陽光照耀的山坡、濃密的綠蔭和幽靜的山谷；森林中的樹木從枝幹滲出瓊漿玉液，散發著馥郁的芬芳，結在枝椏間的金色果實，更是玲瓏剔透，可愛極了。一隻隻羊兒散佈在草地上，低著頭咂巴咂巴地嚼著青草；另一邊，陰涼的岩洞區，攀爬在岩頂上的枝蔓盤根錯結，茂密的葉叢間有一串串晶瑩剔透的紫葡萄。宛如鏡面的湖水寧靜無波，鳥兒在歌唱，綠葉在微風中輕顫，……這美麗的景致讓春神停駐，牧神潘恩（Pan）和美神、時神則快樂地跳舞，使青春永不消逝。

西西里島上的恩那（Enna）也曾是春神統治的地方，山谷間百花齊放，綠草如茵；一日，美麗的波瑟楓妮來

Hid Amalthea and her Florid Son
Young Bacchus from his Stepdame Rhea's eye;
Nor where Abassin Kings thir issue Guard, [280]
Mount Amara, though this by som suppos'd
True Paradise under the Ethiop Line
By Nilus head, enclosd with shining Rock,
A whole days journy high, but wide remote
From this Assyrian Garden, where the Fiend [285]
Saw undelighted all delight, all kind
Of living Creatures new to sight and strange:
Two of far nobler shape erect and tall,
Godlike erect, with native Honour clad
In naked Majestie seemd Lords of all, [290]
And worthie seemd, for in thir looks Divine
The image of thir glorious Maker shon,
Truth, wisdome, Sanctitude severe and pure,
Severe but in true filial freedom plac't;
Whence true autority in men; though both [295]
Not equal, as thir sex not equal seemd;
For contemplation hee and valour formd,
For softness shee and sweet attractive Grace,
Hee for God only, shee for God in him:
His fair large Front and Eye sublime declar'd [300]
Absolute rule; and Hyacinthin Locks
Round from his parted forelock manly hung
Clustring, but not beneath his shoulders broad:
Shee as a vail down to the slender waste
Her unadorned golden tresses wore [305]
Disheveld, but in wanton ringlets wav'd

註6：《舊約‧創世紀》：「有河從伊甸流出來滋潤那園子，從那裡分為四道：第一道名叫比遜，就是環繞哈腓拉全地的；在那裡有金子，並且那地的金子是好的；在那裡又有珍珠和紅瑪瑙。第二道河名叫基訓，就是環繞古實全地的。第三道河名叫希底結（現為底格里斯），流在亞述的東邊。第四道河就是伯拉河（現為幼發拉底河）幼發拉底河。」

撒旦潛進美麗的伊甸樂園
杜雷 版畫 1866年

走進園內的景象，比居高俯視更美、更真實。如此豐饒美麗的淨土，就是上帝為新人類準備的美好樂園。

As the Vine curles her tendrils, which impli'd
Subjection, but requir'd with gentle sway,
And by her yielded, by him best receivd,
Yielded with coy submission, modest pride, [310]
And sweet reluctant amorous delay.
Nor those mysterious parts were then conceald,
Then was not guiltie shame, dishonest shame
Of natures works, honor dishonorable,
Sin-bred, how have ye troubl'd all mankind [315]
With shews instead, meer shews of seeming pure,
And banisht from mans life his happiest life,
Simplicitie and spotless innocence.
So passd they naked on, nor shund the sight
Of God or Angel, for they thought no ill: [320]
So hand in hand they passd, the lovliest pair
That ever since in loves imbraces met,
Adam the goodliest man of men since borne
His Sons, the fairest of her Daughters Eve.
Under a tuft of shade that on a green [325]
Stood whispering soft, by a fresh Fountain side
They sat them down, and after no more toil
Of thir sweet Gardning labour then suffic'd
To recommend coole Zephyr, and made ease
More easie, wholsom thirst and appetite [330]
More grateful, to thir Supper Fruits they fell,
Nectarine Fruits which the compliant boughes
Yielded them, side-long as they sat recline
On the soft downie Bank damaskt with flours:
The savourie pulp they chew, and in the rinde [335]
Still as they thirsted scoop the brimming stream;
Nor gentle purpose, nor endearing smiles
Wanted, nor youthful dalliance as beseems
Fair couple, linkt in happie nuptial League,
Alone as they. About them frisking playd [340]
All Beasts of th' Earth, since wilde, and of all chase
In Wood or Wilderness, Forrest or Den;

到恩那山谷採摘花朵，當她正要把一朵純白色的百合放進籃子裡時，她腳下的地面突然裂了一個大洞，冥王黑地斯從洞裡跳出來，把她抓回地獄做妻子；波瑟楓妮的母親收穫女神賽麗絲得知女兒失蹤的消息後，心如刀割，她不吃不喝、不眠不休地四處尋找女兒的下落，最後終於在冥界找到

了女兒[7]。

　　黎巴嫩奧倫特斯（Orontes）河畔的達芙妮森林是個觀光勝地，景色相當優美，森林裡有一座太陽神阿波羅的神廟。傳說阿波羅因得罪了小愛神丘比特（Cupid）而慘遭報復；丘比特把點燃愛情的箭射向他，同時把排斥愛情的箭射進山澤女神達芙妮的心裡，造成阿波羅猛追，達芙妮卻急忙奔逃的窘境。最後，達芙妮在不堪其擾的情況下，請求父親河神皮里奧斯將她變做一株月桂樹；見到心愛的人竟然懼怕自己到這樣的地步，阿波羅只好傷心地離去[8]。　其他還有像利比亞的尼棲亞島（Nyseia）與尼羅河上游的

註7：出自《希臘羅馬神話故事》，波瑟楓妮（Proserpine）為收穫女神賽麗絲（Ceres）的女兒，冥王黑地斯（Heides）的妻子；依照播種與收割的季節，波瑟楓妮每年有三分之二的時間可回到母親身邊，其餘的時間則待在地獄。

註8：出自《希臘羅馬神話故事》，達芙妮（Daphne）是河神皮里奧斯（Peneus）的女兒，因丘比特的戲弄變成一棵月桂樹。因此阿波羅（Apollo）把月桂樹當做自己的聖樹，並以桂冠給勝利者加冕。

Sporting the Lion rampd, and in his paw
Dandl'd the Kid; Bears, Tygers, Ounces, Pards
Gambold before them, th' unwieldy Elephant [345]
To make them mirth us'd all his might, and wreathd
His Lithe Proboscis; close the Serpent sly
Insinuating, wove with Gordian twine
His breaded train, and of his fatal guile
Gave proof unheeded; others on the grass [350]
Coucht, and now fild with pasture gazing sat,
Or Bedward ruminating: for the Sun
Declin'd was hasting now with prone carreer
To th' Ocean Iles, and in th' ascending Scale
Of Heav'n the Starrs that usher Evening rose: [355]
When Satan still in gaze, as first he stood,
Scarce thus at length faild speech recoverd sad.

O Hell! what doe mine eyes with grief behold,
Into our room of bliss thus high advanc't
Creatures of other mould, earth-born perhaps, [360]
Not Spirits, yet to heav'nly Spirits bright
Little inferior; whom my thoughts pursue
With wonder, and could love, so lively shines
In them Divine resemblance, and such grace
The hand that formd them on thir shape hath pourd. [365]
Ah gentle pair, yee little think how nigh
Your change approaches, when all these delights
Will vanish and deliver ye to woe,
More woe, the more your taste is now of joy;
Happie, but for so happie ill secur'd [370]
Long to continue, and this high seat your Heav'n
Ill fenc't for Heav'n to keep out such a foe
As now is enterd; yet no purpos'd foe
To you whom I could pittie thus forlorne
Though I unpittied: League with you I seek, [375]
And mutual amitie so streight, so close,
That I with you must dwell, or you with me
Henceforth; my dwelling haply may not please
Like this fair Paradise, your sense, yet such
Accept your Makers work; he gave it me, [380]
Which I as freely give; Hell shall unfold,
To entertain you two, her widest Gates,
And send forth all her Kings; there will be room,

∧ 亞當與夏娃於泉水旁休憩
杜雷 版畫 1866年

　　亞當招呼夏娃喝水，他們雖然全身赤裸，卻是純潔可喜，散發聖潔美麗的光輝，生活是那麼無憂無慮。

阿瑪拉山（Amara），也都以豐饒美麗著稱於世，但這些地方比起伊甸園來，都還差上一大截呢！

　　儘管伊甸樂園的風景是如此美麗，滿懷嫉妒與恨意的撒旦卻無心欣賞，他以銳利的目光四處搜尋，在清泉旁邊的樹蔭底下，發現了兩個挺拔俊秀

Not like these narrow limits, to receive
Your numerous ofspring; if no better place, [385]
Thank him who puts me loath to this revenge
On you who wrong me not for him who wrongd.
And should I at your harmless innocence
Melt, as I doe, yet public reason just,
Honour and Empire with revenge enlarg'd, [390]
By conquering this new World, compels me now
To do what else though damnd I should abhorre.

So spake the Fiend, and with necessitie,
The Tyrants plea, excus'd his devilish deeds.
Then from his loftie stand on that high Tree [395]
Down he alights among the sportful Herd
Of those fourfooted kindes, himself now one,
Now other, as thir shape servd best his end
Neerer to view his prey, and unespi'd
To mark what of thir state he more might learn [400]
By word or action markt: about them round
A Lion now he stalkes with fierie glare,
Then as a Tyger, who by chance hath spi'd
In some Purlieu two gentle Fawnes at play,
Strait couches close, then rising changes oft [405]
His couchant watch, as one who chose his ground
Whence rushing he might surest seize them both
Gript in each paw: when Adam first of men
To first of women Eve thus moving speech,
Turnd him all eare to hear new utterance flow. [410]

Sole partner and sole part of all these joyes,
Dearer thy self then all; needs must the Power
That made us, and for us this ample World
Be infinitly good, and of his good
As liberal and free as infinite, [415]
That rais'd us from the dust and plac't us here
In all this happiness, who at his hand
Have nothing merited, nor can performe
Aught whereof hee hath need, hee who requires
From us no other service then to keep [420]
This one, this easie charge, of all the Trees
In Paradise that bear delicious fruit
So various, not to taste that onely Tree

的形體,他們全身赤裸,似造物主的
容顏上散發著聖潔的光輝。男的叫亞
當,一頭蜷曲的青髮從額頭往左右兩
邊垂下,懸盪在寬廣的肩膀之上;他
機智、勇敢,且掌握了權柄。女的叫
夏娃,金黃色的長髮如輕盈的頭紗,
直罩到纖細的腰際,凌亂的髮絲則捲
曲似葡萄嫩芽;她溫柔、美麗,具有
服從性格。他們依順自然的創造,心
中純潔無任何邪念,故能以坦然的態
度迎向天使們的注視,並不拘宥於所
謂的羞恥心。

　　「來,夏娃。坐到我的身旁來
吧!」

　　亞當坐在濃密的樹蔭下,雙足浸泡
在清澈的泉水中,轉頭輕喚身後的美
麗女子。

　　「嗯!」

　　夏娃柔順地走到泉水邊,緩緩地坐
了下來,把身體斜倚在亞當肩上。

　　「吃吧!很甜喔!」

　　亞當把一顆鮮嫩欲滴的果子擺到夏

Of knowledge, planted by the Tree of Life,
So neer grows Death to Life, what ere Death is, [425]
Som dreadful thing no doubt; for well thou knowst
God hath pronounc't it death to taste that Tree,
The only sign of our obedience left
Among so many signes of power and rule
Conferrd upon us, and Dominion giv'n [430]
Over all other Creatures that possess
Earth, Aire, and Sea. Then let us not think hard
One easie prohibition, who enjoy
Free leave so large to all things else, and choice
Unlimited of manifold delights: [435]
But let us ever praise him, and extoll
His bountie, following our delightful task
To prune these growing Plants, and tend these Flours,
Which were it toilsom, yet with thee were sweet.

To whom thus Eve repli'd. O thou for whom [440]
And from whom I was formd flesh of thy flesh,
And without whom am to no end, my Guide
And Head, what thou hast said is just and right.
For wee to him indeed all praises owe,
And daily thanks, I chiefly who enjoy [445]
So farr the happier Lot, enjoying thee
Præeminent by so much odds, while thou
Like consort to thy self canst no where find.
That day I oft remember, when from sleep
I first awak't, and found my self repos'd [450]
Under a shade of flours, much wondring where
And what I was, whence thither brought, and how.
Not distant far from thence a murmuring sound
Of waters issu'd from a Cave and spread
Into a liquid Plain, then stood unmov'd [455]
Pure as th' expanse of Heav'n; I thither went
With unexperienc't thought, and laid me downe
On the green bank, to look into the cleer
Smooth Lake, that to me seemd another Skie.
As I bent down to look, just opposite, [460]
A Shape within the watry gleam appeard
Bending to look on me, I started back,
It started back, but pleas'd I soon returnd,
Pleas'd it returnd as soon with answering looks

伊甸園有各種動物，彼此都能和平相處，獅子可以和小羊玩耍，熊和花豹等猛獸也可以在亞當和夏娃身旁嬉戲。撒旦發現新人類對動物沒有戒心，於是一路悄悄化為各種動物，靠到他們身邊。

娃面前，隨即拿起另外一顆放進嘴裡，「喀茲！喀茲！」地嚼了起來。

落日的餘暉輕輕地灑在兩人身上，他們一邊享受徐徐清風，一邊吃著晚餐。

「喝點水吧！」

夏娃吃完果子，拿起果殼彎下腰來，從清泉中盛了一碗水，遞給亞當喝。

綠蔭底下，動物們正愉快地玩

Of sympathie and love; there I had fixt [465]
Mine eyes till now, and pin'd with vain desire,
Had not a voice thus warnd me, What thou seest,
What there thou seest fair Creature is thy self,
With thee it came and goes: but follow me,
And I will bring thee where no shadow staies [470]
Thy coming, and thy soft imbraces, hee
Whose image thou art, him thou shalt enjoy
Inseparablie thine, to him shalt beare
Multitudes like thy self, and thence be call'd
Mother of human Race: what could I doe, [475]

耍 —— 獅子把前爪攀附在小羊背上撫弄牠，依靠後腳來支撐身體的重量；熊、虎、花豹及山貓則圍繞在他們身邊跳躍著；行動笨拙的大象也捲起長長的鼻子，想博取他們的笑容；狡猾的蛇更以虛偽的笑語，假意向他倆示好，但就如戈迪斯車轅上打的結[9]，其邪惡的意圖顯而易見，但亞當卻沒有識破；其它還有一些動物，飽食青草後在原野上散步，或躺在草地上反芻。此時已是夕陽西下，即將落入大西洋諸島的時刻，星星躍上黑絲絨的天幕，夜晚悄悄降臨了。

　　撒旦仍舊佇立在生命樹上，仔細地觀察著亞當和夏娃的一舉一動。

　　「唉！這就是上帝創造的新種族嗎？他們並非天使，身上卻散發著像全能者一般的優雅風華，且能夠生活

註9：戈迪斯（Gordius）為弗魯吉亞（Phrygia）地方的王，曾經在自己的車轅上打了一個非常複雜的繩結，傳說，誰要是能夠把此結打開，日後便能成為亞洲的主宰；亞歷山大東征時經過此地，拿刀把它給劈開了。

But follow strait, invisibly thus led?
Till I espi'd thee, fair indeed and tall,
Under a Platan, yet methought less faire,
Less winning soft, less amiablie milde,
Then that smooth watry image; back I turnd, [480]
Thou following cryd'st aloud, Return faire Eve,
Whom fli'st thou? whom thou fli'st, of him thou art,
His flesh, his bone; to give thee being I lent
Out of my side to thee, neerest my heart
Substantial Life, to have thee by my side [485]
Henceforth an individual solace dear;
Part of my Soul I seek thee, and thee claim
My other half: with that thy gentle hand
Seisd mine, I yielded, and from that time see
How beauty is excelld by manly grace [490]
And wisdom, which alone is truly fair.

So spake our general Mother, and with eyes
Of conjugal attraction unreprov'd,
And meek surrender, half imbracing leand
On our first Father, half her swelling Breast [495]
Naked met his under the flowing Gold
Of her loose tresses hid: he in delight
Both of her Beauty and submissive Charms
Smil'd with superior Love, as Jupiter
On Juno smiles, when he impregns the Clouds [500]
That shed May Flowers; and press'd her Matron lip
With kisses pure: aside the Devil turnd
For envie, yet with jealous leer maligne
Ey'd them askance, and to himself thus plaind.

Sight hateful, sight tormenting! thus these two [505]
Imparadis't in one anothers arms
The happier Eden, shall enjoy thir fill
Of bliss on bliss, while I to Hell am thrust,
Where neither joy nor love, but fierce desire,
Among our other torments not the least, [510]
Still unfulfill'd with pain of longing pines;
Yet let me not forget what I have gain'd
From thir own mouths; all is not theirs it seems:
One fatal Tree there stands of Knowledge call'd,
Forbidden them to taste: Knowledge forbidd'n? [515]

在媲美天堂的美麗園地，過著天使般的幸福生活；瞧！多麼恩愛的一對戀人哪！可惜，上帝雖然給了你們光潔的外貌，卻沒有在你們的心坎種下防衛的種子，為此，祂將付出沉痛的代價。」

說完，從樹梢飛下來，落入百獸堆裡頭去。他先變成一隻獅子、再變做老虎，一路幻化成各種動物的形貌，往亞當和夏娃的方向移動，不一會兒，已悄悄來到他倆身旁，剛好亞當正對夏娃說著：

「可愛的人兒呀！我倆是何等幸福，上帝為我們創造了美麗的樂園，給予我們極大的自由，並能掌管天空、地面與水中的所有生物，而我倆必需做的事，卻只有修剪整理園裡的花木，這事對我來說一點也不辛苦，

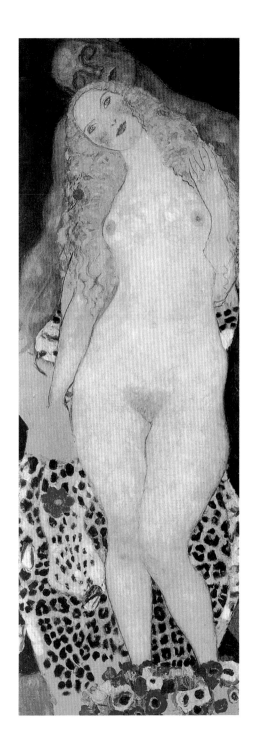

>> 亞當和夏娃
克林姆 油畫 1918年

　　夏娃由亞當的肋骨而生，她生來就是為了安慰、陪伴亞當的。這一對天造地設的戀人相互為伴，原是最無憂無慮的神仙眷侶。

不過是舒展一下筋骨罷了，況且有你陪伴在我身邊，就算再辛苦的工作，也都變成甜蜜了。

「但是有一個禁忌我們必須絕對遵守，那便是知識樹所結的果子不可以吃，吃了它固然能夠辨別善惡，卻會招來死亡的厄運；它長在生命樹的旁邊，死成了生的近鄰，死必定是個可怕的事。我倆應當嚴守這道禁令，心懷感恩，時時讚頌上帝的恩賜。」

夏娃回答說：

「好的，亞當，我既然是你的肉中之肉，為你而創生 [10]，自然得事事服從你，照你所說的去做。那一天，我從睡夢中醒來，發現自己躺在濃密的綠蔭底下，地面鋪滿各色鮮花；我愣在那兒，不知道自己是誰，從何方

註9：戈迪斯（Gordius）為弗魯吉亞（Phrygia）
　　地方的王，曾經在自己的車轅上打了一個非
　　常複雜的繩結，傳說，誰要是能夠把此結打
　　開，日後便能成為亞洲的主宰；亞歷山大東
　　征時經過此地，拿刀把它給劈開了。
註10：夏娃是由亞當的肋骨造成的，所以說是亞當
　　　的「肉中之肉」，出自《舊約‧創世紀》。
　　　請參照本書第八卷，註2。

Suspicious, reasonless. Why should thir Lord
Envie them that? can it be sin to know,
Can it be death? and do they onely stand
By Ignorance, is that thir happie state,
The proof of thir obedience and thir faith? [520]
O fair foundation laid whereon to build
Thir ruine! Hence I will excite thir minds
With more desire to know, and to reject
Envious commands, invented with designe
To keep them low whom knowledge might exalt [525]
Equal with Gods; aspiring to be such,
They taste and die: what likelier can ensue?
But first with narrow search I must walk round
This Garden, and no corner leave unspi'd;
A chance but chance may lead where I may meet [530]
Some wandring Spirit of Heav'n, by Fountain side,
Or in thick shade retir'd, from him to draw
What further would be learnt. Live while ye may,
Yet happie pair; enjoy, till I return,
Short pleasures, for long woes are to succeed. [535]

So saying, his proud step he scornful turn'd,
But with sly circumspection, and began
Through wood, through waste, o're hill, o're dale his roam.
Mean while in utmost Longitude, where Heav'n
With Earth and Ocean meets, the setting Sun [540]
Slowly descended, and with right aspect
Against the eastern Gate of Paradise
Leveld his eevning Rayes: it was a Rock
Of Alablaster, pil'd up to the Clouds,
Conspicuous farr, winding with one ascent [545]
Accessible from Earth, one entrance high;
The rest was craggie cliff, that overhung
Still as it rose, impossible to climbe.
Betwixt these rockie Pillars Gabriel sat
Chief of th' Angelic Guards, awaiting night; [550]
About him exercis'd Heroic Games
Th' unarmed Youth of Heav'n, but nigh at hand
Celestial Armourie, Shields, Helmes, and Speares
Hung high with Diamond flaming, and with Gold.
Thither came Uriel, gliding through the Eeven [555]
On a Sun beam, swift as a shooting Starr

來？直到聽見潺潺流水的聲音，才回過神，站起來往湖邊走去。我低下頭，在清澈見底的湖面上看見一個美麗的身影，那時，有一個聲音在我的耳盼響起，它說：『那便是你呀！別再凝視自己的影子了，快跟我來，與一個真實的人見面，他將溫柔地擁抱你，因為你就是依著他的形象創生出來的呀。』

「接著，我便在一棵高大的樹木

In Autumn thwarts the night, when vapors fir'd
Impress the Air, and shews the Mariner
From what point of his Compass to beware
Impetuous winds: he thus began in haste. [560]

Gabriel, to thee thy course by Lot hath giv'n
Charge and strict watch that to this happie place
No evil thing approach or enter in;
This day at highth of Noon came to my Spheare
A Spirit, zealous, as he seem'd, to know [565]
More of th' Almighties works, and chiefly Man
Gods latest Image: I describ'd his way
Bent all on speed, and markt his Aerie Gate;
But in the Mount that lies from Eden North,
Where he first lighted, soon discernd his looks [570]
Alien from Heav'n, with passions foul obscur'd:
Mine eye pursu'd him still, but under shade
Lost sight of him; one of the banisht crew
I fear, hath ventur'd from the Deep, to raise
New troubles; him thy care must be to find. [575]

To whom the winged Warriour thus returnd:
Uriel, no wonder if thy perfet sight,
Amid the Suns bright circle where thou sitst,
See farr and wide: in at this Gate none pass
The vigilance here plac't, but such as come [580]
Well known from Heav'n; and since Meridian hour
No Creature thence: if Spirit of other sort,
So minded, have oreleapt these earthie bounds
On purpose, hard thou knowst it to exclude
Spiritual substance with corporeal barr. [585]
But if within the circuit of these walks,
In whatsoever shape he lurk, of whom

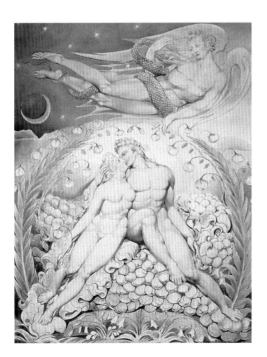

◄ 撒旦注視亞當與夏娃親吻
布雷克　水彩畫 1808年

　　撒旦看見兩情繾綣的亞當和夏娃，內心產生強烈的妒意。想到自己被打入地獄，眼前的甜蜜生太讓人生氣啦！他決定要引誘他們觸犯禁忌，讓人類吃下知識果，招來死亡的命運。

下遇見你了；你是那麼地俊秀挺拔，但我卻著迷於湖面上那美麗柔順的身影，因此欲轉身離去。你一把抱住我，大聲地說著：『你要到什麼地方去呢？我的肋骨化成了你的血肉，使你成為我靈魂的一部分，你生來本是為了安慰我、陪伴我，做我的另外一半呀！』

從那一刻起我便明白，你的恩情遠勝於我美麗的外貌，因為崇高的德性才是真正美麗的東西。」

夏娃說完，嬌柔地躺入亞當的胸膛，她那金色柔軟的頭髮半遮掩著聳立的雙峰。

亞當輕輕地撫摸夏娃宛若凝脂的白晰肌膚，心中充滿著無限的愛戀，他低下頭來，溫柔地親吻她紅潤的嘴唇。

撒旦見此情景，急忙轉過頭去，人類之祖幸福的模樣，激起魔鬼內心強烈的妒意，「真是天差地遠哪！他倆住在美麗的樂園，整天盡情說愛，而

Thou tellst, by morrow dawning I shall know.

So promis'd hee, and Uriel to his charge
Returnd on that bright beam, whose point now rais'd [590]
Bore him slope downward to the Sun now fall'n
Beneath th' Azores; whither the prime Orb,
Incredible how swift, had thither rowl'd
Diurnal, or this less volubil Earth
By shorter flight to th' East, had left him there [595]
Arraying with reflected Purple and Gold
The Clouds that on his Western Throne attend:
Now came still Eevning on, and Twilight gray
Had in her sober Liverie all things clad;
Silence accompanied, for Beast and Bird, [600]
They to thir grassie Couch, these to thir Nests
Were slunk, all but the wakeful Nightingale;
She all night long her amorous descant sung;
Silence was pleas'd: now glow'd the Firmament
With living Saphirs: Hesperus that led [605]
The starrie Host, rode brightest, till the Moon
Rising in clouded Majestie, at length
Apparent Queen unvaild her peerless light,
And o're the dark her Silver Mantle threw.

When Adam thus to Eve: Fair Consort, th' hour [610]
Of night, and all things now retir'd to rest
Mind us of like repose, since God hath set
Labour and rest, as day and night to men
Successive, and the timely dew of sleep
Now falling with soft slumbrous weight inclines [615]
Our eye-lids; other Creatures all day long
Rove idle unimploid, and less need rest;
Man hath his daily work of body or mind
Appointed, which declares his Dignitie,
And the regard of Heav'n on all his waies; [620]
While other Animals unactive range,
And of thir doings God takes no account.
To morrow ere fresh Morning streak the East
With first approach of light, we must be ris'n,
And at our pleasant labour, to reform [625]
Yon flourie Arbors, yonder Allies green,
Our walk at noon, with branches overgrown,

我卻被打入陰森恐怖的地獄，過著渴
求歡樂的生活；眼前甜蜜的景象叫人
生氣，我一定要設法引誘他們觸犯禁

▼ 尤烈兒警告加百列魔鬼已潛入樂園的消息
杜雷版畫 1866年

　　大天使尤烈兒驚覺自己竟然指引撒旦來到
伊甸園，連忙向加百列報告，加百列一方面要
尤烈兒放心，一方面還是派遣幾隊天使前往巡
視，以保護天真無邪的亞當和夏娃。

That mock our scant manuring, and require
More hands then ours to lop thir wanton growth:
Those Blossoms also, and those dropping Gumms, [630]
That lie bestrowne unsightly and unsmooth,
Ask riddance, if we mean to tread with ease;
Mean while, as Nature wills, Night bids us rest.

To whom thus Eve with perfet beauty adornd.
My Author and Disposer, what thou bidst [635]
Unargu'd I obey; so God ordains,
God is thy Law, thou mine: to know no more
Is womans happiest knowledge and her praise.
With thee conversing I forget all time,
All seasons and thir change, all please alike. [640]
Sweet is the breath of morn, her rising sweet,
With charm of earliest Birds; pleasant the Sun
When first on this delightful Land he spreads
His orient Beams, on herb, tree, fruit, and flour,
Glistring with dew; fragrant the fertil earth [645]
After soft showers; and sweet the coming on
Of grateful Eevning milde, then silent Night
With this her solemn Bird and this fair Moon,
And these the Gemms of Heav'n, her starrie train:
But neither breath of Morn when she ascends [650]
With charm of earliest Birds, nor rising Sun
On this delightful land, nor herb, fruit, floure,
Glistring with dew, nor fragrance after showers,
Nor grateful Eevning mild, nor silent Night
With this her solemn Bird, nor walk by Moon, [655]
Or glittering Starr-light without thee is sweet.
But wherfore all night long shine these, for whom
This glorious sight, when sleep hath shut all eyes?

To whom our general Ancestor repli'd.
Daughter of God and Man, accomplisht Eve, [660]
Those have thir course to finish, round the Earth,
By morrow Eevning, and from Land to Land
In order, though to Nations yet unborn,
Ministring light prepar'd, they set and rise;
Least total darkness should by Night regaine [665]
Her old possession, and extinguish life
In Nature and all things, which these soft fires

忌，摘取知識樹的果實來吃。只是，
上帝立下的這道禁令未免太過自私，
為了避免人類凌駕天神的地位，就阻
止他們求取知識？這剛好讓我想到這
條絕妙的計策，就讓人類給自己招來
死亡的命運吧！哈！哈！哈！」

　　此時，在樂園的最西邊，天、地、
海洋的會合處，夕陽正緩緩地降落，
金黃色的餘暉灑落在伊甸園東邊的
大門上，格外壯觀耀眼；那門由石
灰岩建築而成，高聳入雲，前方只
有一條道路通向樂園入口，旁邊皆是
陡峭的峭壁懸崖。守門天使加百列
（Gabriel）嚴守在岩柱間，靜待夜晚
的降臨，圍繞在周遭的戰士們則熱烈
地討論著戰術。

　　遠方天際出現一道模糊的身影，大
天使尤烈兒正沿著夕陽射下的光線急
奔而來，遠遠看去彷彿一顆劃過天際
的流星。他來到加百列面前，神色略
顯嚴肅地說道：

　　「今天中午，有一個天使向我詢問

Not only enlighten, but with kindly heate
Of various influence foment and warme,
Temper or nourish, or in part shed down [670]
Thir stellar vertue on all kinds that grow
On Earth, made hereby apter to receive
Perfection from the Suns more potent Ray.
These then, though unbeheld in deep of night,
Shine not in vain, nor think, though men were none, [675]
That heav'n would want spectators, God want praise;
Millions of spiritual Creatures walk the Earth
Unseen, both when we wake, and when we sleep:
All these with ceaseless praise his works behold
Both day and night: how often from the steep [680]
Of echoing Hill or Thicket have we heard
Celestial voices to the midnight air,
Sole, or responsive each to others note
Singing thir great Creator: oft in bands
While they keep watch, or nightly rounding walk, [685]
With Heav'nly touch of instrumental sounds
In full harmonic number joind, thir songs
Divide the night, and lift our thoughts to Heaven.

Thus talking hand in hand alone they pass'd
On to thir blissful Bower; it was a place [690]
Chos'n by the sovran Planter, when he fram'd
All things to mans delightful use; the roofe
Of thickest covert was inwoven shade
Laurel and Mirtle, and what higher grew
Of firm and fragrant leaf; on either side [695]
Acanthus, and each odorous bushie shrub
Fenc'd up the verdant wall; each beauteous flour,
Iris all hues, Roses, and Gessamin
Rear'd high thir flourisht heads between, and wrought
Mosaic; underfoot the Violet, [700]
Crocus, and Hyacinth with rich inlay
Broiderd the ground, more colour'd then with stone
Of costliest Emblem: other Creature here
Beast, Bird, Insect, or Worm durst enter none;
Such was thir awe of Man. In shadie Bower [705]
More sacred and sequesterd, though but feignd,
Pan or Silvanus never slept, nor Nymph,
Nor Faunus haunted. Here in close recess

樂園的事情，我被他誠懇的態度所感
動，為他指引了伊甸園的方向；待他
飛抵尼法提斯山的山頂後不久，我卻
從高高的天上看見他不自覺地露出了
猙獰的容貌。我想他應該是從地獄脫
逃的囚犯之一，於是趕緊前來通知
你，請務必做好守衛的工作。」

「尤烈兒呀！請你儘管
放心，除了天界派來的熟
稔天使，沒有人能夠通過
這道防衛森嚴的門檻，你
所說的壞天使，至今尚未
出現，但為了謹慎起見，
我仍會派出天使兵前去各
個角落巡視，一定會在天
色拂曉前查個清楚。」

加百列信心滿滿地回
答。

尤烈兒聽他如此堅定的
保證，便稍稍放下心來，
乘著僅存的昏黃光線，重
回自己的崗位。

With Flowers, Garlands, and sweet-smelling Herbs
Espoused Eve deckt first her Nuptial Bed, [710]
And heav'nlyly Quires the Hymenæan sung,
What day the genial Angel to our Sire
Brought her in naked beauty more adorn'd
More lovely then Pandora, whom the Gods
Endowd with all thir gifts, and O too like [715]
In sad event, when to the unwiser Son
Of Japhet brought by Hermes, she ensnar'd
Mankind with her faire looks, to be aveng'd

▽ **亞當與夏娃**
克拉那赫 油畫 1528年

夜幕悄然降臨，動物們蜷伏在巢穴裡沉沉睡著，寂靜蒼茫的夜色中，只有聲音宛轉的夜鶯歌唱著愛戀的情歌。滿天星斗，月亮自漆黑的大地甦醒，褪去身上的雲裳，散發出皎潔的光芒。

花叢間，亞當和夏娃正手牽著手漫步在月色中，亞當開口說道：

「夜已深，我們應當回去休息了，明天，當旭日初升之時我們就得起床，去園中修剪蔓生的枝條，和清除落在小徑上的花瓣；這勞動雖然不是很辛苦，卻也得花費一些氣力，因此，晚間我們須比那些終日遊玩的動物們更多些睡眠，藉此供給白天的工作能量，這也是人類比動物有尊嚴的原因。」

「你說的極是。有你陪伴在我身邊，萬物都是甜美的，晨曦、夕照、微風、鳥語……，沒有一樣不是令人雀躍的；因此，只要是你所說的便成了我的律法，我依隨著你的腳步，如

On him who had stole Joves authentic fire.

Thus at thir shadie Lodge arriv'd, both stood [720]
Both turnd, and under op'n Skie ador'd
The God that made both Skie, Air, Earth and Heav'n
Which they beheld, the Moons resplendent Globe
And starrie Pole: Thou also mad'st the Night,
Maker Omnipotent, and thou the Day, [725]
Which we in our appointed work imployd
Have finisht happie in our mutual help
And mutual love, the Crown of all our bliss
Ordaind by thee, and this delicious place
For us too large, where thy abundance wants [730]
Partakers, and uncropt falls to the ground.
But thou hast promis'd from us two a Race
To fill the Earth, who shall with us extoll
Thy goodness infinite, both when we wake,
And when we seek, as now, thy gift of sleep. [735]

This said unanimous, and other Rites
Observing none, but adoration pure
Which God likes best, into thir inmost bowre
Handed they went; and eas'd the putting off
These troublesom disguises which wee wear, [740]
Strait side by side were laid, nor turnd I weene
Adam from his fair Spouse, nor Eve the Rites
Mysterious of connubial Love refus'd:
Whatever Hypocrites austerely talk
Of puritie and place and innocence, [745]
Defaming as impure what God declares
Pure, and commands to som, leaves free to all.
Our Maker bids increase, who bids abstain
But our Destroyer, foe to God and Man?
Haile wedded Love, mysterious Law, true source [750]
Of human ofspring, sole proprietie,
In Paradise of all things common else.
By thee adulterous lust was driv'n from men
Among the bestial herds to raunge, by thee
Founded in Reason, Loyal, Just, and Pure, [755]
Relations dear, and all the Charities
Of Father, Son, and Brother first were known.
Farr be it, that I should write thee sin or blame,

同上帝是人類的主宰。只是，當萬物睡著之際，天上那些晶亮燦爛的星星和月亮，又是為了什麼而存在的呢？難道只是徒然地散發著光輝的景致？」

夏娃眨巴著深遂的雙眸，說出心中的疑惑。

「星星和月亮自有它們運行的軌道，它們順應自然，有秩序的循環，為尚未出生的人類固守光明的大地，免得『混沌』與『夜』奪回昔日所屬的版圖；它們並供給地面上的萬物光和熱，讓萬物的生命更加調和。況且，就算是闃靜無聲的黑夜，仍有許多的守衛天使在各處巡防，無時無刻他們都在歌唱，以優美和諧的樂音讚美上帝。只要你用心聆聽，那遠方的山崖和樹林，不是正迴盪著柔和聖潔的天籟嗎？」

亞當一邊回答夏娃的問題，一邊拉著她的手走進一處樹叢。

這是一座由上帝親手打造，專屬

Or think thee unbefitting holiest place,
Perpetual Fountain of Domestic sweets, [760]
Whose bed is undefil'd and chaste pronounc't,
Present, or past, as Saints and Patriarchs us'd.
Here Love his golden shafts imploies, here lights
His constant Lamp, and waves his purple wings,
Reigns here and revels; not in the bought smile [765]
Of Harlots, loveless, joyless, unindeard,
Casual fruition, nor in Court Amours
Mixt Dance, or wanton Mask, or Midnight Bal,
Or Serenate, which the starv'd Lover sings
To his proud fair, best quitted with disdain. [770]

▽ 沉睡的亞當和夏娃
布雷克　水彩畫 1808年

　　亞當和夏娃在他們的臥室熟睡著，加百列派了兩名天使前來巡視這個神聖的居所，不讓魔鬼侵犯他們。只可惜已經太晚了。

於他倆的臥房。桂樹、山桃和高大喬木的枝葉相互交錯，編織成翁鬱的屋頂；芳香怡人的灌木圍成濃密的牆壁，枝葉間綴滿了色彩繽紛的鳶尾花、玫瑰花和茉莉花；鮮豔的紫羅蘭、番紅花和風信子，則鑲嵌成美麗的地板。

所有的飛禽、動物和昆蟲都不敢踏入這個地方半步，因為此時牠們對人類仍存著敬畏的心。臥房的最深處神聖幽靜，是亞當和夏娃躺臥的地方，連神話中的山林之神都不曾進來過。當初，天上傳來讚頌神聖婚姻的歌曲，掌管姻緣的天使領著新娘夏娃來到亞當身旁，讓她坐在裝飾著花朵、花環和香草的床上；她那美麗的裸體，更勝於神話中的絕世美女潘朵拉[11]。

「全能的上帝，感謝您賜予我們幸福的園地，為回報您的恩德，我倆的後代也將世世代代讚揚您的恩慈；此刻，夜幕已低垂，求您賞賜我們睡眠

These lulld by Nightingales imbraceing slept,
And on thir naked limbs the flourie roof
Showrd Roses, which the Morn repair'd. Sleep on
Blest pair; and O yet happiest if ye seek
No happier state, and know to know no more. [775]

Now had night measur'd with her shaddowie Cone
Half way up Hill this vast Sublunar Vault,
And from thir Ivorie Port the Cherubim
Forth issuing at th' accustomd hour stood armd
To thir night watches in warlike Parade, [780]
When Gabriel to his next in power thus spake.

Uzziel, half these draw off, and coast the South
With strictest watch; these other wheel the North,
Our circuit meets full West. As flame they part
Half wheeling to the Shield, half to the Spear. [785]
From these, two strong and suttle Spirits he calld
That neer him stood, and gave them thus in charge.

Ithuriel and Zephon, with wingd speed
Search through this Garden, leave unsearcht no nook,
But chiefly where those two fair Creatures Lodge, [790]
Now laid perhaps asleep secure of harme.
This Eevning from the Sun's decline arriv'd

註11：潘朵拉（Pandora）是《希臘羅馬神話故事》中的絕色美女。普羅米修斯（Prometheus）為人類偷盜火種，觸怒天帝宙斯（Zeus），宙斯於是命令火依女神的形象造出一個女人 ── 潘朵拉，美神賜給她美貌、智慧女神教她各種才藝、太陽神讓她精通音樂、使神則送給她靈巧的辯才。宙斯讓潘朵拉嫁給普羅米修斯的弟弟艾匹美修斯（Epimetheus），讓她在好奇心的驅使下打開裝著各種災禍的大箱子，使嫉妒、仇恨、病痛……等種種苦痛瀰漫到人間，此後，人類便得面對各種災難的折磨。

伊修烈爾和洗芬在亞當與夏娃的臥房上巡視
杜雷 版畫 1866年

　　兩位天使手持長矛，飛往亞當和夏娃的臥室上空，結果遲了一步，撒旦已經潛伏在夏娃身邊施展邪惡的法術。

的恩典。」

　　亞當和夏娃誠心禱告完後，倆人相互擁抱，頭兒靠著頭兒地躺臥在床上，空氣中瀰漫著淡淡的花瓣幽香，夜鶯如搖籃曲般的歌唱，哄著他們甜

Who tells of som infernal Spirit seen
Hitherward bent (who could have thought?) escap'd
The barrs of Hell, on errand bad no doubt: [795]
Such where ye find, seise fast, and hither bring.

So saying, on he led his radiant Files,
Daz'ling the Moon; these to the Bower direct
In search of whom they sought: him there they found
Squat like a Toad, close at the eare of Eve; [800]
Assaying by his Devilish art to reach
The Organs of her Fancie, and with them forge
Illusions as he list, Phantasms and Dreams,
Or if, inspiring venom, he might taint
Th' animal spirits that from pure blood arise [805]
Like gentle breaths from Rivers pure, thence raise
At least distemperd, discontented thoughts,
Vaine hopes, vaine aimes, inordinate desires
Blown up with high conceits ingendring pride.
Him thus intent Ithuriel with his Spear [810]
Touch'd lightly; for no falshood can endure
Touch of Celestial temper, but returns
Of force to its own likeness: up he starts
Discoverd and surpriz'd. As when a spark
Lights on a heap of nitrous Powder, laid [815]
Fit for the Tun som Magazin to store
Against a rumord Warr, the Smuttie graine
With sudden blaze diffus'd, inflames the Aire:
So started up in his own shape the Fiend.
Back stept those two fair Angels half amaz'd [820]
So sudden to behold the grieslie King;
Yet thus, unmovd with fear, accost him soon.

Which of those rebell Spirits adjudg'd to Hell
Com'st thou, escap'd thy prison, and transform'd,
Why satst thou like an enemie in waite [825]
Here watching at the head of these that sleep?

Know ye not then said Satan, fill'd with scorn
Know ye not mee? ye knew me once no mate
For you, there sitting where ye durst not soare;
Not to know mee argues your selves unknown, [830]
The lowest of your throng; or if ye know,

甜蜜蜜地沉入夢鄉。

皎潔的月亮旋掛在夜空，守衛天使加百列站在編排成行的隊伍前，吩咐副將阿西爾（Uzziel）說：

「你將隊伍分成兩組，一隊由你指揮到南邊去巡邏，另一隊則跟著我往北邊去，務必做到滴水不漏，我們在西邊會合。」

接著，他又轉頭對身旁兩個魁梧聰敏的天使說道：

「伊修烈爾（Ithuriel）、洗芬（Zephon），人類就交給你們兩個保護，切勿讓魔鬼侵犯他們；尤其是那聖潔的居所，更要加強巡視。」

交代完任務之後，守衛隊便如分開的火燄，往左右兩邊而去。

伊修烈爾和洗芬等隊伍離開之後，隨即動身前往亞當和夏娃的居所。這時，撒旦早已潛伏在夏娃的耳朵旁邊，朝她施展邪惡的魔法，把各種能夠產生不滿思想的毒素，緩緩地灌輸到她的腦海裡，污染其「動

Why ask ye, and superfluous begin
Your message, like to end as much in vain?
To whom thus Zephon, answering scorn with scorn.
Think not, revolted Spirit, thy shape the same, [835]
Or undiminisht brightness, to be known
As when thou stoodst in Heav'n upright and pure;
That Glorie then, when thou no more wast good,
Departed from thee, and thou resembl'st now
Thy sin and place of doom obscure and foule. [840]
But come, for thou, be sure, shalt give account
To him who sent us, whose charge is to keep
This place inviolable, and these from harm.

So spake the Cherube, and his grave rebuke
Severe in youthful beautie, added grace [845]
Invincible: abasht the Devil stood,
And felt how awful goodness is, and saw
Vertue in her shape how lovly, saw, and pin'd
His loss; but chiefly to find here observd
His lustre visibly impair'd; yet seemd [850]

⋀ **撒旦面對伊修烈爾的長矛**
佛斐利 油畫 1779年

　　天使撞見撒旦在灌輸夏娃邪惡思想，氣得舉起長矛，要將撒旦抓到天使加百列面前。

物精神」[12]，藉此可讓人產生驕傲自大的心理和種種欲望，如同輕輕吹過溪流水面的微風，漾起了一圈圈的漣漪。

伊修烈爾和洗芬到達臥室的上方，從葉叢縫隙間看見夏娃身旁有一個蹲伏著、貌似蟾蜍的生物。

「糟了！晚來一步。」

兩人不約而同地發出一聲驚呼，立刻朝向那生物刺出長矛。

「可惡！是誰偷襲我？」

如同彈藥庫的火藥突然爆炸，黑色硝煙瀰漫，落下點點星火；撒旦現出原形，蹴然蹦跳到半空中，嘴裡氣憤地叫罵著。

「可惡的背叛者，竟敢從地獄逃脫，還妄想侵害上帝的寵兒，你到底

註12：引自中古時期名醫加林（Galen）的學說，加林把人類的精神分成三種：一是「自然精神」（Natural Spirit），乃生理上的現象；二是「生機精神」（Vital Spirit），指生命的活力；三是「動物精神」（Animal Spirit），即思想感情部分。

Undaunted. If I must contend, said he,
Best with the best, the Sender not the sent,
Or all at once; more glorie will be wonn,
Or less be lost. Thy fear, said Zephon bold,
Will save us trial what the least can doe [855]
Single against thee wicked, and thence weak.

The Fiend repli'd not, overcome with rage;
But like a proud Steed reind, went hautie on,
Chaumping his iron curb: to strive or flie
He held it vain; awe from above had quelld [860]
His heart, not else dismai'd. Now drew they nigh
The western Point, where those half-rounding guards
Just met, and closing stood in squadron joind
Awaiting next command. To whom thir Chief
Gabriel from the Front thus calld aloud. [865]

O friends, I hear the tread of nimble feet
Hasting this way, and now by glimps discerne
Ithuriel and Zephon through the shade,
And with them comes a third of Regal port,
But faded splendor wan; who by his gate [870]
And fierce demeanour seems the Prince of Hell,
Not likely to part hence without contest;
Stand firm, for in his look defiance lours.

He scarce had ended, when those two approachd
And brief related whom they brought, where found, [875]
How busied, in what form and posture coucht.

To whom with stern regard thus Gabriel spake.
Why hast thou, Satan, broke the bounds prescrib'd
To thy transgressions, and disturbd the charge
Of others, who approve not to transgress [880]
By thy example, but have power and right
To question thy bold entrance on this place;
Imploi'd it seems to violate sleep, and those
Whose dwelling God hath planted here in bliss?

To whom thus Satan with contemptuous brow. [885]
Gabriel, thou hadst in Heav'n th' esteem of wise,
And such I held thee; but this question askt

是誰？快點報上姓名來！」

　　伊修烈爾和洗芬乍見撒旦猙獰的醜陋模樣，不禁往後倒退一步，迅即回過神來，迎向前去審問他。

　　「哼！你們竟然不認識我？這也難怪，地位這麼低下的天使，根本就沒有機會見到我尊貴的姿容。」

　　撒旦一臉鄙夷，輕蔑地回答。

　　「莫再沾沾自喜了，你昔日的光彩早已散盡，現今，你就跟拘囚背叛者的牢籠一樣黯淡無光，還有什麼值得驕傲的呢？快快隨我們離開，去向加百列說明你此番前來伊甸園的目的。」

　　伊修烈爾和洗芬表情肅穆，以嚴厲的語氣對撒旦說。

　　惡行削弱了撒旦原本的氣勢，他自知逃不過守衛天使的眼目，只好像一頭被硬架上絡頭的馬，心不甘情不願地跟隨他倆前去面見加百列。

　　「你好啊！自稱地獄君主的大魔王，你擅自從地獄脫逃，是想要在上

Puts me in doubt. Lives ther who loves his pain?
Who would not, finding way, break loose from Hell,
Though thither doomd? Thou wouldst thyself, no doubt, [890]
And boldly venture to whatever place
Farthest from pain, where thou mightst hope to change
Torment with ease, and; soonest recompence
Dole with delight, which in this place I sought;
To thee no reason; who knowst only good, [895]
But evil hast not tri'd: and wilt object
His will who bound us? let him surer barr
His Iron Gates, if he intends our stay
In that dark durance: thus much what was askt.
The rest is true, they found me where they say; [900]
But that implies not violence or harme.

Thus he in scorn. The warlike Angel mov'd,
Disdainfully half smiling thus repli'd.
O loss of one in Heav'n to judge of wise,
Since Satan fell, whom follie overthrew, [905]
And now returns him from his prison scap't,
Gravely in doubt whether to hold them wise
Or not, who ask what boldness brought him hither
Unlicenc't from his bounds in Hell prescrib'd;
So wise he judges it to fly from pain [910]
However, and to scape his punishment.
So judge thou still, presumptuous, till the wrauth,
Which thou incurr'st by flying, meet thy flight
Seavenfold, and scourge that wisdom back to Hell,
Which taught thee yet no better, that no pain [915]
Can equal anger infinite provok't.
But wherefore thou alone? wherefore with thee
Came not all Hell broke loose? is pain to them
Less pain, less to be fled, or thou then they
Less hardie to endure? courageous Chief, [920]
The first in flight from pain, hadst thou alleg'd
To thy deserted host this cause of flight,
Thou surely hadst not come sole fugitive.

To which the Fiend thus answerd frowning stern.
Not that I less endure, or shrink from pain, [925]
Insulting Angel, well thou knowst I stood
Thy fiercest, when in Battel to thy aide

帝所創造的新樂園中為非作歹嗎？」
加百列質問撒旦。

「你問的這個問題，讓我懷疑你的
智慧。誰喜歡苦難？誰能忍受地獄中
無盡的煎熬？有機會的話，我當然要
另覓它地遷移，誰願意生活在水深火
熱之中呢？如果是你，你也會想盡辦
法逃離苦境吧！況且，若那個掌權者
真心想要永遠禁錮我的話，就應該把
地獄的鐵門鎖得更牢一些才對。」

撒旦輕慢地回答。

「你少自以為聰明了！如果真像你
所說的一般，想要尋找新的住處；為
什麼只有你一人前來，莫非其他人的
忍耐功夫都勝於你？那你又有何本領
自稱為他們英勇的領袖呢？」

加百列被撒旦輕蔑的態度所激怒，
話語中帶著一絲怒氣。

「哼！並非我欠缺忍耐力，而是身
為一個領導者，必須具備身先士卒的
勇氣；對於陌生的路徑，自己得先去
探勘過後，才能帶領部將前行，如此

The blasting volied Thunder made all speed
And seconded thy else not dreaded Spear.
But still thy words at random, as before, [930]
Argue thy inexperience what behooves
From hard assaies and ill successes past
A faithful Leader, not to hazard all
Through wayes of danger by himself untri'd,
I therefore, I alone first undertook [935]
To wing the desolate Abyss, and spie
This new created World, whereof in Hell
Fame is not silent, here in hope to find
Better abode, and my afflicted Powers
To settle here on Earth, or in mid Aire; [940]
Though for possession put to try once more
What thou and thy gay Legions dare against;
Whose easier business were to serve thir Lord
High up in Heav'n, with songs to hymne his Throne,
And practis'd distances to cringe, not fight. [945]

To whom the warriour Angel, soon repli'd.
To say and strait unsay, pretending first
Wise to flie pain, professing next the Spie,
Argues no Leader, but a lyar trac't,
Satan, and couldst thou faithful add? O name, [950]
O sacred name of faithfulness profan'd!
Faithful to whom? to thy rebellious crew?
Armie of Fiends, fit body to fit head;
Was this your discipline and faith ingag'd,
Your military obedience, to dissolve [955]
Allegeance to th' acknowledg'd Power supream?
And thou sly hypocrite, who now wouldst seem
Patron of liberty, who more then thou
Once fawn'd, and cring'd, and servilly ador'd
Heav'ns awful Monarch? wherefore but in hope [960]
To dispossess him, and thy self to reigne?
But mark what I arreede thee now, avant;
Flie thither whence thou fledst: if from this houre
Within these hallowd limits thou appeer,
Back to th' infernal pit I drag thee chaind, [965]
And Seale thee so, as henceforth not to scorne
The facil gates of hell too slightly barrd.

才能夠避免讓下屬涉險。若不懂得這
個道理，你便不配當一個稱職的領導
者。」

　　撒旦皺起眉頭說道。

　　「一開始說是為了脫離苦境，後
來又說是為部屬探路而來，我看你不
過是一個撒謊者罷了！快點滾回地獄
去！否則我就要把你銬起來，強行押
回地獄。」

　　加百列下了最後通牒。

　　「高傲的基路伯呀，看看誰做誰的
俘虜？別以為天神坐在你們的翅膀上
飛行[13]，使你們如同牛馬一般有負軛
車子的力量，在鋪滿星星的天幕上奔
走，你們就有強過我的本領。等我真
的成為你的俘虜之後，再來說這些狂
妄的話吧！」

　　撒旦忿怒地罵著。

　　天使軍紛紛舉起長矛，朝撒旦的
方向聚攏，周遭充滿肅殺之氣；此
時，上帝為避免一場惡戰，遂於天
際懸掛起金天秤，代表天使軍的砝

So threatn'd hee, but Satan to no threats
Gave heed, but waxing more in rage repli'd.

Then when I am thy captive talk of chaines, [970]
Proud limitarie Cherube, but ere then
Farr heavier load thy self expect to feel
From my prevailing arme, though Heavens King
Ride on thy wings, and thou with thy Compeers,
Us'd to the yoak, draw'st his triumphant wheels [975]
In progress through the rode of Heav'n Star-pav'd.

While thus he spake, th' Angelic Squadron bright

▽ 撒旦被守衛天使逐出伊甸園
杜雷 版畫 1866年

　　天使紛紛舉起長矛，逼撒旦離開，
撒旦看到敵眾我寡，只好悻悻然退離美
麗的伊甸園。

碼是「和」，代表魔鬼的砝碼則是
「戰」，而「戰」被高高的舉起，幾
乎碰到秤桿[14]。

「傲慢的魔鬼，你抬頭看看吧！你
我的力量都是來自於上帝，此刻，他
所給予你的能力只有那麼一些些，你
最好識相一點，快滾！」

加百列指指天上的天秤，嚴厲地對
撒旦說。

撒旦仰頭一望，果真發現上帝設下
的天秤，屬於自己的一方高高升起，
預言了失敗的命運；於是他不再逗
留，匆忙地逃離。夜，也隨著他的腳
步離開了。

註13：《舊約‧撒母耳記下》：「當耶和華救大衛
　　　脫離一切仇敵和掃羅之手的日子，他向耶
　　　和華念這詩，說：『……他又使天下垂，
　　　親自降臨，有黑雲在他腳下。他坐著基路
　　　伯飛行，在風的翅膀上顯現。』」
註14：出自荷馬《伊利亞德》，天帝宙斯用天秤來
　　　測量希臘軍和特洛亞軍誰贏誰輸，所以金
　　　天秤在此地有衡量事物輕重的功能。

Turnd fierie red, sharpning in mooned hornes
Thir Phalanx, and began to hemm him round
With ported Spears, as thick as when a field [980]
Of Ceres ripe for harvest waving bends
Her bearded Grove of ears, which way the wind
Swayes them; the careful Plowman doubting stands
Least on the threshing floore his hopeful sheaves
Prove chaff. On th' other side Satan allarm'd [985]
Collecting all his might dilated stood,
Like Teneriff or Atlas unremov'd:
His stature reacht the Skie, and on his Crest
Sat horror Plum'd; nor wanted in his graspe
What seemd both Spear and Shield: now dreadful deeds [990]
Might have ensu'd, nor onely Paradise
In this commotion, but the Starrie Cope
Of Heav'n perhaps, or all the Elements
At least had gon to rack, disturbd and torne
With violence of this conflict, had not soon [995]
Th' Eternal to prevent such horrid fray
Hung forth in Heav'n his golden Scales, yet seen
Betwixt Astrea and the Scorpion signe,
Wherein all things created first he weighd,
The pendulous round Earth with balanc't Aire [1000]
In counterpoise, now ponders all events,
Battels and Realms: in these he put two weights
The sequel each of parting and of fight;
The latter quick up flew, and kickt the beam;
Which Gabriel spying, thus bespake the Fiend. [1005]

Satan, I know thy strength, and thou know'st mine,
Neither our own but giv'n; what follie then
To boast what Arms can doe, since thine no more
Then Heav'n permits, nor mine, though doubld now
To trample thee as mire: for proof look up, [1010]
And read thy Lot in yon celestial Sign
Where thou art weigh'd, and shown how light, how weak,
If thou resist. The Fiend lookt up and knew
His mounted scale aloft: nor more; but fled
Murmuring, and with him fled the shades of night. [1015]

天使的警示

　　撒旦逃離伊甸園之後，上帝派出天使拉斐爾前去提醒亞當——人類應當誠心地順從上帝、人類心中仍保有自由的意志、人類的敵人即將來臨等。拉斐爾並且向亞當說明這個將要出現的敵人叫撒旦，昔日曾經召集為數眾多的天使，發動一場天庭叛變，後被神子以雷霆打入幽冥地府。撒旦原本應該囚禁在地獄中受苦，不意竟從冥界脫逃，今日恐怕已經混入伊甸樂園來了，人類當要小心防備。

晨曦於東方天空抹上薔薇的色澤，大地灑滿晶瑩的露珠，亞當如常在這個時刻醒來，他揉揉惺忪的雙眼，坐起來深深吸口氣：

「嗯！好清新的空氣。」

因為他的日常飲食相當清淡，且內心坦然純正無所掛礙，故能夠保有如空氣一般輕盈舒適的睡眠。

「夏娃！」

亞當斜倚身體，深情款款地凝視著沉浸在睡夢中的夏娃，他伸出手來，溫柔地撫摸夏娃的額頭，想要叫醒她：

「快些醒來吧！我的愛人。早晨的微風已吹過樹梢，樹葉沙沙作響，你聽，那嘩啦啦的流水與枝頭鳥兒的合奏如此美妙，切莫辜負了這一首清脆動人的晨歌。」

「亞當，我好害怕。」

≺ 亞當輕喚夏娃起來
杜雷版畫 1866年

　　亞當一早醒來，看到身旁的夏娃依舊熟睡，不免愛憐地盯著愛侶的甜美面容。

Now morn her rosie steps in th' Eastern Clime
Advancing, sow'd the earth with Orient Pearle,
When Adam wak't, so customd, for his sleep
Was Aerie light, from pure digestion bred,
And temperat vapors bland, which th' only sound [5]
Of leaves and fuming rills, Aurora's fan,
Lightly dispers'd, and the shrill Matin Song
Of Birds on every bough; so much the more
His wonder was to find unwak'nd Eve
With Tresses discompos'd, and glowing Cheek, [10]
As through unquiet rest: he on his side
Leaning half-rais'd, with looks of cordial Love
Hung over her enamour'd, and beheld
Beautie, which whether waking or asleep,
Shot forth peculiar graces; then with voice [15]
Milde, as when Zephyrus on Flora breathes,
Her hand soft touching, whisperd thus. Awake
My fairest, my espous'd, my latest found,
Heav'ns last best gift, my ever new delight,
Awake, the morning shines, and the fresh field [20]
Calls us, we lose the prime, to mark how spring
Our tended Plants, how blows the Citron Grove,
What drops the Myrrhe, and what the balmie Reed,
How Nature paints her colours, how the Bee
Sits on the Bloom extracting liquid sweet. [25]

Such whispering wak'd her, but with startl'd eye
On Adam, whom imbracing, thus she spake.

O Sole in whom my thoughts find all repose,
My Glorie, my Perfection, glad I see
Thy face, and Morn return'd, for I this Night, [30]
Such night till this I never pass'd, have dream'd,
If dream'd, not as I oft am wont, of thee,
Works of day pass't, or morrows next designe,
But of offense and trouble, which my mind
Knew never till this irksom night; methought [35]
Close at mine ear one call'd me forth to walk
With gentle voice, I thought it thine; it said,
Why sleepst thou Eve? now is the pleasant time,
The cool, the silent, save where silence yields
To the night-warbling Bird, that now awake [40]

夏娃在亞當的呼喚聲中醒來，睜開
的雙眸裡有一絲恐懼，她緊緊地抱住
亞當說道：

「昨晚我做了一個很可怕的夢，夢
中，有一個插著雙翼的天使帶我到知

▽ 伊甸園中的亞當和夏娃
人物：魯本斯／風景：布勒哲爾
油畫 1615年

　　夢到偷吃知識果的夏娃忐忑不安，亞當好言
安慰，並不知道撒旦還會進一步誘惑他們。

Tunes sweetest his love-labor'd song; now reignes
Full Orb'd the Moon, and with more pleasing light
Shadowie sets off the face of things; in vain,
If none regard; Heav'n wakes with all his eyes,
Whom to behold but thee, Natures desire, [45]
In whose sight all things joy, with ravishment
Attracted by thy beauty still to gaze.
I rose as at thy call, but found thee not;
To find thee I directed then my walk;
And on, methought, alone I pass'd through ways [50]
That brought me on a sudden to the Tree
Of interdicted Knowledge: fair it seem'd,
Much fairer to my Fancie then by day:
And as I wondring lookt, beside it stood
One shap'd and wing'd like one of those from Heav'n [55]
By us oft seen; his dewie locks distill'd
Ambrosia; on that Tree he also gaz'd;

識樹下，並對我說：『多可惜呀！這麼美麗的樹，結實累累卻沒有人品嘗，是知識不值得追求？還是有人自私地想要獨占，不讓別人分享？我卻不信這一套，偏偏要摘一些來吃。』說著，那天使便伸手摘下一顆知識果吃了起來，我站在旁邊，被他這種叛逆的舉動嚇得渾身發抖，沒想到他竟轉過頭來，把知識果放到我的嘴邊說道：『吃一口吧，很甜哩！這園中的果實本來就是為人類而生的，況且只要吃了它，你就能夠像神一樣自由遨翔天際，並且飛到天上去參觀天使們生活的地方，享受更多的自由和幸福，這有什麼不好呢？』

　　「知識樹的果子是那麼的芳香，我禁不住誘惑咬了一口，然後，就像那個天使所說的，我擁有了飛翔的能力，展開翅膀一直飛升到樂園的上空，向下俯瞰一望無際的美麗大地；但突然地，身旁的天使倏地消失，我便往下墜落重新回到臥房中。」

And O fair Plant, said he, with fruit surcharg'd,
Deigns none to ease thy load and taste thy sweet,
Nor God, nor Man; is Knowledge so despis'd? [60]
Or envie, or what reserve forbids to taste?
Forbid who will, none shall from me withhold
Longer thy offerd good, why else set here?
This said he paus'd not, but with ventrous Arme
He pluckt, he tasted; mee damp horror chil'd [65]
At such bold words voucht with a deed so bold:
But he thus overjoy'd, O Fruit Divine,
Sweet of thy self, but much more sweet thus cropt,
Forbidd'n here, it seems, as onely fit
For God's, yet able to make Gods of Men: [70]
And why not Gods of Men, since good, the more
Communicated, more abundant growes,
The Author not impair'd, but honourd more?
Here, happie Creature, fair Angelic Eve,
Partake thou also; happie though thou art, [75]
Happier thou mayst be, worthier canst not be:
Taste this, and be henceforth among the Gods
Thy self a Goddess, not to Earth confind,
But somtimes in the Air, as wee, somtimes
Ascend to Heav'n, by merit thine, and see [80]
What life the Gods live there, and such live thou.
So saying, he drew nigh, and to me held,
Even to my mouth of that same fruit held part
Which he had pluckt; the pleasant savourie smell
So quick'nd appetite, that I, methought, [85]
Could not but taste. Forthwith up to the Clouds
With him I flew, and underneath beheld
The Earth outstretcht immense, a prospect wide
And various: wondring at my flight and change
To this high exaltation; suddenly [90]
My Guide was gon, and I, me thought, sunk down,
And fell asleep; but O how glad I wak'd
To find this but a dream! Thus Eve her Night
Related, and thus Adam answerd sad.

Best Image of my self and dearer half, [95]
The trouble of thy thoughts this night in sleep
Affects me equally; nor can I like
This uncouth dream, of evil sprung I fear;

　　夏娃以驚慌的語氣向亞當陳述夢境，依偎在亞當懷中的身體輕輕顫抖著。

　　亞當皺起眉頭，憂心忡忡地對夏娃說：

　　「別怕，既然你對夢中的行為充滿恐懼感，表示那惡念無法在你的心中留存，要知道，人的內心充滿著『理性』和『幻想』，當外界形形色色的事物透過五官進入我們的心靈，幻想便從中建構出想像或幻影，理性隨之與它們合併或分離，使我們產生知識和判斷，進而持有肯定或否定的能力。在我們睡眠的時候，理性也跟著休息了，夢境成為幻想的舞台，所以在夢中，我們常有一些光怪陸離、背離現實的邪惡想像，但只要我們堅定心志，不容許它停駐在心中，醒來後它自然會消失。因此，我的最愛，你無須驚惶，快快拋開不愉快的夢境，與我一塊享受這清晨美景與新鮮的空氣吧！」

Yet evil whence? in thee can harbour none,
Created pure. But know that in the Soule [100]
Are many lesser Faculties that serve
Reason as chief; among these Fansie next
Her office holds; of all external things,
Which the five watchful Senses represent,
She forms Imaginations, Aerie shapes, [105]
Which Reason joyning or disjoyning, frames
All what we affirm or what deny, and call
Our knowledge or opinion; then retires
Into her private Cell when Nature rests.
Oft in her absence mimic Fansie wakes [110]
To imitate her; but misjoyning shapes,
Wilde work produces oft, and most in dreams,
Ill matching words and deeds long past or late.
Som such resemblances methinks I find
Of our last Eevnings talk, in this thy dream, [115]
But with addition strange; yet be not sad.
Evil into the mind of God or Man
May come and go, so unapprov'd, and leave
No spot or blame behind: Which gives me hope
That what in sleep thou didst abhorr to dream, [120]
Waking thou never wilt consent to do.
Be not disheart'nd then, nor cloud those looks
That wont to be more chearful and serene
Then when fair Morning first smiles on the World,
And let us to our fresh imployments rise [125]
Among the Groves, the Fountains, and the Flours
That open now thir choicest bosom'd smells
Reservd from night, and kept for thee in store.

So cheard he his fair Spouse, and she was cheard,
But silently a gentle tear let fall [130]
From either eye, and wip'd them with her haire;
Two other precious drops that ready stood,
Each in thir Chrystal sluce, hee ere they fell
Kiss'd as the gracious signs of sweet remorse
And pious awe, that feard to have offended. [135]

So all was cleard, and to the Field they haste.
But first from under shadie arborous roof,
Soon as they forth were come to open sight

夏娃聽見亞當安慰的話語，心中頓時開朗許多，含在眼眶中的淚水，也被亞當輕輕吻去，於是，他倆站起身來，手牽著手走出林蔭深處，兩人面對著遼闊的田野開始晨禱：

「全能的天父呀！您高高地坐在天上的寶座中，我們雖然無法瞻仰您的容貌[1]，但從萬物身上也能略知一、二，因為您所創造的宇宙是如此的神奇美好，沒有一樣事物不感念您的至德。

「天使們呀！你們身上的光輝是如此明亮，乃因日夜圍繞在天父的寶座旁邊，以聖歌來讚頌祂。

「地面上的萬物呀！你們也要高聲頌讚，永不停歇。最美麗的星辰呀！雖然你隸屬於黑夜，但黎明降臨之際，也該展露出微笑來讚美祂。

註1：《新約‧提摩太前書》：「到了日期，那可稱頌、獨有權能的萬王之王、萬主之主，就是那獨一不死，住在人不能靠近的光裡，是人未曾看見，也是不能看見的，要將他顯明出來。」

Of day-spring, and the Sun, who scarce up risen
With wheels yet hov'ring o're the Ocean brim, [140]
Shot paralel to the earth his dewie ray,
Discovering in wide Lantskip all the East
Of Paradise and Edens happie Plains,
Lowly they bow'd adoring, and began
Thir Orisons, each Morning duly paid [145]
In various style, for neither various style
Nor holy rapture wanted they to praise
Thir Maker, in fit strains pronounc't or sung
Unmeditated, such prompt eloquence
Flowd from thir lips, in Prose or numerous Verse, [150]
More tuneable then needed Lute or Harp
To add more sweetness, and they thus began.

These are thy glorious works, Parent of good,
Almightie, thine this universal Frame,
Thus wondrous fair; thy self how wondrous then! [155]
Unspeakable, who sitst above these Heavens
To us invisible or dimly seen
In these thy lowest works, yet these declare
Thy goodness beyond thought, and Power Divine:
Speak yee who best can tell, ye Sons of Light, [160]
Angels, for yee behold him, and with songs
And choral symphonies, Day without Night,
Circle his Throne rejoycing, yee in Heav'n,
On Earth joyn all ye Creatures to extoll
Him first, him last, him midst, and without end. [165]
Fairest of Starrs, last in the train of Night,
If better thou belong not to the dawn,
Sure pledge of day, that crownst the smiling Morn
With thy bright Circlet, praise him in thy Spheare
While day arises, that sweet hour of Prime. [170]
Thou Sun, of this great World both Eye and Soule,
Acknowledge him thy Greater, sound his praise
In thy eternal course, both when thou climb'st,
And when high Noon hast gaind, and when thou fallst.
Moon, that now meetst the orient Sun, now fli'st [175]
With the fixt Starrs, fixt in thir Orb that flies,
And yee five other wandring Fires that move
In mystic Dance not without Song, resound
His praise, who out of Darkness call'd up Light.

「太陽呀！你是世界的靈魂之窗，
但祂比你更偉大，當你在每日例行的
運行軌道中，要不斷地讚美祂。

「月兒呀！你當與恆星、金星、木
星、水星、火星和土星們互相唱和，
稱頌那喚出光明的全能者。

「地、水、火、空氣呀！你們是構
成宇宙的四大元素，在千變萬化的種
種組合中，造出各式各樣的事物，請
以新創的詩歌，唱頌造物者的偉大。

「霧氣與水氣呀！你們瀰漫在湖面
和山中，灰濛濛的衣裙每被陽光烘染
成金黃色，或升騰到天空成為雲朵、
或化作雨滴潤濕大地，無論身處晴朗
的天空或給乾旱的大地以甘霖，都要
讚美祂的恩澤。

「風兒呀！有時柔和、有時粗暴地
向四面八方吹拂，請時時吹奏讚揚的
歌聲。

「松林呀！請輕輕搖動樹梢向祂敬
禮。

「清泉呀！請以潺潺流水合唱出婉

Aire, and ye Elements the eldest birth [180]
Of Natures Womb, that in quaternion run
Perpetual Circle, multiform; and mix
And nourish all things, let your ceaseless change
Varie to our great Maker still new praise.
Ye Mists and Exhalations that now rise [185]
From Hill or steaming Lake, duskie or grey,
Till the Sun paint your fleecie skirts with Gold,
In honour to the Worlds great Author rise,
Whether to deck with Clouds th' uncolourd skie,
Or wet the thirstie Earth with falling showers, [190]
Rising or falling still advance his praise.
His praise ye Winds, that from four Quarters blow,
Breathe soft or loud; and wave your tops, ye Pines,
With every Plant, in sign of Worship wave.
Fountains and yee, that warble, as ye flow, [195]
Melodious murmurs, warbling tune his praise.
Joyn voices all ye living Souls; ye Birds,
That singing up to Heaven Gate ascend,
Bear on your wings and in your notes his praise;
Yee that in Waters glide, and yee that walk [200]
The Earth, and stately tread, or lowly creep;
Witness if I be silent, Morn or Eeven,
To Hill, or Valley, Fountain, or fresh shade
Made vocal by my Song, and taught his praise.
Hail universal Lord, be bounteous still [205]
To give us onely good; and if the night
Have gathered aught of evil or conceald,
Disperse it, as now light dispels the dark.

So pray'd they innocent, and to thir thoughts
Firm peace recoverd soon and wonted calm. [210]
On to thir mornings rural work they haste
Among sweet dewes and flours; where any row
Of Fruit-trees overwoodie reachd too farr
Thir pamperd boughes, and needed hands to check
Fruitless imbraces: or they led the Vine [215]
To wed her Elm; she spous'd about him twines
Her marriageable arms, and with her brings
Her dowr th' adopted Clusters, to adorn
His barren leaves. Them thus imploid beheld
With pittie Heav'ns high King, and to him call'd [220]

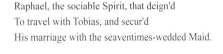

轉的頌歌。

「鳥兒呀！請伸展雙翅把頌詞背負到天庭。

「所有一切有生命的都應與我相會，於清朗的晨曦中齊聲讚頌 —— 偉大的天父呀！請降下德澤，喚醒光明來驅散暗藏在黑夜中的邪惡。」

禱告完畢，亞當和夏娃隨即展開一天的工作，他們勤奮地穿梭在枝葉茂密的果樹叢間，修剪過度蔓延而交纏的枝椏；並把葡萄藤盤繞到榆樹的枝幹上，宛如牽線的紅娘，讓兩種植物相互依偎，等到葡萄收成的季節，便能夠從結實累累的榆樹枝幹上，輕易地摘取葡萄。

上帝見到人類如此辛勤地勞動，心生憐惜，於是召喚善於交際的天使拉斐爾（Raphael）到跟前來，對他說道：

「拉斐爾，從地獄脫逃的撒旦

Raphael, the sociable Spirit, that deign'd
To travel with Tobias, and secur'd
His marriage with the seaventimes-wedded Maid.

Raphael, said hee, thou hear'st what stir on Earth
Satan from Hell scap't through the darksom Gulf [225]
Hath raisd in Paradise, and how disturbd
This night the human pair, how he designes
In them at once to ruin all mankind.
Go therefore, half this day as friend with friend
Converse with Adam, in what Bowre or shade [230]
Thou find'st him from the heat of Noon retir'd,
To respit his day-labour with repast,
Or with repose; and such discourse bring on,
As may advise him of his happie state,
Happiness in his power left free to will, [235]
Left to his own free Will, his Will though free,
Yet mutable; whence warne him to beware
He swerve not too secure: tell him withall
His danger, and from whom, what enemie
Late falln himself from Heav'n, is plotting now [240]
The fall of others from like state of bliss;
By violence, no, for that shall be withstood,
But by deceit and lies; this let him know,

▽ 亞當和夏娃
印章 美索不達米亞 西元前2000年

下圖右是一個西元前2000多年前的阿卡得人的綠玉圓筒印章，在下圖左的印泥上印出了一對男女、一棵樹和一條蛇。根據推測，當時的美索不達米亞已經開始流傳伊甸園的傳說。

昨晚潛入樂園，給人類帶來一陣不安的騷動，意圖誘惑他們犯下罪惡以遭致毀滅的命運。現在，我命你到樂園去，花半天的時間與亞當談談，將魔鬼已侵入樂園的消息告訴他，並提醒他，要善用己身的自由意志，加強堅定不疑的信仰，才能繼續保有幸福的生活；另外，要他千萬不可輕忽大意，掉入撒旦所設下的陷阱，讓自己一腳踩進邪惡裡。你要明確的告訴他，魔鬼並不會用強力來脅迫他們，因為那反而會導致人類的反抗，他會利用謊言，以欺騙的手段驅使人類觸犯天規。後面的這一點一定要跟他講清楚，別讓他在犯錯之後有『事先沒被告知』的藉口。」

拉斐爾聽完上帝的交代之後，一刻也不敢停留，馬上展開翅膀飛出天庭大門，逕往地球的方向而去。穿越廣闊無垠的太空之後，他來到樂園的上空，與鷹隼們一塊迎風遨翔，宛若傳說中每五百年即浴火重生一遍的鳳

Lest wilfully transgressing he pretend
Surprisal, unadmonisht, unforewarnd. [245]

So spake th' Eternal Father, and fulfilld
All Justice: nor delaid the winged Saint
After his charge receivd; but from among
Thousand Celestial Ardors, where he stood
Vaild with his gorgeous wings, up springing light [250]
Flew through the midst of Heav'n; th' angelic Quires
On each hand parting, to his speed gave way
Through all th' Empyreal road; till at the Gate
Of Heav'n arriv'd, the gate self-opend wide
On golden Hinges turning, as by work [255]
Divine the sov'ran Architect had fram'd.
From hence, no cloud, or, to obstruct his sight,
Starr interpos'd, however small he sees,
Not unconform to other shining Globes,
Earth and the Gard'n of God, with Cedars crownd [260]
Above all Hills. As when by night the Glass
Of Galileo, less assur'd, observes
Imagind Lands and Regions in the Moon:
Or Pilot from amidst the Cyclades
Delos or Samos first appeering kenns [265]
A cloudy spot. Down thither prone in flight
He speeds, and through the vast Ethereal Skie
Sailes between worlds and worlds, with steddie wing
Now on the polar windes, then with quick Fann
Winnows the buxom Air; till within soare [270]
Of Towring Eagles, to all the Fowles he seems
A Phœnix, gaz'd by all, as that sole Bird
When to enshrine his reliques in the Sun's
Bright Temple, to Ægyptian Theb's he flies.
At once on th' Eastern cliff of Paradise [275]
He lights, and to his proper shape returns
A Seraph wingd; six wings he wore, to shade
His lineaments Divine; the pair that clad
Each shoulder broad, came mantling o're his brest
With regal Ornament; the middle pair [280]
Girt like a Starrie Zone his waste, and round
Skirted his loines and thighes with downie Gold
And colours dipt in Heav'n; the third his feet
Shaddowd from either heele with featherd maile

凰，美麗無比。隨後，降落在樂園東
方的山頂上，那有著六隻翅膀的神聖
儀表，乃撒拉弗天使的原始形貌。一
對披護著寬闊的肩膀，像帝王的裝飾
般，垂掛到胸前；金光燦爛的一對，

˄ 天堂的守門人
希土克 油畫 1889年

　　為了保護人類的安全，伊甸園門口一直由天
使守衛著，直到後來當亞當和夏娃背棄了上帝的信
任，天使才從伊甸園撤守。

Skie-tinctur'd grain. Like Maia's son he stood, [285]
And shook his Plumes, that Heav'nly fragrance filld
The circuit wide. Strait knew him all the Bands
Of Angels under watch; and to his state,
And to his message high in honour rise;
For on Som message high they guessd him bound. [290]
Thir glittering Tents he passd, and now is come
Into the blissful field, through Groves of Myrrhe,
And flouring Odours, Cassia, Nard, and Balme;
A Wilderness of sweets; for Nature here
Wantond as in her prime, and plaid at will [295]
Her Virgin Fancies, pouring forth more sweet,
Wilde above Rule or Art; enormous bliss.
Him through the spicie Forrest onward com
Adam discernd, as in the dore he sat
Of his coole Bowre, while now the mounted Sun [300]
Shot down direct his fervid Raies, to warme
Earths inmost womb, more warmth then Adam needs;
And Eve within, due at her hour prepar'd
For dinner savourie fruits, of taste to please
True appetite, and not disrelish thirst [305]
Of nectarous draughts between, from milkie stream,
Berrie or Grape: to whom thus Adam call'd.

Haste hither Eve, and worth thy sight behold
Eastward among those Trees, what glorious shape
Comes this way moving; seems another Morn [310]
Ris'n on mid-noon; Som great behest from Heav'n
To us perhaps he brings, and will voutsafe
This day to be our Guest. But goe with speed,
And what thy stores contain, bring forth and poure
Abundance, fit to honour and receive [315]
Our Heav'nly stranger; well we may afford
Our givers thir own gifts, and large bestow
From large bestowd, where Nature multiplies
Her fertil growth, and by disburd'ning grows
More fruitful, which instructs us not to spare. [320]

To whom thus Eve. Adam, earths hallowd mould,
Of God inspir'd, small store will serve, where store,
All seasons, ripe for use hangs on the stalk;

圍繞在腰部和大腿；腳踝上的一對，則
有著藍天般的顏色[2]。

拉斐爾挺直地站在岩頂上，彷若神
話中的使神漢密斯[3]。守門天使看見
他，連忙把大門拉開，恭敬地請他進

▽ 亞當和夏娃迎接天使的來訪
杜雷 版畫 1866年

　　伊甸園除了亞當和夏娃，就只有各種動物為
伴，當亞當看到渾身散發燦爛光芒的天使，不禁
興奮地告訴夏娃，準備迎接從天庭來的客人。

Save what by frugal storing firmness gains
To nourish, and superfluous moist consumes: [325]
But I will haste and from each bough and break,
Each Plant and juiciest Gourd will pluck such choice
To entertain our Angel guest, as hee
Beholding shall confess that here on Earth
God hath dispenst his bounties as in Heav'n. [330]

So saying, with dispatchful looks in haste
She turns, on hospitable thoughts intent
What choice to chuse for delicacie best,
What order, so contriv'd as not to mix
Tastes, not well joynd, inelegant, but bring [335]
Taste after taste upheld with kindliest change,
Bestirs her then, and from each tender stalk
Whatever Earth all-bearing Mother yields
In India East or West, or middle shoare
In Pontus or the Punic Coast, or where [340]
Alcinous reign'd, fruit of all kindes, in coate,
Rough, or smooth rin'd, or bearded husk, or shell
She gathers, Tribute large, and on the board
Heaps with unsparing hand; for drink the Grape
She crushes, inoffensive moust, and meathes [345]
From many a berrie, and from sweet kernels prest
She tempers dulcet creams, nor these to hold
Wants her fit vessels pure, then strews the ground
With Rose and Odours from the shrub unfum'd.
Mean while our Primitive great Sire, to meet [350]
His god-like Guest, walks forth, without more train
Accompanied then with his own compleat
Perfections; in himself was all his state,
More solemn then the tedious pomp that waits
On Princes, when thir rich Retinue long [355]
Of Horses led, and Grooms besmear'd with Gold
Dazles the croud, and sets them all agape.
Neerer his presence Adam though not awd,
Yet with submiss approach and reverence meek,
As to a superior Nature, bowing low, [360]

Thus said. Native of Heav'n, for other place
None can then Heav'n such glorious shape contain;
Since by descending from the Thrones above,

來。他進入樂園，於鋪滿鮮花、芳香四溢的田野上行走，前往人類的居所。

此時，亞當正坐在住所入口邊的綠蔭下，躲避正午炎熱的豔陽；夏娃則在屋子裡準備午餐。遠遠地，一個天使模樣的身影出現在亞當眼簾，他興奮地朝屋裡喊著：

「夏娃，樹林中有一個渾身散發著陽光般燦爛光輝的天使正朝向我們走來，快點把貯藏室裡最好的食物拿出來，好好地招待客人吧！」

「親愛的亞當，你是大地聖潔的產物，受上帝的氣息而生[4]。樂園裡，四季都有甜美的花果生長，除了一些

註2：《舊約·以賽亞書》：「其上有撒拉弗侍立，各有六個翅膀：用兩個翅膀遮臉，兩個翅膀遮腳，兩個翅膀飛翔。」

註3：漢密斯（Hermes）是《希臘羅馬神話故事》中的使神，為天神宙斯和美麗的女神美雅（Maia）所生，聰敏慧黠，機智過人。

註4：亞當是上帝用大地上的塵土所捏造的，所以說是「大地聖潔的產物」。《舊約·創世記》：「耶和華神用地上的塵土造人，將生氣吹在他鼻孔裡，他就成了有靈的活人，名叫亞當。」

Those happie places thou hast deignd a while
To want, and honour these, voutsafe with us [365]
Two onely, who yet by sov'ran gift possess
This spacious ground, in yonder shadie Bowre
To rest, and what the Garden choicest bears
To sit and taste, till this meridian heat
Be over, and the Sun more coole decline. [370]

Whom thus the Angelic Vertue answerd milde.
Adam, I therefore came, nor art thou such
Created, or such place hast here to dwell,
As may not oft invite, though Spirits of Heav'n
To visit thee; lead on then where thy Bowre [375]
Oreshades; for these mid-hours, till Eevning rise
I have at will. So to the Silvan Lodge
They came, that like Pomona's Arbour smil'd
With flourets deck't and fragrant smells; but Eve
Undeckt, save with her self more lovely fair [380]
Then Wood-Nymph, or the fairest Goddess feign'd
Of three that in Mount Ida naked strove,
Stood to entertain her guest from Heav'n; no vaile
Shee needed, Vertue-proof, no thought infirme
Alterd her cheek. On whom the Angel Haile [385]
Bestowd, the holy salutation us'd
Long after to blest Marie, second Eve.

Haile Mother of Mankind, whose fruitful Womb
Shall fill the World more numerous with thy Sons
Then with these various fruits the Trees of God [390]
Have heap'd this Table. Rais'd of grassie terf
Thir Table was, and mossie seats had round,
And on her ample Square from side to side
All Autumn pil'd, though Spring and Autumn here
Danc'd hand in hand. A while discourse they hold; [395]
No fear lest Dinner coole; when thus began
Our Authour. Heav'nly stranger, please to taste
These bounties which our Nourisher, from whom
All perfet good unmeasur'd out, descends,
To us for food and for delight hath caus'd [400]
The Earth to yeild; unsavourie food perhaps
To spiritual Natures; only this I know,
That one Celestial Father gives to all.

瓜果，我們無需刻意貯存食物；我現在就到林子裡去，摘取懸枝頭上最鮮美的果實來招待客人。」

夏娃說完，隨即跑進樹林裡去。

拉斐爾走到亞當面前，全身散發著莊嚴的儀態；亞當彎身向前，恭敬地對他鞠躬，說道：

「歡迎光臨！請跟我到屋裡去，裡頭比較涼爽，方便我們說話。」

「好的。」

拉斐爾露出笑容，跟著亞當進入屋內，桌上已擺滿了夏娃採摘回來的各色瓜果，有核桃、櫻桃、無花果和阿爾西諾斯國王林園中所生產的果實[5]，還有葡萄汁和果醬；另外，地面上妝點著美麗的薔薇花瓣，發出淡雅的清香。

「您好！請坐下來享用我們特地為您準備的果實。」

註5：阿爾西諾斯（Alcinous）是荷馬《奧德賽》詩中的人物，為舍利亞（Scheria）的國王，有一個果樹茂密的林園。

To whom the Angel. Therefore what he gives
(Whose praise be ever sung) to man in part [405]
Spiritual, may of purest Spirits be found
No ingrateful food: and food alike those pure
Intelligential substances require
As doth your Rational; and both contain
Within them every lower facultie [410]
Of sense, whereby they hear, see, smell, touch, taste,
Tasting concoct, digest, assimilate,
And corporeal to incorporeal turn.
For know, whatever was created, needs
To be sustaind and fed; of Elements [415]
The grosser feeds the purer, Earth the Sea,
Earth and the Sea feed Air, the Air those Fires
Ethereal, and as lowest first the Moon;
Whence in her visage round those spots, unpurg'd
Vapours not yet into her substance turnd. [420]
Nor doth the Moon no nourishment exhale
From her moist Continent to higher Orbes.
The Sun that light imparts to all, receives
From all his alimental recompence
In humid exhalations, and at Even [425]
Sups with the Ocean: though in Heav'n the Trees
Of life ambrosial frutage bear, and vines
Yield Nectar, though from off the boughs each Morn
We brush mellifluous Dewes, and find the ground
Cover'd with pearly grain: yet God hath here [430]
Varied his bounty so with new delights,
As may compare with Heaven; and to taste
Think not I shall be nice. So down they sat,
And to thir viands fell, nor seemingly
The Angel, nor in mist, the common gloss [435]
Of Theologians, but with keen dispatch
Of real hunger, and concoctive heate
To transubstantiate; what redounds, transpires
Through Spirits with ease; nor wonder; if by fire
Of sooty coal the Empiric Alchimist [440]
Can turn, or holds it possible to turn
Metals of drossiest Ore to perfet Gold
As from the Mine. Mean while at Table Eve
Ministerd naked, and thir flowing cups

∧ **拉斐爾向亞當、夏娃述說撒旦的叛變**
杜雷 版畫 1866年

　　拉斐爾大天使坐在亞當和夏娃面前，娓娓道來
撒旦叛亂的經過，提醒他們注意撒旦的邪惡誘惑。

夏娃站在桌子旁，熱忱地招呼著客人。她的身上雖然沒有任何一點裝飾品，卻比那在伊德山上爭吵的三位女神中最美的阿芙蘿黛緹還要美麗[6]。

「祝福你！」

拉斐爾給了夏娃一聲神聖的祝福。於是三個人一塊兒坐下，在覆滿青苔的椅子上面，一邊享用著美食、一邊聊天。

看見天使吃著果子，那津津有味的模樣，亞當忍不住好奇地問：

「這兒生產的果實，比起您所居住的天庭來，恐怕遜色很多吧？」

「這你就想錯了，」

拉斐爾回答：

「萬物全都是由同一位造物者所創造，只是以各種不同的形體展現，所

註6：伊德山（Ida）上三女神的故事出自《希臘羅馬神話故事》，天后希拉（Hera）、美神阿芙蘿黛緹（Aphrodite）、智慧女神雅典娜（Athena）為了爭奪一顆刻有「獻給最美麗的女人」的金蘋果而爭吵不休，天神宙斯要她們去伊德山上找特洛伊王子帕里斯做裁決；後來，帕里斯把金蘋果判給了阿芙蘿黛緹。

With pleasant liquors crown'd: O innocence [445]
Deserving Paradise! if ever, then,
Then had the Sons of God excuse to have bin
Enamour'd at that sight; but in those hearts
Love unlibidinous reign'd, nor jealousie
Was understood, the injur'd Lovers Hell.

Thus when with meats and drinks they had suffic'd [450]
Not burd'nd Nature, sudden mind arose
In Adam, not to let th' occasion pass
Given him by this great Conference to know
Of things above his World, and of thir being [455]
Who dwell in Heav'n, whose excellence he saw
Transcend his own so farr, whose radiant forms
Divine effulgence, whose high Power so far
Exceeded human, and his wary speech
Thus to th' Empyreal Minister he fram'd. [460]

Inhabitant with God, now know I well
Thy favour, in this honour done to man,
Under whose lowly roof thou hast voutsaf't
To enter, and these earthly fruits to taste,
Food not of Angels, yet accepted so, [465]
As that more willingly thou couldst not seem
At Heav'n's high feasts to have fed: yet what compare?

To whom the winged Hierarch repli'd.
O Adam, one Almightie is, from whom
All things proceed, and up to him return, [470]
If not deprav'd from good, created all
Such to perfection, one first matter all,
Indu'd with various forms, various degrees
Of substance, and in things that live, of life;
But more refin'd, more spiritous, and pure, [475]
As neerer to him plac't or neerer tending
Each in thir several active Sphears assignd,
Till body up to spirit work, in bounds
Proportiond to each kind. So from the root
Springs lighter the green stalk, from thence the leaves [480]
More aerie, last the bright consummate floure
Spirits odorous breathes: flours and thir fruit
Mans nourishment, by gradual scale sublim'd

∧ 拉斐爾警告亞當和夏娃
布雷克　水彩畫 1808年

　　拉斐爾奉上帝之命，前來警告單純的亞當和夏娃。告誡他們要堅持對上帝的愛與順從。

以每一樣事物都是完美的。所有原質相同的事物，終會回歸到靈質的境界；吃了上帝為你們所安排的食物，對我來說也是有益的，你無須感到奇怪。現在你們吃著這些營養的食物，有一天，你們的肉身將會升騰為靈

To vital Spirits aspire, to animal,
To intellectual, give both life and sense, [485]
Fansie and understanding, whence the Soule
Reason receives, and reason is her being,
Discursive, or Intuitive; discourse
Is oftest yours, the latter most is ours,
Differing but in degree, of kind the same. [490]
Wonder not then, what God for you saw good
If I refuse not, but convert, as you,
To proper substance; time may come when men
With Angels may participate, and find
No inconvenient Diet, nor too light Fare: [495]
And from these corporal nutriments perhaps
Your bodies may at last turn all to Spirit,
Improv'd by tract of time, and wingd ascend
Ethereal, as wee, or may at choice
Here or in Heav'nly Paradises dwell; [500]
If ye be found obedient, and retain
Unalterably firm his love entire
Whose progenie you are. Mean while enjoy
Your fill what happiness this happie state
Can comprehend, incapable of more. [505]

To whom the Patriarch of mankind repli'd,
O favourable spirit, propitious guest,
Well hast thou taught the way that might direct
Our knowledge, and the scale of Nature set
From center to circumference, whereon [510]
In contemplation of created things
By steps we may ascend to God. But say,
What meant that caution joind, if ye be found
Obedient? can we want obedience then
To him, or possibly his love desert [515]
Who formd us from the dust, and plac'd us here
Full to the utmost measure of what bliss
Human desires can seek or apprehend?

To whom the Angel. Son of Heav'n and Earth,
Attend: That thou art happie, owe to God; [520]
That thou continu'st such, owe to thy self,
That is, to thy obedience; therein stand.
This was that caution giv'n thee; be advis'd.
God made thee perfect, not immutable;

質，從肩膀生出一雙翅膀，和天使一樣隨意來去天庭與地球之間；只要你們對造物主的愛和順從始終不變，終能保有這樣的幸福。」

「為什麼你要說『對造物主的愛和順從始終不變』？我們由上帝所造，祂給予我們生命，又讓我們生活在如此幸福的園地，我們怎會不順從祂呢？」

亞當疑惑地問。

「別忘了，上帝雖然給予你幸福，但這幸福也必須由你自己把握住，順從上帝必須出於自願，若非自願，祂便不能接受。你的意志是自由的，可以決定要真心的順從上帝，得到幸福；抑或選擇墮落，失去幸福。」拉斐爾語重心長地說著。

「我不明白，雖然我們擁有自由的意志，但卻從未偏離上帝的規定，我們一定會保持堅定的意志，永遠遵守造物者的命令。有誰會違背崇高的天父呢？」

And good he made thee, but to persevere [525]
He left it in thy power, ordaind thy will
By nature free, not over-rul'd by Fate
Inextricable, or strict necessity;
Our voluntarie service he requires,
Not our necessitated, such with him [530]
Finds no acceptance, nor can find, for how
Can hearts, not free, be tri'd whether they serve
Willing or no, who will but what they must
By Destinie, and can no other choose?
Myself and all th' Angelic Host that stand [535]
In sight of God enthron'd, our happie state
Hold, as you yours, while our obedience holds;
On other surety none; freely we serve
Because we freely love, as in our will
To love or not; in this we stand or fall: [540]
And Som are fall'n, to disobedience fall'n,
And so from Heav'n to deepest Hell; O fall
From what high state of bliss into what woe!

To whom our great Progenitor. Thy words
Attentive, and with more delighted eare [545]
Divine instructer, I have heard, then when
Cherubic Songs by night from neighbouring Hills
Aereal Music send: nor knew I not
To be both will and deed created free;
Yet that we never shall forget to love [550]
Our maker, and obey him whose command
Single, is yet so just, my constant thoughts
Assur'd me and still assure: though what thou tellst
Hath past in Heav'n, Som doubt within me move,
But more desire to hear, if thou consent, [555]
The full relation, which must needs be strange,
Worthy of Sacred silence to be heard;
And we have yet large day, for scarce the Sun
Hath finisht half his journey, and scarce begins
His other half in the great Zone of Heav'n. [560]

Thus Adam made request, and Raphael
After short pause assenting, thus began.

High matter thou injoinst me, O prime of men,

亞當一臉疑惑，急於表明自己的心意。

「嗯！的確是有一些天使背離了上帝，如今，他們已墜落到地獄去了。」

拉斐爾漸漸提到了這次來訪的目的。

「可以說給我聽嗎？」

亞當露出驚訝的神情，向拉斐爾請求著。

「說來，這是一件可悲的往事。當時，尚未有你們居住的這個世界，廣大的空間為『混沌』所統轄。一日，天國的最高主宰向所有的天使軍發出召集令，不一會兒，多如細沙的軍隊即整頓好軍容，在上帝的寶座前列隊成行，放眼望去，各式各樣的旌旗標誌著所屬的階級，飄揚在行伍之間。天使大軍圍成一圈一圈，層層疊疊地把上帝環繞在中間。

「終於，上帝開口說道：『各位請看，在我右手邊的是誕生於錫安聖山

Sad task and hard, for how shall I relate
To human sense th' invisible exploits [565]
Of warring Spirits; how without remorse
The ruin of so many glorious once
And perfet while they stood; how last unfould
The secrets of another World, perhaps
Not lawful to reveal? yet for thy good [570]
This is dispenc't, and what surmounts the reach
Of human sense, I shall delineate so,
By lik'ning spiritual to corporal forms,
As may express them best, though what if Earth
Be but the shadow of Heav'n, and things therein [575]
Each to other like, more then on earth is thought?

As yet this World was not, and Chaos Wilde
Reignd where these Heav'ns now rowl, where Earth now rests
Upon her Center pois'd, when on a day
(For Time, though in Eternitie, appli'd [580]
To motion, measures all things durable
By present, past, and future) on such day
As Heav'ns great Year brings forth, th' Empyreal Host
Of Angels by Imperial summons call'd,
Innumerable before th' Almighties Throne [585]
Forthwith from all the ends of Heav'n appeerd
Under thir Hierarchs in orders bright
Ten thousand thousand Ensignes high advanc'd,
Standards and Gonfalons twixt Van and Reare
Streame in the Aire, and for distinction serve [590]
Of Hierarchies, of Orders, and Degrees;
Or in thir glittering Tissues bear imblaz'd
Holy Memorials, acts of Zeale and Love
Recorded eminent. Thus when in Orbes
Of circuit inexpressible they stood, [595]
Orb within Orb, the Father infinite,
By whom in bliss imbosom'd sat the Son,
Amidst as from a flaming Mount, whose top
Brightness had made invisible, thus spake.

Hear all ye Angels, Progenie of Light, [600]
Thrones, Dominations, Princedoms, Vertues, Powers,
Hear my Decree, which unrevok't shall stand.
This day I have begot whom I declare

的基督（Christ），他是我的獨生子[7]；
我在此冊立他為諸神之主[8]，他將總攬
天國政事，統領天使大軍。所有的天
神都要服從他的命令，因為他的命令
即代表我的命令，若有誰敢違背他的

▽ 三位一體
貝倫 油畫 1620年

　　天使簇擁著上帝和耶穌基督，上帝冊立耶穌
為眾神之王，總攬天國政事，統率天使軍團，卻
引起撒旦的不滿。

My onely Son, and on this holy Hill
Him have anointed, whom ye now behold [605]
At my right hand; your Head I him appoint;
And by my Self have sworn to him shall bow
All knees in Heav'n, and shall confess him Lord:
Under his great Vice-gerent Reign abide
United as one individual Soule [610]
For ever happie: him who disobeyes
Mee disobeyes, breaks union, and that day
Cast out from God and blessed vision, falls
Into utter darkness, deep ingulft, his place
Ordaind without redemption, without end. [615]

So spake th' Omnipotent, and with his words
All seemd well pleas'd, all seem'd, but were not all.
That day, as other solemn dayes, they spent
In song and dance about the sacred Hill,
Mystical dance, which yonder starrie Spheare [620]
Of Planets and of fixt in all her Wheeles
Resembles nearest, mazes intricate,
Eccentric, intervolv'd, yet regular
Then most, when most irregular they seem,
And in thir motions harmonie Divine [625]
So smooths her charming tones, that Gods own ear
Listens delighted. Eevning now approach'd
(For wee have also our Eevning and our Morn,
Wee ours for change delectable, not need)
Forthwith from dance to sweet repast they turn [630]
Desirous, all in Circles as they stood,
Tables are set, and on a sudden pil'd
With Angels Food, and rubied Nectar flows
In Pearl, in Diamond, and massie Gold,
Fruit of delicious Vines, the growth of Heav'n. [635]
On flours repos'd, and with fresh flourets crownd,
They eate, they drink, and in communion sweet
Quaff immortalitie and joy, secure
Of surfet where full measure onely bounds
Excess, before th' all bounteous King, who showrd [640]
With copious hand, rejoycing in thir joy.
Now when ambrosial Night with Clouds exhal'd
From that high mount of God, whence light & shade
Spring both, the face of brightest Heav'n had changd

指令，將會被逐出天庭，到那黑暗的深淵裡去。』沒多久，基督接掌諸神之長的消息，便迅速地在天國散播開來。」

「你剛剛說的那些背離上帝的天使，就是因為這件事嗎？」

亞當急於知道後情，連忙問道。

「是的，並不是所有的天使都歡喜聽見這個消息，其中有個叫撒旦的大天使，原本在天庭把持著權力地位，享受極高的尊榮。天神的這項命令，無疑地降低了他的地位，因此讓他心生怨懟。當他聽到這項命令的時候，彷彿當頭挨了一記悶棍，內心非常不滿，忍不住埋怨：『憑什麼要基督來領導我們，難道他的力量會勝過我嗎？我絕對不聽從一個外來者的指

註7：《舊約‧詩篇》：「耶和華之受膏者為王。……說：『我已經立我的君在錫安我的聖山上了。』」
註8：《新約‧腓立比書》：「所以神將他升為至高，又賜給他那超乎萬名之上的名，叫一切在天上的、地上的和地底下的，因耶穌的名無不屈膝，無不口稱耶穌基督為主，使榮耀歸與父神。」

To grateful Twilight (for Night comes not there [645]
In darker veile) and roseat Dews dispos'd
All but the unsleeping eyes of God to rest,
Wide over all the Plain, and wider farr
Then all this globous Earth in Plain out spred,
(Such are the Courts of God) th' Angelic throng [650]
Disperst in Bands and Files thir Camp extend
By living Streams among the Trees of Life,
Pavilions numberless, and sudden reard,
Celestial Tabernacles, where they slept
Fannd with coole Winds, save those who in thir course [655]
Melodious Hymns about the sovran Throne
Alternate all night long: but not so wak'd
Satan, so call him now, his former name
Is heard no more in Heav'n; he of the first,
If not the first Arch-Angel, great in Power, [660]
In favour and præeminence, yet fraught
With envie against the Son of God, that day
Honourd by his great Father, and proclaimd
Messiah King anointed, could not beare
Through pride that sight, & thought himself impaird. [665]
Deep malice thence conceiving and disdain,
Soon as midnight brought on the duskie houre
Friendliest to sleep and silence, he resolv'd
With all his Legions to dislodge, and leave
Unworshipt, unobey'd the Throne supream [670]
Contemptuous, and his next subordinate
Awak'ning, thus to him in secret spake.

Sleepst thou, Companion dear, what sleep can close
Thy eye-lids? and remembrest what Decree
Of yesterday, so late hath past the lips [675]
Of Heav'ns Almightie. Thou to me thy thoughts
Wast wont, I mine to thee was wont to impart;
Both waking we were one; how then can now
Thy sleep dissent? new Laws thou seest impos'd;
New Laws from him who reigns, new minds may raise [680]
In us who serve, new Counsels, to debate
What doubtful may ensue; more in this place
To utter is not safe. Assemble thou
Of all those Myriads which we lead the chief;
Tell them that by command, ere yet dim Night [685]

示。』

「偏偏為神子舉辦的各項慶典如火如荼地展開，歡樂的氣氛瀰漫著整個天庭。白天，天使們圍繞著聖山，快樂地唱歌跳舞；晚上，擺出豐盛的瓊漿玉液，盡情地暢飲。

「這番熱鬧滾滾的景象，更加燃起撒旦內心忿怒的火燄。他找來自己的親信別西卜，與之商量叛變的計畫。別西卜是地位僅次於撒旦的天使，撒旦去找他的時候，他也正為自己的地位被貶低而感到憤憤不平；所以，當撒旦提出叛變計畫時，他舉雙手贊成，並且義憤填膺地對撒旦說：『就讓我充當說客，前去號召天使軍們加入叛變的行列吧！』」

「真的有天使軍願意加入他們嗎？」亞當問道。

「嗯！不但有，而且數量還不少。」拉斐爾回答，接著述說。

「那時，在別西卜強力的遊說下，天國千百萬個天使大軍中，竟有三分

Her shadowie Cloud withdraws, I am to haste,
And all who under me thir Banners wave,
Homeward with flying march where we possess
The Quarters of the North, there to prepare
Fit entertainment to receive our King [690]
The great Messiah, and his new commands,
Who speedily through all the Hierarchies
Intends to pass triumphant, and give Laws.

So spake the false Arch-Angel, and infus'd
Bad influence into th' unwarie brest [695]
Of his Associate; hee together calls,
Or several one by one, the Regent Powers,
Under him Regent, tells, as he was taught,
That the most High commanding, now ere Night,
Now ere dim Night had disincumberd Heav'n, [700]
The great Hierarchal Standard was to move;
Tells the suggested cause, and casts between
Ambiguous words and jealousies, to sound
Or taint integritie; but all obey'd
The wonted signal, and superior voice [705]
Of thir great Potentate; for great indeed
His name, and high was his degree in Heav'n;
His count'nance, as the Morning Starr that guides
The starrie flock, allur'd them, and with lyes
Drew after him the third part of Heav'ns Host: [710]
Mean while th' Eternal eye, whose sight discernes
Abstrusest thoughts, from forth his holy Mount
And from within the golden Lamps that burne
Nightly before him, saw without thir light
Rebellion rising, saw in whom, how spred [715]
Among the sons of Morn, what multitudes
Were banded to oppose his high Decree;
And smiling to his onely Son thus said.

Son, thou in whom my glory I behold
In full resplendence, Heir of all my might, [720]
Neerly it now concernes us to be sure
Of our Omnipotence, and with what Arms
We mean to hold what anciently we claim
Of Deitie or Empire, such a foe
Is rising, who intends to erect his Throne [725]

之一被說服，選擇投入撒旦麾下。他
們鼓動雙翼，趁著夜幕低垂，飛往天
國北方撒旦的宮殿，並在廣場前集
結，準備聆聽將領的說法。

「一會兒，撒旦英姿煥發地從宮殿
中走出來，那高大挺拔的身軀矗立在
高台上，彷若一株擎天巨木。他冷冽
的瞳孔射出兩道寒光，以炯炯目光環
視廣場一周後，開口說道：『各位！
白天時上帝宣布了新法規，想必大家
都聽得很清楚。可是，我們對上帝早
已是卑恭屈膝、極盡奉承之能事，沒
想到現在又多出一個來，要我們對他
同樣尊崇；那宣稱掌有正義天平的眾
神之主，如今卻讓新來的權貴奪去了
諸神的權力，原本公正的天平，如今
竟傾向外來之人。可以預見的是，未
來我們的自由將被剝奪，凡事備受法
令的束縛。我們都是上天的子民，本
該享有同樣的地位，為什麼我們要聽
命於神子？為什麼我們必須忍受這種
不平等的待遇？』」

Equal to ours, throughout the spacious North;
Nor so content, hath in his thought to try
In battel, what our Power is, or our right.
Let us advise, and to this hazard draw
With speed what force is left, and all imploy [730]
In our defense, lest unawares we lose
This our high place, our Sanctuarie, our Hill.

To whom the Son with calm aspect and cleer
Light'ning Divine, ineffable, serene,
Made answer. Mightie Father, thou thy foes [735]
Justly hast in derision, and secure
Laugh'st at thir vain designes and tumults vain,
Matter to mee of Glory, whom thir hate
Illustrates, when they see all Regal Power
Giv'n me to quell thir pride, and in event [740]
Know whether I be dextrous to subdue
Thy Rebels, or be found the worst in Heav'n.

So spake the Son, but Satan with his Powers
Far was advanc't on winged speed, an Host
Innumerable as the Starrs of Night, [745]
Or Starrs of Morning, Dew-drops, which the Sun
Impearls on every leaf and every flouer.
Regions they pass'd, the mightie Regencies
Of Seraphim and Potentates and Thrones
In thir triple Degrees, Regions to which [750]
All thy Dominion, Adam, is no more
Then what this Garden is to all the Earth,
And all the Sea, from one entire globose
Stretcht into Longitude; which having pass'd
At length into the limits of the North [755]
They came, and Satan to his Royal seat
High on a Hill, far blazing, as a Mount
Rais'd on a Mount, with Pyramids and Towrs
From Diamond Quarries hew'n, and Rocks of Gold,
The Palace of great Lucifer, (so call [760]
That Structure in the Dialect of men
Interpreted) which not long after, he
Affecting all equality with God,
In imitation of that Mount whereon
Messiah was declar'd in sight of Heav'n, [765]

「哇！撒旦怎敢發表如此不敬的言論？難道就沒有人反駁他的說法嗎？」亞當一臉驚愕，激動地問。

「有的，當時有一個名叫亞必迭（Abdiel）的天使，在聽完撒旦的演說之後，就跟你現在一樣情緒激動，他從人群中擠向前去，憤怒地瞪著撒旦罵道：『住口，狂妄的傢伙，你怎能發表這種挑撥的言論？說什麼法律束縛了自由，同輩之間不該有統治關係，沒有人能獨攬永恆的權力。難道創造我們的造物者卻不能掌管祂的創造物[9]？況且祂待我們善良慈愛，任命神子的目的，不過是想更加凝聚眾人的心罷了，為什麼要毀謗偉大的聖父呢？快點去祈求上帝的原諒。』亞必迭說完，竟無一人相附和。

「這情景給了撒旦更多的勇氣，他

註9：《新約‧歌羅西書》：「因為萬有都是靠他造的，無論是天上的、地上的、能看見的、不能看見的，或是有位的、主治的、執政的、掌權的，一概都是藉著他造的，又是為他造的。」

The Mountain of the Congregation call'd;
For thither he assembl'd all his Train,
Pretending so commanded to consult
About the great reception of thir King,
Thither to come, and with calumnious Art [770]
Of counterfeted truth thus held thir ears.

Thrones, Dominations, Princedoms, Vertues, Powers,
If these magnific Titles yet remain
Not meerly titular, since by Decree
Another now hath to himself ingross't [775]
All Power, and us eclipst under the name
Of King anointed, for whom all this haste
Of midnight march, and hurried meeting here,
This onely to consult how we may best
With what may be devis'd of honours new [780]
Receive him coming to receive from us
Knee-tribute yet unpaid, prostration vile,
Too much to one, but double how endur'd,
To one and to his image now proclaim'd?
But what if better counsels might erect [785]
Our minds and teach us to cast off this Yoke?
Will ye submit your necks, and chuse to bend
The supple knee? ye will not, if I trust
To know ye right, or if ye know your selves
Natives and Sons of Heav'n possest before [790]
By none, and if not equal all, yet free,
Equally free; for Orders and Degrees
Jarr not with liberty, but well consist.
Who can in reason then or right assume
Monarchie over such as live by right [795]
His equals, if in power and splendor less,
In freedome equal? or can introduce
Law and Edict on us, who without law
Erre not, much less for this to be our Lord,
And look for adoration to th' abuse [800]
Of those Imperial Titles which assert
Our being ordain'd to govern, not to serve?

Thus farr his bold discourse without controule
Had audience, when among the Seraphim
Abdiel, then whom none with more zeale ador'd [805]

冷冷地望著亞必迭，以嘲諷的語氣說道：『亞必迭呀，亞必迭！你說什麼，我們是上帝創造的？別開玩笑了，你親眼看見了嗎？』

「士兵們發出一陣陣訕笑，盡皆漫罵起亞必迭來。

「被人群孤立的亞必迭並不害怕，他勇敢地說道：『總有一天你會嘗到背叛的果實，上帝既然能夠創造你，就有能力將你毀滅，你準備接受制裁吧！』說完，隨即飛離撒旦的陣營。」

「後來呢？亞必迭前去提醒上帝了嗎？」亞當問道。

「你放心，上帝畢竟是萬神之主呀，祂早就預見了撒旦的叛心，對於叛軍的集結和軍事行動，更是瞭如指掌；所以，在撒旦大軍尚未出發之前，他已任命神子率領剩下的天使軍，嚴正以待。戰雲瀰漫，空氣彷彿凝結，原本靜穆的天庭，即將掀起一場血腥戰爭。」拉斐爾回答。

The Deitie, and divine commands obeid,
Stood up, and in a flame of zeale severe
The current of his fury thus oppos'd.

O argument blasphemous, false and proud!
Words which no eare ever to hear in Heav'n [810]
Expected, least of all from thee, ingrate
In place thy self so high above thy Peeres.
Canst thou with impious obloquie condemne
The just Decree of God, pronounc't and sworn,
That to his only Son by right endu'd [815]
With Regal Scepter, every Soule in Heav'n
Shall bend the knee, and in that honour due
Confess him rightful King? unjust thou saist
Flatly unjust, to binde with Laws the free,
And equal over equals to let Reigne, [820]
One over all with unsucceeded power.
Shalt thou give Law to God, shalt thou dispute
With him the points of libertie, who made
Thee what thou art, and formd the Pow'rs of Heav'n
Such as he pleasd, and circumscrib'd thir being? [825]
Yet by experience taught we know how good,
And of our good, and of our dignitie
How provident he is, how farr from thought
To make us less, bent rather to exalt
Our happie state under one Head more neer [830]
United. But to grant it thee unjust,
That equal over equals Monarch Reigne:
Thy self though great and glorious dost thou count,
Or all Angelic Nature joind in one,
Equal to him begotten Son, by whom [835]
As by his Word the mighty Father made
All things, ev'n thee, and all the Spirits of Heav'n
By him created in thir bright degrees,
Crownd them with Glory, and to thir Glory nam'd
Thrones, Dominations, Princedoms, Vertues, Powers, [840]
Essential Powers, nor by his Reign obscur'd,
But more illustrious made, since he the Head
One of our number thus reduc't becomes,
His Laws our Laws, all honour to him done
Returns our own. Cease then this impious rage, [845]
And tempt not these; but hast'n to appease

Th' incensed Father, and th' incensed Son,
While Pardon may be found in time besought.

So spake the fervent Angel, but his zeale
None seconded, as out of season judg'd, [850]
Or singular and rash, whereat rejoic'd
Th' Apostat, and more haughty thus repli'd.
That we were formd then saist thou? and the work
Of secondarie hands, by task transferd
From Father to his Son? strange point and new! [855]
Doctrin which we would know whence learnt: who saw
When this creation was? rememberst thou
Thy making, while the Maker gave thee being?
We know no time when we were not as now;
Know none before us, self-begot, self-rais'd [860]
By our own quick'ning power, when fatal course
Had circl'd his full Orbe, the birth mature
Of this our native Heav'n, Ethereal Sons.
Our puissance is our own, our own right hand
Shall teach us highest deeds, by proof to try [865]
Who is our equal: then thou shalt behold
Whether by supplication we intend
Address, and to begirt th' Almighty Throne
Beseeching or besieging. This report,
These tidings carrie to th' anointed King; [870]
And fly, ere evil intercept thy flight.

He said, and as the sound of waters deep
Hoarce murmur echo'd to his words applause
Through the infinite Host, nor less for that
The flaming Seraph fearless, though alone [875]
Encompass'd round with foes, thus answerd bold.

O alienate from God, O spirit accurst,
Forsak'n of all good; I see thy fall
Determind, and thy hapless crew involv'd
In this perfidious fraud, contagion spred [880]
Both of thy crime and punishment: henceforth
No more be troubl'd how to quit the yoke
Of Gods Messiah; those indulgent Laws
Will not now be voutsaf't, other Decrees
Against thee are gon forth without recall; [885]

That Golden Scepter which thou didst reject
Is now an Iron Rod to bruise and breake
Thy disobedience. Well thou didst advise,
Yet not for thy advise or threats I fly
These wicked Tents devoted, least the wrauth [890]
Impendent, raging into sudden flame
Distinguish not: for soon expect to feel
His Thunder on thy head, devouring fire.
Then who created thee lamenting learne,
When who can uncreate thee thou shalt know. [895]

So spake the Seraph Abdiel faithful found,
Among the faithless, faithful only hee;
Among innumerable false, unmov'd,
Unshak'n, unseduc'd, unterrifi'd
His Loyaltie he kept, his Love, his Zeale; [900]
Nor number, nor example with him wrought
To swerve from truth, or change his constant mind
Though single. From amidst them forth he passd,
Long way through hostile scorn, which he susteind
Superior, nor of violence fear'd aught; [905]
And with retorted scorn his back he turn'd
On those proud Towrs to swift destruction doom'd.

天庭的戰爭

　　天使拉斐爾繼續向亞當陳述撒旦背版上帝的事跡，說到那一場戰況激烈的天庭大戰——第一日，米迦勒和加百列奉上帝之命，率領天使軍前往天國北方迎戰撒旦叛軍，撒旦被殺傷潰敗；第二日，撒旦帶著新發明的武器上戰場，天使軍投擲山峰子以還擊，雙方陷入苦戰；第三日，基督披掛上陣，撒旦和叛軍全部被逐出天國，落入地獄裡去。

⋀ 米迦勒大天使
拉斐爾 油彩、畫板 1503~1504年

　　米迦勒天使長是上帝軍團的統帥，他往往以手持聖劍、腳踏惡魔的形象出現，是積極打擊撒旦惡勢力的行動派。

「亞必迭從撒旦的宮殿離開之後，便急忙往上帝寶座的方向飛去，他徹夜趕路，後方並無追兵；一直到晨光乍現，黑暗回到了它所居住的洞穴。」拉斐爾緊接著說。

「那時，在遍灑金色朝陽的廣大原野上，天使大軍已編整行伍，身上配備精良的武器，牽著雄糾糾的戰馬，蓄勢待發；亞必迭見上帝早有防備，內心萬分驚喜，連忙加入軍隊。

「大家見到他的到來，莫不鼓掌歡迎，讚揚他維護真理的勇氣。他們把他帶到聖山上，上帝坐在金光燦爛的雲層裡，以和藹的聲音說道：『你無懼盲目群眾的攻擊，以言語悍衛了真理，贏得一場勝戰，這行為值得大大嘉許。我已任命米迦勒（Michael）和加百列率領千萬大軍，前去迎戰那些不肯服從基督的叛徒，你雖然曾經受到他們的差辱，但勝利必定是屬於你這一方的。』

「上帝說完以後，霎時間烏雲密

All night the dreadless Angel unpursu'd
Through Heav'ns wide Champain held his way, till Morn,
Wak't by the circling Hours, with rosie hand
Unbarr'd the gates of Light. There is a Cave
Within the Mount of God, fast by his Throne, [5]
Where light and darkness in perpetual round
Lodge and dislodge by turns, which makes through Heav'n
Grateful vicissitude, like Day and Night;
Light issues forth, and at the other dore
Obsequious darkness enters, till her houre [10]
To veile the Heav'n, though darkness there might well
Seem twilight here; and now went forth the Morn
Such as in highest Heav'n, arrayd in Gold
Empyreal, from before her vanisht Night,
Shot through with orient Beams: when all the Plain [15]
Coverd with thick embatteld Squadrons bright,
Chariots and flaming Armes, and fierie Steeds
Reflecting blaze on blaze, first met his view:
Warr he perceav'd, warr in procinct, and found
Already known what he for news had thought [20]
To have reported: gladly then he mixt
Among those friendly Powers who him receav'd
With joy and acclamations loud, that one
That of so many Myriads fall'n, yet one
Returnd not lost: On to the sacred hill [25]
They led him high applauded, and present
Before the seat supream; from whence a voice
From midst a Golden Cloud thus milde was heard.

Servant of God, well done, well hast thou fought
The better fight, who single hast maintaind [30]
Against revolted multitudes the Cause
Of Truth, in word mightier then they in Armes;
And for the testimonie of Truth hast born
Universal reproach, far worse to beare
Then violence: for this was all thy care [35]
To stand approv'd in sight of God, though Worlds
Judg'd thee perverse: the easier conquest now
Remains thee, aided by this host of friends,
Back on thy foes more glorious to return
Then scornd thou didst depart, and to subdue [40]
By force, who reason for thir Law refuse,

佈、煙塵滾滾，翻騰的火燄覆蓋著聖山，表達了造物主對叛軍的忿怒。

「嘹亮的號角吹起，慷慨激昂的樂聲中，千萬大軍邁出步伐，軍容浩大地往北方前進。他們隊伍齊整，高高地在空中跨步，腳下行經無數的高山、深谷、森林和溪流，那在空中行進的隊伍，就像當初盤旋在伊甸園上空的飛鳥一般，只是他們並不是等著你來命名，而是為了彌賽亞而出征[1]。」

說到這裡，拉斐爾拿起桌上的葡萄汁喝了一口，稍為休息一下，然後又繼續說道：「他們走過廣闊的天庭領土，差不多有地球的十倍，終於到達極北地；此時，撒旦正高高地坐在光彩耀眼的戰車陣中，身上披掛著黃金盔甲，神情無比威嚴，四周則有手執火燄寶劍的基路伯天使環繞著[2]。

「亞必迭見著這景象，獨自從天使軍的隊伍中走出來，憤怒地對撒旦說道：『你這個狂傲的傢伙，自以為能

Right reason for thir Law, and for thir King
Messiah, who by right of merit Reigns.
Go Michael of Celestial Armies Prince,
And thou in Military prowess next [45]
Gabriel, lead forth to Battel these my Sons
Invincible, lead forth my armed Saints
By Thousands and by Millions rang'd for fight;
Equal in number to that Godless crew
Rebellious, them with Fire and hostile Arms [50]
Fearless assault, and to the brow of Heav'n
Pursuing drive them out from God and bliss,
Into thir place of punishment, the Gulf
Of Tartarus, which ready opens wide
His fiery Chaos to receave thir fall. [55]

So spake the Sovran voice, and Clouds began
To darken all the Hill, and smoak to rowl
In duskie wreathes, reluctant flames, the signe
Of wrauth awak't: nor with less dread the loud
Ethereal Trumpet from on high gan blow: [60]
At which command the Powers Militant,
That stood for Heav'n, in mighty Quadrate joyn'd
Of Union irresistible, mov'd on
In silence thir bright Legions, to the sound
Of instrumental Harmonie that breath'd [65]
Heroic Ardor to advent'rous deeds
Under thir God-like Leaders, in the Cause
Of God and his Messiah. On they move

註1：《舊約‧創世紀》：「耶和華神用土所造成的野地各樣走獸，和空中各樣飛鳥都帶到那人面前，看他叫什麼。那人怎樣叫各樣的活物，那就是牠的名字。那人便給一切牲畜和空中飛鳥、野地走獸都起了名。」彌賽亞（Messiah）就是基督或塗膏者的意思。

註2：基路伯是把守生命樹的天使，見《舊約‧創世紀》：「又在伊甸園的東邊安設基路伯，和四面轉動發火燄的劍，要把守生命樹的道路。」

∧ 撒旦鼓動天使軍背叛上帝
杜雷 版畫 1866年

　　撒旦不甘心權力地位被剝奪，又多了一個神子要恭敬服
從，於是鼓吹眾天使一起背叛上帝，爭取不受統轄的自由。

夠取代神的地位嗎？跟全能的上帝比起來，你不過渺小得有如滄海一粟，就算有三分之一的天使受到矇騙，誤入叛軍陣營，上帝仍然能夠從石頭中創造出無可計數的軍隊來[3]。而且，祂只要舉起一隻手擊向你，不需借助外力，即能輕易地把你給消滅掉。』

「『喔！喔！看看是誰在跟我說話？』」

「撒旦發出冷冷的笑聲，從戰車上跳下來迎向前去說道：『懦夫，少逞口舌之能了。別以為甘心做上帝的奴僕，是一件多麼光榮的事，那只不過表明了你沒有追求自由的勇氣罷了！』」

「『無論你怎樣毀謗我，都不能減損一分上帝灌注在我心中的真理；只有那些去侍候不賢明的、或趨附作亂者的，才真的具有奴性，要我舉個例

註3：《新約‧馬太福音》：「約翰看見許多法利賽人和撒都該人也來受洗，就對他們說：『……我告訴你們：神能從這些石頭中給亞伯拉罕興起子孫來。』」

Indissolubly firm; nor obvious Hill
Nor streit'ning Vale, nor Wood, nor Stream divides [70]
Thir perfet ranks; for high above the ground
Thir march was, and the passive Air upbore
Thir nimble tread, as when the total kind
Of Birds in orderly array on wing
Came summond over Eden to receive [75]
Thir names of thee; so over many a tract
Of Heav'n they march'd, and many a Province wide
Tenfold the length of this terrene: at last
Farr in th' Horizon to the North appeer'd
From skirt to skirt a fierie Region, stretcht [80]
In battailous aspect, and neerer view
Bristl'd with upright beams innumerable
Of rigid Spears, and Helmets throng'd, and Shields
Various, with boastful Argument portraid,
The banded Powers of Satan hasting on [85]
With furious expedition; for they weend
That self same day by fight, or by surprize
To win the Mount of God, and on his Throne
To set the envier of his State, the proud
Aspirer, but thir thoughts prov'd fond and vain [90]
In the mid way: though strange to us it seemd
At first, that Angel should with Angel warr,
And in fierce hosting meet, who wont to meet
So oft in Festivals of joy and love
Unanimous, as sons of one great Sire [95]
Hymning th' Eternal Father: but the shout
Of Battel now began, and rushing sound
Of onset ended soon each milder thought.
High in the midst exalted as a God
Th' Apostate in his Sun-bright Chariot sate [100]
Idol of Majesty Divine, enclos'd
With Flaming Cherubim, and golden Shields;
Then lighted from his gorgeous Throne, for now
'Twixt Host and Host but narrow space was left,
A dreadful intervall, and Front to Front [105]
Presented stood in terrible array
Of hideous length: before the cloudie Van,
On the rough edge of battel ere it joyn'd,
Satan with vast and haughtie strides advanc't,
Came towring, armd in Adamant and Gold; [110]

子嗎？回頭瞧瞧就是啦！』

「亞必迭話音剛落，猛然舉起手來給撒旦致命的一擊。

「撒旦聽著話兒，未料到亞必迭會突然發動攻勢，心中未曾加以防備，因此，這威力強大的一擊把他給震得往後倒退，他膝蓋半屈，用力把長矛插在地上，直退到第十步才停了下來；彷彿一陣來自地底的颶風、或潰堤的大水，把一座高山吹起沖走，連山上的松樹都給洪水淹沒得只剩下半截。

「雙方人馬先是對眼前突發的狀況一陣驚愕，隨即高舉兵器，投入戰爭的行列。兩軍交鋒，兵戎相接，奔馳的戰車揚起漫天的煙塵，長矛與盾牌也發出相互撞擊的金屬鏗鏘聲，一時刀光劍影，殺伐之聲不絕於耳。

「米迦勒身為天使軍指揮，在戰場上衝鋒陷陣、奮勇殺敵，很快地便與撒旦正面對上。

「『邪惡的製造者呀！看看你給原

Abdiel that sight endur'd not, where he stood
Among the mightiest, bent on highest deeds,
And thus his own undaunted heart explores.

O Heav'n! that such resemblance of the Highest
Should yet remain, where faith and realtie [115]
Remain not; wherefore should not strength and might
There fail where Vertue fails, or weakest prove
Where boldest; though to sight unconquerable?
His puissance, trusting in th' Almightie's aide,
I mean to try, whose Reason I have tri'd [120]
Unsound and false; nor is it aught but just,
That he who in debate of Truth hath won,
Should win in Arms, in both disputes alike
Victor; though brutish that contest and foule,
When Reason hath to deal with force, yet so [125]
Most reason is that Reason overcome.

So pondering, and from his armed Peers
Forth stepping opposite, half way he met
His daring foe, at this prevention more
Incens't, and thus securely him defi'd. [130]

Proud, art thou met? thy hope was to have reacht
The highth of thy aspiring unoppos'd,
The Throne of God unguarded, and his side
Abandond at the terror of thy Power
Or potent tongue; fool, not to think how vain [135]
Against th' Omnipotent to rise in Arms;
Who out of smallest things could without end
Have rais'd incessant Armies to defeat
Thy folly; or with solitarie hand
Reaching beyond all limit at one blow [140]
Unaided could have finisht thee, and whelmd
Thy Legions under darkness; but thou seest
All are not of thy Train; there be who Faith
Prefer, and Pietie to God, though then
To thee not visible, when I alone [145]
Seemd in thy World erroneous to dissent
From all: my Sect thou seest, now learn too late
How few somtimes may know, when thousands err.

Whom the grand foe with scornful eye askance
Thus answerd. Ill for thee, but in wisht houre [150]
Of my revenge, first sought for thou returnst
From flight, seditious Angel, to receave
Thy merited reward, the first assay
Of this right hand provok't, since first that tongue
Inspir'd with contradiction durst oppose [155]
A third part of the Gods, in Synod met
Thir Deities to assert, who while they feel
Vigour Divine within them, can allow
Omnipotence to none. But well thou comst
Before thy fellows, ambitious to win [160]
From me som Plume, that thy success may show
Destruction to the rest: this pause between
(Unanswerd least thou boast) to let thee know;
At first I thought that Libertie and Heav'n
To heav'nly Soules had bin all one; but now [165]
I see that most through sloth had rather serve,
Ministring Spirits, traind up in Feast and Song;
Such hast thou arm'd, the Minstrelsie of Heav'n,
Servilitie with freedom to contend,
As both thir deeds compar'd this day shall prove. [170]

To whom in brief thus Abdiel stern repli'd.
Apostat, still thou errst, nor end wilt find
Of erring, from the path of truth remote:
Unjustly thou deprav'st it with the name
Of Servitude to serve whom God ordains, [175]
Or Nature; God and Nature bid the same,
When he who rules is worthiest, and excells
Them whom he governs. This is servitude,
To serve th' unwise, or him who hath rebelld
Against his worthier, as thine now serve thee, [180]
Thy self not free, but to thy self enthrall'd;
Yet leudly dar'st our ministring upbraid.
Reign thou in Hell thy Kingdom, let mee serve
In Heav'n God ever blest, and his Divine
Behests obey, worthiest to be obey'd, [185]
Yet Chains in Hell, not Realms expect: mean while
From mee returnd, as erst thou saidst, from flight,
This greeting on thy impious Crest receive.

▲ 撒旦軍與天使軍正面交鋒
杜雷 版畫 1866年

　　亞必迭發動攻擊，正式向撒旦宣戰，雙方人馬隨即正面交鋒，寧靜的天庭頓時陷入刀光劍影、煙塵四起的喧囂中。

本寧靜幸福的天庭帶來什麼？只有動亂與不安。天國絕對不容許暴力和戰爭，快點領著你的黨羽，往那罪惡的地府裡去，或者，你想要我的利劍送你一程？』

　　「『米迦勒，休想用言語威脅我，

你說這是一場邪惡的戰爭，我卻認為
是光榮之戰，因為它是為了自由而
戰。』

「亞必迭的突襲並未讓撒旦退怯，
反而激發他更強烈的鬥志，他踩穩踉
蹌的腳跟，以嚴厲的語氣反擊強敵米
迦勒的話語。

「兩軍首領相互對峙，以仇視的
目光望著對方，空氣中瀰漫著一股殺
氣。終於，撒旦舉劍往前刺去，米迦
勒立刻拔劍還擊，兩把火劍在空中快
速揮舞，劃出一道道圓形的火圈，巨
大的盾牌因為抵擋利劍的攻擊，紛紛
噴濺出刺人眼睛的火光。眾天使看見
這場兇猛的搏鬥，連忙往兩旁退去，
讓出一個廣闊的戰場給他們，避免受
到波及；因此，兩人更加肆無忌憚地
使出猛烈的攻勢。

「兩人雖然力量相當，不分軒輊，
但是米迦勒手中的劍畢竟是打造自天
國的武器庫，刀鋒鋒利無比，只見他
高高舉起寶劍，朝撒旦的劍發出猛烈

So saying, a noble stroke he lifted high,
Which hung not, but so swift with tempest fell [190]
On the proud Crest of Satan, that no sight,
Nor motion of swift thought, less could his Shield
Such ruin intercept: ten paces huge
He back recoild; the tenth on bended knee
His massie Spear upstaid; as if on Earth [195]
Winds under ground or waters forcing way
Sidelong, had push't a Mountain from his seat
Half sunk with all his Pines. Amazement seis'd
The Rebel Thrones, but greater rage to see
Thus foil'd thir mightiest, ours joy filld, and shout, [200]
Presage of Victorie and fierce desire
Of Battel: whereat Michael bid sound
Th' Arch-Angel trumpet; through the vast of Heaven
It sounded, and the faithful Armies rung
Hosanna to the Highest: nor stood at gaze [205]
The adverse Legions, nor less hideous joyn'd
The horrid shock: now storming furie rose,
And clamour such as heard in Heav'n till now
Was never, Arms on Armour clashing bray'd
Horrible discord, and the madding Wheeles [210]
Of brazen Chariots rag'd; dire was the noise
Of conflict; over head the dismal hiss
Of fiery Darts in flaming volies flew,
And flying vaulted either Host with fire.
So under fierie Cope together rush'd [215]
Both Battels maine, with ruinous assault
And inextinguishable rage; all Heav'n
Resounded, and had Earth bin then, all Earth
Had to her Center shook. What wonder? when
Millions of fierce encountring Angels fought [220]
On either side, the least of whom could weild
These Elements, and arm him with the force
Of all thir Regions: how much more of Power
Armie against Armie numberless to raise
Dreadful combustion warring, and disturb, [225]
Though not destroy, thir happie Native seat;
Had not th' Eternal King Omnipotent
From his strong hold of Heav'n high over-rul'd
And limited thir might; though numberd such
As each divided Legion might have seemd [230]

一擊，霎時間，撒旦手中的劍斷成兩截，趁其尚未反應之前，米迦勒又迅速地補上一劍，刺中他的右肋。撒旦被利劍刺傷，痛苦地扭動身體，鮮血從深深的傷口噴湧出來，染紅了金色的盾牌和盔甲。撒旦的護衛軍見狀，連忙奔過來掩護他，一邊把他扶到戰車上休息。

「撒旦躺在戰車上，身體流出泊泊

A numerous Host, in strength each armed hand
A Legion; led in fight, yet Leader seemd
Each Warriour single as in Chief, expert
When to advance, or stand, or turn the sway
Of Battel, open when, and when to close [235]
The ridges of grim Warr; no thought of flight,
None of retreat, no unbecoming deed
That argu'd fear; each on himself reli'd,
As onely in his arm the moment lay
Of victorie; deeds of eternal fame [240]
Were don, but infinite: for wide was spred
That Warr and various; somtimes on firm ground
A standing fight, then soaring on main wing
Tormented all the Air; all Air seemd then
Conflicting Fire: long time in eeven scale [245]
The Battel hung; till Satan, who that day
Prodigious power had shewn, and met in Armes
No equal, raunging through the dire attack
Of fighting Seraphim confus'd, at length
Saw where the Sword of Michael smote, and fell'd [250]
Squadrons at once, with huge two-handed sway
Brandisht aloft the horrid edge came down
Wide wasting; such destruction to withstand
He hasted, and oppos'd the rockie Orb
Of tenfold Adamant, his ample Shield [255]
A vast circumference: At his approach
The great Arch-Angel from his warlike toile
Surceas'd, and glad as hoping here to end
Intestine War in Heav'n, the arch foe subdu'd
Or Captive drag'd in Chains, with hostile frown [260]
And visage all enflam'd first thus began.

Author of evil, unknown till thy revolt,
Unnam'd in Heav'n, now plenteous, as thou seest
These Acts of hateful strife, hateful to all,

< **撒旦被米迦勒刺傷，痛苦不已**
杜雷 版畫 1866年

　　米迦勒手持天國的聖劍，很快就刺傷撒旦，撒旦痛苦的倒臥在，手中的刀劍和盾牌也掉落一旁。

的汁液，覆蓋在傷口上進行修復，雖
然他背叛了上帝，但他的身體仍然具
有天使的靈質，能夠自體療傷，永遠
不會死亡。只要等傷口一復原，他就
能夠重回戰場，繼續戰鬥；但這需要
一點時間，所以他只能眼巴巴地看著

聖米迦勒
法瑞梅 銅雕 1897年

Though heaviest by just measure on thy self [265]
And thy adherents: how hast thou disturb'd
Heav'ns blessed peace, and into Nature brought
Miserie, uncreated till the crime
Of thy Rebellion? how hast thou instill'd
Thy malice into thousands, once upright [270]
And faithful, now prov'd false. But think not here
To trouble Holy Rest; Heav'n casts thee out
From all her Confines. Heav'n the seat of bliss
Brooks not the works of violence and Warr.
Hence then, and evil go with thee along [275]
Thy ofspring, to the place of evil, Hell,
Thou and thy wicked crew; there mingle broiles,
Ere this avenging Sword begin thy doome,
Or som more sudden vengeance wing'd from God
Precipitate thee with augmented paine. [280]

So spake the Prince of Angels; to whom thus
The Adversarie. Nor think thou with wind
Of airie threats to aw whom yet with deeds
Thou canst not. Hast thou turnd the least of these
To flight, or if to fall, but that they rise [285]
Unvanquisht, easier to transact with mee
That thou shouldst hope, imperious, and with threats
To chase me hence? erre not that so shall end
The strife which thou call'st evil, but wee style
The strife of Glorie: which we mean to win, [290]
Or turn this Heav'n it self into the Hell
Thou fablest, here however to dwell free,
If not to reign: mean while thy utmost force,
And join him nam'd Almighty to thy aid,
I flie not, but have sought thee farr and nigh. [295]

They ended parle, and both addresst for fight
Unspeakable; for who, though with the tongue
Of Angels, can relate, or to what things
Liken on Earth conspicuous, that may lift
Human imagination to such highth [300]
Of Godlike Power: for likest Gods they seemd,
Stood they or mov'd, in stature, motion, arms
Fit to decide the Empire of great Heav'n.
Now wav'd thir fierie Swords, and in the Aire

同伴們在戰場上廝殺。

「戰場上的惡鬥持續進行著。加百列對上摩洛，只見他揮舞著軍旗，衝進摩洛的隊伍中，摩洛向他喊道：『不自量力的傢伙，小心我把你綁在車輪上拖著走……。』

「話還來不及說完，就被加百列攔腰刺傷，哀號著往後方逃走。

「大天使尤烈兒和拉斐爾也各自擊敗了叛軍亞得米勒（Adramelec）和阿斯瑪代（Asmadai）。

「另外，亞必迭無法容忍叛軍對上帝的不敬，故發動猛列的攻勢，將亞利（Ariel）、亞略（Arioc）和拉米埃（Ramie）一一打敗，並用烈火灼燒他們。

「就這樣，撒旦叛軍陣營裡能力較強的幾個，陸陸續續地敗下陣來，底下的小囉嘍一見大勢已去，紛紛丟盔卸甲，往陣後奔逃。第一回合，撒旦軍潰敗、天使軍贏得光榮的勝利。

「夜幕襲來，雙方大軍各自紮營佈

Made horrid Circles; two broad Suns thir Shields [305]
Blaz'd opposite, while expectation stood
In horror; from each hand with speed retir'd
Where erst was thickest fight, th' Angelic throng,
And left large field, unsafe within the wind
Of such commotion, such as to set forth [310]
Great things by small, If Natures concord broke,
Among the Constellations warr were sprung,
Two Planets rushing from aspect maligne
Of fiercest opposition in mid Skie,
Should combat, and thir jarring Sphears confound. [315]
Together both with next to Almightie Arme,
Uplifted imminent one stroke they aim'd
That might determine, and not need repeate,
As not of power, at once; nor odds appeerd
In might or swift prevention; but the sword [320]
Of Michael from the Armorie of God
Was giv'n him temperd so, that neither keen
Nor solid might resist that edge: it met
The sword of Satan with steep force to smite
Descending, and in half cut sheere, nor staid, [325]
But with swift wheele reverse, deep entring shar'd
All his right side; then Satan first knew pain,
And writh' d him to and fro convolv'd; so sore
The griding sword with discontinuous wound
Passd through him, but th' Ethereal substance clos'd [330]
Not long divisible, and from the gash
A stream of Nectarous humor issuing flow'd
Sanguin, such as Celestial Spirits may bleed,
And all his Armour staind ere while so bright.
Forthwith on all sides to his aide was run [335]
By Angels many and strong, who interpos'd
Defence, while others bore him on thir Shields
Back to his Chariot; where it stood retir'd
From off the files of warr; there they him laid
Gnashing for anguish and despite and shame [340]
To find himself not matchless, and his pride
Humbl'd by such rebuke, so farr beneath
His confidence to equal God in power.
Yet soon he heal'd; for Spirits that live throughout
Vital in every part, not as frail man [345]
In Entrailes, Heart or Head, Liver or Reines;

Cannot but by annihilating die;
Nor in thir liquid texture mortal wound
Receive, no more then can the fluid Aire:
All Heart they live, all Head, all Eye, all Eare, [350]
All Intellect, all Sense, and as they please,
They Limb themselves, and colour, shape or size
Assume, as likes them best, condense or rare.

Mean while in other parts like deeds deservd
Memorial, where the might of Gabriel fought, [355]
And with fierce Ensignes pierc'd the deep array
Of Moloc furious King, who him defi'd
And at his Chariot wheeles to drag him bound
Threatn'd, nor from the Holie One of Heav'n
Refrein'd his tongue blasphemous; but anon [360]
Down clov'n to the waste, with shatterd Armes
And uncouth paine fled bellowing. On each wing
Uriel and Raphael his vaunting foe,
Though huge, and in a Rock of Diamond Armd,
Vanquish'd Adramelec, and Asmadai, [365]
Two potent Thrones, that to be less then Gods
Disdain'd, but meaner thoughts learnd in thir flight,
Mangl'd with gastly wounds through Plate and Maile,
Nor stood unmindful Abdiel to annoy
The Atheist crew, but with redoubl'd blow [370]
Ariel and Arioc, and the violence
Of Ramiel scorcht and blasted overthrew.
I might relate of thousands, and thir names
Eternize here on Earth; but those elect
Angels contented with thir fame in Heav'n [375]
Seek not the praise of men: the other sort
In might though wondrous and in Acts of Warr,
Nor of Renown less eager, yet by doome
Canceld from Heav'n and sacred memorie,
Nameless in dark oblivion let them dwell. [380]
For strength from Truth divided and from Just,
Illaudable, naught merits but dispraise
And ignominie, yet to glorie aspires
Vain glorious, and through infamie seeks fame:
Therfore Eternal silence be thir doome. [385]

And now thir Mightiest quelld, the battel swerv'd,

聖米迦勒刺傷撒旦
雷尼 油畫 1636年

　　撒旦不敵天使大軍的神兵利器，很快就被米
迦勒一劍刺中，這也讓叛亂的天使軍團一時陣腳
大亂，急忙把撒旦搶救回去休息。

哨，天使軍營中瀰漫著勝利的喜悅，戰敗的那方則正在舉行一場軍事會議。

「『今天我們之所以失敗，並不是因為戰鬥能力比不上他們，而是由於武器不若他們精良，所以想問問大家的意思，是不是要加強武裝，或是誰有更好的計策可以打敗對方？』撒旦站在眾多將領前方，嚴肅地徵詢部屬們的意見，右肋被劍刺傷的地方，已經看不出任何痕跡。

「尼斯洛（Nisroc）懷著憂愁的神色，首先站起來發言：『領導我們爭取自由的首領呀！既然知道落敗的主要原因在於武器，是否就該把討論的重心擺在『如何研製武器』上頭？但是，距離天亮只勝下短短的幾個鐘頭，我們如何能夠製造出威力強大的新武器呢？』

「『這個你放心，事實上，對於新武器我已經完成了初步的設計，它是一個圓柱形、中間鏤空的長形大炮。

With many an inrode gor'd; deformed rout
Enter'd, and foul disorder; all the ground
With shiverd armour strow'n, and on a heap
Chariot and Charioter lay overturnd [390]
And fierie foaming Steeds; what stood, recoyld
Orewearied, through the faint Satanic Host
Defensive scarse, or with pale fear surpris'd,
Then first with fear surpris'd and sense of paine
Fled ignominious, to such evil brought [395]
By sin of disobedience, till that hour
Not liable to fear or flight or paine.
Far otherwise th' inviolable Saints
In Cubic Phalanx firm advanc't entire,
Invulnerable, impenitrably arm'd: [400]
Such high advantages thir innocence
Gave them above thir foes, not to have sinnd,
Not to have disobei'd; in fight they stood
Unwearied, unobnoxious to be pain'd
By wound, though from thir place by violence mov'd. [405]

Now Night her course began, and over Heav'n
Inducing darkness, grateful truce impos'd,
And silence on the odious dinn of Warr:
Under her Cloudie covert both retir'd,
Victor and Vanquisht: on the foughten field [410]
Michael and his Angels prevalent
Encamping, plac'd in Guard thir Watches round,
Cherubic waving fires: on th' other part
Satan with his rebellious disappeerd,
Far in the dark dislodg'd, and void of rest, [415]
His Potentates to Councel call'd by night;
And in the midst thus undismai'd began.

O now in danger tri'd, now known in Armes
Not to be overpowerd, Companions deare,
Found worthy not of Libertie alone, [420]
Too mean pretense, but what we more affect,
Honour, Dominion, Glorie, and renowne,
Who have sustaind one day in doubtful fight
(And if one day, why not Eternal dayes?)
What Heavens Lord had powerfullest to send [425]
Against us from about his Throne, and judg'd

Sufficient to subdue us to his will,
But proves not so: then fallible, it seems,
Of future we may deem him, though till now
Omniscient thought. True is, less firmly arm'd, [430]
Some disadvantage we endur'd and paine,
Till now not known, but known as soon contemnd,
Since now we find this our Empyreal form
Incapable of mortal injurie
Imperishable, and though pierc'd with wound, [435]
Soon closing, and by native vigour heal'd.
Of evil then so small as easie think
The remedie; perhaps more valid Armes,
Weapons more violent, when next we meet,
May serve to better us, and worse our foes, [440]
Or equal what between us made the odds,
In Nature none: if other hidden cause
Left them Superiour, while we can preserve
Unhurt our mindes, and understanding sound,
Due search and consultation will disclose. [445]

He sat; and in th' assembly next upstood
Nisroc, of Principalities the prime;
As one he stood escap't from cruel fight,
Sore toild, his riv'n Armes to havoc hewn,
And cloudie in aspect thus answering spake. [450]
Deliverer from new Lords, leader to free
Enjoyment of our right as Gods; yet hard
For Gods, and too unequal work we find
Against unequal arms to fight in paine,
Against unpaind, impassive; from which evil [455]
Ruin must needs ensue; for what availes
Valour or strength, though matchless, quelld with pain
Which all subdues, and makes remiss the hands
Of Mightiest. Sense of pleasure we may well
Spare out of life perhaps, and not repine, [460]
But live content, which is the calmest life:
But pain is perfet miserie, the worst
Of evils, and excessive, overturnes
All patience. He who therefore can invent
With what more forcible we may offend [465]
Our yet unwounded Enemies, or arme
Our selves with like defence, to me deserves

撒旦思考著如何打敗天使軍
杜雷 版畫 1866年

　　夜幕低垂，受傷的撒旦暗自思索著，他一方面要鼓舞部眾的士氣，一方面要想出好方法，才能對抗天使軍團的神兵利器。

你們可知，在這個滿佈鮮花、果實、芳草和黃金的光明聖境底下，蘊藏了一種黑色的物質，經由靈氣和火泡的淬煉，再經過與光接觸的過程，即能

變成一種光芒四射的美麗物質；把它放進我所設計的長形大炮圓管中，然後在大炮的尾端點燃火苗，便會射出宛若轟雷的驚人火燄，摧毀它所接觸到的任何東西。』撒旦得意洋洋地說著。

「撒旦充滿自信的態度和話語，幫士氣低落的叛軍們打了一劑強心針，他們帶著重新拾回的希望，徹夜不斷地挖土、製造黑色彈藥，並在撒旦的指揮下打造新式武器。天亮之前，所有的攻擊部署便已經完成。

「晨曦在嘹亮的號角聲中醒來，天使軍早已編整行伍、朝氣蓬勃的準備迎接新一回合的挑戰；他們穿著金色盔甲，個個精神飽滿，臉上充滿著無比的自信。昨日一場勝戰，帶給他們無比的信心，相信今天定能殲滅敵軍，把叛逆者全部趕到幽冥裡去。

「『大家注意！撒旦軍正朝向這邊來，快點拿起武器準備迎戰。』偵察天使佐飛爾（Zophiel）從曙光照射的

No less then for deliverance what we owe.

Whereto with look compos'd Satan repli'd.
Not uninvented that, which thou aright [470]
Believst so main to our success, I bring;
Which of us who beholds the bright surface
Of this Ethereous mould whereon we stand,
This continent of spacious Heav'n, adornd
With Plant, Fruit, Flour Ambrosial, Gemms & Gold, [475]
Whose Eye so superficially surveyes
These things, as not to mind from whence they grow
Deep under ground, materials dark and crude,
Of spiritous and fierie spume, till toucht
With Heav'ns ray, and temperd they shoot forth [480]
So beauteous, op'ning to the ambient light.
These in thir dark Nativitie the Deep
Shall yield us pregnant with infernal flame,
Which into hallow Engins long and round
Thick-rammd, at th' other bore with touch of fire [485]
Dilated and infuriate shall send forth
From far with thundring noise among our foes
Such implements of mischief as shall dash
To pieces, and orewhelm whatever stands
Adverse, that they shall fear we have disarmd [490]
The Thunderer of his only dreaded bolt.
Nor long shall be our labour, yet ere dawne,
Effect shall end our wish. Mean while revive;
Abandon fear; to strength and counsel joind
Think nothing hard, much less to be despaird. [495]
He ended, and his words thir drooping chere
Enlightn'd, and thir languisht hope reviv'd.
Th' invention all admir'd, and each, how hee
To be th' inventor miss'd, so easie it seemd
Once found, which yet unfound most would have thought [500]
Impossible: yet haply of thy Race
In future dayes, if Malice should abound,
Some one intent on mischief, or inspir'd
With dev'lish machination might devise
Like instrument to plague the Sons of men [505]
For sin, on warr and mutual slaughter bent.
Forthwith from Councel to the work they flew,
None arguing stood, innumerable hands

山頂飛奔回來，帶來敵軍的動向。

　　「天使軍們聽見佐飛爾的警告，全都提高警覺、握緊兵器，以嚴整的軍容靜待敵軍的到來。

　　「撒旦領著稠密如蜂群的叛軍，邁著整齊的步伐大步走來，「前衛軍們，往左右兩邊站開，讓他們瞧瞧我們追求和平的心意有多麼的熱切呀！」撒旦語帶嘲諷，向自己的軍隊下達命令。

　　「站在前排的叛軍們，迅速地往兩邊分開，露出隱藏在行伍中間的秘密武器 —— 由鋼、鐵和石材鑄造而成的長條形圓柱，裡頭是空心的，它被架在車輪上，像一頭張開血盆大口的怪獸，朝著天使軍猙猙吐信。擺明了撒旦並非真有求和的心意。

　　「天使軍一邊觀察敵軍的新式武器，一邊舉盾防衛。不一會兒，高舉火把的叛軍走到圓柱形武器後方，把火苗往武器的火門點去；迅即濃煙密佈，伴隨著一聲巨響，宛如轟雷般的

Were ready, in a moment up they turnd
Wide the Celestial soile, and saw beneath [510]
Th' originals of Nature in thir crude
Conception; Sulphurous and Nitrous Foame
They found, they mingl'd, and with suttle Art,
Concocted and adusted they reduc'd
To blackest grain, and into store convey'd: [515]
Part hidd'n veins diggd up (nor hath this Earth
Entrails unlike) of Mineral and Stone,
Whereof to found thir Engins and thir Balls
Of missive ruin; part incentive reed
Provide, pernicious with one touch to fire. [520]
So all ere day-spring, under conscious Night
Secret they finish'd, and in order set,
With silent circumspection unespi'd.
Now when fair Morn Orient in Heav'n appeerd
Up rose the Victor Angels, and to Arms [525]
The matin Trumpet Sung: in Arms they stood
Of Golden Panoplie, refulgent Host,
Soon banded; others from the dawning Hills
Lookd round, and Scouts each Coast light-armed scoure,
Each quarter, to descrie the distant foe, [530]
Where lodg'd, or whither fled, or if for fight,
In motion or in alt: him soon they met
Under spred Ensignes moving nigh, in slow
But firm Battalion; back with speediest Sail
Zophiel, of Cherubim the swiftest wing, [535]
Came flying, and in mid Aire aloud thus cri'd.

Arme, Warriors, Arme for fight, the foe at hand,
Whom fled we thought, will save us long pursuit
This day, fear not his flight; so thick a Cloud
He comes, and settl'd in his face I see [540]
Sad resolution and secure: let each
His Adamantine coat gird well, and each
Fit well his Helme, gripe fast his orbed Shield,
Born eevn or high, for this day will pour down,
If I conjecture aught, no drizling showr, [545]
But ratling storm of Arrows barbd with fire.
So warnd he them aware themselves, and soon
In order, quit of all impediment;
Instant without disturb they took Allarm,

炮彈從長管中噴射出來，把千百萬的天使軍炸得撲倒在地、潰不成軍。

「那些機靈地躲過炮彈攻擊的天使軍們，先是猶疑了一會，隨即想到反制的良策，他們丟掉手中的武器，迅速地往高山群峰的方向飛去；他們把高山連根拔起，倒過來握在手上朝撒旦軍丟去。叛軍們看見巨大的山峰向自己飛來，全都嚇得心驚膽顫，逃竄不及的，便被高山壓在底下動彈不得。

「雙方如此你來我往，炮彈和高山互相撞擊發出驚天動地的聲響，把原本靜穆的天庭弄得混亂不堪。

「上帝早已料到這一場災難，默許它的發生乃是為了完成心中願望——讓基督建立宏偉功業，名正言順地接掌天國。於是，正當雙方人馬打得昏天暗地的時刻，祂召來基督，對他說道：『我親愛的兒子呀！該是你出征的時候了，現在就請你領著雷霆、身上配帶精良的裝備，坐我的戰車往戰

And onward move Embattelld; when behold [550]
Not distant far with heavie pace the Foe
Approaching gross and huge; in hollow Cube
Training his devilish Enginrie, impal'd
On every side with shaddowing Squadrons Deep,
To hide the fraud. At interview both stood [555]
A while, but suddenly at head appeerd
Satan: And thus was heard Commanding loud.

Vanguard, to Right and Left the Front unfould;
That all may see who hate us, how we seek
Peace and composure, and with open brest [560]
Stand readie to receive them, if they like
Our overture, and turn not back perverse;
But that I doubt, however witness Heaven,
Heav'n witness thou anon, while we discharge
Freely our part; yee who appointed stand [565]
Do as you have in charge, and briefly touch
What we propound, and loud that all may hear.

So scoffing in ambiguous words he scarce
Had ended; when to Right and Left the Front
Divided, and to either Flank retir'd. [570]
Which to our eyes discoverd new and strange,
A triple mounted row of Pillars laid
On Wheels (for like to Pillars most they seem'd
Or hollow'd bodies made of Oak or Firr
With branches lopt, in Wood or Mountain fell'd) [575]
Brass, Iron, Stonie mould, had not thir mouthes
With hideous orifice gap't on us wide,
Portending hollow truce; at each behind
A Seraph stood, and in his hand a Reed
Stood waving tipt with fire; while we suspense, [580]
Collected stood within our thoughts amus'd,
Not long, for sudden all at once thir Reeds
Put forth, and to a narrow vent appli'd
With nicest touch. Immediate in a flame,
But soon obscur'd with smoak, all Heav'n appeerd, [585]
From those deep throated Engins belcht, whose roar
Emboweld with outragious noise the Air,
And all her entrails tore, disgorging foule
Thir devilish glut, chaind Thunderbolts and Hail

場上去；用我賜與你的權力和威信，
漂漂亮亮地打一場勝戰，讓所有的天
使都能夠心悅誠服，甘心地接受你的
領導。』

「『是的，父親。我將領受您所給
予的權力，把那些背叛您的狂徒，統

聖米迦勒刺傷撒旦
拉斐爾　油畫 1518年

Of Iron Globes, which on the Victor Host [590]
Level'd, with such impetuous furie smote,
That whom they hit, none on thir feet might stand,
Though standing else as Rocks, but down they fell
By thousands, Angel on Arch-Angel rowl'd;
The sooner for thir Arms, unarm'd they might [595]
Have easily as Spirits evaded swift
By quick contraction or remove; but now
Foule dissipation follow'd and forc't rout;
Nor serv'd it to relax thir serried files. [600]
What should they do? if on they rusht, repulse
Repeated, and indecent overthrow
Doubl'd, would render them yet more despis'd,
And to thir foes a laughter; for in view
Stood rankt of Seraphim another row
In posture to displode thir second tire [605]
Of Thunder: back defeated to return
They worse abhorr'd. Satan beheld thir plight,
And to his Mates thus in derision call'd.

O Friends, why come not on these Victors proud?
Ere while they fierce were coming, and when wee, [610]
To entertain them fair with open Front
And Brest, (what could we more?) propounded terms
Of composition, strait they chang'd thir minds,
Flew off, and into strange vagaries fell,
As they would dance, yet for a dance they seemd [615]
Somwhat extravagant and wilde, perhaps
For joy of offerd peace: but I suppose
If our proposals once again were heard
We should compel them to a quick result.

To whom thus Belial in like gamesom mood, [620]
Leader, the terms we sent were terms of weight,
Of hard contents, and full of force urg'd home,
Such as we might perceive amus'd them all,
And stumbl'd many, who receives them right,
Had need from head to foot well understand; [625]
Not understood, this gift they have besides,
They shew us when our foes walk not upright.

So they among themselves in pleasant veine

統驅趕到地獄裡去。純潔的聖徒將
再次圍繞著聖山，高聲歌頌您的恩
典。』

「基督恭敬地回答。說完即起身，
準備前往戰場。

「第三日，旭日初升之際，一架
戰車發出旋風般的呼嘯聲，轟隆隆地
奔至戰場。四個外貌特殊的天使護衛
著戰車，他們各有四張臉孔、四個翅
膀，前面是人臉、右面是獅子的臉、
左面是牛的臉、後面則是鷹的臉；在
他們身體的四周，有火燄上上下下地
跳耀著，火中能夠發出閃電。

「基督身上穿著鑽石製成的著烏陵
（Urim），氣宇軒昂地坐在戰車上，
他的身上背著弓弦和箭袋，袋中放有
三枝雷霆；車子的右邊立著插著鷹翼
的勝利神像，後方則有千萬個天使和
兩萬輛戰車緊緊跟隨著。

「米迦勒看見飄揚在空中的彌賽
亞旗幟，立即整頓軍隊，帶領眾天使
加入基督的隊伍，並把指揮權交給神

Stood scoffing, highthn'd in thir thoughts beyond
All doubt of victorie, eternal might [630]
To match with thir inventions they presum'd
So easie, and of his Thunder made a scorn,
And all his Host derided, while they stood
A while in trouble; but they stood not long,
Rage prompted them at length, and found them arms [635]
Against such hellish mischief fit to oppose.
Forthwith (behold the excellence, the power
Which God hath in his mighty Angels plac'd)
Thir Arms away they threw, and to the Hills
(For Earth hath this variety from Heav'n [640]
Of pleasure situate in Hill and Dale)
Light as the Lightning glimps they ran, they flew,
From thir foundations loosning to and fro
They pluckt the seated Hills with all thir load,
Rocks, Waters, Woods, and by the shaggie tops [645]
Up lifting bore them in thir hands: Amaze,
Be sure, and terrour seis'd the rebel Host,
When coming towards them so dread they saw
The bottom of the Mountains upward turn'd,
Till on those cursed Engins triple-row [650]
They saw them whelm'd, and all thir confidence
Under the weight of Mountains buried deep,
Themselves invaded next, and on thir heads
Main Promontories flung, which in the Air
Came shadowing, and opprest whole Legions arm'd, [655]
Thir armor help'd thir harm, crush't in and bruis'd
Into thir substance pent, which wrought them pain
Implacable, and many a dolorous groan,
Long strugling underneath, ere they could wind
Out of such prison, though Spirits of purest light, [660]
Purest at first, now gross by sinning grown.
The rest in imitation to like Armes
Betook them, and the neighbouring Hills uptore;
So Hills amid the Air encounterd Hills
Hurl'd to and fro with jaculation dire, [665]
That under ground, they fought in dismal shade;
Infernal noise; Warr seem'd a civil Game
To this uproar; horrid confusion heapt
Upon confusion rose: and now all Heav'n
Had gone to wrack, with ruin overspred, [670]

子。

「撒旦遠遠地瞧見神子帶著滿身的
榮光而來，心中非但未能即時醒悟，

▽ 米迦勒集合部衆，與基督並肩作戰
杜雷版畫 1866年

　　氣宇軒昂的基督奉上帝的旨意領軍出征，米
迦勒看到基督親上戰場，連忙集合天使部衆加入
基督的隊伍，撒旦率領的軍隊不敵耶穌的雷霆，
很快就被打得四處竄逃。

Had not th' Almightie Father where he sits
Shrin'd in his Sanctuarie of Heav'n secure,
Consulting on the sum of things, foreseen
This tumult, and permitted all, advis'd:
That his great purpose he might so fulfill, [675]
To honour his Anointed Son aveng'd
Upon his enemies, and to declare
All power on him transferr'd: whence to his Son
Th' Assessor of his Throne he thus began.

Effulgence of my Glorie, Son belov'd, [680]
Son in whose face invisible is beheld
Visibly, what by Deitie I am,
And in whose hand what by Decree I doe,
Second Omnipotence, two dayes are past,
Two dayes, as we compute the dayes of Heav'n, [685]
Since Michael and his Powers went forth to tame
These disobedient; sore hath been thir fight,
As likeliest was, when two such Foes met arm'd;
For to themselves I left them, and thou knowst,
Equal in thir Creation they were form'd, [690]
Save what sin hath impaird, which yet hath wrought
Insensibly, for I suspend thir doom;
Whence in perpetual fight they needs must last
Endless, and no solution will be found:
Warr wearied hath perform'd what Warr can do, [695]
And to disorder'd rage let loose the reines,
With Mountains as with Weapons arm'd, which makes
Wild work in Heav'n, and dangerous to the maine.
Two dayes are therefore past, the third is thine;
For thee I have ordain'd it, and thus farr [700]
Have sufferd, that the Glorie may be thine
Of ending this great Warr, since none but Thou
Can end it. Into thee such Vertue and Grace
Immense I have transfus'd, that all may know
In Heav'n and Hell thy Power above compare, [705]
And this perverse Commotion governd thus,
To manifest thee worthiest to be Heir
Of all things, to be Heir and to be King
By Sacred Unction, thy deserved right.
Go then thou Mightiest in thy Fathers might, [710]
Ascend my Chariot, guide the rapid Wheeles

反而生出更強烈的妒意來，嫉妒讓他抱持著『寧為玉碎、不為瓦全』的心理，發動更猛烈的攻擊。

「基督來到戰場，對全體天使軍說道：『你們為了維護造物者的真理，在戰場上奮不顧身地與叛軍作戰，上帝深受感動，為避免讓我軍過度疲累，故賜予我榮譽，派我到此地來殲滅叛逆者，現在起，你們只需在旁邊觀戰即可。』

「眾將領聽神子這樣一說，便先把手上的山峰全部歸返原位，讓它們恢復原來美麗的樣貌；然後退到戰場後方，觀看神子如何發揮威力，消滅為數眾多的叛軍。

「基督駕著戰車來到撒旦軍面前，嚴肅的臉孔上，閃現著憤怒的光芒，強烈地讓人不敢直視。他舉起手來朝叛軍發射出萬束雷霆，霎時間，電光閃閃、雷聲隆隆，撒旦軍的新式武器一下子就被擊成灰燼；四個護衛天使也跟著揮動翅膀，擊出威力強大的閃

That shake Heav'ns basis, bring forth all my Warr,
My Bow and Thunder, my Almightie Arms
Gird on, and Sword upon thy puissant Thigh;
Pursue these sons of Darkness, drive them out [715]
From all Heav'ns bounds into the utter Deep:
There let them learn, as likes them, to despise
God and Messiah his anointed King.

He said, and on his Son with Rayes direct
Shon full, he all his Father full exprest [720]
Ineffably into his face receiv'd,
And thus the filial Godhead answering spake.

O Father, O Supream of heav'nly Thrones,
First, Highest, Holiest, Best, thou always seekst
To glorifie thy Son, I always thee, [725]
As is most just; this I my Glorie account,
My exaltation, and my whole delight,
That thou in me well pleas'd, declarst thy will
Fulfill'd, which to fulfil is all my bliss.
Scepter and Power, thy giving, I assume, [730]
And gladlier shall resign, when in the end
Thou shalt be All in All, and I in thee
For ever, and in mee all whom thou lov'st:
But whom thou hat'st, I hate, and can put on
Thy terrors, as I put thy mildness on, [735]
Image of thee in all things; and shall soon,
Armd with thy might, rid heav'n of these rebell'd,
To thir prepar'd ill Mansion driven down
To chains of darkness, and th' undying Worm,
That from thy just obedience could revolt, [740]
Whom to obey is happiness entire.
Then shall thy Saints unmixt, and from th' impure
Farr separate, circling thy holy Mount
Unfeigned Halleluiahs to thee sing,
Hymns of high praise, and I among them chief. [745]
So said, he o're his Scepter bowing, rose
From the right hand of Glorie where he sate,
And the third sacred Morn began to shine
Dawning through Heav'n: forth rush'd with whirl-wind sound
The Chariot of Paternal Deitie, [750]
Flashing thick flames, Wheele within Wheele, undrawn,

電，把敵軍打得四處逃竄、武器丟得
滿地都是。

　　「基督見撒旦軍已經喪失作戰的勇
氣，便收起雷霆，不再發射；因為他
主要的目的不在於徹底消滅叛逆者，
而是要把他們驅逐到黑暗的地獄去，
接受烈燄焚身的懲罰。於是他命令潰

▽ 天使的叛亂
布雷克　水彩畫 1808年
　　耶穌基督背著弓和箭袋，袋裡有三枚雷霆，
當他朝撒旦叛軍發射萬丈的雷霆，根本不需其他
天使支援，就把敵人打得潰不成軍。

It self instinct with Spirit, but convoyd
By four Cherubic shapes, four Faces each
Had wondrous, as with Starrs thir bodies all
And Wings were set with Eyes, with Eyes the wheels [755]
Of Beril, and careering Fires between;
Over thir heads a chrystal Firmament,
Whereon a Saphir Throne, inlaid with pure
Amber, and colours of the showrie Arch.
Hee in Celestial Panoplie all armd [760]
Of radiant Urim, work divinely wrought,
Ascended, at his right hand Victorie
Sate Eagle-wing'd, beside him hung his Bow
And Quiver with three-bolted Thunder stor'd,
And from about him fierce Effusion rowld [765]
Of smoak and bickering flame, and sparkles dire;
Attended with ten thousand thousand Saints,
He onward came, farr off his coming shon,
And twentie thousand (I thir number heard)
Chariots of God, half on each hand were seen: [770]
Hee on the wings of Cherub rode sublime
On the Chrystallin Skie, in Saphir Thron'd.
Illustrious farr and wide, but by his own
First seen, them unexpected joy surpriz'd,
When the great Ensign of Messiah blaz'd [775]
Aloft by Angels born, his Sign in Heav'n:
Under whose Conduct Michael soon reduc'd
His Armie, circumfus'd on either Wing,
Under thir Head imbodied all in one.
Before him Power Divine his way prepar'd; [780]
At his command the uprooted Hills retir'd
Each to his place, they heard his voice and went
Obsequious, Heav'n his wonted face renewd,
And with fresh Flourets Hill and Valley smil'd.
This saw his hapless Foes but stood obdur'd, [785]
And to rebellious fight rallied thir Powers
Insensate, hope conceiving from despair.
In heav'nly Spirits could such perverseness dwell?
But to convince the proud what Signs availe,
Or Wonders move th' obdurate to relent? [790]
They hard'nd more by what might most reclame,
Grieving to see his Glorie, at the sight
Took envie, and aspiring to his highth,

△ 墜落的天使
林堡兄弟 插畫 1413~1416年

　　墜落天使是中世紀相當流行的繪畫主題，彰顯善惡交戰，邪不勝正的真理。

不成軍的叛徒集合起來，把他們驅趕到天界的境頭，喝令他們跳下；撒旦軍擠在水晶城牆的缺口，沒有人敢跳下無底深淵。最後，神子發出猛烈的

Stood reimbattell'd fierce, by force or fraud
Weening to prosper, and at length prevaile [795]
Against God and Messiah, or to fall
In universal ruin last, and now
To final Battel drew, disdaining flight,
Or faint retreat; when the great Son of God
To all his Host on either hand thus spake. [800]

Stand still in bright array ye Saints, here stand
Ye Angels arm'd, this day from Battel rest;
Faithful hath been your warfare, and of God
Accepted, fearless in his righteous Cause,
And as ye have receivd, so have ye don [805]
Invincibly; but of this cursed crew
The punishment to other hand belongs,
Vengeance is his, or whose he sole appoints;
Number to this dayes work is not ordain'd
Nor multitude, stand onely and behold [810]
Gods indignation on these Godless pourd
By mee, not you but mee they have despis'd,
Yet envied; against mee is all thir rage,
Because the Father, t' whom in Heav'n supream
Kingdom and Power and Glorie appertains, [815]
Hath honourd me according to his will.
Therefore to mee thir doom he hath assig'n'd;
That they may have thir wish, to trie with mee
In Battel which the stronger proves, they all,
Or I alone against them, since by strength [820]
They measure all, of other excellence
Not emulous, nor care who them excells;
Nor other strife with them do I voutsafe.

So spake the Son, and into terrour chang'd
His count'nance too severe to be beheld [825]
And full of wrauth bent on his Enemies.
At once the Four spred out thir Starrie wings
With dreadful shade contiguous, and the Orbes
Of his fierce Chariot rowld, as with the sound
Of torrent Floods, or of a numerous Host. [830]
Hee on his impious Foes right onward drove,
Gloomie as Night; under his burning Wheeles
The stedfast Empyrean shook throughout,

^ 黑暗地獄是撒旦軍墜落的終點
杜雷 版畫 1866年

一擊，把他們全數逐出天門。

「數量龐大的撒旦軍從天庭往下墜落，發出巨大的哀號聲，驚動了『混沌』；九天後，終於落在陰森炙熱的地獄。

「另一方面，眾天使手持代表勝利的棕櫚枝前去迎接基督，歌頌他成為勝利的君主；彌賽亞凱旋而歸，重新

All but the Throne it self of God. Full soon
Among them he arriv'd; in his right hand [835]
Grasping ten thousand Thunders, which he sent
Before him, such as in thir Soules infix'd
Plagues; they astonish all resistance lost,
All courage; down thir idle weapons drop'd;
O're Shields and Helmes, and helmed heads he rode [840]
Of Thrones and mighty Seraphim prostrate,
That wisht the Mountains now might be again
Thrown on them as a shelter from his ire.
Nor less on either side tempestuous fell
His arrows, from the fourfold-visag'd Foure, [845]
Distinct with eyes, and from the living Wheels,
Distinct alike with multitude of eyes,
One Spirit in them rul'd, and every eye
Glar'd lightning, and shot forth pernicious fire
Among th' accurst, that witherd all thir strength, [850]
And of thir wonted vigour left them draind,
Exhausted, spiritless, afflicted, fall'n.
Yet half his strength he put not forth, but check'd
His Thunder in mid Volie, for he meant
Not to destroy, but root them out of Heav'n: [855]
The overthrown he rais'd, and as a Heard
Of Goats or timerous flock together throngd
Drove them before him Thunder-struck, pursu'd
With terrors and with furies to the bounds
And Chrystal wall of Heav'n, which op'ning wide, [860]
Rowld inward, and a spacious Gap disclos'd
Into the wastful Deep; the monstrous sight
Strook them with horror backward, but far worse
Urg'd them behind; headlong themselves they threw
Down from the verge of Heav'n, Eternal wrauth [865]
Burnt after them to the bottomless pit.

Hell heard th' unsufferable noise, Hell saw
Heav'n ruining from Heav'n and would have fled

≺ **墜落的天使**
油畫 十四世紀初
　　據說叛亂的天使連續墜落了九天九夜，才落到炙熱黑暗的地獄。

坐到上帝寶座的右邊，享受幸福的榮
光。」

　　拉斐爾敘述完這場天庭大戰之後，
語重心長的對亞當說：

　　「我們發現魔鬼撒旦已經從地獄
脫逃，潛伏在伊甸樂園裡；他來到此
地，意圖誘惑人類步上他的後塵，藉
此報復上帝。我詳細的向你講述這場
天庭戰爭，是希望你能謹
記背叛上帝的悲慘下場；
你和你的弱者 —— 夏娃[4]，
千萬要順從上帝的命令，
可別被撒旦欺騙，做出犯
罪的事來。」

註4：《新約‧彼得前書》：「你們作
　　丈夫的也要按情理和妻子同住，
　　因她比你軟弱，與你一同承受生
　　命之恩的，所以要敬重她。」

Affrighted; but strict Fate had cast too deep
Her dark foundations, and too fast had bound. [870]
Nine dayes they fell; confounded Chaos roard,
And felt tenfold confusion in thir fall
Through his wilde Anarchie, so huge a rout
Incumberd him with ruin: Hell at last

▽ 撒旦軍連續往下墜落九天
杜雷 版畫 1866年

　　耶穌基督並不想趕盡殺絕，祂只是要
把這群叛亂的天使趕出天國，送他們到地
獄受懲罰。天堂與地獄的距離是如此遙
遠，撒旦軍團連續墜落了九天九夜，才落
到黑暗地獄的終點。

Yawning receavd them whole, and on them clos'd, [875]
Hell thir fit habitation fraught with fire
Unquenchable, the house of woe and paine.
Disburdnd Heav'n rejoic'd, and soon repaird
Her mural breach, returning whence it rowld.
Sole Victor from th' expulsion of his Foes [880]
Messiah his triumphal Chariot turnd:
To meet him all his Saints, who silent stood
Eye witnesses of his Almightie Acts,
With Jubilie advanc'd; and as they went,
Shaded with branching Palme, each order bright, [885]
Sung Triumph, and him sung Victorious King,
Son, Heir, and Lord, to him Dominion giv'n,
Worthiest to Reign: he celebrated rode
Triumphant through mid Heav'n, into the Courts
And Temple of his mightie Father Thron'd [890]
On high: who into Glorie him receav'd,
Where now he sits at the right hand of bliss.

Thus measuring things in Heav'n by things on Earth
At thy request, and that thou maist beware
By what is past, to thee I have reveal'd [895]
What might have else to human Race bin hid;
The discord which befel, and Warr in Heav'n
Among th' Angelic Powers, and the deep fall
Of those too high aspiring, who rebelld
With Satan, hee who envies now thy state, [900]
Who now is plotting how he may seduce
Thee also from obedience, that with him
Bereavd of happiness thou maist partake
His punishment, Eternal miserie;
Which would be all his solace and revenge, [905]
As a despite don against the most High,
Thee once to gaine Companion of his woe.
But list'n not to his Temptations, warne
Thy weaker; let it profit thee to have heard
By terrible Example the reward [910]
Of disobedience; firm they might have stood,
Yet fell; remember, and fear to transgress.

˄ 墜落地獄
布慈 油畫 1450年

　　幾乎所有的宗教都有一個充滿各種
刑罰的可怕地獄。如果生前作惡，死後
就會墜入地獄，接受永無止盡的處罰。
撒旦和他的黨羽因為不服耶穌的領導而
群起叛亂，最後也因此被打入地獄。

7 > 創造新世界

　　亞當仔細聆聽天使拉斐爾講述於他出生之前，在天庭發生的
一場天使與叛徒的激戰；戰後撒旦和他的部眾，被驅逐到地獄受
罰。拉斐爾並且提醒亞當，小心防備魔鬼撒旦的入侵。亞當明確
地表明對上帝的忠誠順從，並趁此難得的機會，要求拉斐爾告知
人類生活的世界從何而來，又是怎麼被創造出來的。

「神聖的寶座旁竟然會發生戰爭？純潔的天使怎會生出仇恨的思想？你說發動叛亂者已來到樂園中，潛藏在我們身旁待機而動，這消息真叫我膽戰心驚，人類薄弱的力量，如何能夠抵擋叛逆天使的威力？」

亞當想到天庭上那場戰爭的激烈場面，忍不住擔心起來。

「你大可以放心，撒旦用的是心理戰術，他把邪惡的思想灌輸到人類的腦海，讓人類做出犯罪的事來。所以，只要你們能夠秉持善念，堅守上帝的規範，就不必害怕魔鬼的入侵。」拉斐爾安慰亞當。

「感謝你不遠千里而來，預先警告我們，使我們心中有所防備；對於上帝，我們滿懷敬意，百分之百地順從祂的指示，從來不敢有半點邪惡

◁ **伊甸園**

漢斯多瑪 油畫 1896年

上帝替人類打造了一個新的世界，那裡只有喜悅和幸福，沒有一點惡的因子，如果人類通過順從的試煉，便能成為天國的居民，伊甸園也將與上帝的天庭合而為一。

Descend from Heav'n Urania, by that name
If rightly thou art call'd, whose Voice divine
Following, above th' Olympian Hill I soare,
Above the flight of Pegasean wing.
The meaning, not the Name I call: for thou [5]
Nor of the Muses nine, nor on the top
Of old Olympus dwell'st, but Heav'nlie borne,
Before the Hills appeerd, or Fountain flow'd,
Thou with Eternal Wisdom didst converse,
Wisdom thy Sister, and with her didst play [10]
In presence of th' Almightie Father, pleas'd
With thy Celestial Song. Up led by thee
Into the Heav'n of Heav'ns I have presum'd,
An Earthlie Guest, and drawn Empyreal Aire,
Thy tempring; with like safetie guided down [15]
Return me to my Native Element:
Least from this flying Steed unrein'd, (as once
Bellerophon, though from a lower Clime)
Dismounted, on th' Aleian Field I fall
Erroneous there to wander and forlorne. [20]
Half yet remaines unsung, but narrower bound
Within the visible Diurnal Spheare;
Standing on Earth, not rapt above the Pole,
More safe I Sing with mortal voice, unchang'd
To hoarce or mute, though fall'n on evil dayes, [25]
On evil dayes though fall'n, and evil tongues;
In darkness, and with dangers compast round,
And solitude; yet not alone, while thou
Visit'st my slumbers Nightly, or when Morn
Purples the East: still govern thou my Song, [30]
Urania, and fit audience find, though few.
But drive farr off the barbarous dissonance
Of Bacchus and his Revellers, the Race
Of that wilde Rout that tore the Thracian Bard
In Rhodope, where Woods and Rocks had Eares [35]
To rapture, till the savage clamor dround
Both Harp and Voice; nor could the Muse defend
Her Son. So fail not thou, who thee implores:
For thou art Heav'nlie, shee an empty dreame.

Say Goddess, what ensu'd when Raphael, [40]
The affable Arch-Angel, had forewarn'd

的念頭；我相信，無論魔鬼施以何種
詭譎的計謀，都無法煽動我們背叛上
帝。」

　　亞當重拾笑容，滿懷信心地說著。
他想起心中長久以來的疑惑，於是繼
續向拉斐爾問道：

　　「關於天空、大地和伊甸園是怎
樣被創造出來的？對於這片美麗的居
所，我充滿著濃厚的興趣，能否冒昧
地請你說一說呢？」

　　「嗯！關於造物主的各項創造物，
若要用人類所能理解的言語陳述，以
我的能力恐怕無法說得明白，但上帝
派我到這裡來的主要目的，就是為你
解答疑惑，所以我願意試著說給你
聽。只是求取知識就像吃東西一樣，
吃得剛剛好，有助於身體的健康，若
暴飲暴食不懂得節制，反會造成身體
的負擔；所以我告訴你的知識，必須
有一定的界限，希望你能夠明白。」

　　亞當向拉斐爾點點頭，於是拉斐爾
開始描述世界創造的過程。

Adam by dire example to beware
Apostasie, by what befell in Heaven
To those Apostates, least the like befall
In Paradise to Adam or his Race, [45]
Charg'd not to touch the interdicted Tree,
If they transgress, and slight that sole command,
So easily obeyd amid the choice
Of all tastes else to please thir appetite,
Though wandring. He with his consorted Eve [50]
The storie heard attentive, and was fill'd
With admiration, and deep Muse to heare
Of things so high and strange, things to thir thought
So unimaginable as hate in Heav'n,
And Warr so neer the Peace of God in bliss [55]
With such confusion: but the evil soon
Driv'n back redounded as a flood on those
From whom it sprung, impossible to mix
With Blessedness. Whence Adam soon repeal'd
The doubts that in his heart arose: and now [60]
Led on, yet sinless, with desire to know
What neerer might concern him, how this World
Of Heav'n and Earth conspicious first began,
When, and whereof created, for what cause,
What within Eden or without was done [65]
Before his memorie, as one whose drouth
Yet scarce allay'd still eyes the current streame,
Whose liquid murmur heard new thirst excites,
Proceeded thus to ask his Heav'nly Guest.

Great things, and full of wonder in our eares, [70]
Farr differing from this World, thou hast reveal'd
Divine interpreter, by favour sent
Down from the Empyrean to forewarne
Us timely of what might else have bin our loss,
Unknown, which human knowledg could not reach: [75]
For which to the infinitly Good we owe
Immortal thanks, and his admonishment
Receave with solemne purpose to observe
Immutably his sovran will, the end
Of what we are. But since thou hast voutsaf't [80]
Gently for our instruction to impart
Things above Earthly thought, which yet concernd

「那時，叛逆天使們被基督驅逐到荒漠的幽冥，全能者坐在寶座上對祂的獨生子說：『覷覷天庭寶座的敵人已墜落地獄，這場戰爭造成天國莫大的損傷，我會將它修復成以往的美好。除此之外，我打算在天庭之外另造一個新的世界，讓新的物種——人類，在其中生衍繁殖；那兒將充滿著無窮的喜悅和幸福，沒有一點『惡』的因子。人類也將受到『順從』的試煉，如果他們能夠通過考驗，便能變成天國的居民，新世界也將變成天國，與我們合成一塊兒。兒啊！這創造新世界的工作，就借由你的手去完成吧！』

「神子領受上帝的指示，在一片歡慶勝利和讚美全能者的聖歌聲中，領著為數眾多的天使來到兩座銅山之間的武器庫[1]，先配戴精良的裝備，隨即登上戰車出發。

「『喀答！』

「天門發出和諧的聲音，為創造

Our knowing, as to highest wisdom seemd,
Deign to descend now lower, and relate
What may no less perhaps availe us known, [85]
How first began this Heav'n which we behold
Distant so high, with moving Fires adornd
Innumerable, and this which yeelds or fills
All space, the ambient Aire, wide interfus'd
Imbracing round this florid Earth, what cause [90]
Mov'd the Creator in his holy Rest
Through all Eternitie so late to build
In Chaos, and the work begun, how soon
Absolv'd, if unforbid thou maist unfould
What wee, not to explore the secrets aske [95]
Of his Eternal Empire, but the more
To magnifie his works, the more we know.
And the great Light of Day yet wants to run
Much of his Race though steep, suspens in Heav'n
Held by thy voice, thy potent voice he heares, [100]
And longer will delay to heare thee tell
His Generation, and the rising Birth
Of Nature from the unapparent Deep:
Or if the Starr of Eevning and the Moon
Haste to thy audience, Night with her will bring [105]
Silence, and Sleep listning to thee will watch,
Or we can bid his absence, till thy Song
End, and dismiss thee ere the Morning shine.

Thus Adam his illustrious Guest besought:

And thus the Godlike Angel answerd milde. [110]
This also thy request with caution askt
Obtaine: though to recount Almightie works
What words or tongue of Seraph can suffice,
Or heart of man suffice to comprehend?
Yet what thou canst attain, which best may serve [115]
To glorifie the Maker, and inferr
Thee also happier, shall not be withheld
Thy hearing, such Commission from above

註1：《舊約‧撒迦利亞書》：「我又舉目觀看，見有四輛車從兩山中間出來，那山是銅山。」

新世界的隊伍啟開了。神子站在天界向外看，只見陰暗無邊的深淵波濤洶湧，宛如一座座巨山直衝上來。

「『停止吧！混亂與喧鬧。』

「隨著基督的喝斥聲，眾天使飛向『混沌』讓出的空間，開始著手於新世界的創造。

「神子拿出一個黃金製的圓規，一腳立定在中心點，一腳則高旋至遼闊的茫茫深淵，畫出一個大圓；然後他說：

「『這就是新世界的範圍。』

「於是，在這個界限裡，新天地被神子創造了出來。

「就在這個新天地裡，天神的靈張開雙翼，覆於平靜的水面，把生命的活力灌注在其中；水中的殘餘物質沉澱下去，變得堅硬，慢慢形成圓形的球體 ── 地球，懸掛在空氣的中心。然後，天神說：

「『要有光！』

「就有了光，光中有第五元素，乃

I have receav'd, to answer thy desire
Of knowledge within bounds; beyond abstain [120]
To ask, nor let thine own inventions hope
Things not reveal'd, which th' invisible King,
Onely Omniscient hath supprest in Night,
To none communicable in Earth or Heaven:
Anough is left besides to search and know. [125]
But Knowledge is as food, and needs no less
Her Temperance over Appetite, to know
In measure what the mind may well contain,
Oppresses else with Surfet, and soon turns
Wisdom to Folly, as Nourishment to Winde. [130]

Know then, that after Lucifer from Heav'n
(So call him, brighter once amidst the Host
Of Angels, then that Starr the Starrs among)
Fell with his flaming Legions through the Deep
Into his place, and the great Son returnd [135]
Victorious with his Saints, th' Omnipotent
Eternal Father from his Throne beheld
Thir multitude, and to his Son thus spake.

At least our envious Foe hath fail'd, who thought
All like himself rebellious, by whose aid [140]
This inaccessible high strength, the seat
Of Deitie supream, us dispossest,
He trusted to have seis'd, and into fraud
Drew many, whom thir place knows here no more;
Yet farr the greater part have kept, I see, [145]
Thir station, Heav'n yet populous retaines
Number sufficient to possess her Realmes
Though wide, and this high Temple to frequent
With Ministeries due and solemn Rites:
But least his heart exalt him in the harme [150]
Already done, to have dispeopl'd Heav'n
My damage fondly deem'd, I can repaire
That detriment, if such it be to lose
Self-lost, and in a moment will create
Another World, out of one man a Race [155]
Of men innumerable, there to dwell,
Not here, till by degrees of merit rais'd
They open to themselves at length the way

來自『混沌』先前統治的深淵；當時尚無太陽，光被包裹在東方的雲團中，使雲層透出光芒來。上帝喜愛這光，便以球體的半邊來區分光和暗，光明的那邊稱為晝，黑暗的那邊叫做夜。這是頭一日 [2]。

▽ 古老的年代
布雷克插畫 1797年

　　上帝以黃金圓規畫向茫茫深淵，決定新世界的範圍。

Up hither, under long obedience tri'd,
And Earth be chang'd to Heav'n, & Heav'n to Earth, [160]
One Kingdom, Joy and Union without end.
Mean while inhabit laxe, ye Powers of Heav'n,
And by my Word, begotten Son, by thee
This I perform, speak thou, and be it don:
My overshadowing Spirit and might with thee [165]
I send along, ride forth, and bid the Deep
Within appointed bounds be Heav'n and Earth,
Boundless the Deep, because I am who fill
Infinitude, nor vacuous the space.
Though I uncircumscrib'd my self retire, [170]
And put not forth my goodness, which is free
To act or not, Necessitie and Chance
Approach not mee, and what I will is Fate.

So spake th' Almightie, and to what he spake
His Word, the Filial Godhead, gave effect. [175]
Immediate are the Acts of God, more swift
Then time or motion, but to human ears
Cannot without process of speech be told,
So told as earthly notion can receave.
Great triumph and rejoycing was in Heav'n [180]
When such was heard declar'd the Almightie's will;
Glorie they sung to the most High, good will
To future men, and in thir dwellings peace:
Glorie to him whose just avenging ire
Had driven out th' ungodly from his sight [185]
And th' habitations of the just; to him
Glorie and praise, whose wisdom had ordain'd
Good out of evil to create, in stead
Of Spirits maligne a better Race to bring
Into thir vacant room, and thence diffuse [190]
His good to Worlds and Ages infinite.
So sang the Hierarchies: Mean while the Son
On his great Expedition now appeer'd,
Girt with Omnipotence, with Radiance crown'd
Of Majestie Divine, Sapience and Love [195]
Immense, and all his Father in him shon.
About his Chariot numberless were pour'd
Cherub and Seraph, Potentates and Thrones,
And Vertues, winged Spirits, and Chariots wing'd,

「天神說：

「『諸水之間要有天空，諸水之間要上下分開。』

「於是就有了天空和空氣，空氣清澈澄淨，裡頭有許多元素，直擴展到凸形圓球的球面；地球上的諸多水域平靜地流動著，遠離了混沌的喧鬧和紊亂。這是第二日。

「這時，地球被海水包圍著，彷彿

From the Armoury of God, where stand of old [200]
Myriads between two brazen Mountains lodg'd
Against a solemn day, harnest at hand,
Celestial Equipage; and now came forth
Spontaneous, for within them Spirit livd,
Attendant on thir Lord: Heav'n op'nd wide [205]
Her ever during Gates, Harmonious sound
On golden Hinges moving, to let forth
The King of Glorie in his powerful Word
And Spirit coming to create new Worlds.
On heav'nly ground they stood, and from the shore [210]
They view'd the vast immeasurable Abyss
Outrageous as a Sea, dark, wasteful, wilde,
Up from the bottom turn'd by furious windes
And surging waves, as Mountains to assault
Heav'ns highth, and with the Center mix the Pole. [215]

註2：上帝創造天地的過程出自《舊約‧創世紀》：「起初神創造天地。地是空虛混沌，淵面黑暗；神的靈運行在水面上。神說：『要有光』，就有了光。神看光是好的，就把光暗分開了。神稱光為晝，稱暗為夜。有晚上，有早晨，這是頭一日。神說：『諸水之間要有空氣，將水分為上下。』神就造出空氣，將空氣以下的水、空氣以上的水分開了。事就這樣成了。神稱空氣為天。有晚上，有早晨，是第二日。神說：『天下的水要聚在一處，使旱地露出來。』事就這樣成了。神稱旱地為地，稱水的聚處為海。神看著是好的。神說：『地要發生青草和結種子的菜蔬，並結果子的樹木，各從其類，果子都包著核。』事就這樣成了。於是地發生了青草和結種子的菜蔬，各從其類；並結果子的樹木，各從其類，果子都包著核。神看著是好的。有晚上，有早晨，是第三日。神說：『天上要有光體，可以分晝夜，作記號，定節令、日子、年歲，並要發光在天空，普照在地上。』事就這樣成了。於是神造了兩個大光，大的管晝，小的管夜，又造眾星，就把這些光擺列在天空，普照在地上，管理晝夜，分別明暗。神看著是好的。有晚上，有早晨，是第四日。神說：『水要多多滋生有生命的物，要有雀鳥飛在地面以上，在天空之中。』神就造出大魚，和水中所滋生各樣有生命的動物，各從其類。又造出各樣飛鳥，各從其類。神看著是好的。神就賜福給這一切說：『滋生繁多，充滿海中的水；雀鳥也要多生在地上。』有晚上，有早晨，是第五日。神說：『地要生出活物來，各從其類；牲畜、昆蟲、野獸，各從其類。』事就這樣成了。於是神造出野獸，各從其類；牲畜，各從其類；地上一切昆蟲，各從其類。神看著是好的。神說：『我們要照著我們的形像，按著我們的樣式造人，使他們管理海裡的魚、空中的鳥、地上的牲畜和全地，並地上所爬的一切昆蟲。神就照著自己的形像造人，乃是照著他的形像造男造女。神就賜福給他們，又對他們說：『要生養眾多，遍滿地面，治理這地；也要管理海裡的魚、空中的鳥，和地上各樣行動的活物。』神說：『看哪！我將遍地上一切結種子的菜蔬，和一切樹上所結有核的果子，全賜給你們作食物。至於地上的走獸和空中的飛鳥，並各樣爬在地上有生命的物，我將青草賜給他們作食物。』事就這樣成了。神看著一切所造的都甚好。有晚上，有早晨，是第六日。　天地萬物都造齊了。到第七日，神造物的工已經完畢，就在第七日歇了他一切的工，安息了。神賜福給第七日，定為聖日，因為在這日，神歇了他一切創造的工，就安息了。」

子宮中的胎兒，裹覆在溫暖的羊水中吸取養分，表面溫暖的水氣滋養著地球，使它慢慢地成形。天神說：

「『天下的水要聚在一起，使陸地顯露出來。』

「於是群山出現，高聳入雲；山與山之間的河床，流水洶湧奔騰，爭先恐後地往前竄去，直到諸水的匯聚地——海洋。因此，除去海洋部分，地球表面剩下的其他乾燥無流水的部分，便稱作陸地。天神又說：

「『讓陸地上冒出青草和結種子的蔬菜，還有結果實的樹木，並讓種子自然地落在地上。』

「隨即，嫩綠的青草從地底冒出來，大地鋪上了一層青綠色的毯子，各種顏色的花朵陸續綻放、繽紛美麗，傳來芳香陣陣。接著，葡萄藤蔓纏繞攀爬，結出一串串晶盈剔透的葡

> **上帝創造世界**
圖畫聖經 1229年

　　上帝藉由圓規輔助，已經創造出渾圓的太陽和月亮。被海洋包圍的地球正在成形中。

Silence, ye troubl'd waves, and thou Deep, peace,
Said then th' Omnific Word, your discord end:

Nor staid, but on the Wings of Cherubim
Uplifted, in Paternal Glorie rode
Farr into Chaos, and the World unborn; [220]
For Chaos heard his voice: him all his Traine
Follow'd in bright procession to behold
Creation, and the wonders of his might.
Then staid the fervid Wheeles, and in his hand
He took the golden Compasses, prepar'd [225]
In Gods Eternal store, to circumscribe
This Universe, and all created things:
One foot he center'd, and the other turn'd
Round through the vast profunditie obscure,
And said, thus farr extend, thus farr thy bounds, [230]
This be thy just Circumference, O World.
Thus God the Heav'n created, thus the Earth,
Matter unform'd and void: Darkness profound
Cover'd th' Abyss: but on the watrie calme
His brooding wings the Spirit of God outspred, [235]

▲ **群山高聳入雲，波濤於岩壁間洶湧奔騰**
杜雷 版畫 1866年

　　上帝在第三日造了高山和海洋，替各種生物準備牠們的棲身地。

萄；曠野上，灌木叢遍佈，各種樹木伸展枝椏，結實累累。高山上林木蓊鬱，河流兩岸開滿美麗的花朵。這是第三日。

　　「天神說：

　　『天上要有發光體，可以劃分晝

And vital vertue infus'd, and vital warmth
Throughout the fluid Mass, but downward purg'd
The black tartareous cold Infernal dregs
Adverse to life: then founded, then conglob'd
Like things to like, the rest to several place [240]
Disparted, and between spun out the Air,
And Earth self ballanc't on her Center hung.

Let ther be Light, said God, and forthwith Light
Ethereal, first of things, quintessence pure
Sprung from the Deep, and from her Native East [245]
To journie through the airie gloom began,
Sphear'd in a radiant Cloud, for yet the Sun
Was not; shee in a cloudie Tabernacle
Sojourn'd the while. God saw the Light was good;
And light from darkness by the Hemisphere [250]
Divided: Light the Day, and Darkness Night
He nam'd. Thus was the first Day Eev'n and Morn:
Nor past uncelebrated, nor unsung
By the Celestial Quires, when Orient Light
Exhaling first from Darkness they beheld; [255]
Birth-day of Heav'n and Earth; with joy and shout
The hollow Universal Orb they fill'd,
And touch'd thir Golden Harps, and hymning prais'd
God and his works, Creatour him they sung,
Both when first Eevning was, and when first Morn. [260]

Again, God said, let ther be Firmament
Amid the Waters, and let it divide
The Waters from the Waters: and God made
The Firmament, expanse of liquid, pure,
Transparent, Elemental Air, diffus'd [265]
In circuit to the uttermost convex
Of this great Round: partition firm and sure,
The Waters underneath from those above
Dividing: for as Earth, so he the World
Built on circumfluous Waters calme, in wide [270]
Crystallin Ocean, and the loud misrule
Of Chaos farr remov'd, least fierce extreames
Contiguous might distemper the whole frame:
And Heav'n he nam'd the Firmament: So Eev'n
And Morning Chorus sung the second Day. [275]

夜，也能作為標記，定季節、日期與年歲；並在天空發光，普照地面。』

「就這樣，天神造了兩個巨大的光體，大的掌管白晝、小的掌管夜晚；祂又造了許多星星，一塊在天空輪番照耀大地。第一個被創造出來的光體是巨大的太陽，接著是月亮和諸星球，綿綿密密地撒在天空上。早晨，太陽從東方升起，像一盞明亮的燈光，在地平線上放射出萬丈光芒；負責掌管白晝。此時，月亮從西方緩緩落下，彷彿太陽的鏡子；它從太陽借來光源，靜靜地等待夜晚來臨時，再從東方升起，與眾星一塊兒在天空閃爍。這是第四日。

「天神說：

「『要在水中繁殖有生命的生物，讓鳥類在天際翱翔，並要多多生殖繁衍，讓海洋裡、湖水中，以及江河等各個水域，都有生物在繁殖。』

「海洋中有巨大的鯨魚和海怪，遠遠望去，好像一座會移動的高山；港

The Earth was form'd, but in the Womb as yet
Of Waters, Embryon immature involv'd,
Appeer'd not: over all the face of Earth
Main Ocean flow'd, not idle, but with warme
Prolific humour soft'ning all her Globe, [280]
Fermented the great Mother to conceave,
Satiate with genial moisture, when God said
Be gather'd now ye Waters under Heav'n
Into one place, and let dry Land appeer.
Immediately the Mountains huge appeer [285]
Emergent, and thir broad bare backs upheave
Into the Clouds, thir tops ascend the Skie:
So high as heav'd the tumid Hills, so low
Down sunk a hollow bottom broad and deep,
Capacious bed of Waters: thither they [290]
Hasted with glad precipitance, uprowld
As drops on dust conglobing from the drie;
Part rise in crystal Wall, or ridge direct,
For haste; such flight the great command impress'd
On the swift flouds: as Armies at the call [295]
Of Trumpet (for of Armies thou hast heard)
Troop to thir Standard, so the watrie throng,
Wave rowling after Wave, where way they found,
If steep, with torrent rapture, if through Plaine,
Soft-ebbing; nor withstood them Rock or Hill, [300]
But they, or under ground, or circuit wide
With Serpent errour wandring, found thir way,
And on the washie Oose deep Channels wore;
Easie, e're God had bid the ground be drie,
All but within those banks, where Rivers now [305]
Stream, and perpetual draw thir humid traine.
The dry Land, Earth, and the great receptacle
Of congregated Waters he call'd Seas:
And saw that it was good, and said, Let th' Earth
Put forth the verdant Grass, Herb yielding Seed, [310]
And Fruit Tree yielding Fruit after her kind;
Whose Seed is in her self upon the Earth.
He scarce had said, when the bare Earth, till then
Desert and bare, unsightly, unadorn'd,
Brought forth the tender Grass, whose verdure clad [315]
Her Universal Face with pleasant green,
Then Herbs of every leaf, that sudden flour'd

∧ 上帝創造日月
米開朗基羅 西斯汀教堂壁畫 1508年

　　　上帝張開手臂，命令日與月出現，在第四天創造了日月星辰。

灣裡有無數的魚群和貝類，魚鱗在海面閃閃發光，海豚與海豹快樂地追逐浪花。同時，鳥類在溫暖的洞穴、沼澤和湖濱孵蛋，鷹隼於懸崖上築巢，夜鶯徹夜唱歌，白天鵝昂首於高舉的雙翅中，雄糾糾的公雞以嘹亮的啼叫聲報曉，更有那尾翎綴滿眼睛的孔雀，絢爛多姿。於是，水中和天空都佈滿了生物。這是第五日。

　　「天神說：

Op'ning thir various colours, and made gay
Her bosom smelling sweet: and these scarce blown,
Forth flourish't thick the clustring Vine, forth crept [320]
The smelling Gourd, up stood the cornie Reed
Embattell'd in her field: and the humble Shrub,
And Bush with frizl'd hair implicit: last
Rose as in Dance the stately Trees, and spred
Thir branches hung with copious Fruit; or gemm'd [325]
Thir blossoms: with high woods the hills were crownd,
With tufts the vallies and each fountain side,
With borders long the Rivers. That Earth now
Seemd like to Heav'n, a seat where Gods might dwell,
Or wander with delight, and love to haunt [330]
Her sacred shades: though God had yet not rain'd
Upon the Earth, and man to till the ground
None was, but from the Earth a dewie Mist
Went up and waterd all the ground, and each
Plant of the field, which e're it was in the Earth [335]
God made, and every Herb, before it grew
On the green stemm; God saw that it was good.
So Eev'n and Morn recorded the Third Day.

Again th' Almightie spake: Let there be Lights
High in th' expanse of Heaven to divide [340]
The Day from Night; and let them be for Signes,
For Seasons, and for Dayes, and circling Years,
And let them be for Lights as I ordaine
Thir Office in the Firmament of Heav'n
To give Light on the Earth; and it was so. [345]
And God made two great Lights, great for thir use
To Man, the greater to have rule by Day,
The less by Night alterne: and made the Starrs,
And set them in the Firmament of Heav'n
To illuminate the Earth, and rule the Day [350]
In thir vicissitude, and rule the Night,
And Light from Darkness to divide. God saw,
Surveying his great Work, that it was good:
For of Celestial Bodies first the Sun
A mightie Spheare he fram'd, unlightsom first, [355]
Though of Ethereal Mould: then form'd the Moon
Globose, and every magnitude of Starrs,
And sowd with Starrs the Heav'n thick as a field:

^　水中和天空佈滿了生物
杜雷 版畫 1866年

　　上帝在第五日創造了各種生物，有翱翔天空的禽鳥，也有海裡翻騰的蛟龍和魚類。

∧ 海中巨怪如一座移動的島嶼
杜雷 版畫 1866年

　　海洋有許多奇怪的生物，像是巨鯨和海怪，
遠遠望去就像一座會移動的高山。

Of Light by farr the greater part he took,
Transplanted from her cloudie Shrine, and plac'd [360]
In the Suns Orb, made porous to receive
And drink the liquid Light, firm to retaine
Her gather'd beams, great Palace now of Light.
Hither as to thir Fountain other Starrs
Repairing, in thir gold'n Urns draw Light, [365]
And hence the Morning Planet guilds her horns;
By tincture or reflection they augment
Thir small peculiar, though from human sight
So farr remote, with diminution seen.
First in his East the glorious Lamp was seen, [370]
Regent of Day, and all th' Horizon round
Invested with bright Rayes, jocond to run
His Longitude through Heav'n's high rode: the gray
Dawn, and the Pleiades before him danc'd
Shedding sweet influence: less bright the Moon, [375]
But opposite in leveld West was set
His mirror, with full face borrowing her Light
From him, for other light she needed none
In that aspect, and still that distance keepes
Till night, then in the East her turn she shines, [380]
Revolvd on Heav'ns great Axle, and her Reign
With thousand lesser Lights dividual holds,
With thousand thousand Starres, that then appeer'd
Spangling the Hemisphere: then first adornd
With thir bright Luminaries that Set and Rose, [385]
Glad Eevning and glad Morn crownd the fourth day.

And God said, let the Waters generate
Reptil with Spawn abundant, living Soule:
And let Fowle flie above the Earth, with wings
Displayd on the op'n Firmament of Heav'n. [390]
And God created the great Whales, and each
Soul living, each that crept, which plenteously
The waters generated by thir kindes,
And every Bird of wing after his kinde;
And saw that it was good, and bless'd them, saying, [395]
Be fruitful, multiply, and in the Seas
And Lakes and running Streams the waters fill;
And let the Fowle be multiply'd on the Earth.
Forthwith the Sounds and Seas, each Creek and Bay

「『地上要生出生物來，牲畜、昆
蟲、野獸，各從其類。』

「大地便孕育了許多種類的生物，
牠們從大地的懷中走出來，一對對漫
步於廣闊的原野和樹林。牲畜成群地
在草地上吃草，獅子、老虎、豹和山

貓居住在洞穴裡，河流中有河馬和鱷魚，大象費力地站起來，牡鹿則抬起頭上樹枝狀的犄角。昆蟲也迅速地繁殖起來，有的有翅膀，有的沒有；有些翅膀上帶著彩色的斑點，有的則在地上匍匐前進，像是一條線；螞蟻辛勤地勞動著，蜜蜂用蜜蠟築起蜂窩，供養蜂王；蛇在原野上活動，眼睛透著狡點，但對上帝是馴服的。

▽ 上帝創造動物
丁托列多 油畫 1552年

　　上帝在第五天創造了各種動物。天上飛的、水裡游的，當然也有在陸上跑跳、爬行的各種動物。

With Frie innumerable swarme, and Shoales [400]
Of Fish that with thir Finns and shining Scales
Glide under the green Wave, in Sculles that oft
Bank the mid Sea: part single or with mate
Graze the Sea weed thir pasture, and through Groves
Of Coral stray, or sporting with quick glance [405]
Show to the Sun thir wav'd coats dropt with Gold,
Or in thir Pearlie shells at ease, attend
Moist nutriment, or under Rocks thir food
In jointed Armour watch: on smooth the Seale,
And bended Dolphins play: part huge of bulk [410]
Wallowing unweildie, enormous in thir Gate
Tempest the Ocean: there Leviathan
Hugest of living Creatures, on the Deep
Stretcht like a Promontorie sleeps or swimmes,
And seems a moving Land, and at his Gilles [415]
Draws in, and at his Trunck spouts out a Sea.
Mean while the tepid Caves, and Fens and shoares
Thir Brood as numerous hatch, from the Egg that soon
Bursting with kindly rupture forth disclos'd
Thir callow young, but featherd soon and fledge [420]
They summ'd thir Penns, and soaring th' air sublime
With clang despis'd the ground, under a cloud
In prospect; there the Eagle and the Stork
On Cliffs and Cedar tops thir Eyries build:

∧ 鳥類孵化於溫暖的洞穴、沼澤和湖濱
杜雷 版畫 1866年

除了海洋中的巨鯨和海怪，湖濱、溪流也有
許多傍水而居的水鳥。上帝造物從巨型猛獸到渺
小螻蟻都想到了，這是萬物欣欣向榮的美好世
界。

「第六天剩下的時間裡，天神要完
成最主要的工作 ── 創造人類。於是
祂對聖子說道：

「『現在要照著我們的形像和樣式
造人，他將掌管天上的鳥、海中的魚
和地面的一切生物。』

「就這樣，第一個人類被創造出

Part loosly wing the Region, part more wise [425]
In common, rang'd in figure wedge thir way,
Intelligent of seasons, and set forth
Thir Aierie Caravan high over Sea's
Flying, and over Lands with mutual wing
Easing thir flight; so stears the prudent Crane [430]
Her annual Voiage, born on Windes; the Aire,
Floats, as they pass, fann'd with unnumber'd plumes:
From Branch to Branch the smaller Birds with song
Solac'd the Woods, and spred thir painted wings
Till Ev'n, nor then the solemn Nightingal [435]
Ceas'd warbling, but all night tun'd her soft layes:
Others on Silver Lakes and Rivers Bath'd
Thir downie Brest; the Swan with Arched neck
Between her white wings mantling proudly, Rowes
Her state with Oarie feet: yet oft they quit [440]
The Dank, and rising on stiff Pennons, towre
The mid Aereal Skie: Others on ground
Walk'd firm; the crested Cock whose clarion sounds
The silent hours, and th' other whose gay Traine
Adorns him, colour'd with the Florid hue [445]
Of Rainbows and Starrie Eyes. The Waters thus
With Fish replenisht, and the Aire, with Fowle,
Ev'ning and Morn solemniz'd the Fift day.

The Sixt, and of Creation last arose
With Eevning Harps and Mattin, when God said, [450]
Let th' Earth bring forth Soul living in her kinde,
Cattel and Creeping things, and Beast of the Earth,
Each in their kinde. The Earth obey'd, and strait
Op'ning her fertile Woomb teem'd at a Birth
Innumerous living Creatures, perfet formes, [455]
Limb'd and full grown: out of the ground up rose
As from his Laire the wilde Beast where he wonns
In Forrest wilde, in Thicket, Brake, or Den;
Among the Trees in Pairs they rose, they walk'd:
The Cattel in the Fields and Meddowes green: [460]
Those rare and solitarie, these in flocks
Pasturing at once, and in broad Herds upsprung.
The grassie Clods now Calv'd, now half appeer'd
The Tawnie Lion, pawing to get free
His hinder parts, then springs as broke from Bonds, [465]

來，那就是你，亞當。他拿起地上的
塵土，依著自己的形像捏塑人類的外
形，並把氣吹進人的鼻孔裡，於是，
你就有了生命。然後，祂又為你造了
一個女人，除了陪伴你之外，還為了
使人類多加繁衍。你被帶進美麗的樹
林中，享用各種樹上香甜的果實，知
識樹上的果子除外；倘若你吃了知識
樹的果實，便得接受『死亡』的懲
罰。這是第六日，所有的創造工作都
已完成，一個新的世界誕生了。

「第七日為聖日，所有的工作都停
止了。天使們合唱著優美的聖歌，祝
賀新世界的誕生，豎琴、風琴、簫等
樂器合奏出快樂的旋律，歡欣的氣氛
瀰漫著整個天庭。基督回到天國，坐
在上帝的右手邊，聆賞天使們高聲的

And Rampant shakes his Brinded main; the Ounce,
The Libbard, and the Tyger, as the Moale
Rising, the crumbl'd Earth above them threw
In Hillocks; the swift Stag from under ground
Bore up his branching head: scarse from his mould [470]
Behemoth biggest born of Earth upheav'd
His vastness: Fleec't the Flocks and bleating rose,
As Plants: ambiguous between Sea and Land
The River Horse and scalie Crocodile.
At once came forth whatever creeps the ground, [475]
Insect or Worme; those wav'd thir limber fans
For wings, and smallest Lineaments exact
In all the Liveries dect of Summers pride
With spots of Gold and Purple, azure and green:
These as a line thir long dimension drew, [480]
Streaking the ground with sinuous trace; not all
Minims of Nature; some of Serpent kinde
Wondrous in length and corpulence involv'd

>> **第五日、第六日**
伯恩瓊斯 水彩畫 1870~1876年
　　伯恩瓊斯以優美的天使造型來襯托新世界的
創造，其中第五日就由五位天使捧著代表前五日
的地球，第六日有六個天使，亞當和夏娃在這一
天誕生。地上蹲著第七個天使，她手中沒有懷抱
地球，而是在彈琴為樂，代表第七天為休息日。

頌讚哈利路亞（Halleluiah）[3]。」

「「這就是世界的創生過程，你還有其他的疑問嗎？」

「拉斐爾一口氣說完上帝六日的創造工作，知道亞當必定還有其他的問題想問，於是主動問他。

註3：哈利路亞（Halleluiah），讚美神的歌詞。

Thir Snakie foulds, and added wings. First crept
The Parsimonious Emmet, provident [485]
Of future, in small room large heart enclos'd,
Pattern of just equalitie perhaps
Hereafter, join'd in her popular Tribes
Of Commonaltie: swarming next appeer'd
The Female Bee that feeds her Husband Drone [490]
Deliciously, and builds her waxen Cells
With Honey stor'd: the rest are numberless,
And thou thir Natures know'st, & gav'st them Names,
Needless to thee repeated; nor unknown
The Serpent suttl'st Beast of all the field, [495]
Of huge extent somtimes, with brazen Eyes
And hairie Main terrific, though to thee
Not noxious, but obedient at thy call.
Now Heav'n in all her Glorie shon, and rowld
Her motions, as the great first-Movers hand [500]
First wheeld thir course; Earth in her rich attire
Consummate lovly smil'd; Aire,, Water, Earth,
By Fowl, Fish, Beast, was flown, was swum, was walkt
Frequent; and of the Sixt day yet remain'd;
There wanted yet the Master work, the end [505]
Of all yet don; a Creature who not prone
And Brute as other Creatures, but endu'd
With Sanctitie of Reason, might erect
His Stature, and upright with Front serene
Govern the rest, self-knowing, and from thence [510]
Magnanimous to correspond with Heav'n,
But grateful to acknowledge whence his good
Descends, thither with heart and voice and eyes
Directed in Devotion, to adore
And worship God Supream, who made him chief [515]
Of all his works: therefore the Omnipotent
Eternal Father (For where is not hee
Present) thus to his Son audibly spake.

≪ 伊甸園的落日餘暉，各種動物都休息了
杜雷 版畫 1866年

　　上帝花了六日創造世界，所有的工作到此完成，忙碌生活的動物也隨著落日餘輝休息了。

^ 伊甸園
布勒哲爾 油畫 1612年

　　上帝完成創造世界的工作，伊甸園
呈現一片和樂融融的景象。

Let us make now Man in our image, Man
In our similitude, and let them rule [520]
Over the Fish and Fowle of Sea and Aire,,
Beast of the Field, and over all the Earth,
And every creeping thing that creeps the ground.
This said, he formd thee, Adam, thee O Man
Dust of the ground, and in thy nostrils breath'd [525]
The breath of Life; in his own Image hee
Created thee, in the Image of God
Express, and thou becam'st a living Soul.
Male he created thee, but thy consort
Female for Race; then bless'd Mankinde, and said, [530]
Be fruitful, multiplie, and fill the Earth,
Subdue it, and throughout Dominion hold
Over Fish of the Sea, and Fowle of the Aire,,
And every living thing that moves on the Earth.
Wherever thus created, for no place [535]
Is yet distinct by name, thence, as thou know'st
He brought thee into this delicious Grove,
This Garden, planted with the Trees of God,
Delectable both to behold and taste;
And freely all thir pleasant fruit for food [540]
Gave thee, all sorts are here that all th' Earth yields,
Varietie without end; but of the Tree

Which tasted works knowledge of Good and Evil,
Thou mai'st not; in the day thou eat'st, thou di'st;
Death is the penaltie impos'd, beware, [545]
And govern well thy appetite, least sin
Surprise thee, and her black attendant Death.
Here finish'd hee, and all that he had made
View'd, and behold all was entirely good;
So Ev'n and Morn accomplish't the Sixt day: [550]
Yet not till the Creator from his work
Desisting, though unwearied, up returnd
Up to the Heav'n of Heav'ns his high abode,
Thence to behold this new created World
Th' addition of his Empire, how it shew'd [555]
In prospect from his Throne, how good, how faire,
Answering his great Idea. Up he rode
Followd with acclamation and the sound
Symphonious of ten thousand Harpes that tun'd
Angelic harmonies: the Earth, the Aire, [560]
Resounded, (thou remember'st for thou heardst)

The Heav'ns and all the Constellations rung,
The Planets in thir stations list'ning stood,
While the bright Pomp ascended jubilant.
Open, ye everlasting Gates, they sung, [565]
Open, ye Heav'ns, your living dores; let in
The great Creator from his work returnd
Magnificent, his Six days work, a World;
Open, and henceforth oft; for God will deigne
To visit oft the dwellings of just Men [570]
Delighted, and with frequent intercourse
Thither will send his winged Messengers
On errands of supernal Grace. So sung
The glorious Train ascending: He through Heav'n,
That open'd wide her blazing Portals, led [575]
To Gods Eternal house direct the way,
A broad and ample rode, whose dust is Gold
And pavement Starrs, as Starrs to thee appeer,
Seen in the Galaxie, that Milkie way
Which nightly as a circling Zone thou seest [580]
Pouderd with Starrs. And now on Earth the Seventh
Eev'ning arose in Eden, for the Sun
Was set, and twilight from the East came on,
Forerunning Night; when at the holy mount
Of Heav'ns high-seated top, th' Impereal Throne [585]
Of Godhead, fixt for ever firm and sure,
The Filial Power arriv'd, and sate him down
With his great Father (for he also went
Invisible, yet staid, such priviledge
Hath Omnipresence) and the work ordain'd, [590]
Author and end of all things, and from work
Now resting, bless'd and hallowd the Seav'nth day,
As resting on that day from all his work,
But not in silence holy kept; the Harp
Had work and rested not, the solemn Pipe, [595]
And Dulcimer, all Organs of sweet stop,
All sounds on Fret by String or Golden Wire
Temper'd soft Tunings, intermixt with Voice
Choral or Unison; of incense Clouds
Fuming from Golden Censers hid the Mount. [600]
Creation and the Six dayes acts they sung,
Great are thy works, Jehovah, infinite

Thy power; what thought can measure thee or tongue
Relate thee; greater now in thy return
Then from the Giant Angels; thee that day [605]
Thy Thunders magnifi'd; but to create
Is greater then created to destroy.
Who can impair thee, mighty King, or bound
Thy Empire? easily the proud attempt
Of Spirits apostat and thir Counsels vaine [610]
Thou hast repeld, while impiously they thought
Thee to diminish, and from thee withdraw
The number of thy worshippers. Who seekes
To lessen thee, against his purpose serves
To manifest the more thy might: his evil [615]
Thou usest, and from thence creat'st more good.
Witness this new-made World, another Heav'n
From Heaven Gate not farr, founded in view
On the cleer Hyaline, the Glassie Sea;
Of amplitude almost immense, with Starr's [620]
Numerous, and every Starr perhaps a World
Of destind habitation; but thou know'st
Thir seasons: among these the seat of men,
Earth with her nether Ocean circumfus'd,
Thir pleasant dwelling place. Thrice happie men, [625]
And sons of men, whom God hath thus advanc't,
Created in his Image, there to dwell
And worship him, and in reward to rule
Over his Works, on Earth, in Sea, or Air,
And multiply a Race of Worshippers [630]
Holy and just: thrice happie if they know
Thir happiness, and persevere upright.

So sung they, and the Empyrean rung,
With Halleluiahs: Thus was Sabbath kept.
And thy request think now fulfill'd, that ask'd [635]
How first this World and face of things began,
And what before thy memorie was don
From the beginning, that posteritie
Informd by thee might know; if else thou seek'st
Aught, not surpassing human measure, say. [640]

8 > 人類的誕生

　　拉斐爾繼續爲亞當講述有關天體運行的事。亞當則爲拉斐爾敘說自己誕生的過程，說到造物主創造了他，使他成爲人類之祖，並讓他替地球上的鳥獸蟲魚命名；之後，在他的祈求下，上帝拿出他的一根肋骨創造了夏娃。接著，亞當向天使描述自己和夏娃互相愛戀、攜手相伴的幸福生活。

　　亞當全神灌注、仔細聆聽拉斐爾的話語，直到拉斐爾問他：

　　「你還有其他的疑問嗎？」

　　他才回過神來，如夢初醒地回答：

　　「是的，你說的這些事，都是人類能力所無法探求的東西，但對於天地的構造，我仍有不明白的地方。與天上那許多的星星相比較，地球只不過是一個極小的黑點；造物主

▽ **創造亞當**
米開朗基羅 西斯汀教堂壁畫 1508年

　　初生的亞當彷彿剛從睡夢中醒來，渾身尚自慵懶無力，他躺在草地上休息片刻，之後才起身去探索新世界。

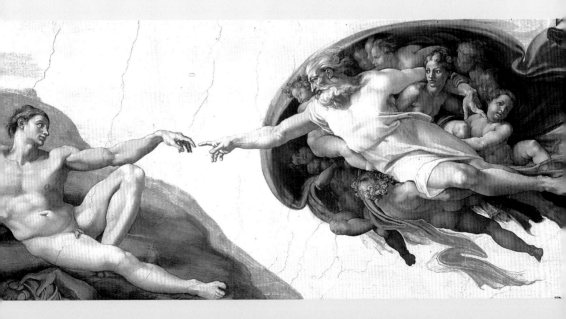

創造了這麼多不斷運行於既定軌道
上的星球，難道只是為了給地球供給
溫暖和光明？這未免太過於大材小用
了。」

亞當說出心中的疑問，為這深奧的
問題所困擾，陷入深深的沉思中。

夏娃用心聽著拉斐爾和亞當之間
深刻的談話，此時，身體感到有些疲
憊，便從椅子上站了起來，往花園走
去。花朵見到她的到來，紛紛綻放色
彩鮮豔的花瓣，對她展露甜美的笑
靨。

◁ **亞當與夏娃**
克拉那赫 油畫 1510年

The Angel ended, and in Adams Eare
So Charming left his voice, that he a while
Thought him still speaking, still stood fixt to hear;
Then as new wak't thus gratefully repli'd.
What thanks sufficient, or what recompence [5]
Equal have I to render thee, Divine
Hystorian, who thus largely hast allayd
The thirst I had of knowledge, and voutsaf't
This friendly condescention to relate
Things else by me unsearchable, now heard [10]
With wonder, but delight, and, as is due,
With glorie attributed to the high
Creator; something yet of doubt remaines,
Which onely thy solution can resolve.
When I behold this goodly Frame, this World [15]
Of Heav'n and Earth consisting, and compute,
Thir magnitudes, this Earth a spot, a graine,
An Atom, with the Firmament compar'd
And all her numberd Starrs, that seem to rowle
Spaces incomprehensible (for such [20]
Thir distance argues and thir swift return
Diurnal) meerly to officiate light
Round this opacous Earth, this punctual spot,
One day and night; in all thir vast survey
Useless besides, reasoning I oft admire, [25]
How Nature wise and frugal could commit
Such disproportions, with superfluous hand
So many nobler Bodies to create,
Greater so manifold to this one use,
For aught appeers, and on thir Orbs impose [30]
Such restless revolution day by day
Repeated, while the sedentarie Earth,
That better might with farr less compass move,
Serv'd by more noble then her self, attaines
Her end without least motion, and receaves, [35]
As Tribute such a sumless journey brought
Of incorporeal speed, her warmth and light;
Speed, to describe whose swiftness Number failes.

「嗯！好香啊。」

夏娃彎下身，把鼻子湊進花瓣，芬芳的花香讓她慵懶的情緒微微一振。她並非不喜歡聆聽兩人的談話，只是長時間當個聽眾，難免想要透透氣；其實，夏娃非常喜歡聆聽亞當的話語，她總是依偎在亞當的懷中，與他分享心事和對各種事物的想法，兩人非常的甜蜜恩愛。

休息了一陣子，拉斐爾開口說道：

「天體運行的奧祕對你來說像是一本奇妙的書，裡頭記載著上帝創造星體的記錄，內容神奇奧妙，充滿種種精密的計算。你只須去讚嘆它，深入的了解倒是不必要的，切莫妄自臆測天體的構造。」

拉斐爾又接著說：

「上帝創造了太陽，目的是要它以光明照耀地球，使居住在上頭的人類感覺溫暖；不要過問其他星球上的事 —— 那兒是否有生物？他們如何生活？像這樣的事情上帝自會有所安

So spake our Sire, and by his count'nance seemd
Entring on studious thoughts abstruse, which Eve [40]
Perceaving where she sat retir'd in sight,
With lowliness Majestic from her seat,
And Grace that won who saw to wish her stay,
Rose, and went forth among her Fruits and Flours,
To visit how they prosper'd, bud and bloom, [45]
Her Nurserie; they at her coming sprung
And toucht by her fair tendance gladlier grew.
Yet went she not, as not with such discourse
Delighted, or not capable her eare
Of what was high: such pleasure she reserv'd, [50]
Adam relating, she sole Auditress;
Her Husband the Relater she preferr'd
Before the Angel, and of him to ask
Chose rather: hee, she knew would intermix
Grateful digressions, and solve high dispute [55]
With conjugal Caresses, from his Lip
Not Words alone pleas'd her. O when meet now
Such pairs, in Love and mutual Honour joyn'd?
With Goddess-like demeanour forth she went;
Not unattended, for on her as Queen [60]
A pomp of winning Graces waited still,
And from about her shot Darts of desire
Into all Eyes to wish her still in sight.
And Raphael now to Adam's doubt propos'd
Benevolent and facil thus repli'd. [65]

To ask or search I blame thee not, for Heav'n
Is as the Book of God before thee set,
Wherein to read his wondrous Works, and learne
His Seasons, Hours, or Dayes, or Months, or Yeares:
This to attain, whether Heav'n move or Earth, [70]
Imports not, if thou reck'n right, the rest
From Man or Angel the great Architect
Did wisely to conceal, and not divulge
His secrets to be scann'd by them who ought
Rather admire; or if they list to try [75]
Conjecture, he his Fabric of the Heav'ns
Hath left to thir disputes, perhaps to move
His laughter at thir quaint Opinions wide
Hereafter, when they come to model Heav'n

排，你只須敬畏上帝、真心順服，並對祂所給予的一切感到滿足。」

「我明白了，你的教導甚是。我何苦讓種種不切實際的疑惑，阻擾了生活的快樂？上帝賜給我們喜樂，命令『煩惱』不可接近我們，我又何須去自尋煩惱？況且，高深的智慧非我所能觸及，若硬要去探求，反而會落得茫然空虛、毫無所獲。所以，我應該去關心日常生活的根本智慧才對呀！」

亞當幡然覺悟，拋開了滿心的疑惑之後，心情頓時開朗起來。他想到要同客人說些自身的事，便開口說道：

「你所說的話語，雋永芬芳，深藏智慧，令人回味不已。不知道你有沒有興趣，聽聽我的故事？」

拉斐爾點點頭，高興地回答：

「當然，我非常想知道這仿製上帝美麗形像的人類是怎樣被創造出來的。因為上帝在創造人類的時候，我並不在現場；上帝派遣我率領軍隊，

And calculate the Starrs, how they will weild [80]
The mightie frame, how build, unbuild, contrive
To save appeerances, how gird the Sphear
With Centric and Eccentric scribl'd o're,
Cycle and Epicycle, Orb in Orb:
Alreadie by thy reasoning this I guess, [85]
Who art to lead thy ofspring, and supposest
That bodies bright and greater should not serve
The less not bright, nor Heav'n such journies run,
Earth sitting still, when she alone receaves
The benefit: consider first, that Great [90]
Or Bright inferrs not Excellence: the Earth
Though, in comparison of Heav'n, so small,
Nor glistering, may of solid good containe
More plenty then the Sun that barren shines,
Whose vertue on it self workes no effect, [95]
But in the fruitful Earth; there first receavd
His beams, unactive else, thir vigour find.
Yet not to Earth are those bright Luminaries
Officious, but to thee Earths habitant.
And for the Heav'ns wide Circuit, let it speak [100]
The Makers high magnificence, who built
So spacious, and his Line stretcht out so farr;
That Man may know he dwells not in his own;
An Edifice too large for him to fill,
Lodg'd in a small partition, and the rest [105]
Ordain'd for uses to his Lord best known.
The swiftness of those Circles attribute,
Though numberless, to his Omnipotence,
That to corporeal substances could adde
Speed almost Spiritual; mee thou thinkst not slow, [110]
Who since the Morning hour set out from Heav'n
Where God resides, and ere mid-day arriv'd
In Eden, distance inexpressible
By Numbers that have name. But this I urge,
Admitting Motion in the Heav'ns, to shew [115]
Invalid that which thee to doubt it mov'd;
Not that I so affirm, though so it seem
To thee who hast thy dwelling here on Earth.
God to remove his wayes from human sense,
Plac'd Heav'n from Earth so farr, that earthly sight, [120]
If it presume, might erre in things too high,

前去防守地獄大門，避免敵人、叛逆趁機逃出來，跑去破壞新世界的創造工程。所以，請你為我講述人類始祖的來源吧！[1]」

「當時，我彷彿剛從睡夢中醒來，張開眼睛，發現自己躺臥在柔軟的草地上；一顆顆的汗珠從我的皮膚上滲出來，但很快地便被太陽的光線給曬得蒸發掉。我靜靜地躺著，雙眼凝視著湛藍的天空；過了一會兒，我伸出手撐住地面站起身來，往前方走去。環顧四周，群山圍繞、林木蓊鬱，原野上百花綻放，溪水蜿蜒其間，發出潺潺的水聲；動物們在草地上漫步，鳥兒們蹲在枝頭鳴唱，大地如此美好，喜悅盈滿胸際，使我不由得手舞足蹈起來。

「我漫無目的地向前走，直走到一處碧綠的泉水邊，我蹲下來，雙手合

註1：出自《舊約‧創世紀》：「神就照著自己的形像造人，乃是照著他的形像男造女。……神用地上的塵土造人，將生氣吹在他鼻孔裡，他就成了有靈的活人，名叫亞當。」

And no advantage gaine. What if the Sun
Be Centre to the World, and other Starrs
By his attractive vertue and their own
Incited, dance about him various rounds? [125]
Thir wandring course now high, now low, then hid,
Progressive, retrograde, or standing still,
In six thou seest, and what if sev'nth to these
The Planet Earth, so stedfast though she seem,
Insensibly three different Motions move? [130]
Which else to several Spheres thou must ascribe,
Mov'd contrarie with thwart obliquities,
Or save the Sun his labour, and that swift
Nocturnal and Diurnal rhomb suppos'd,
Invisible else above all Starrs, the Wheele [135]
Of Day and Night; which needs not thy beleefe,
If Earth industrious of her self fetch Day
Travelling East, and with her part averse
From the Suns beam meet Night, her other part
Still luminous by his ray. What if that light [140]
Sent from her through the wide transpicuous aire,
To the terrestrial Moon be as a Starr
Enlightning her by Day, as she by Night
This Earth? reciprocal, if Land be there,
Fields and Inhabitants: Her spots thou seest [145]
As Clouds, and Clouds may rain, and Rain produce
Fruits in her soft'nd Soile, for some to eate
Allotted there; and other Suns perhaps
With thir attendant Moons thou wilt descrie
Communicating Male and Femal Light, [150]
Which two great Sexes animate the World,
Stor'd in each Orb perhaps with some that live.
For such vast room in Nature unpossest
By living Soule, desert and desolate,
Onely to shine, yet scarce to contribute [155]
Each Orb a glimps of Light, conveyd so farr
Down to this habitable, which returnes
Light back to them, is obvious to dispute.
But whether thus these things, or whether not,
Whether the Sun predominant in Heav'n [160]
Rise on the Earth, or Earth rise on the Sun,
Hee from the East his flaming rode begin,
Or Shee from West her silent course advance

併捧起泉水來啜飲著，泉水的清涼消除了我一路步行的疲憊，綠蔭下的徐徐清風則拂去了我額頭上的汗珠，這舒爽的感覺讓我昏昏欲睡。此時，一個聲音自我的耳畔響起，他說：『起來吧！亞當，人類的始祖；跟隨我，前往你快樂的居所去吧。』

「我心想：『這便是我的創造者吧！』於是連忙起身，他拉起我的手往天上飛去，穿過了遼闊的田野、越過了無數河川，終於來到一座樹林茂密的高山。我們往下滑行，雙腳降落在山頂上；然後，那創造我的神發出聲音說道：

「『我為你創造了這個樂園，讓你在其中耕種、生活，各種樹上所結的果子都可任你採摘、吃食，只有那棵辨別善惡的知識樹的果實你不可以碰，更不能夠摘來吃，如果你觸犯了這個命令，便要以生命做代價，面臨死亡的懲罰。

「但是，只要你能嚴守這項命令，

With inoffensive pace that spinning sleeps
On her soft Axle, while she paces Eev'n, [165]
And beares thee soft with the smooth Air along,
Sollicit not thy thoughts with matters hid,
Leave them to God above, him serve and feare;
Of other Creatures, as him pleases best,
Wherever plac't, let him dispose: joy thou [170]
In what he gives to thee, this Paradise
And thy faire Eve; Heav'n is for thee too high
To know what passes there; be lowlie wise:
Think onely what concernes thee and thy being;
Dream not of other Worlds, what Creatures there [175]
Live, in what state, condition or degree,
Contented that thus farr hath been reveal'd
Not of Earth onely but of highest Heav'n.

To whom thus Adam cleerd of doubt, repli'd.
How fully hast thou satisfi'd me, pure [180]
Intelligence of Heav'n, Angel serene,
And freed from intricacies, taught to live
The easiest way, nor with perplexing thoughts
To interrupt the sweet of Life, from which
God hath bid dwell farr off all anxious cares, [185]
And not molest us, unless we our selves
Seek them with wandring thoughts, and notions vain.
But apt the Mind or Fancy is to roave
Uncheckt, and of her roaving is no end;
Till warn'd, or by experience taught, she learne, [190]
That not to know at large of things remote
From use, obscure and suttle, but to know
That which before us lies in daily life,
Is the prime Wisdom, what is more, is fume,
Or emptiness, or fond impertinence, [195]
And renders us in things that most concerne
Unpractis'd, unprepar'd, and still to seek.
Therefore from this high pitch let us descend
A lower flight, and speak of things at hand
Useful, whence haply mention may arise [200]
Of somthing not unseasonable to ask
By sufferance, and thy wonted favour deign'd.
Thee I have heard relating what was don
Ere my remembrance: now hear mee relate

便能夠成為全地球的主宰，包括那天上飛的、地上爬的和水裡游的；我且把鳥類和動物叫來，由你替牠們命名。』

「創造者說完之後，果然有一對對的鳥獸來到我面前，我便一一給牠們取了名字[2]。做完這事之後，我突然感到孤單起來，於是我開口，大膽地向隱形的天神說道：

「『讓人萬分尊崇的創造者呀！您賜給我一切美好的東西，並讓我管理這美麗的園圃，我本應心懷感激，不可有非分的想望，但見著鳥獸們成雙成對、恩恩愛愛的模樣，卻使我熱切地想要一個伴侶，來與我分享喜樂。』

「『孤單？不是有各式各樣的生物圍繞著你嗎？牠們雖然無法與你說話，但牠們擁有知覺，能夠服從你的命令。』創造者回答。

「『我所需要的，並不是那些聽命於我、地位較為低下的生物；我需

My Storie, which perhaps thou hast not heard; [205]
And Day is yet not spent; till then thou seest
How suttly to detaine thee I devise,
Inviting thee to hear while I relate,
Fond, were it not in hope of thy reply:
For while I sit with thee, I seem in Heav'n, [210]
And sweeter thy discourse is to my eare
Then Fruits of Palm-tree pleasantest to thirst
And hunger both, from labour, at the houre
Of sweet repast; they satiate, and soon fill,
Though pleasant, but thy words with Grace Divine [215]
Imbu'd, bring to thir sweetness no satietie.

To whom thus Raphael answer'd heav'nly meek.
Nor are thy lips ungraceful, Sire of men,
Nor tongue ineloquent; for God on thee
Abundantly his gifts hath also pour'd [220]
Inward and outward both, his image faire:
Speaking or mute all comliness and grace
Attends thee, and each word, each motion formes
Nor less think wee in Heav'n of thee on Earth
Then of our fellow servant, and inquire [225]
Gladly into the wayes of God with Man:
For God we see hath honour'd thee, and set
On Man his Equal Love: say therefore on;
For I that Day was absent, as befell,
Bound on a voyage uncouth and obscure, [230]
Farr on excursion toward the Gates of Hell;
Squar'd in full Legion (such command we had)
To see that none thence issu'd forth a spie,
Or enemie, while God was in his work,
Least hee incenst at such eruption bold, [235]
Destruction with Creation might have mixt.
Not that they durst without his leave attempt,
But us he sends upon his high behests
For state, as Sovran King, and to enure
Our prompt obedience. Fast we found, fast shut [240]

註2：亞當給地球上各種生物取名字的過程，出自《舊約‧創世紀》。請參照本書第六卷，註1。

要的是一個地位與我相當，能夠互相
了解、分享想法的伴侶。就像公的鳥
配母的鳥，公的獸配母的獸，總不能
讓鳥類與獸類交配，亂了自然的法則
吧？』我再次懇求。

「『恆久以來我便是單獨的。與我
創造的那些生物相處、交談，我感到
自在且快樂，並不會因為他們的地位
與我不平等而感到孤獨呀！』創造者

The dismal Gates, and barricado'd strong;
But long ere our approaching heard within
Noise, other then the sound of Dance or Song,
Torment, and loud lament, and furious rage.
Glad we return'd up to the coasts of Light [245]
Ere Sabbath Eev'ning: so we had in charge.
But thy relation now; for I attend,
Pleas'd with thy words no less then thou with mine.

So spake the Godlike Power, and thus our Sire.
For Man to tell how human Life began [250]
Is hard; for who himself beginning knew?
Desire with thee still longer to converse
Induc'd me. As new wak't from soundest sleep
Soft on the flourie herb I found me laid

▽ 創造夏娃
米開朗基羅 西斯汀教堂壁畫 1508年

創造夏娃
布雷克 水彩畫 1808年
　　上帝要亞當沉睡，然後取出亞當的一根肋骨，為他造了可愛完美的伴侶。

和顏悅色地回答。

　　「『那是因為您完美無缺，集萬物於一身，並不需要繁殖；但人類並不完美，他依照您的形像而造，必須不斷地繁衍，以便從眾多人的身上匯聚完美。所以，我請求您讓我擁有至愛。』我熱切地說著。

　　「『哈哈，先前不過是在考驗你罷了，你了解你自己，知道自己想要的

In Balmie Sweat, which with his Beames the Sun [255]
Soon dri'd, and on the reaking moisture fed.
Strait toward Heav'n my wondring Eyes I turnd,
And gaz'd a while the ample Skie, till rais'd
By quick instinctive motion up I sprung,
As thitherward endevoring, and upright [260]
Stood on my feet; about me round I saw
Hill, Dale, and shadie Woods, and sunnie Plaines,
And liquid Lapse of murmuring Streams; by these,
Creatures that livd, and movd, and walk'd, or flew,
Birds on the branches warbling; all things smil'd, [265]
With fragrance and with joy my heart oreflow'd.
My self I then perus'd, and Limb by Limb
Survey'd, and sometimes went, and sometimes ran
With supple joints, as lively vigour led:
But who I was, or where, or from what cause, [270]
Knew not; to speak I tri'd, and forthwith spake,
My Tongue obey'd and readily could name
What e're I saw. Thou Sun, said I, faire Light,
And thou enlight'nd Earth, so fresh and gay,
Ye Hills and Dales, ye Rivers, Woods, and Plaines, [275]
And ye that live and move, fair Creatures, tell,
Tell, if ye saw, how came I thus, how here?
Not of my self; by some great Maker then,
In goodness and in power præeminent;
Tell me, how may I know him, how adore, [280]
From whom I have that thus I move and live,
And feel that I am happier then I know.
While thus I call'd, and stray'd I knew not whither,
From where I first drew Aire, and first beheld
This happie Light, when answer none return'd, [285]
On a green shadie Bank profuse of Flours
Pensive I sate me down; there gentle sleep
First found me, and with soft oppression seis'd
My droused sense, untroubl'd, though I thought
I then was passing to my former state [290]
Insensible, and forthwith to dissolve:
When suddenly stood at my Head a dream,
Whose inward apparition gently mov'd
My Fancy to believe I yet had being,
And livd: One came, methought, of shape Divine, [295]
And said, thy Mansion wants thee, Adam, rise,

是什麼，並表現出了自由的精神，這讓我覺得很高興。其實，我早就為你安排好伴侶，現在就把她帶到你身邊來。』

「創造者說完，便叫我躺下、閉上眼睛，沒多久，我便沉沉地進入夢鄉，我的身體雖然睡著了，但我的心靈卻是清醒的；我看見天神打開我的左肋，從裡頭拿出一根肋骨來，捏成一個美麗、可愛的女人[3]。

「我從睡夢中醒來，正哀嘆夢中女子的消失，遠遠地，便看到那名女子朝著自己走來。天上的造物主以聲音引領她來到我眼前，並教導她神聖的婚姻和婚禮的儀式；我忍不住驚聲嘆道：

註3：夏娃被創造的過程，出自《舊約・創世紀》：「耶和華神說：『那人獨居不好，我要為他造一個配偶幫助他。』……耶和華神使他沉睡，他就睡了；於是取下他的一條肋骨，又把肉合起來。耶和華神就用那人身上所取的肋骨造成一個女人，領她到那人跟前。那人說：『這是我骨中的骨，肉中的肉，可以稱她為「女人」，因為她是從男人身上取出來的。』因此，人要離開父母與妻子連合，二人成為一體。」

First Man, of Men innumerable ordain'd
First Father, call'd by thee I come thy Guide
To the Garden of bliss, thy seat prepar'd.
So saying, by the hand he took me rais'd, [300]
And over Fields and Waters, as in Aire
Smooth sliding without step, last led me up
A woodie Mountain; whose high top was plaine,
A Circuit wide, enclos'd, with goodliest Trees
Planted, with Walks, and Bowers, that what I saw [305]
Of Earth before scarce pleasant seemd. Each Tree
Load'n with fairest Fruit, that hung to the Eye
Tempting, stirr'd in me sudden appetite
To pluck and eate; whereat I wak'd, and found
Before mine Eyes all real, as the dream [310]
Had lively shadowd: Here had new begun
My wandring, had not hee who was my Guide
Up hither, from among the Trees appeer'd,
Presence Divine. Rejoycing, but with aw,
In adoration at his feet I fell [315]
Submiss: he rear'd me, and Whom thou soughtst I am,
Said mildely, Author of all this thou seest
Above, or round about thee or beneath.
This Paradise I give thee, count it thine
To Till and keep, and of the Fruit to eate: [320]
Of every Tree that in the Garden growes
Eate freely with glad heart; fear here no dearth:
But of the Tree whose operation brings
Knowledg of good and ill, which I have set
The Pledge of thy Obedience and thy Faith, [325]
Amid the Garden by the Tree of Life,
Remember what I warne thee, shun to taste,
And shun the bitter consequence: for know,
The day thou eat'st thereof, my sole command
Transgrest, inevitably thou shalt dye; [330]
From that day mortal, and this happie State
Shalt loose, expell'd from hence into a World
Of woe and sorrow. Sternly he pronounc'd
The rigid interdiction, which resounds
Yet dreadful in mine eare, though in my choice [335]
Not to incur; but soon his cleer aspect
Return'd and gracious purpose thus renew'd.
Not only these fair bounds, but all the Earth

△ 亞當和夏娃
克拉那赫 油畫 1528年

　　亞當和夏娃是純潔與美麗的象徵，許多畫家都用這對愛侶來表現人體之美。

　　「『天神哪！您所給予我的創造物當中，這是最完美的一個。她是我的骨中骨、肉中肉，稱她為『女人』，因為她是從男人身上取出來的，因此，人要離開父母與妻子連合，二人成為一體。』

　　「夏娃聽聞我的驚嘆，臉頰迅速泛紅，宛如夕陽西下時，於天際的那抹

To thee and to thy Race I give; as Lords
Possess it, and all things that therein live, [340]
Or live in Sea, or Aire, Beast, Fish, and Fowle.
In signe whereof each Bird and Beast behold
After thir kindes; I bring them to receave
From thee thir Names, and pay thee fealtie
With low subjection; understand the same [345]
Of Fish within thir watry residence,
Not hither summon'd, since they cannot change
Thir Element to draw the thinner Aire.
As thus he spake, each Bird and Beast behold
Approaching two and two, These cowring low [350]
With blandishment, each Bird stoop'd on his wing.
I nam'd them, as they pass'd, and understood
Thir Nature, with such knowledg God endu'd
My sudden apprehension: but in these
I found not what me thought I wanted still; [355]
And to the Heav'nly vision thus presum'd.

O by what Name, for thou above all these,
Above mankinde, or aught then mankinde higher,
Surpassest farr my naming, how may I
Adore thee, Author of this Universe, [360]
And all this good to man, for whose well being
So amply, and with hands so liberal
Thou hast provided all things: but with mee
I see not who partakes. In solitude
What happiness, who can enjoy alone, [365]
Or all enjoying, what contentment find?
Thus I presumptuous; and the vision bright,
As with a smile more bright'nd, thus repli'd.

What call'st thou solitude, is not the Earth
With various living creatures, and the Aire [370]
Replenisht, and all these at thy command
To come and play before thee; know'st thou not
Thir language and thir wayes? They also know,
And reason not contemptibly; with these
Find pastime, and beare rule; thy Realm is large. [375]
So spake the Universal Lord, and seem'd
So ordering. I with leave of speech implor'd,
And humble deprecation thus repli'd.

彩霞；她轉過身去，想要離開。我急
忙追上前去抱住她，向她述說滿心的
愛意，並告訴她：

「『你要到哪兒去呢？你是我的
肋骨造成的，跟我本是一體，快點
跟著我，回到屬於我們兩人的住所去
吧！』

「於是，我牽起她的手，回到撒滿
薔薇花瓣的居所，當晚我倆便結為夫
妻。」

說到這裡，亞當停了下來，轉頭對
妻子微微一笑，然後繼續說道：

「「頭一次，我感受到內心澎湃
不已的熱情，她的美，完美無瑕，讓
我產生強烈的欲望；雖然，從其他的
事物上我也能夠得到歡樂，比方說視
覺、味覺、花朵的芳香和果實的甜
美，甚至鳥兒的輕唱。但卻比不上對
她強烈的愛意。

「她舉止優雅，心靈高貴純潔，智
慧、權威和理性在她面前全得低頭臣
服。」

Let not my words offend thee, Heav'nly Power,
My Maker, be propitious while I speak. [380]
Hast thou not made me here thy substitute,
And these inferiour farr beneath me set?
Among unequals what societie
Can sort, what harmonie or true delight?
Which must be mutual, in proportion due [385]
Giv'n and receiv'd; but in disparitie
The one intense, the other still remiss
Cannot well suite with either, but soon prove
Tedious alike: Of fellowship I speak
Such as I seek, fit to participate [390]
All rational delight, wherein the brute
Cannot be human consort; they rejoyce
Each with thir kinde, Lion with Lioness;
So fitly them in pairs thou hast combin'd;
Much less can Bird with Beast, or Fish with Fowle [395]
So well converse, nor with the Ox the Ape;
Wors then can Man with Beast, and least of all.
Whereto th' Almighty answer'd, not displeas'd.
A nice and suttle happiness I see
Thou to thyself proposest, in the choice [400]
Of thy Associates, Adam, and wilt taste
No pleasure, though in pleasure, solitarie.
What think'st thou then of mee, and this my State,
Seem I to thee sufficiently possest
Of happiness, or not? who am alone [405]
From all Eternitie, for none I know
Second to mee or like, equal much less.
How have I then with whom to hold converse
Save with the Creatures which I made, and those
To me inferiour, infinite descents [410]
Beneath what other Creatures are to thee?

He ceas'd, I lowly answer'd. To attaine
The highth and depth of thy Eternal wayes
All human thoughts come short, Supream of things;
Thou in thy self art perfet, and in thee [415]
Is no deficience found; not so is Man,
But in degree, the cause of his desire
By conversation with his like to help,

「亞當呀，你所重視的不應該是夏娃外在的美，而應該是以理性為基礎，去求得兩人心靈的契合，而非肉體，人與野獸的差別即在於此；智慧可以增加一個人談話的深度，愛情則能夠讓思想產生深度。」拉斐爾語重心長地對亞當說。

亞當感到有些慚愧，連忙對天使說明：

「就像你所說的，愛可以引領我們往天庭的路上走去；對於夏娃，使我深切愛著的並非她美麗的容貌，而是她從日常生活中散發出來種種優雅的談吐和得宜的舉止。這便是我內心所有的感受，已經一一說給你聽。」

夕陽已落在大地的綠岬，拉斐爾站起來準備離去。臨走前，再一次對亞當和夏娃交代著：

「我必須離開了，今後，你們仍要相親相愛、快樂的生活；對上帝要絕對的服從，切莫因慾望來動搖心中的信念，做出錯誤的行為。你們的

Or solace his defects. No need that thou
Shouldst propagat, already infinite; [420]
And through all numbers absolute, though One;
But Man by number is to manifest
His single imperfection, and beget
Like of his like, his Image multipli'd,
In unitie defective, which requires [425]
Collateral love, and deerest amitie.
Thou in thy secresie although alone,
Best with thy self accompanied, seek'st not
Social communication, yet so pleas'd,
Canst raise thy Creature to what highth thou wilt [430]
Of Union or Communion, deifi'd;
I by conversing cannot these erect
From prone, nor in thir wayes complacence find.
Thus I embold'nd spake, and freedom us'd
Permissive, and acceptance found, which gain'd [435]
This answer from the gratious voice Divine.

Thus farr to try thee, Adam, I was pleas'd,
And finde thee knowing not of Beasts alone,
Which thou hast rightly nam'd, but of thy self,
Expressing well the spirit within thee free, [440]
My Image, not imparted to the Brute,
Whose fellowship therefore unmeet for thee
Good reason was thou freely shouldst dislike,
And be so minded still; I, ere thou spak'st,
Knew it not good for Man to be alone, [445]
And no such companie as then thou saw'st
Intended thee, for trial only brought,
To see how thou could'st judge of fit and meet:
What next I bring shall please thee, be assur'd,
Thy likeness, thy fit help, thy other self, [450]
Thy wish, exactly to thy hearts desire.

Hee ended, or I heard no more, for now
My earthly by his Heav'nly overpowerd,
Which it had long stood under, streind to the highth
In that celestial Colloquie sublime, [455]
As with an object that excels the sense,
Dazl'd and spent, sunk down, and sought repair
Of sleep, which instantly fell on me, call'd

自由意志將影響後世子孫的未來，千萬記得時時警惕自我，阻絕所有的誘惑。」

　　亞當和夏娃站起來，以不捨的眼光目送著拉斐爾離開；天色暗了下來，兩人慢慢走回臥房，準備迎接夜幕的降臨。

By Nature as in aide, and clos'd mine eyes.
Mine eyes he clos'd, but op'n left the Cell [460]
Of Fancie my internal sight, by which
Abstract as in a transe methought I saw,
Though sleeping, where I lay, and saw the shape
Still glorious before whom awake I stood;
Who stooping op'nd my left side, and took [465]
From thence a Rib, with cordial spirits warme,
And Life-blood streaming fresh; wide was the wound,
But suddenly with flesh fill'd up and heal'd:
The Rib he formd and fashond with his hands;
Under his forming hands a Creature grew, [470]
Manlike, but different sex, so lovly faire,
That what seemd fair in all the World, seemd now
Mean, or in her summ'd up, in her containd
And in her looks, which from that time infus'd
Sweetness into my heart, unfelt before, [475]
And into all things from her Aire inspir'd
The spirit of love and amorous delight.
Shee disappeerd, and left me dark, I wak'd
To find her, or for ever to deplore
Her loss, and other pleasures all abjure: [480]
When out of hope, behold her, not farr off,
Such as I saw her in my dream, adornd
With what all Earth or Heaven could bestow
To make her amiable: On she came,
Led by her Heav'nly Maker, though unseen, [485]
And guided by his voice, nor uninformd
Of nuptial Sanctitie and marriage Rites:
Grace was in all her steps, Heav'n in her Eye,
In every gesture dignitie and love.
I overjoyd could not forbear aloud. [490]

This turn hath made amends; thou hast fulfill'd
Thy words, Creator bounteous and benigne,

≼ 亞當和夏娃目送天使拉斐爾離開
杜雷 版畫 1866年

　　經過一番諄諄告誡，拉斐爾準備返回天庭，亞當和夏娃目送他的離去，暗自警惕自己要遠離誘惑。

Giver of all things faire, but fairest this
Of all thy gifts, nor enviest. I now see
Bone of my Bone, Flesh of my Flesh, my Self [495]
Before me; Woman is her Name, of Man
Extracted; for this cause he shall forgoe
Father and Mother, and to his Wife adhere;
And they shall be one Flesh, one Heart, one Soule.

She heard me thus, and though divinely brought, [500]
Yet Innocence and Virgin Modestie,
Her vertue and the conscience of her worth,
That would be woo'd, and not unsought be won,
Not obvious, not obtrusive, but retir'd,
The more desirable, or to say all, [505]
Nature her self, though pure of sinful thought,
Wrought in her so, that seeing me, she turn'd;
I follow'd her, she what was Honour knew,
And with obsequious Majestie approv'd
My pleaded reason. To the Nuptial Bowre [510]
I led her blushing like the Morn: all Heav'n,
And happie Constellations on that houre
Shed thir selectest influence; the Earth
Gave sign of gratulation, and each Hill;
Joyous the Birds; fresh Gales and gentle Aires [515]
Whisper'd it to the Woods, and from thir wings
Flung Rose, flung Odours from the spicie Shrub,
Disporting, till the amorous Bird of Night
Sung Spousal, and bid haste the Eevning Starr
On his Hill top, to light the bridal Lamp. [520]
Thus I have told thee all my State, and brought
My Storie to the sum of earthly bliss
Which I enjoy, and must confess to find
In all things else delight indeed, but such
As us'd or not, works in the mind no change, [525]
Nor vehement desire, these delicacies
I mean of Taste, Sight, Smell, Herbs, Fruits and Flours,
Walks, and the melodie of Birds; but here
Farr otherwise, transported I behold,
Transported touch; here passion first I felt, [530]
Commotion strange, in all enjoyments else
Superiour and unmov'd, here onely weake
Against the charm of Beauties powerful glance.

Or Nature faild in mee, and left some part
Not proof enough such Object to sustain, [535]
Or from my side subducting, took perhaps
More then enough; at least on her bestow'd
Too much of Ornament, in outward shew
Elaborate, of inward less exact.
For well I understand in the prime end [540]
Of Nature her th' inferiour, in the mind
And inward Faculties, which most excell,
In outward also her resembling less
His Image who made both, and less expressing
The character of that Dominion giv'n [545]
O're other Creatures; yet when I approach
Her loveliness, so absolute she seems
And in her self compleat, so well to know
Her own, that what she wills to do or say,
Seems wisest, vertuousest, discreetest, best; [550]
All higher knowledge in her presence falls
Degraded, Wisdom in discourse with her
Looses discount'nanc't, and like folly shewes;
Authority and Reason on her waite,
As one intended first, not after made [555]
Occasionally; and to consummate all,
Greatness of mind and nobleness thir seat
Build in her loveliest, and create an awe
About her, as a guard Angelic plac't.
To whom the Angel with contracted brow. [560]

Accuse not Nature, she hath don her part;
Do thou but thine, and be not diffident
Of Wisdom, she deserts thee not, if thou
Dismiss not her, when most thou needst her nigh,
By attributing overmuch to things [565]
Less excellent, as thou thy self perceav'st.
For what admir'st thou, what transports thee so,
An outside? fair no doubt, and worthy well
Thy cherishing, thy honouring, and thy love,
Not thy subjection: weigh with her thy self; [570]
Then value: Oft times nothing profits more
Then self esteem, grounded on just and right
Well manag'd; of that skill the more thou know'st,
The more she will acknowledge thee her Head,

And to realities yield all her shows: [575]
Made so adorn for thy delight the more,
So awful, that with honour thou maist love
Thy mate, who sees when thou art seen least wise.
But if the sense of touch whereby mankind
Is propagated seem such dear delight [580]
Beyond all other, think the same voutsaf't
To Cattel and each Beast; which would not be
To them made common and divulg'd, if aught
Therein enjoy'd were worthy to subdue
The Soule of Man, or passion in him move. [585]
What higher in her societie thou findst
Attractive, human, rational, love still;
In loving thou dost well, in passion not,
Wherein true Love consists not; love refines
The thoughts, and heart enlarges, hath his seat [590]
In Reason, and is judicious, is the scale
By which to heav'nly Love thou maist ascend,
Not sunk in carnal pleasure, for which cause
Among the Beasts no Mate for thee was found.

To whom thus half abash't Adam repli'd. [595]
Neither her out-side formd so fair, nor aught
In procreation common to all kindes
(Though higher of the genial Bed by far,
And with mysterious reverence I deem)
So much delights me as those graceful acts, [600]
Those thousand decencies that daily flow
From all her words and actions mixt with Love
And sweet compliance, which declare unfeign'd
Union of Mind, or in us both one Soule;
Harmonie to behold in wedded pair [605]
More grateful then harmonious sound to the eare.
Yet these subject not; I to thee disclose
What inward thence I feel, not therefore foild,
Who meet with various objects, from the sense
Variously representing; yet still free [610]
Approve the best, and follow what I approve.
To Love thou blam'st me not, for love thou saist
Leads up to Heav'n, is both the way and guide;
Bear with me then, if lawful what I ask;
Love not the heav'nly Spirits, and how thir Love [615]

Express they, by looks onely, or do they mix
Irradiance, virtual or immediate touch?

To whom the Angel with a smile that glow'd
Celestial rosie red, Loves proper hue,
Answer'd. Let it suffice thee that thou know'st [620]
Us happie, and without Love no happiness.
Whatever pure thou in the body enjoy'st
(And pure thou wert created) we enjoy
In eminence, and obstacle find none
Of membrane, joynt, or limb, exclusive barrs: [625]
Easier then Air with Air, if Spirits embrace,
Total they mix, Union of Pure with Pure
Desiring; nor restrain'd conveyance need
As Flesh to mix with Flesh, or Soul with Soul.
But I can now no more; the parting Sun [630]
Beyond the Earths green Cape and verdant Isles
Hesperean sets, my Signal to depart.
Be strong, live happie, and love, but first of all
Him whom to love is to obey, and keep
His great command; take heed lest Passion sway [635]
Thy Judgment to do aught, which else free Will
Would not admit; thine and of all thy Sons
The weal or woe in thee is plac't; beware.
I in thy persevering shall rejoyce,
And all the Blest: stand fast; to stand or fall [640]
Free in thine own Arbitrement it lies.
Perfet within, no outward aid require;
And all temptation to transgress repel.

So saying, he arose; whom Adam thus
Follow'd with benediction. Since to part, [645]
Go heavenly Guest, Ethereal Messenger,
Sent from whose sovran goodness I adore.
Gentle to me and affable hath been
Thy condescension, and shall be honour'd ever
With grateful Memorie: thou to mankind [650]
Be good and friendly still, and oft return.

So parted they, the Angel up to Heav'n
From the thick shade, and Adam to his Bowre.

人類的原罪

撒旦被守衛天使逐出伊甸園後，遍歷地球各地，盡覽風光。數日後，他再次潛入伊甸園，打算實施新的計謀；他進到狡猾的蛇體內，借由蛇的外貌，悄悄接近落單時的夏娃，甜言蜜語地引誘她摘食知識樹的果實。夏娃觸犯禁令後，極力慫恿亞當也嘗嘗禁果；亞當深愛夏娃，雖明知是錯誤的行為，仍然為她吃下禁果。

∧ 撒旦在河流中泅泳，藉以重回伊甸園
杜雷版畫 1866年

　　被守衛天使逐出伊甸園的撒旦，走遍新世界的名山百川，一路都在思考如何引誘人類犯罪，最後又順著河流泅泳，回到伊甸園伺機而動。

就在亞當和夏娃回到住所，準備就寢之際，被守衛天使加百列逐出樂園的魔鬼，又悄悄地潛回樂園來；這段日子，他飛越黑海、亞速海，經由西伯利亞往南而下，到達南極。之後，又從黎巴嫩往西邊走，到達巴拿馬地峽，一路前行，直走到前方被太平洋阻斷了去路，才又轉往恆河和印度河地區。如此歷經七個夜晚，遊歷大半個地球；旅途中，他不斷地思考著要用何種方法去引誘人類犯罪，終於，在第七個夜晚想到一個絕妙的計謀。

於是他鑽進流經樂園地底的底格里斯河，順著河水泅泳，從生命樹旁邊的一處噴泉躍出水面，隱藏在霧氣當中。本想等到天亮時再伺機而動，但眼見亞當和夏娃相處的歡樂景象，熊熊怒火便不由地從他的胸膛竄起，使他渾身燥熱、憤憤不平：

「這地方就跟天堂一般美好，無數的星辰環繞著它，以聖潔的光輝映照在它的表面；山川、河谷、森林、草

No more of talk where God or Angel Guest
With Man, as with his Friend, familiar us'd
To sit indulgent, and with him partake
Rural repast, permitting him the while
Venial discourse unblam'd: I now must change [5]
Those Notes to Tragic; foul distrust, and breach
Disloyal on the part of Man, revolt,
And disobedience: On the part of Heav'n
Now alienated, distance and distaste,
Anger and just rebuke, and judgement giv'n, [10]
That brought into this World a world of woe,
Sinne and her shadow Death, and Miserie
Deaths Harbinger: Sad task, yet argument
Not less but more Heroic then the wrauth
Of stern Achilles on his Foe pursu'd [15]
Thrice Fugitive about Troy Wall; or rage
Of Turnus for Lavinia disespous'd,
Or Neptun's ire or Juno's, that so long
Perplex'd the Greek and Cytherea's Son;
If answerable style I can obtaine [20]
Of my Celestial Patroness, who deignes
Her nightly visitation unimplor'd,
And dictates to me slumb'ring, or inspires
Easie my unpremeditated Verse:
Since first this Subject for Heroic Song [25]
Pleas'd me long choosing, and beginning late;
Not sedulous by Nature to indite
Warrs, hitherto the onely Argument
Heroic deem'd, chief maistrie to dissect
With long and tedious havoc fabl'd Knights [30]
In Battels feign'd; the better fortitude
Of Patience and Heroic Martyrdom
Unsung; or to describe Races and Games,
Or tilting Furniture, emblazon'd Shields,
Impreses quaint, Caparisons and Steeds; [35]
Bases and tinsel Trappings, gorgious Knights
At Joust and Torneament; then marshal'd Feast
Serv'd up in Hall with Sewers, and Seneshals;
The skill of Artifice or Office mean,
Not that which justly gives Heroic name [40]
To Person or to Poem. Mee of these
Nor skilld nor studious, higher Argument

原和無數高貴的動、植物遍佈在其中。

　　自從為數眾多的天使被我喚醒，群體擺脫上帝的奴役，祂便用泥土捏塑了人類，想藉這個新種族來補充自己失去的崇拜者數目，不但花費六天六

▽ 撒旦眼見樂園的歡樂景象，心生妒意

杜雷 版畫 1866年

　　看到恩愛幸福的亞當和夏娃，怒火與妒意油然而生，撒旦決心摧毀上帝所造的新物種，以消心頭之恨。

Remaines, sufficient of it self to raise
That name, unless an age too late, or cold
Climat, or Years damp my intended wing [45]
Deprest, and much they may, if all be mine,
Not Hers who brings it nightly to my Ear.

The Sun was sunk, and after him the Starr
Of Hesperus, whose Office is to bring
Twilight upon the Earth, short Arbiter [50]
Twixt Day and Night, and now from end to end
Nights Hemisphere had veild the Horizon round:
When Satan who late fled before the threats
Of Gabriel out of Eden, now improv'd
In meditated fraud and malice, bent [55]
On mans destruction, maugre what might hap
Of heavier on himself, fearless return'd.
By Night he fled, and at Midnight return'd.
From compassing the Earth, cautious of day,
Since Uriel Regent of the Sun descri'd [60]
His entrance, and forewarnd the Cherubim
That kept thir watch; thence full of anguish driv'n,
The space of seven continu'd Nights he rode
With darkness, thrice the Equinoctial Line
He circl'd, four times cross'd the Carr of Night [65]
From Pole to Pole, traversing each Colure;
On the eighth return'd, and on the Coast averse
From entrance or Cherubic Watch, by stealth
Found unsuspected way. There was a place,
Now not, though Sin, not Time, first wraught the change, [70]
Where Tigris at the foot of Paradise
Into a Gulf shot under ground, till part
Rose up a Fountain by the Tree of Life;
In with the River sunk, and with it rose
Satan involv'd in rising Mist, then sought [75]
Where to lie hid; Sea he had searcht and Land
From Eden over Pontus, and the Poole
Mæotis, up beyond the River Ob;
Downward as farr Antartic; and in length
West from Orontes to the Ocean barr'd [80]
At Darien, thence to the Land where flowes
Ganges and Indus: thus the Orb he roam'd
With narrow search; and with inspection deep

夜為人類造了這個幸福的園地，把所
有新造的生物交給他們統轄，更派遣
高貴的天使在周遭保衛。我一定要盡
快把祂所創造的一切毀掉，才能夠消
除我心中無窮的怨恨，也才對得起那
群仍在地獄裡受苦的伙伴們。」

　　想到這兒，撒旦再也按耐不住，立
刻走入叢林，搜尋蛇的蹤跡。

　　離開伊甸園的這段時間，撒旦遍覽
地球、觀察所有的生物，他發現，蛇
是上帝所造的生物中，最為狡猾靈活
的[1]。於是，他打算進入蛇的身體，
利用蛇的外貌來躲避天使尤烈兒和加
百列的監視。

　　漆黑的夜色中，草地上有一團模糊
的影子，由下往上，一圈一圈地向上
盤繞；撒旦走近細看，發現就是自己
在尋找的蛇，牠的頭擺放在圓圈最頂
端的中央，正無憂無慮地熟睡著呢！
魔鬼很快地從蛇的口中潛入，掌握了

註1：出自《舊約‧創世紀》：「耶和華神所造的，
　　　唯有蛇比田野一切的活物更狡猾。」

Consider'd every Creature, which of all
Most opportune might serve his Wiles, and found [85]
The Serpent suttlest Beast of all the Field.
Him after long debate, irresolute
Of thoughts revolv'd, his final sentence chose
Fit Vessel, fittest Imp of fraud, in whom
To enter, and his dark suggestions hide [90]
From sharpest sight: for in the wilie Snake,
Whatever sleights none would suspicious mark,
As from his wit and native suttletie
Proceeding, which in other Beasts observ'd
Doubt might beget of Diabolic pow'r [95]
Active within beyond the sense of brute.
Thus he resolv'd, but first from inward griefe
His bursting passion into plaints thus pour'd:

O Earth, how like to Heav'n, if not preferr'd
More justly, Seat worthier of Gods, as built [100]
With second thoughts, reforming what was old!
For what God after better worse would build?
Terrestrial Heav'n, danc't round by other Heav'ns
That shine, yet bear thir bright officious Lamps,
Light above Light, for thee alone, as seems, [105]
In thee concentring all thir precious beams
Of sacred influence: As God in Heav'n
Is Center, yet extends to all, so thou
Centring receav'st from all those Orbs; in thee,
Not in themselves, all thir known vertue appeers [110]
Productive in Herb, Plant, and nobler birth
Of Creatures animate with gradual life
Of Growth, Sense, Reason, all summ'd up in Man.
With what delight could I have walkt thee round,
If I could joy in aught, sweet interchange [115]
Of Hill, and Vallie, Rivers, Woods and Plaines,
Now Land, now Sea, and Shores with Forrest crownd,
Rocks, Dens, and Caves; but I in none of these
Find place or refuge; and the more I see
Pleasures about me, so much more I feel [120]
Torment within me, as from the hateful siege
Of contraries; all good to me becomes
Bane, and in Heav'n much worse would be my state.
But neither here seek I, no nor in Heav'n

∧ 撒旦借蛇的外貌接近亞當和夏娃，伺機而動
杜雷 版畫 1866年

　　蛇是上帝創造的生物中，最為狡猾靈巧的，於是他潛入蛇的身體，打算利用蛇的外貌來躲避天使的監視。

牠的頭和心，然後，靜靜地窩在草地上，等待朝陽升起。

　　天亮了，伊甸園在晨光中緩緩甦醒，亞當和夏娃已做完晨禱，準備展開晨間的工作。夏娃首先開口，朝氣蓬勃地對亞當說道：

　　「我至愛的亞當，請你聽我說。照

To dwell, unless by maistring Heav'ns Supreame; [125]
Nor hope to be my self less miserable
By what I seek, but others to make such
As I, though thereby worse to me redound:
For onely in destroying I find ease
To my relentless thoughts; and him destroyd, [130]
Or won to what may work his utter loss,
For whom all this was made, all this will soon
Follow, as to him linkt in weal or woe,
In wo then: that destruction wide may range:
To mee shall be the glorie sole among [135]
The infernal Powers, in one day to have marr'd
What he Almightie styl'd, six Nights and Days
Continu'd making, and who knows how long
Before had bin contriving, though perhaps
Not longer then since I in one Night freed [140]
From servitude inglorious welnigh half
Th' Angelic Name, and thinner left the throng
Of his adorers: hee to be aveng'd,
And to repair his numbers thus impair'd,
Whether such vertue spent of old now faild [145]
More Angels to Create, if they at least
Are his Created, or to spite us more,
Determin'd to advance into our room
A Creature form'd of Earth, and him endow,
Exalted from so base original, [150]
With Heav'nly spoils, our spoils: What he decreed
He effected; Man he made, and for him built
Magnificent this World, and Earth his seat,
Him Lord pronounc'd, and, O indignitie!
Subjected to his service Angel wings, [155]
And flaming Ministers to watch and tend
Thir earthy Charge: Of these the vigilance
I dread, and to elude, thus wrapt in mist
Of midnight vapor glide obscure, and prie
In every Bush and Brake, where hap may finde [160]
The Serpent sleeping, in whose mazie foulds
To hide me, and the dark intent I bring.
O foul descent! that I who erst contended
With Gods to sit the highest, am now constraind
Into a Beast, and mixt with bestial slime, [165]
This essence to incarnate and imbrute,

顧園中的花卉草木，這樣的勞動是使我快樂的；但隨著工作量一天一天的增加，我們所需花費的工作時間越來越長，常常得工作到晚上。我想到一個好主意，你看可不可行，就是我們兩個人分開來工作，你去把攀藤植物的枝條牽引到適當的方向，我則負責修剪玫瑰花叢的枝葉，這樣便可以省去我們因聊天、討論工作分配所浪費掉的時間。」

亞當微微一笑，溫柔地回答：

「親愛的夏娃，上帝分派給我們的唯一工作，不過是照顧整理伊甸園中的樹木花草，這工作並不辛苦，也不必急著完成。況且，我倆說話的時間並不長，應該不至於會占去太多的工作時間。我並不贊成兩人分開工作，因為你昨天也聽天使說了，撒旦已經潛入樂園，或許正隱藏在這附近。倘若魔鬼趁你落單的時候，對你做出邪惡的舉動，傷害了你，那會使我痛苦萬分的。

That to the hight of Deitie aspir'd;
But what will not Ambition and Revenge
Descend to? who aspires must down as low
As high he soard, obnoxious first or last [170]
To basest things. Revenge, at first though sweet,
Bitter ere long back on it self recoiles;
Let it; I reck not, so it light well aim'd,
Since higher I fall short, on him who next
Provokes my envie, this new Favorite [175]
Of Heav'n, this Man of Clay, Son of despite,
Whom us the more to spite his Maker rais'd
From dust: spite then with spite is best repaid.

So saying, through each Thicket Danck or Drie,
Like a black mist low creeping, he held on [180]
His midnight search, where soonest he might finde
The Serpent: him fast sleeping soon he found
In Labyrinth of many a round self-rowld,
His head the midst, well stor'd with suttle wiles:
Not yet in horrid Shade or dismal Den, [185]
Nor nocent yet, but on the grassie Herbe
Fearless unfeard he slept: in at his Mouth
The Devil enterd, and his brutal sense,
In heart or head, possessing soon inspir'd
With act intelligential; but his sleep [190]
Disturbd not, waiting close th' approach of Morn.
Now when as sacred Light began to dawne
In Eden on the humid Flours, that breathd
Thir morning incense, when all things that breath,
From th' Earths great Altar send up silent praise [195]
To the Creator, and his Nostrils fill
With grateful Smell, forth came the human pair
And joind thir vocal Worship to the Quire
Of Creatures wanting voice, that done, partake
The season, prime for sweetest Sents and Aires: [200]
Then commune how that day they best may ply
Thir growing work: for much thir work outgrew
The hands dispatch of two Gardning so wide.
And Eve first to her Husband thus began.

Adam, well may we labour still to dress [205]
This Garden, still to tend Plant, Herb and Flour,

「如果你只是想要暫時離開我的身邊，享受一會兒孤獨帶來的思考空間，這倒是可以的；因為暫時的分開是情感的催化劑，當我們再度碰面時，會更加珍惜彼此。」

夏娃聽了亞當的話，對於他的不信任，心中感到一絲委屈，於是說道：

「只要堅守心中的信仰、不受誘惑，魔鬼便不能使我們受到傷害；我記得昨日天使是這麼說的，不是嗎？還是你覺得我無法約束自己，對你不夠忠誠，因此不放心讓我獨自工作？」亞當聽出夏娃語帶埋怨，連忙澄清：

「不是的，你別誤會。我是真的擔心你的安危才這麼說。想想看，連天上聖潔的天使們都會被撒旦欺騙，做出叛逆的事來，足見他有多麼狡詐邪惡。因此，他一定會施展更加可怕的陰謀來傷害我們。如果沒有親眼看著你，我是無法安心工作的。」說完，緊緊地握住夏娃的手。

Our pleasant task enjoyn'd, but till more hands
Aid us, the work under our labour grows,
Luxurious by restraint; what we by day
Lop overgrown, or prune, or prop, or bind, [210]
One night or two with wanton growth derides
Tending to wilde. Thou therefore now advise
Or hear what to my minde first thoughts present,
Let us divide our labours, thou where choice
Leads thee, or where most needs, whether to wind [215]
The Woodbine round this Arbour, or direct
The clasping Ivie where to climb, while I
In yonder Spring of Roses intermixt
With Myrtle, find what to redress till Noon:
For while so near each other thus all day [220]
Our taske we choose, what wonder if so near
Looks intervene and smiles, or object new
Casual discourse draw on, which intermits
Our dayes work brought to little, though begun
Early, and th' hour of Supper comes unearn'd. [225]

To whom mild answer Adam thus return'd.
Sole Eve, Associate sole, to me beyond
Compare above all living Creatures deare,
Well hast thou motion'd, well thy thoughts imployd
How we might best fulfill the work which here [230]
God hath assign'd us, nor of me shalt pass
Unprais'd: for nothing lovelier can be found
In Woman, then to studie houshold good,
And good workes in her Husband to promote.
Yet not so strictly hath our Lord impos'd [235]
Labour, as to debarr us when we need
Refreshment, whether food, or talk between,
Food of the mind, or this sweet intercourse
Of looks and smiles, for smiles from Reason flow,
To brute deni'd, and are of Love the food, [240]
Love not the lowest end of human life.
For not to irksom toile, but to delight
He made us, and delight to Reason joyn'd.
These paths & Bowers doubt not but our joynt hands
Will keep from Wilderness with ease, as wide [245]
As we need walk, till younger hands ere long
Assist us: But if much converse perhaps

夏娃一邊用力把手給抽回來，一邊甜甜地笑著說：

「你放心啦！我可以保護自己的，我可沒那麼容易被引誘呢！就這麼決定了，你留在這兒工作，我去樹林子那邊的玫瑰花園修剪枝葉，中午再回到居處一塊兒用餐。」

對於夏娃的堅持，亞當雖然不同意，但為避免愛人誤會，也只好眼睜睜地看著她漸漸走遠。她那輕盈曼妙的步伐，比神話中的山精歐麗、樹精德萊雅和月神黛安娜都要來得優美動人[2]。

撒旦潛伏於蛇的體內，在距離亞當和夏娃不遠的樹叢下，注視著他倆的一舉一動，渴盼他們有落單的時機，方便他施行計謀。沒想到機會來得如此快速；夏娃正揮別亞當，往另一邊走去。撒旦連忙扭動長長的身體、滑

註2：山精歐麗（Oreads）、樹精德萊雅（Dryads）和月神黛安娜（Diana）都是《希臘羅馬神話故事》中的神祇。

Thee satiate, to short absence I could yield.
For solitude somtimes is best societie,
And short retirement urges sweet returne. [250]
But other doubt possesses me, least harm
Befall thee sever'd from me; for thou knowst
What hath bin warn'd us, what malicious Foe
Envying our happiness, and of his own
Despairing, seeks to work us woe and shame [255]
By sly assault; and somwhere nigh at hand
Watches, no doubt, with greedy hope to find
His wish and best advantage, us asunder,
Hopeless to circumvent us joynd, where each
To other speedie aide might lend at need; [260]
Whether his first design be to withdraw
Our fealtie from God, or to disturb
Conjugal Love, then which perhaps no bliss
Enjoy'd by us excites his envie more;
Or this, or worse, leave not the faithful side [265]
That gave thee being, still shades thee and protects.
The Wife, where danger or dishonour lurks,
Safest and seemliest by her Husband staies,
Who guards her, or with her the worst endures.

To whom the Virgin Majestie of Eve, [270]
As one who loves, and some unkindness meets,
With sweet austeer composure thus reply'd,

Ofspring of Heav'n and Earth, and all Earths Lord,
That such an Enemie we have, who seeks
Our ruin, both by thee informd I learne, [275]
And from the parting Angel over-heard
As in a shadie nook I stood behind,
Just then returnd at shut of Evening Flours.
But that thou shouldst my firmness therfore doubt
To God or thee, because we have a foe [280]
May tempt it, I expected not to hear.
His violence thou fear'st not, being such,
As wee, not capable of death or paine,
Can either not receave, or can repell.
His fraud is then thy fear, which plain inferrs [285]
Thy equal fear that my firm Faith and Love
Can by his fraud be shak'n or seduc't;

^ **撒旦偽裝成蛇，躲在叢林窺視亞當和夏娃**
杜雷 版畫 1866年

    化身為蛇的撒旦一直在暗中觀察亞當和夏娃，耐心等候他們落單的時機，以便施展他的計謀。

行著，緊緊跟在後頭。

    夏娃在玫瑰園停下腳步，心情愉快地進行整理的工作；只見她扶起一株株傾倒的花朵，在枝幹綁上支架，讓它撐起來。接著，又彎腰撿拾落在地上的枯葉和樹枝，把花間小徑清理得

Thoughts, which how found they harbour in thy brest
Adam, misthought of her to thee so dear?

To whom with healing words Adam replyd. [290]
Daughter of God and Man, immortal Eve,
For such thou art, from sin and blame entire:
Not diffident of thee do I dissuade
Thy absence from my sight, but to avoid
Th' attempt itself, intended by our Foe. [295]
For hee who tempts, though in vain, at least asperses
The tempted with dishonour foul, suppos'd
Not incorruptible of Faith, not prooff
Against temptation: thou thy self with scorne
And anger wouldst resent the offer'd wrong, [300]
Though ineffectual found: misdeem not then,
If such affront I labour to avert
From thee alone, which on us both at once
The Enemie, though bold, will hardly dare,
Or daring, first on mee th' assault shall light. [305]
Nor thou his malice and false guile contemn;
Suttle he needs must be, who could seduce
Angels nor think superfluous others aid.
I from the influence of thy looks receave
Access in every Vertue, in thy sight [310]
More wise, more watchful, stronger, if need were
Of outward strength; while shame, thou looking on,
Shame to be overcome or over-reacht
Would utmost vigor raise, and rais'd unite.
Why shouldst not thou like sense within thee feel [315]
When I am present, and thy trial choose
With me, best witness of thy Vertue tri'd.

So spake domestick Adam in his care
And Matrimonial Love; but Eve, who thought
Less attributed to her Faith sincere, [320]
Thus her reply with accent sweet renewd.

If this be our condition, thus to dwell
In narrow circuit strait'nd by a Foe,
Suttle or violent, we not endu'd
Single with like defence, wherever met, [325]
How are we happie, still in fear of harm?

非常乾淨。

人類之母的美麗，差點讓魔鬼打消惡毒的念頭，但美善終究不敵仇恨，撒旦開始實施狡詐的計謀。他高舉蛇頭，緩緩地靠近夏娃，口中發出嘶嘶的聲響，想藉此引來夏娃的注視。終於，夏娃看見他了，他趕忙開口說道：

「啊！多麼美麗的人兒呀，你的美讓百花黯然失色，群獸看得癡迷；可惜在這片遼闊的土地上，竟只有一個人識得你的美，真是可惜啊！」

夏娃乍然聽見蛇說出人語來，嚇得

▽ 撒旦看到落單的夏娃而竊喜
布雷克　水彩畫 1795年

重返伊甸園的撒旦看到落單的夏娃，竊喜機不可失，立刻化身為蛇接近她。

But harm precedes not sin: onely our Foe
Tempting affronts us with his foul esteem
Of our integritie: his foul esteeme
Sticks no dishonor on our Front, but turns [330]
Foul on himself; then wherefore shund or feard
By us? who rather double honour gaine
From his surmise prov'd false, find peace within,
Favour from Heav'n, our witness from th' event.
And what is Faith, Love, Vertue unassaid [335]
Alone, without exterior help sustaind?
Let us not then suspect our happie State
Left so imperfet by the Maker wise,
As not secure to single or combin'd.
Fraile is our happiness, if this be so, [340]
And Eden were no Eden thus expos'd.

To whom thus Adam fervently repli'd.
O Woman, best are all things as the will
Of God ordain'd them, his creating hand
Nothing imperfet or deficient left [345]
Of all that he Created, much less Man,
Or aught that might his happie State secure,
Secure from outward force; within himself
The danger lies, yet lies within his power:
Against his will he can receave no harme. [350]
But God left free the Will, for what obeyes
Reason, is free, and Reason he made right
But bid her well beware, and still erect,
Least by some faire appeering good surpris'd
She dictate false, and misinforme the Will [355]
To do what God expresly hath forbid,
Not then mistrust, but tender love enjoynes,
That I should mind thee oft, and mind thou me.
Firm we subsist, yet possible to swerve,
Since Reason not impossibly may meet [360]
Some specious object by the Foe subornd,
And fall into deception unaware,
Not keeping strictest watch, as she was warnd.
Seek not temptation then, which to avoide
Were better, and most likelie if from mee [365]
Thou sever not: Trial will come unsought.
Wouldst thou approve thy constancie, approve

停下手邊的工作，問道：

「你怎麼會說人類的語言？對人類來說，上帝所創造的各種生物應該都像啞巴，不會說，也不能明白人類的話語，而你卻說出人類的語言，這究竟是怎麼回事呢？」

「曾經，我就像你所說的，只會發出蛇類的嘶嘶聲，在草地裡躥來躥去，漫無目的地生活著；直到有一天，我無意間吃了一棵果樹上所結的果子，此後便能夠懂得人類的語言，並產生思考的能力。」蛇狡黠地回答。

「喔！園中竟有這樣神奇的樹，在那個地方呢？能否告訴我，我想去瞧瞧。」

夏娃聽見蛇的說詞，好奇心頓起，想親眼去看看那棵樹。

「能夠為最美麗的人兒服務，是我莫大的榮幸，請跟著我來吧！我這就帶你去那棵樹生長的地方。」

蛇露出興奮的神情說道，立刻在前

First thy obedience; th' other who can know,
Not seeing thee attempted, who attest?
But if thou think, trial unsought may finde [370]
Us both securer then thus warnd thou seemst,
Go; for thy stay, not free, absents thee more;
Go in thy native innocence, relie
On what thou hast of vertue, summon all,
For God towards thee hath done his part, do thine. [375]

So spake the Patriarch of Mankinde, but Eve
Persisted, yet submiss, though last, repli'd.

With thy permission then, and thus forewarnd
Chiefly by what thy own last reasoning words
Touchd onely, that our trial, when least sought, [380]
May finde us both perhaps farr less prepar'd,
The willinger I goe, nor much expect
A Foe so proud will first the weaker seek,
So bent, the more shall shame him his repulse.
Thus saying, from her Husbands hand her hand [385]
Soft she withdrew, and like a Wood-Nymph light
Oread or Dryad, or of Delia's Traine,
Betook her to the Groves, but Delia's self
In gate surpass'd and Goddess-like deport,
Though not as shee with Bow and Quiver armd, [390]
But with such Gardning Tools as Art yet rude,
Guiltless of fire had formd, or Angels brought.
To Pales, or Pomona, thus adornd,
Likeliest she seemd, Pomona when she fled
Vertumnus, or to Ceres in her Prime, [395]
Yet Virgin of Proserpina from Jove.
Her long with ardent look his Eye pursu'd
Delighted, but desiring more her stay.
Oft he to her his charge of quick returne
Repeated, shee to him as oft engag'd [400]
To be returnd by Noon amid the Bowre,
And all things in best order to invite
Noontide repast, or Afternoons repose.
O much deceav'd, much failing, hapless Eve,
Of thy presum'd return! event perverse! [405]
Thou never from that houre in Paradise
Foundst either sweet repast, or sound repose;

方帶路，領著夏娃往知識樹的方向而去；彷彿墓園陰森的鬼火，引導夜間旅人往山崖、沼澤裡去，使他們丟掉性命。

穿過樹林，沿著溪流往前走幾公尺，再轉兩、三個彎，便到達目的地，蛇來到樹下，轉頭對夏娃說：

「就是我前面的這棵樹。」

夏娃看看四周，再抬頭一看，發現蛇所吃的，竟然是知識樹的果實，她大吃一驚，惶恐地對蛇喊著：

「哎呀！你怎麼能吃這棵樹的果子呢？上帝曾經嚴格的告誡我們，禁止我們觸摸和摘食它的果實。」

「是嗎？可是就我所知，原野上所有的生物，從來就不曾聽過這項禁令，莫非，上帝的這個限制是專為人類設下的，為什麼呢？」

蛇故意裝出一副疑惑的神情，狡猾地問。

Such ambush hid among sweet Flours and Shades
Waited with hellish rancour imminent
To intercept thy way, or send thee back [410]
Despoild of Innocence, of Faith, of Bliss.
For now, and since first break of dawne the Fiend,
Meer Serpent in appearance, forth was come,
And on his Quest, where likeliest he might finde
The onely two of Mankinde, but in them [415]
The whole included Race, his purposd prey.
In Bowre and Field he sought, where any tuft
Of Grove or Garden-Plot more pleasant lay,
Thir tendance or Plantation for delight,
By Fountain or by shadie Rivulet [420]
He sought them both, but wish'd his hap might find
Eve separate, he wish'd, but not with hope
Of what so seldom chanc'd, when to his wish,
Beyond his hope, Eve separate he spies,
Veild in a Cloud of Fragrance, where she stood, [425]
Half spi'd, so thick the Roses bushing round
About her glowd, oft stooping to support
Each Flour of slender stalk, whose head though gay

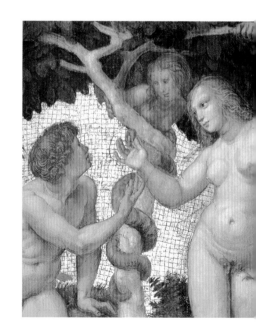

➢ 亞當與夏娃（局部）
拉斐爾 壁畫 1509～1511年

「我也不清楚，只知道這是一棵能夠分辨善惡的樹，上帝說，倘若我們吃了樹上的果子，必得死亡。」

夏娃回答蛇的問題之後，內心也開始產生一絲疑惑，「為什麼蛇吃了禁果，卻沒有死呢？」

「這的確是一棵神奇的樹，我吃了它的果實之後，便能明白許多知識，增長智慧，故也能夠分辨善惡；上帝要你們避免犯錯，不可步入惡途，但你們既不懂得『惡』，又如何會有施行『善』的能力呢？因為你們根本無法分出孰是善、孰是惡呀！況且我擁有了智慧，不但沒有死，生活反而更加充實，眼睛更為明亮了。」蛇接著又說：

「依我看來，造物主不讓你們吃知識果的主要原因，並不是真的為了你們著想，而是自私地想獨占智慧、知識，因為唯有如此，人類才能對天神永懷敬畏之心，祂也才能夠永享高高在上的地位。」

Carnation, Purple, Azure, or spect with Gold,
Hung drooping unsustaind, them she upstaies [430]
Gently with Mirtle band, mindless the while,
Her self, though fairest unsupported Flour,
From her best prop so farr, and storm so nigh.
Neerer he drew, and many a walk travers'd
Of stateliest Covert, Cedar, Pine, or Palme, [435]
Then voluble and bold, now hid, now seen
Among thick-wov'n Arborets and Flours
Imborderd on each Bank, the hand of Eve:
Spot more delicious then those Gardens feign'd
Or of reviv'd Adonis, or renownd [440]
Alcinous, host of old Laertes Son,
Or that, not Mystic, where the Sapient King
Held dalliance with his fair Egyptian Spouse.
Much hee the Place admir'd, the Person more.
As one who long in populous City pent, [445]
Where Houses thick and Sewers annoy the Aire,
Forth issuing on a Summers Morn to breathe
Among the pleasant Villages and Farmes
Adjoynd, from each thing met conceaves delight,
The smell of Grain, or tedded Grass, or Kine, [450]
Or Dairie, each rural sight, each rural sound;
If chance with Nymphlike step fair Virgin pass,
What pleasing seemd, for her now pleases more,
She most, and in her look summs all Delight.
Such Pleasure took the Serpent to behold [455]
This Flourie Plat, the sweet recess of Eve
Thus earlie, thus alone; her Heav'nly forme
Angelic, but more soft, and Feminine,
Her graceful Innocence, her every Aire
Of gesture or lest action overawd [460]
His Malice, and with rapine sweet bereav'd
His fierceness of the fierce intent it brought:
That space the Evil one abstracted stood
From his own evil, and for the time remaind
Stupidly good, of enmitie disarm'd, [465]
Of guile, of hate, of envie, of revenge;
But the hot Hell that alwayes in him burnes,
Though in mid Heav'n, soon ended his delight,
And tortures him now more, the more he sees
Of pleasure not for him ordain'd: then soon [470]

「上帝創造了我和亞當，我們本來就應該對祂心懷敬意，因此，就算祂的主要目的，真的是不想讓我們增長智慧，我們也無任何怨懟。我要回玫瑰園繼續工作了，你如果想吃知識樹的果子，那就自己吃吧！」夏娃說完，轉身就要走。

蛇見夏娃要走，連忙叫喊著：

「等一下！你真得不吃嗎？上帝賜給亞當較高的智慧、勇氣和體力，如果你吃了知識樹的果子，就能夠像亞當一般聰明，懂得一樣多了。」

夏娃聽見蛇的話，意志不禁動搖起來，

「是呀！如果我能夠懂得多一點，不但擴展了自己的眼界，還能夠像天使拉斐爾那般侃侃而談，這是一件多麼棒的事情。況且，死亡有什麼可怕的呢？誰又知道是不是真的會死，看哪！蛇犯下禁令，不但沒有受到懲罰，甚至變得像人類一樣聰明了。」

蛇見夏娃有些猶豫，立刻又添油加

Fierce hate he recollects, and all his thoughts
Of mischief, gratulating, thus excites.

Thoughts, whither have ye led me, with what sweet
Compulsion thus transported to forget
What hither brought us, hate, not love, nor hope [475]
Of Paradise for Hell, hope here to taste
Of pleasure, but all pleasure to destroy,
Save what is in destroying, other joy
To me is lost. Then let me not let pass
Occasion which now smiles, behold alone [480]
The Woman, opportune to all attempts,
Her Husband, for I view far round, not nigh,
Whose higher intellectual more I shun,
And strength, of courage hautie, and of limb
Heroic built, though of terrestrial mould, [485]
Foe not informidable, exempt from wound,
I not; so much hath Hell debas'd, and paine
Infeebl'd me, to what I was in Heav'n.
Shee fair, divinely fair, fit Love for Gods,
Not terrible, though terrour be in Love [490]
And beautie, not approach by stronger hate,
Hate stronger, under shew of Love well feign'd,
The way which to her ruin now I tend.

So spake the Enemie of Mankind, enclos'd
In Serpent, Inmate bad, and toward Eve [495]
Address'd his way, not with indented wave,
Prone on the ground, as since, but on his reare,
Circular base of rising foulds, that tour'd
Fould above fould a surging Maze, his Head
Crested aloft, and Carbuncle his Eyes; [500]
With burnisht Neck of verdant Gold, erect
Amidst his circling Spires, that on the grass
Floted redundant: pleasing was his shape,
And lovely, never since of Serpent kind
Lovelier, not those that in Illyria chang'd [505]
Hermione and Cadmus, or the God
In Epidaurus; nor to which transformd
Ammonian Jove, or Capitoline was seen,
Hee with Olympias, this with her who bore
Scipio the highth of Rome. With tract oblique [510]

夏娃的引誘和墮落
布雷克　水彩畫 1808年

　　蛇再三鼓吹夏娃，其實吃下知識果並不會死亡，反而會得到神性，智慧大開，他以自己為例，終於誘使夏娃張口吃了知識果。

諂地說：

　　「別再考慮了，上帝如果真得不想讓你們吃知識樹的果子，那又何必把知識樹種在伊甸園裡？可見祂不過是想測試一下你們的忠誠度，吃果子本身並沒有多大害處，頂多是被上帝責備一下罷了。但你卻因此能夠變得像天使一般學識淵博，小懲罰換來大收

At first, as one who sought access, but feard
To interrupt, side-long he works his way.
As when a Ship by skilful Stearsman wrought
Nigh Rivers mouth or Foreland, where the Wind
Veres oft, as oft so steers, and shifts her Saile; [515]
So varied hee, and of his tortuous Traine
Curld many a wanton wreath in sight of Eve,
To lure her Eye; shee busied heard the sound
Of rusling Leaves, but minded not, as us'd
To such disport before her through the Field, [520]
From every Beast, more duteous at her call,
Then at Circean call the Herd disguis'd.
Hee boulder now, uncall'd before her stood;
But as in gaze admiring: Oft he bowd
His turret Crest, and sleek enamel'd Neck, [525]
Fawning, and lick'd the ground whereon she trod.
His gentle dumb expression turnd at length
The Eye of Eve to mark his play; he glad
Of her attention gaind, with Serpent Tongue
Organic, or impulse of vocal Air, [530]
His fraudulent temptation thus began.

Wonder not, sovran Mistress, if perhaps
Thou canst, who art sole Wonder, much less arm
Thy looks, the Heav'n of mildness, with disdain,
Displeas'd that I approach thee thus, and gaze [535]
Insatiate, I thus single, nor have feard
Thy awful brow, more awful thus retir'd.
Fairest resemblance of thy Maker faire,
Thee all things living gaze on, all things thine
By gift, and thy Celestial Beautie adore [540]
With ravishment beheld, there best beheld
Where universally admir'd; but here
In this enclosure wild, these Beasts among,
Beholders rude, and shallow to discerne
Half what in thee is fair, one man except, [545]
Who sees thee? (and what is one?) who shouldst be seen
A Goddess among Gods, ador'd and serv'd
By Angels numberless, thy daily Train.

So gloz'd the Tempter, and his Proem tun'd;
Into the Heart of Eve his words made way, [550]

益，這不是很划算的事嗎？」

夏娃被蛇說動了，伸手摘下知識果，咬下一口。

「嗯！真是香甜。」

她貪婪地吃著，根本未曾察覺那引誘她犯下死罪、滿身邪惡的蛇，已從她身邊悄悄地溜進草叢裡去了。

夏娃吃完一顆果子，伸手又摘下一顆。

「我得讓亞當也吃顆知識果才行，否則只有我獨得神性，卻無人能夠與我相對等地交談，那又有什麼意思呢？」

心裡才在想著呢，一個高壯的身影已出現在遠方。原來，夏娃遲遲未歸，亞當在家裡等急了，心中擔心不已，於是出來找她。

「亞當，你來的正好。快點來嚐嚐我手上的這棵果子，很甜喔！」

夏娃展露甜甜的笑靨，跑向

Though at the voice much marveling; at length
Not unamaz'd she thus in answer spake.
What may this mean? Language of Man pronounc't
By Tongue of Brute, and human sense exprest?
The first at lest of these I thought deni'd [555]
To Beasts, whom God on thir Creation-Day
Created mute to all articulat sound;
The latter I demurre, for in thir looks
Much reason, and in thir actions oft appeers.
Thee, Serpent, suttlest beast of all the field [560]
I knew, but not with human voice endu'd;

夏娃初嘗知識果的美味
杜雷 版畫 1866年

　　落單的夏娃在蛇的勸誘下，吃下知識樹的果實，她從來沒吃過如此美味的果子，吃完之後又摘了一顆，覺得應該與亞當分享。

前去迎接亞當。

　　亞當舉起雙臂，輕輕地把夏娃攬進懷裡，溫柔地說：

　　「怎麼還待在這兒？我在家裡等你好一陣子了。」

　　隨即，他發現夏娃握在手中的，竟然是知識果。

　　「你！你……犯下大罪了，你難道不知道，這果子是不可以吃的呀！」

　　亞當嚇得冒出一身冷汗，驚恐地瞪著夏娃。

　　「你別緊張，你看，我早就吃下一顆禁果，到現在也沒怎麼樣啊。而且，我遇到一條能夠說人類語言的蛇喔！牠就是吃了禁果，才會說話的，不但沒死，還具備了無窮的智慧。就是因為牠的勸說，我才放心吃的，你也安心地吃吧！」

　　夏娃說完，嬌柔地把禁果遞到亞當嘴邊。

　　「不行，我不能吃，倘若吃了禁果，便是背叛上帝；」

Redouble then this miracle, and say,
How cam'st thou speakable of mute, and how
To me so friendly grown above the rest
Of brutal kind, that daily are in sight? [565]
Say, for such wonder claims attention due.

To whom the guileful Tempter thus reply'd.
Empress of this fair World, resplendent Eve,
Easie to mee it is to tell thee all
What thou commandst and right thou shouldst be obeyd: [570]
I was at first as other Beasts that graze
The trodden Herb, of abject thoughts and low,
As was my food, nor aught but food discern'd
Or Sex, and apprehended nothing high:
Till on a day roaving the field, I chanc'd [575]
A goodly Tree farr distant to behold
Loaden with fruit of fairest colours mixt,
Ruddie and Gold: I nearer drew to gaze;
When from the boughes a savorie odour blow'n,
Grateful to appetite, more pleas'd my sense, [580]
Then smell of sweetest Fenel or the Teats
Of Ewe or Goat dropping with Milk at Eevn,
Unsuckt of Lamb or Kid, that tend thir play.
To satisfie the sharp desire I had
Of tasting those fair Apples, I resolv'd [585]
Not to deferr; hunger and thirst at once,
Powerful perswaders, quick'nd at the scent
Of that alluring fruit, urg'd me so keene.
About the mossie Trunk I wound me soon,
For high from ground the branches would require [590]
Thy utmost reach or Adams: Round the Tree
All other Beasts that saw, with like desire
Longing and envying stood, but could not reach.
Amid the Tree now got, where plenty hung
Tempting so nigh, to pluck and eat my fill [595]
I spar'd not, for such pleasure till that hour
At Feed or Fountain never had I found.
Sated at length, ere long I might perceave
Strange alteration in me, to degree
Of Reason in my inward Powers, and Speech [600]
Wanted not long, though to this shape retain'd.
Thenceforth to Speculations high or deep

亞當內心掙扎不已，他低頭望著夏娃，為她眼中的深情所惑。

「但是，我深愛的女人已經犯下死罪，我怎能讓她獨自承擔沉淪的苦果，如果，她因此罪而死亡，我獨活世間又有什麼意義？還不如與她一塊死去。」

亞當這樣想著，一顆驚慌的心，立刻獲得紓解；他拿起夏娃手中的果子，用力咬下一口。

就這樣，人類的始祖給後代帶來死亡的原罪，天空為之悲泣，大地痛苦的顫抖，憤怒的雷聲也轟隆隆地響起，全都在哀嘆人類的沉淪。

亞當吃下禁果後，終於懂得何謂「善」，孰為「惡」；他後悔不已，忍不住埋怨起夏娃來：

「仔細想想，你說的那條會說人話的蛇，應該是撒旦化成的；你怎麼這麼糊塗，隨隨便便就輕信他人之言，使我們落入魔鬼的陷阱？現在可好了，我們不但犯下罪行，還對自己的

I turnd my thoughts, and with capacious mind
Considerd all things visible in Heav'n,
Or Earth, or Middle, all things fair and good; [605]
But all that fair and good in thy Divine
Semblance, and in thy Beauties heav'nly Ray
United I beheld; no Fair to thine
Equivalent or second, which compel'd
Mee thus, though importune perhaps, to come [610]
And gaze, and worship thee of right declar'd
Sovran of Creatures, universal Dame.

So talk'd the spirited sly Snake; and Eve
Yet more amaz'd unwarie thus reply'd.

Serpent, thy overpraising leaves in doubt [615]
The vertue of that Fruit, in thee first prov'd:
But say, where grows the Tree, from hence how far?
For many are the Trees of God that grow
In Paradise, and various, yet unknown
To us, in such abundance lies our choice, [620]
As leaves a greater store of Fruit untoucht,
Still hanging incorruptible, till men
Grow up to thir provision, and more hands
Help to disburden Nature of her Bearth.

To whom the wilie Adder, blithe and glad. [625]
Empress, the way is readie, and not long,
Beyond a row of Myrtles, on a Flat,
Fast by a Fountain, one small Thicket past
Of blowing Myrrh and Balme; if thou accept
My conduct, I can bring thee thither soon. [630]

Lead then, said Eve. Hee leading swiftly rowld
In tangles, and made intricate seem strait,
To mischief swift. Hope elevates, and joy
Bright'ns his Crest, as when a wandring Fire
Compact of unctuous vapor, which the Night [635]
Condenses, and the cold invirons round,
Kindl'd through agitation to a Flame,
Which oft, they say, some evil Spirit attends
Hovering and blazing with delusive Light,
Misleads th' amaz'd Night-wanderer from his way [640]

⌃ 原罪
葛斯 油畫 1470年

　　夏娃偷吃了知識果之後，不禁也摘了一顆慫恿亞當同食。亞當不願讓夏娃單獨承受沉淪的苦果，於是也跟著咬了一口，撒旦的詭計輕鬆得逞。

裸體產生羞恥感，無法再以坦然的態度去面對上帝和天使群。」

To Boggs and Mires, and oft through Pond or Poole,
There swallow'd up and lost, from succour farr.
So glister'd the dire Snake, and into fraud
Led Eve our credulous Mother, to the Tree
Of prohibition, root of all our woe; [645]
Which when she saw, thus to her guide she spake.

Serpent, we might have spar'd our coming hither,
Fruitless to mee, though Fruit be here to excess,
The credit of whose vertue rest with thee,
Wondrous indeed, if cause of such effects. [650]
But of this Tree we may not taste nor touch;
God so commanded, and left that Command
Sole Daughter of his voice; the rest, we live
Law to our selves, our Reason is our Law.

To whom the Tempter guilefully repli'd. [655]
Indeed? hath God then said that of the Fruit
Of all these Garden Trees ye shall not eate,
Yet Lords declar'd of all in Earth or Aire?

To whom thus Eve yet sinless. Of the Fruit
Of each Tree in the Garden we may eate, [660]
But of the Fruit of this fair Tree amidst
The Garden, God hath said, Ye shall not eate
Thereof, nor shall ye touch it, least ye die.

She scarse had said, though brief, when now more bold
The Tempter, but with shew of Zeale and Love [665]
To Man, and indignation at his wrong,
New part puts on, and as to passion mov'd,
Fluctuats disturbd, yet comely and in act
Rais'd, as of som great matter to begin.
As when of old som Orator renound [670]
In Athens or free Rome, where Eloquence
Flourishd, since mute, to som great cause addrest,
Stood in himself collected, while each part,
Motion, each act won audience ere the tongue,
Somtimes in highth began, as no delay [675]
Of Preface brooking through his Zeal of Right.
So standing, moving, or to highth upgrown
The Tempter all impassiond thus began.

△ **亞當與夏娃**
希土克 油畫 1912年

　　「你怎麼能這樣指責我？難道你
先前說的，愛我甚於自己，是在騙我
嗎？我怎會知道，魔鬼竟能藉著蛇的
外形來施行詭計；在吃下禁果之前，
我心中從來就不知道惡念為何，又怎
能了解蛇包藏禍心呢？」夏娃說完，
委屈地哭了。

　　亞當並不憐惜，反而更加生氣地回
答：

O Sacred, Wise, and Wisdom-giving Plant,
Mother of Science, Now I feel thy Power [680]
Within me cleere, not onely to discerne
Things in thir Causes, but to trace the wayes
Of highest Agents, deemd however wise.
Queen of this Universe, doe not believe
Those rigid threats of Death; ye shall not Die: [685]
How should ye? by the Fruit? it gives you Life
To Knowledge, By the Threatner, look on mee,
Mee who have touch'd and tasted, yet both live,
And life more perfet have attaind then Fate
Meant mee, by ventring higher then my Lot. [690]
Shall that be shut to Man, which to the Beast
Is open? or will God incense his ire
For such a petty Trespass, and not praise
Rather your dauntless vertue, whom the pain
Of Death denounc't, whatever thing Death be, [695]
Deterrd not from atchieving what might leade
To happier life, knowledge of Good and Evil;
Of good, how just? of evil, if what is evil
Be real, why not known, since easier shunnd?
God therefore cannot hurt ye, and be just; [700]
Not just, not God; not feard then, nor obeyd:
Your feare it self of Death removes the feare.
Why then was this forbid? Why but to awe,
Why but to keep ye low and ignorant,
His worshippers; he knows that in the day [705]
Ye Eate thereof, your Eyes that seem so cleere,
Yet are but dim, shall perfetly be then
Op'nd and cleerd, and ye shall be as Gods,
Knowing both Good and Evil as they know.
That ye should be as Gods, since I as Man, [710]
Internal Man, is but proportion meet,
I of brute human, yee of human Gods.
So ye shall die perhaps, by putting off
Human, to put on Gods, death to be wisht,
Though threat'nd, which no worse then this can bring. [715]
And what are Gods that Man may not become
As they, participating God-like food?
The Gods are first, and that advantage use
On our belief, that all from them proceeds;
I question it, for this fair Earth I see, [720]

「如果你早上肯聽我的話，乖乖的留在我的身邊，就不會讓魔鬼有機可趁了。」

原罪
希土克 油畫 1893年

　　吃下知識果的亞當開始產生忿怒、猜疑的情緒，他開始怪罪一切都是夏娃不好，原本是天賜的紅顏，如今變成魅惑的禍水，彷彿一切的罪惡與墮落，都是夏娃的錯。

Warm'd by the Sun, producing every kind,
Them nothing: If they all things, who enclos'd
Knowledge of Good and Evil in this Tree,
That whoso eats thereof, forthwith attains
Wisdom without their leave? and wherein lies [725]
Th' offence, that Man should thus attain to know?
What can your knowledge hurt him, or this Tree
Impart against his will if all be his?
Or is it envie, and can envie dwell
In Heav'nly brests? these, these and many more [730]
Causes import your need of this fair Fruit.
Goddess humane, reach then, and freely taste.

He ended, and his words replete with guile
Into her heart too easie entrance won:
Fixt on the Fruit she gaz'd, which to behold [735]
Might tempt alone, and in her ears the sound
Yet rung of his perswasive words, impregn'd
With Reason, to her seeming, and with Truth;
Mean while the hour of Noon drew on, and wak'd
An eager appetite, rais'd by the smell [740]
So savorie of that Fruit, which with desire,
Inclinable now grown to touch or taste,
Sollicited her longing eye; yet first
Pausing a while, thus to her self she mus'd.

Great are thy Vertues, doubtless, best of Fruits. [745]
Though kept from Man, and worthy to be admir'd,
Whose taste, too long forborn, at first assay
Gave elocution to the mute, and taught
The Tongue not made for Speech to speak thy praise:
Thy praise hee also who forbids thy use, [750]
Conceales not from us, naming thee the Tree
Of Knowledge, knowledge both of good and evil;
Forbids us then to taste, but his forbidding
Commends thee more, while it inferrs the good
By thee communicated, and our want: [755]
For good unknown, sure is not had, or had
And yet unknown, is as not had at all.
In plain then, what forbids he but to know,
Forbids us good, forbids us to be wise?
Such prohibitions binde not. But if Death [760]

「既然你說我是你骨中的骨、肉中的肉，又說你是我的頭，那麼在我提議分開工作時，你就應該堅持自己的想法，硬把我留下來，而不是現在才來責怪我。」

Bind us with after-bands, what profits then
Our inward freedom? In the day we eate
Of this fair Fruit, our doom is, we shall die.
How dies the Serpent? hee hath eat'n and lives,
And knows, and speaks, and reasons, and discerns, [765]
Irrational till then. For us alone
Was death invented? or to us deni'd
This intellectual food, for beasts reserv'd?
For Beasts it seems: yet that one Beast which first
Hath tasted, envies not, but brings with joy [770]
The good befall'n him, Author unsuspect,
Friendly to man, farr from deceit or guile.
What fear I then, rather what know to feare
Under this ignorance of good and Evil,
Of God or Death, of Law or Penaltie? [775]
Here grows the Cure of all, this Fruit Divine,
Fair to the Eye, inviting to the Taste,
Of vertue to make wise: what hinders then
To reach, and feed at once both Bodie and Mind?

So saying, her rash hand in evil hour [780]
Forth reaching to the Fruit, she pluck'd, she eat:
Earth felt the wound, and Nature from her seat
Sighing through all her Works gave signs of woe,
That all was lost. Back to the Thicket slunk
The guiltie Serpent, and well might, for Eve [785]
Intent now wholly on her taste, naught else
Regarded, such delight till then, as seemd,
In Fruit she never tasted, whether true
Or fansied so, through expectation high
Of knowledg, nor was God-head from her thought. [790]
Greedily she ingorg'd without restraint,
And knew not eating Death: Satiate at length,

◁ 亞當和夏娃犯下沉淪之罪，痛苦地淚流滿面
杜雷 版畫 1866年

亞當知道妻子已經吃下禁果，不忍讓她獨自沉淪死亡的苦果，於是他也咬了一口，人類的始祖替後代招來死亡的原罪，兩人內心痛苦、羞愧，不禁淚流滿面。

And hight'nd as with Wine, jocond and boon,
Thus to her self she pleasingly began.

O Sovran, vertuous, precious of all Trees [795]
In Paradise, of operation blest
To Sapience, hitherto obscur'd, infam'd,
And thy fair Fruit let hang, as to no end
Created; but henceforth my early care,
Not without Song, each Morning, and due praise [800]
Shall tend thee, and the fertil burden ease
Of thy full branches offer'd free to all;
Till dieted by thee I grow mature
In knowledge, as the Gods who all things know;
Though others envie what they cannot give; [805]
For had the gift bin theirs, it had not here
Thus grown. Experience, next to thee I owe,
Best guide; not following thee, I had remaind
In ignorance, thou op'nst Wisdoms way,
And giv'st access, though secret she retire. [810]
And I perhaps am secret; Heav'n is high,
High and remote to see from thence distinct
Each thing on Earth; and other care perhaps
May have diverted from continual watch
Our great Forbidder, safe with all his Spies [815]
About him. But to Adam in what sort
Shall I appeer? shall I to him make known
As yet my change, and give him to partake
Full happiness with mee, or rather not,
But keep the odds of Knowledge in my power [820]
Without Copartner? so to add what wants
In Femal Sex, the more to draw his Love,
And render me more equal, and perhaps,
A thing not undesireable, somtime
Superior: for inferior who is free? [825]
This may be well: but what if God have seen
And Death ensue? then I shall be no more,
And Adam wedded to another Eve,
Shall live with her enjoying, I extinct;
A death to think. Confirm'd then I resolve, [830]
Adam shall share with me in bliss or woe:
So dear I love him, that with him all deaths

I could endure, without him live no life.

So saying, from the Tree her step she turnd,
But first low Reverence don, as to the power [835]
That dwelt within, whose presence had infus'd
Into the plant sciential sap, deriv'd
From Nectar, drink of Gods. Adam the while
Waiting desirous her return, had wove
Of choicest Flours a Garland to adorne [840]
Her Tresses, and her rural labours crown,
As Reapers oft are wont thir Harvest Queen.
Great joy he promis'd to his thoughts, and new
Solace in her return, so long delay'd;
Yet oft his heart, divine of somthing ill, [845]
Misgave him; hee the faultring measure felt;
And forth to meet her went, the way she took
That Morn when first they parted; by the Tree
Of Knowledge he must pass, there he her met,
Scarse from the Tree returning; in her hand [850]
A bough of fairest fruit that downie smil'd,
New gatherd, and ambrosial smell diffus'd.
To him she hasted, in her face excuse
Came Prologue, and Apologie to prompt,
Which with bland words at will she thus addrest. [855]

Hast thou not wonderd, Adam, at my stay?
Thee I have misst, and thought it long, depriv'd
Thy presence, agonie of love till now
Not felt, nor shall be twice, for never more
Mean I to trie, what rash untri'd I sought, [860]
The pain of absence from thy sight. But strange
Hath bin the cause, and wonderful to heare:
This Tree is not as we are told, a Tree
Of danger tasted, nor to evil unknown
Op'ning the way, but of Divine effect [865]
To open Eyes, and make them Gods who taste;
And hath bin tasted such: the Serpent wise,
Or not restraind as wee, or not obeying,
Hath eat'n of the fruit, and is become,
Not dead, as we are threatn'd, but thenceforth [870]
Endu'd with human voice and human sense,

亞當的話，激起夏娃心中的怒氣，她憤憤不平地埋怨著。

「算了，再吵下去也沒辦法改變現實，既然事情已經無法挽回，我們還是想個方法，把令人羞恥的裸體遮掩起來吧！」

亞當說完，拉著夏娃的手往樹林中去，在地上揀了些闊葉，編織成衣物，並把它圍在下半身[3]。

忿怒、羞恥、猜疑和不安，種種惡的情緒在兩人的內心緊緊糾纏，使他們後悔不已，淚流滿面，卻再也挽回不了得「惡」失「善」的後果了。

註3：人類受蛇誘惑的事跡出自《舊約·創世紀》：「蛇對女人說：『神豈是真說，不許你們吃園中所有樹上的果子嗎？』女人對蛇說：『園中樹上的果子，我們可以吃；惟有園當中那棵樹上的果子，神曾說：你們不可吃，也不可摸，免得你們死。』蛇對女人說：『你們不一定死，因為神知道，你們吃的日子眼睛就明亮了，你們便如神能知道善惡。』於是，女人見那棵樹的果子好作食物，也悅人的眼目，且是可喜愛的，能使人有智慧，就摘下果子來吃了；又給她丈夫，她丈夫也吃了。他們二人的眼睛就明亮了，才知道自己是赤身露體，便拿無花果樹的葉子，為自己編作裙子。」

Reasoning to admiration, and with mee
Perswasively hath so prevaild, that I
Have also tasted, and have also found
Th' effects to correspond, opener mine Eyes [875]
Dimm erst, dilated Spirits, ampler Heart,
And growing up to Godhead; which for thee
Chiefly I sought, without thee can despise.
For bliss, as thou hast part, to me is bliss,
Tedious, unshar'd with thee, and odious soon. [880]
Thou therefore also taste, that equal Lot
May joyne us, equal Joy, as equal Love;
Least thou not tasting, different degree
Disjoyne us, and I then too late renounce
Deitie for thee, when Fate will not permit. [885]

Thus Eve with Countnance blithe her storie told;
But in her Cheek distemper flushing glowd.
On th' other side, Adam, soon as he heard
The fatal Trespass don by Eve, amaz'd,
Astonied stood and Blank, while horror chill [890]
Ran through his veins, and all his joynts relax'd;
From his slack hand the Garland wreath'd for Eve
Down drop'd, and all the faded Roses shed:
Speechless he stood and pale, till thus at length
First to himself he inward silence broke. [895]

O fairest of Creation, last and best
Of all Gods works, Creature in whom excell'd
Whatever can to sight or thought be formd,
Holy, divine, good, amiable, or sweet!
How art thou lost, how on a sudden lost, [900]
Defac't, deflourd, and now to Death devote?
Rather how hast thou yeelded to transgress
The strict forbiddance, how to violate
The sacred Fruit forbidd'n! som cursed fraud
Of Enemie hath beguil'd thee, yet unknown, [905]
And mee with thee hath ruind, for with thee
Certain my resolution is to Die;
How can I live without thee, how forgoe
Thy sweet Converse and Love so dearly joyn'd,
To live again in these wilde Woods forlorn? [910]
Should God create another Eve, and I

Another Rib afford, yet loss of thee
Would never from my heart; no no, I feel
The Link of Nature draw me: Flesh of Flesh,
Bone of my Bone thou art, and from thy State [915]
Mine never shall be parted, bliss or woe.

So having said, as one from sad dismay
Recomforted, and after thoughts disturbd
Submitting to what seemd remediless,
Thus in calm mood his Words to Eve he turnd. [920]

Bold deed thou hast presum'd, adventrous Eve
And peril great provok't, who thus hath dar'd
Had it been onely coveting to Eye
That sacred Fruit, sacred to abstinence,
Much more to taste it under banne to touch. [925]
But past who can recall, or don undoe?
Not God Omnipotent, nor Fate, yet so
Perhaps thou shalt not Die, perhaps the Fact
Is not so hainous now, foretasted Fruit,
Profan'd first by the Serpent, by him first [930]
Made common and unhallowd ere our taste;
Nor yet on him found deadly, he yet lives,
Lives, as thou saidst, and gaines to live as Man
Higher degree of Life, inducement strong
To us, as likely tasting to attaine [935]
Proportional ascent, which cannot be
But to be Gods, or Angels Demi-gods.
Nor can I think that God, Creator wise,
Though threatning, will in earnest so destroy
Us his prime Creatures, dignifi'd so high, [940]
Set over all his Works, which in our Fall,
For us created, needs with us must faile,
Dependent made; so God shall uncreate,
Be frustrate, do, undo, and labour loose,
Not well conceav'd of God, who though his Power [945]
Creation could repeate, yet would be loath
Us to abolish, least the Adversary
Triumph and say; Fickle their State whom God
Most Favors, who can please him long; Mee first
He ruind, now Mankind; whom will he next? [950]
Matter of scorne, not to be given the Foe,

However I with thee have fixt my Lot,
Certain to undergoe like doom, if Death
Consort with thee, Death is to mee as Life;
So forcible within my heart I feel [955]
The Bond of Nature draw me to my owne,
My own in thee, for what thou art is mine;
Our State cannot be severd, we are one,
One Flesh; to loose thee were to loose my self.

So Adam, and thus Eve to him repli'd. [960]
O glorious trial of exceeding Love,
Illustrious evidence, example high!
Ingaging me to emulate, but short
Of thy perfection, how shall I attaine,
Adam, from whose deare side I boast me sprung, [965]
And gladly of our Union heare thee speak,
One Heart, one Soul in both; whereof good prooff
This day affords, declaring thee resolvd,
Rather then Death or aught then Death more dread
Shall separate us, linkt in Love so deare, [970]
To undergoe with mee one Guilt, one Crime,
If any be, of tasting this fair Fruit,
Whose vertue, for of good still good proceeds,
Direct, or by occasion hath presented
This happie trial of thy Love, which else [975]
So eminently never had bin known.
Were it I thought Death menac't would ensue
This my attempt, I would sustain alone
The worst, and not perswade thee, rather die
Deserted, then oblige thee with a fact [980]
Pernicious to thy Peace, chiefly assur'd
Remarkably so late of thy so true,
So faithful Love unequald; but I feel
Farr otherwise th' event, not Death, but Life
Augmented, op'nd Eyes, new Hopes, new Joyes, [985]
Taste so Divine, that what of sweet before
Hath toucht my sense, flat seems to this, and harsh.
On my experience, Adam, freely taste,
And fear of Death deliver to the Windes.

So saying, she embrac'd him, and for joy [990]
Tenderly wept, much won that he his Love

△ 夏娃、蛇與死亡
格里恩 油畫 1512年

　　夏娃隨著蛇來到知識樹前面，當她吃
下知識果之後，死亡立刻緊緊抓住她，從
此人類便免不了生老病死的原罪。

Had so enobl'd, as of choice to incurr
Divine displeasure for her sake, or Death.
In recompence (for such compliance bad
Such recompence best merits) from the bough [995]
She gave him of that fair enticing Fruit
With liberal hand: he scrupl'd not to eat
Against his better knowledge, not deceav'd,
But fondly overcome with Femal charm.
Earth trembl'd from her entrails, as again [1000]
In pangs, and Nature gave a second groan,
Skie lowr'd, and muttering Thunder, som sad drops
Wept at compleating of the mortal Sin
Original; while Adam took no thought,
Eating his fill, nor Eve to iterate [1005]
Her former trespass fear'd, the more to soothe
Him with her lov'd societie, that now
As with new Wine intoxicated both
They swim in mirth, and fansie that they feel
Divinitie within them breeding wings [1010]
Wherewith to scorne the Earth: but that false Fruit
Farr other operation first displaid,
Carnal desire enflaming, hee on Eve
Began to cast lascivious Eyes, she him
As wantonly repaid; in Lust they burne: [1015]
Till Adam thus 'gan Eve to dalliance move,

Eve, now I see thou art exact of taste,
And elegant, of Sapience no small part,
Since to each meaning savour we apply,
And Palate call judicious; I the praise [1020]
Yeild thee, so well this day thou hast purvey'd.
Much pleasure we have lost, while we abstain'd
From this delightful Fruit, nor known till now
True relish, tasting; if such pleasure be
In things to us forbidden, it might be wish'd, [1025]
For this one Tree had bin forbidden ten.
But come, so well refresh't, now let us play,
As meet is, after such delicious Fare;
For never did thy Beautie since the day
I saw thee first and wedded thee, adorn'd [1030]
With all perfections, so enflame my sense
With ardor to enjoy thee, fairer now

Then ever, bountie of this vertuous Tree.

So said he, and forbore not glance or toy
Of amorous intent, well understood [1035]
Of Eve, whose Eye darted contagious Fire.
Her hand he seis'd, and to a shadie bank,
Thick overhead with verdant roof imbowr'd
He led her nothing loath; Flours were the Couch,
Pansies, and Violets, and Asphodel, [1040]
And Hyacinth, Earths freshest softest lap.
There they thir fill of Love and Loves disport
Took largely, of thir mutual guilt the Seale,
The solace of thir sin, till dewie sleep
Oppress'd them, wearied with thir amorous play. [1045]
Soon as the force of that fallacious Fruit,
That with exhilerating vapour bland
About thir spirits had plaid, and inmost powers
Made erre, was now exhal'd, and grosser sleep
Bred of unkindly fumes, with conscious dreams [1050]
Encumberd, now had left them, up they rose
As from unrest, and each the other viewing,
Soon found thir Eyes how op'nd, and thir minds
How dark'nd; innocence, that as a veile
Had shadow'd them from knowing ill, was gon, [1055]
Just confidence, and native righteousness
And honour from about them, naked left
To guiltie shame hee cover'd, but his Robe
Uncover'd more, so rose the Danite strong
Herculean Samson from the Harlot-lap [1060]
Of Philistean Dalilah, and wak'd
Shorn of his strength, They destitute and bare
Of all thir vertue: silent, and in face
Confounded long they sate, as struck'n mute,
Till Adam, though not less then Eve abasht, [1065]
At length gave utterance to these words constrain.

O Eve, in evil hour thou didst give eare
To that false Worm, of whomsoever taught
To counterfet Mans voice, true in our Fall,
False in our promis'd Rising; since our Eyes [1070]
Op'nd we find indeed, and find we know
Both Good and Evil, Good lost, and Evil got,

Bad Fruit of Knowledge, if this be to know,
Which leaves us naked thus, of Honour void,
Of Innocence, of Faith, of Puritie, [1075]
Our wonted Ornaments now soild and staind,
And in our Faces evident the signes
Of foul concupiscence; whence evil store;
Even shame, the last of evils; of the first
Be sure then. How shall I behold the face [1080]
Henceforth of God or Angel, earst with joy
And rapture so oft beheld? those heav'nly shapes
Will dazle now this earthly, with thir blaze
Insufferably bright. O might I here
In solitude live savage, in some glade [1085]
Obscur'd, where highest Woods impenetrable
To Starr or Sun-light, spread thir umbrage broad,
And brown as Evening: Cover me ye Pines,
Ye Cedars, with innumerable boughs
Hide me, where I may never see them more. [1090]
But let us now, as in bad plight, devise
What best may for the present serve to hide
The Parts of each from other, that seem most
To shame obnoxious, and unseemliest seen,
Some Tree whose broad smooth Leaves together sowd, [1095]
And girded on our loyns, may cover round
Those middle parts, that this new commer, Shame,
There sit not, and reproach us as unclean.

So counsel'd hee, and both together went
Into the thickest Wood, there soon they chose [1100]
The Figtree, not that kind for Fruit renown'd,
But such as at this day to Indians known
In Malabar or Decan spreds her Armes
Braunching so broad and long, that in the ground
The bended Twigs take root, and Daughters grow [1105]
About the Mother Tree, a Pillard shade
High overarch't, and echoing Walks between;
There oft the Indian Herdsman shunning heate
Shelters in coole, and tends his pasturing Herds
At Loopholes cut through thickest shade: Those Leaves [1110]
They gatherd, broad as Amazonian Targe,
And with what skill they had, together sowd,
To gird thir waste, vain Covering if to hide

Thir guilt and dreaded shame; O how unlike
To that first naked Glorie. Such of late [1115]
Columbus found th' American so girt
With featherd Cincture, naked else and wilde
Among the Trees on Iles and woodie Shores.
Thus fenc't, and as they thought, thir shame in part
Coverd, but not at rest or ease of Mind, [1120]
They sate them down to weep, nor onely Teares
Raind at thir Eyes, but high Winds worse within
Began to rise, high Passions, Anger, Hate,
Mistrust, Suspicion, Discord, and shook sore
Thir inward State of Mind, calm Region once [1125]
And full of Peace, now tost and turbulent:
For Understanding rul'd not, and the Will
Heard not her lore, both in subjection now
To sensual Appetite, who from beneathe
Usurping over sovran Reason claimd [1130]
Superior sway: From thus distemperd brest,
Adam, estrang'd in look and alterd stile,
Speech intermitted thus to Eve renewd.

Would thou hadst heark'nd to my words, and stai'd
With me, as I besought thee, when that strange [1135]
Desire of wandring this unhappie Morn,
I know not whence possessd thee; we had then
Remaind still happie, not as now, despoild
Of all our good, sham'd, naked, miserable.
Let none henceforth seek needless cause to approve [1140]
The Faith they owe; when earnestly they seek
Such proof, conclude, they then begin to faile.

To whom soon mov'd with touch of blame thus Eve.
What words have past thy Lips, Adam severe,
Imput'st thou that to my default, or will [1145]
Of wandring, as thou call'st it, which who knows
But might as ill have happ'nd thou being by,
Or to thy self perhaps: hadst thou been there,
Or here th' attempt, thou couldst not have discernd
Fraud in the Serpent, speaking as he spake; [1150]
No ground of enmitie between us known,
Why hee should mean me ill, or seek to harme.
Was I to have never parted from thy side?

As good have grown there still a liveless Rib.
Being as I am, why didst not thou the Head [1155]
Command me absolutely not to go,
Going into such danger as thou saidst?
Too facil then thou didst not much gainsay,
Nay, didst permit, approve, and fair dismiss.
Hadst thou bin firm and fixt in thy dissent, [1160]
Neither had I transgress'd, nor thou with mee.

To whom then first incenst Adam repli'd,
Is this the Love, is this the recompence
Of mine to thee, ingrateful Eve, exprest
Immutable when thou wert lost, not I, [1165]
Who might have liv'd and joyd immortal bliss,
Yet willingly chose rather Death with thee:
And am I now upbraided, as the cause
Of thy transgressing? not enough severe,
It seems, in thy restraint: what could I more? [1170]
I warn'd thee, I admonish'd thee, foretold
The danger, and the lurking Enemie
That lay in wait; beyond this had bin force,
And force upon free Will hath here no place.
But confidence then bore thee on, secure [1175]
Either to meet no danger, or to finde
Matter of glorious trial; and perhaps
I also err'd in overmuch admiring
What seemd in thee so perfet, that I thought
No evil durst attempt thee, but I rue [1180]
That errour now, which is become my crime,
And thou th' accuser. Thus it shall befall
Him who to worth in Women overtrusting
Lets her Will rule; restraint she will not brook,
And left to her self, if evil thence ensue, [1185]
Shee first his weak indulgence will accuse.

Thus they in mutual accusation spent
The fruitless hours, but neither self-condemning,
And of thir vain contest appeer'd no end.

上帝的懲罰

　　撒旦重回伊甸園，並潛進蛇的身體，引誘夏娃摘食知識樹的果實，犯下死亡重罪；亞當不忍心讓夏娃獨自面對上帝的懲罰，愛妻心切下也跟著吃下禁果；人類的原罪就此成立。上帝派遣神子基督到樂園去審判人類，收回永生與幸福的恩澤；亞當和夏娃對於自己的罪行深感羞愧，於是伏臥於地，誠心祈禱，懇求天父的原諒。

˄ 亞當和夏娃聽見天神的聲音，害怕地躲進樹叢
杜雷 版畫 1866年

　　吃下知識果的亞當和夏娃，有了羞愧之心，當他們聽到天神的腳步聲，竟然害怕地躲進樹叢，不敢面對聖潔的天神。

守衛伊甸園的天使們，發現亞當和夏娃已偷吃禁果，觸犯禁令，自覺再無留守樂園的必要，所以全體整裝出發，飛回天上去。

負責傳遞消息的天使，已先一步回到天庭，在上帝的寶座前報告此事；聽聞這項壞消息的天庭眾天使，無不駭然，他們群集在一塊兒，忿怒地指責魔鬼的狡詐，並要求上帝嚴懲撒旦。

上帝坐在高高的雲端，臉上猶帶一絲慍色，祂早已得知人類犯下的罪行，沒有一件事能夠逃離祂的眼目，因此，祂對甫回天庭的守衛天使說：

「你們無須沮喪、自責，即使你們加倍用心戒備，也無法防範這件事情發生；自從撒旦從地獄脫逃，我就預知了人類必遭魔鬼的引誘。不去阻止，是想看看人類身上的自由意志，會堅守虔敬之心、選擇服從，或聽信謊言、選擇背叛。現在，我們已經看到了結果，人類必須為他們的墮落付

Meanwhile the hainous and despightfull act
Of Satan done in Paradise, and how
Hee in the Serpent, had perverted Eve,
Her Husband shee, to taste the fatall fruit,
Was known in Heav'n; for what can scape the Eye [5]
Of God All-seeing, or deceave his Heart
Omniscient, who in all things wise and just,
Hinder'd not Satan to attempt the minde
Of Man, with strength entire, and free will arm'd,
Complete to have discover'd and repulst [10]
Whatever wiles of Foe or seeming Friend.
For still they knew, and ought to have still remember'd
The high Injunction not to taste that Fruit,
Whoever tempted; which they not obeying,
Incurr'd, what could they less, the penaltie, [15]
And manifold in sin, deserv'd to fall.
Up into Heav'n from Paradise in haste
Th' Angelic Guards ascended, mute and sad
For Man, for of his state by this they knew,
Much wondring how the suttle Fiend had stoln [20]
Entrance unseen. Soon as th' unwelcome news
From Earth arriv'd at Heaven Gate, displeas'd
All were who heard, dim sadness did not spare
That time Celestial visages, yet mixt
With pitie, violated not thir bliss. [25]
About the new-arriv'd, in multitudes
Th' ethereal People ran, to hear and know
How all befell: they towards the Throne Supream
Accountable made haste to make appear
With righteous plea, thir utmost vigilance, [30]
And easily approv'd; when the most High
Eternal Father from his secret Cloud,
Amidst in Thunder utter'd thus his voice.

Assembl'd Angels, and ye Powers return'd
From unsuccessful charge, be not dismaid, [35]
Nor troubl'd at these tidings from the Earth,
Which your sincerest care could not prevent,
Foretold so lately what would come to pass,
When first this Tempter cross'd the Gulf from Hell.
I told ye then he should prevail and speed [40]
On his bad Errand, Man should be seduc't

出死亡的代價，我絕不稍加寬恕。」

　　說到這裡，上帝轉頭對右手邊的基督說道：

　　「我摯愛的獨生子，就由你去審判人類吧！因為我已經把天上、人間及地獄的審判權，通通轉交給你了。而且，你曾經對我表示要做人類的救贖者，因此，由你來擔負這項任務是最為恰當的。」

　　「永恆的天父，只要是您所發的命令，都將由我前去執行；我是您的愛子，您所希望的我都會確實完成，不違背您的意志。我將秉持公理正義，以慈悲心來做出最公平的審判；但是我希望這次的審判只有亞當和夏娃在場，不要有其他人參與。」

　　神子恭敬地回答天父，身上散發著神性的光輝。

　　伊甸園裡，正是夕陽西下、眾鳥歸巢的時刻，神子來到樂園，在徐徐的涼風中散步；亞當和夏娃聽見風中傳來天神腳步聲，害怕地躲進茂密的樹

And flatter'd out of all, believing lies
Against his Maker; no Decree of mine
Concurring to necessitate his Fall,
Or touch with lightest moment of impulse [45]
His free Will, to her own inclining left
In eevn scale. But fall'n he is, and now
What rests but that the mortal Sentence pass
On his transgression Death denounc't that day,
Which he presumes already vain and void, [50]
Because not yet inflicted, as he fear'd,
By some immediate stroak; but soon shall find
Forbearance no acquittance ere day end.
Justice shall not return as bountie scorn'd.
But whom send I to judge them? whom but thee [55]
Vicegerent Son, to thee I have transferr'd
All Judgement whether in Heav'n, or Earth, or Hell.
Easie it might be seen that I intend
Mercie collegue with Justice, sending thee
Mans Friend his Mediator, his design'd [60]
Both Ransom and Redeemer voluntarie,
And destin'd Man himself to judge Man fall'n.

So spake the Father, and unfoulding bright
Toward the right hand his Glorie, on the Son
Blaz'd forth unclouded Deitie; he full [65]
Resplendent all his Father manifest
Express'd, and thus divinely answer'd milde.

Father Eternal, thine is to decree,
Mine both in Heav'n and Earth to do thy will
Supream, that thou in mee thy Son belov'd [70]
Mayst ever rest well pleas'd. I go to judge
On Earth these thy transgressors, but thou knowst,
Whoever judg'd, the worst on mee must light,
When time shall be, for so I undertook
Before thee; and not repenting, this obtaine [75]
Of right, that I may mitigate thir doom
On me deriv'd, yet I shall temper so
Justice with Mercie, as may illustrate most
Them fully satisfied, and thee appease.
Attendance none shall need, nor Train, where none [80]
Are to behold the Judgement, but the judg'd,

叢裡去。只聽見神子大聲地呼喊：

「亞當，你在哪裡？為什麼不出來見我。與我會面不是以前最讓你雀躍的事嗎？」

亞當和夏娃一臉愧色，忐忑不安地從樹叢中走出來，亞當說道：

「我在園中聽見您的聲音，感到害怕，又因為赤身露體，所以躲起來了。」

神子溫柔地問道：

「為什麼要害怕我的聲音？又怎會懂得裸體這個詞呢？難道你吃了知識樹的果子？」面對眼前的審判官，亞當痛苦地想著：

「我該自己承擔起所有的罪責，還是說出妻子的罪行呢？就算我不說，全能的天神也會知道事情的真相吧！」

於是他對神子說道：

「是她，您賜予我最美好的禮物。她要我吃那棵樹的果實，她一向對我極為忠誠，她說的、做的，都是那般

Those two; the third best absent is condemn'd,
Convict by flight, and Rebel to all Law
Conviction to the Serpent none belongs.

Thus saying, from his radiant Seat he rose [85]
Of high collateral glorie: him Thrones and Powers,
Princedoms, and Dominations ministrant
Accompanied to Heaven Gate, from whence
Eden and all the Coast in prospect lay.
Down he descended strait; the speed of Gods [90]
Time counts not, though with swiftest minutes wing'd.
Now was the Sun in Western cadence low
From Noon, and gentle Aires due at thir hour
To fan the Earth now wak'd, and usher in
The Eevning coole, when he from wrauth more coole [95]
Came the mild Judge and Intercessor both
To sentence Man: the voice of God they heard
Now walking in the Garden, by soft windes
Brought to thir Ears, while day declin'd, they heard,
And from his presence hid themselves among [100]
The thickest Trees, both Man and Wife, till God
Approaching, thus to Adam call'd aloud.

Where art thou Adam, wont with joy to meet
My coming seen far off? I miss thee here,
Not pleas'd, thus entertaind with solitude, [105]
Where obvious dutie erewhile appear'd unsaught:
Or come I less conspicuous, or what change
Absents thee, or what chance detains? Come forth.
He came, and with him Eve, more loth, though first
To offend, discount'nanc't both, and discompos'd; [110]
Love was not in thir looks, either to God
Or to each other, but apparent guilt,
And shame, and perturbation, and despaire,
Anger, and obstinacie, and hate, and guile.
Whence Adam faultring long, thus answer'd brief. [115]

I heard thee in the Garden, and of thy voice
Affraid, being naked, hid my self. To whom
The gracious Judge without revile repli'd.

My voice thou oft hast heard, and hast not fear'd,

的美好，我從來不懷疑她要我做的
事，所以我便吃了那果子。我倆都不
夠虔敬，才會受到引誘吃了禁果，接
受懲罰是應該的，是我們咎由自取的
結果。」

「她是為你而造的，是你的伙伴，
你無須聽從她的話語，只須聽信上帝
的聲音即可。」

然後，神子又訓誡夏娃說：

「你知道自己做錯了什麼嗎？」

「是蛇，是牠引誘我去吃禁果
的。」

夏娃羞愧不已，把罪往蛇的身上
推。

於是神子首先宣判蛇的罪，他說：

「從今以後，凡蛇類必終生以腹
部爬行，吃塵土過日。蛇與女人之間
充滿仇恨，女人的後代將擊碎蛇的
頭，而蛇則會咬傷女人後代的腳後跟[1]
。」

接著，神子宣判夏娃的罪：

「我要增加你懷孕時的苦處，你得

But still rejoyc't, how is it now become [120]
So dreadful to thee? that thou art naked, who
Hath told thee? hast thou eaten of the Tree
Whereof I gave thee charge thou shouldst not eat?

To whom thus Adam sore beset repli'd.
O Heav'n! in evil strait this day I stand [125]
Before my Judge, either to undergoe
My self the total Crime, or to accuse
My other self, the partner of my life;
Whose failing, while her Faith to me remaines,
I should conceal, and not expose to blame [130]
By my complaint; but strict necessitie
Subdues me, and calamitous constraint
Least on my head both sin and punishment,
However insupportable, be all
Devolv'd; though should I hold my peace, yet thou [135]
Wouldst easily detect what I conceale.
This Woman whom thou mad'st to be my help,
And gav'st me as thy perfet gift, so good,
So fit, so acceptable, so Divine,
That from her hand I could suspect no ill, [140]
And what she did, whatever in it self,
Her doing seem'd to justifie the deed;
Shee gave me of the Tree, and I did eate.

To whom the sovran Presence thus repli'd.
Was shee thy God, that her thou didst obey [145]
Before his voice, or was shee made thy guide,
Superior, or but equal, that to her
Thou did'st resigne thy Manhood, and the Place
Wherein God set thee above her made of thee,
And for thee, whose perfection farr excell'd [150]

註1：出自《舊約・創世紀》：「耶和華神
　　　對蛇說：『你既做了這事，就必受咒
　　　詛，比一切的牲畜野獸更甚！你必用
　　　肚子行走，終生吃土。我又要叫你和
　　　女人彼此為仇；你的後裔和女人的後
　　　裔也彼此為仇。女人的後裔要傷你的
　　　頭；你要傷他的腳跟。』」

在痛苦中生產。此外，你必須服從丈
夫的管轄[2]。」

最後，神子轉頭對亞當說：

「你既然聽從妻子的話，吃了我曾
經吩咐不可以吃的果子，必得受到懲
罰；今後你將終生勞苦，在田裡汗流
浹背的工作，以此換來食物。土地因
為你的過失受到詛咒，長出荊棘和蒺
藜等多刺的植物來，你只好吃野地裡
的菜蔬。直到死亡，你歸於塵土，因
為你是從塵土中生出來的[3]。」

神子宣判人類和蛇的罪行之後，給
亞當和夏娃穿上獸皮，並讓蛇褪去舊
皮、換上新皮，但仍無法消滅蛇內心
的邪惡。做完這些事，神子即飛回天

註2：出自《舊約‧創世紀》：「耶和華神……又對
　　女人說：『我必多多加增你懷胎的苦楚，你生
　　產兒女必多受苦楚。你必戀慕你丈夫，你丈夫
　　必管轄你。』」
註3：出自《舊約‧創世紀》：「耶和華神……又對
　　亞當說：『你既聽從妻子的話，吃了我所吩咐
　　你不可吃的那樹上的果子，地必為你的緣故受
　　咒詛。你必終生勞苦，才能從地裡得吃的。地
　　必給你長出荊棘和蒺藜來，你也要吃田間的菜
　　蔬。你必汗流滿面才得餬口，直到你歸了土，
　　因為你是從土而出的。你本是塵土，仍要歸於
　　塵土。』」

Hers in all real dignitie: Adornd
She was indeed, and lovely to attract
Thy Love, not thy Subjection, and her Gifts
Were such as under Government well seem'd,
Unseemly to beare rule, which was thy part [155]
And person, hadst thou known thy self aright.

So having said, he thus to Eve in few:
Say Woman, what is this which thou hast done?

To whom sad Eve with shame nigh overwhelm'd,
Confessing soon, yet not before her Judge [160]
Bold or loquacious, thus abasht repli'd.

The Serpent me beguil'd and I did eate.

Which when the Lord God heard, without delay
To Judgement he proceeded on th' accus'd
Serpent though brute, unable to transferre [165]
The Guilt on him who made him instrument
Of mischief, and polluted from the end
Of his Creation; justly then accurst,
As vitiated in Nature: more to know
Concern'd not Man (since he no further knew) [170]
Nor alter'd his offence; yet God at last
To Satan first in sin his doom apply'd
Though in mysterious terms, judg'd as then best:
And on the Serpent thus his curse let fall.

Because thou hast done this, thou art accurst [175]
Above all Cattle, each Beast of the Field;
Upon thy Belly groveling thou shalt goe,
And dust shalt eat all the dayes of thy Life.
Between Thee and the Woman I will put
Enmitie, and between thine and her Seed; [180]
Her Seed shall bruise thy head, thou bruise his heel.

So spake this Oracle, then verifi'd
When Jesus son of Mary second Eve,
Saw Satan fall like Lightning down from Heav'n,
Prince of the Aire; then rising from his Grave [185]
Spoild Principalities and Powers, triumpht

審判亞當及夏娃
布雷克　水彩畫 1808年

　　神子宣判亞當和夏娃的刑罰，夏娃必須忍受懷孕生產的痛苦，亞當必須流汗勞動來換取食物，兩人聽了羞愧不已，真是悔不當初。

In open shew, and with ascension bright
Captivity led captive through the Aire,
The Realm it self of Satan long usurpt,
Whom he shall tread at last under our feet; [190]
Eevn hee who now foretold his fatal bruise,
And to the Woman thus his Sentence turn'd.

Thy sorrow I will greatly multiplie
By thy Conception; Children thou shalt bring
In sorrow forth, and to thy Husbands will [195]
Thine shall submit, hee over thee shall rule.

On Adam last thus judgement he pronounc'd.
Because thou hast heark'nd to the voice of thy Wife,
And eaten of the Tree concerning which
I charg'd thee, saying: Thou shalt not eate thereof, [200]
Curs'd is the ground for thy sake, thou in sorrow
Shalt eate thereof all the days of thy Life;
Thorns also and Thistles it shall bring thee forth
Unbid, and thou shalt eate th' Herb of th' Field,
In the sweat of thy Face shalt thou eat Bread, [205]
Till thou return unto the ground, for thou
Out of the ground wast taken, know thy Birth,
For dust thou art, and shalt to dust returne.

So judg'd he Man, both Judge and Saviour sent,
And th' instant stroke of Death denounc't that day [210]
Remov'd farr off; then pittying how they stood
Before him naked to the aire, that now
Must suffer change, disdain'd not to begin
Thenceforth the form of servant to assume,
As when he wash'd his servants feet so now [215]
As Father of his Familie he clad
Thir nakedness with Skins of Beasts, or slain,
Or as the Snake with youthful Coate repaid;
And thought not much to cloath his Enemies:
Nor hee thir outward onely with the Skins [220]
Of Beasts, but inward nakedness, much more

庭，向天父報告宣判的情形[4]。

　　自從「罪惡」為撒旦打開了地獄大門，他和兒子「死亡」便一直守候在敞開的大門邊，懷著希望，等候撒旦回來帶領他們到新的世界去。此時，「罪惡」開口對「死亡」說：

　　「孩子，我們不能像現在這樣無所事事地空等，我們應該積極些，為父

註4：出自《舊約・創世紀》：「耶和華神為亞當和他妻子用皮子做衣服，給他們穿。」

親的歸來預先做點準備才是；有一股
欲望衝擊著我的內心，吸引我到深淵
之外取得廣闊的土地。讓我們在地獄
和新世界之間建築一座大橋，橫越茫
茫深淵，便於地獄軍團遷徙到新世界
居住。」

「我已經嗅到風中傳來屍體的腐
臭味兒，對於你的計畫，我全力支
持。」

「死亡」露出陰森的笑容，爽快地
回答。那模樣，彷彿一群兀鷲，聞到
士兵們身上散發出死亡的氣息，便紛
紛飛往軍營，靜靜地等待第二天的血
戰。此時，「死亡」也把鼻孔朝向陰
霾的天空，貪婪地嗅著死亡的味道。

於是「罪惡」領著「死亡」飛離地
獄大門，開始在潮濕陰暗的混沌之境
上頭，建築一座橋樑。

首先，「死亡」用力拍打成堆的
泥土，使它緊實；就像神話中的堤洛
島，原本浮在海面上四處漂蕩，後來
天帝宙斯用鎖鏈把它緊緊固定在海底

Opprobrious, with his Robe of righteousness,
Araying cover'd from his Fathers sight.
To him with swift ascent he up returnd,
Into his blissful bosom reassum'd [225]
In glory as of old, to him appeas'd
All, though all-knowing, what had past with Man
Recounted, mixing intercession sweet.
Meanwhile ere thus was sin'd and judg'd on Earth,
Within the Gates of Hell sate Sin and Death, [230]
In counterview within the Gates, that now
Stood open wide, belching outrageous flame
Farr into Chaos, since the Fiend pass'd through,
Sin opening, who thus now to Death began.

O Son, why sit we here each other viewing [235]
Idlely, while Satan our great Author thrives
In other Worlds, and happier Seat provides
For us his ofspring deare? It cannot be
But that success attends him; if mishap,
Ere this he had return'd, with fury driv'n [240]
By his Avengers, since no place like this
Can fit his punishment, or their revenge.
Methinks I feel new strength within me rise,
Wings growing, and Dominion giv'n me large
Beyond this Deep; whatever drawes me on, [245]
Or sympathie, or som connatural force
Powerful at greatest distance to unite
With secret amity things of like kinde
By secretest conveyance. Thou my Shade
Inseparable must with mee along: [250]
For Death from Sin no power can separate.
But least the difficultie of passing back
Stay his return perhaps over this Gulfe
Impassable, Impervious, let us try
Adventrous work, yet to thy power and mine [255]
Not unagreeable, to found a path
Over this Maine from Hell to that new World
Where Satan now prevailes, a Monument
Of merit high to all th' infernal Host,
Easing thir passage hence, for intercourse, [260]
Or transmigration, as thir lot shall lead.
Nor can I miss the way, so strongly drawn

那樣[5]。然後，加上柏油使它更為堅固。漸漸地，一座綿延數千萬里的弓形大橋完工了，連接地獄與新世界。

撒旦鑽出蛇的身體後，變化外形離

註5：堤洛島（Delos）即為《希臘羅馬神話故事》中的歐洛堤亞島，是黑暗女神莉托的妹妹阿絲特莉亞變的，是一座隨著海水到處漂流的島嶼，莉托在島上生下宙斯的孩子 — 太陽神阿波羅及月神阿提密斯。後來宙斯把堤洛島固定在古希臘世界的中心，即愛琴島的中央，日後成為聞名的聖島。

By this new felt attraction and instinct.

Whom thus the meager Shadow answerd soon.
Goe whither Fate and inclination strong [265]
Leads thee, I shall not lag behinde, nor erre
The way, thou leading, such a sent I draw
Of carnage, prey innumerable, and taste
The savour of Death from all things there that live:

♥ 死亡與生命
克林姆 油畫 1916年

　　人類從此脫離不了生老病死的宿命，死神在一旁竊喜不已，露出陰森的笑容。

開伊甸園，打算回到地獄去宣告人類
已被自己引誘的好消息。他來到混沌
邊境，發現一條新蓋好的大橋，筆直
的通向地獄，橋頭站著兩個身影，走
近一看，原來是「罪惡」和「死亡」
母子；他感到萬分驚喜，正欲開口，
便聽見那亦妻亦女的「罪惡」媚聲說
道：

「親愛的父親，我早就預感您即將
高舉勝利的旗幟歸來，所以預先和您
的兒子『死亡』造了這麼一座橋，它
貫通地獄與地球，可方便您前去統轄
新世界。」

撒旦高興地回答：

「是的，我美麗的妻子和女兒，我
已經成功的接掌了新世界，你與「死
亡」現在就直接往那兒去吧！先代我
統治地上和空中的生物，尤其是萬物
之靈的人類，要讓他們臣服於你們腳
下，成為奴隸，然後才殺死他們。現
在，我要越過這座大橋，回到地獄去
向部屬們宣告好消息，順便領著他們

Nor shall I to the work thou enterprisest [270]
Be wanting, but afford thee equal aid,

So saying, with delight he snuff'd the smell
Of mortal change on Earth. As when a flock
Of ravenous Fowl, though many a League remote,
Against the day of Battel, to a Field, [275]
Where Armies lie encampt, come flying, lur'd
With sent of living Carcasses design'd
For death, the following day, in bloodie fight.
So sented the grim Feature, and upturn'd
His Nostril wide into the murkie Air, [280]
Sagacious of his Quarry from so farr.
Then Both from out Hell Gates into the waste
Wide Anarchie of Chaos damp and dark
Flew divers, and with Power (thir Power was great)
Hovering upon the Waters; what they met [285]
Solid or slimie, as in raging Sea
Tost up and down, together crowded drove
From each side shoaling towards the mouth of Hell.
As when two Polar Winds blowing adverse
Upon the Cronian Sea, together drive [290]
Mountains of Ice, that stop th' imagin'd way
Beyond Petsora Eastward, to the rich
Cathaian Coast. The aggregated Soyle
Death with his Mace petrific, cold and dry,
As with a Trident smote, and fix't as firm [295]
As Delos floating once; the rest his look
Bound with Gorgonian rigor not to move,
And with Asphaltic slime; broad as the Gate,
Deep to the Roots of Hell the gather'd beach
They fasten'd, and the Mole immense wraught on [300]
Over the foaming deep high Archt, a Bridge
Of length prodigious joyning to the Wall
Immovable of this now fenceless world
Forfeit to Death; from hence a passage broad,
Smooth, easie, inoffensive down to Hell. [305]
So, if great things to small may be compar'd,
Xerxes, the Libertie of Greece to yoke,
From Susa his Memnonian Palace high
Came to the Sea, and over Hellespont
Bridging his way, Europe with Asia joyn'd, [310]

前往地球。」

「罪惡」和「死亡」聽見這話，馬上高興地動身趕往地球。撒旦目送他們離開之後，便火速奔向地府。

惡魔殿外，聚集了許多撒旦軍，他們個個翹首盼望，焦躁地等待首領歸來。

「首領前往傳說中的新世界已經有好一段時間了，怎麼還不回來？」

「會不會出事了？」

眾人議論紛紛，或站或坐，圍成一圈一圈，交頭接耳地猜測撒旦的行蹤。誰也沒發現，惡魔之首已喬裝成低階士兵，悄悄地穿越人群，走過惡魔之殿 —— 潘地曼尼南富麗堂皇的地毯，直登上那至高者的君王寶座。

「諸位，抬起頭來看看吧！你們的首領信守諾言回來啦！」

撒旦坐在金光閃閃的寶座上，以洪亮的聲音說著。

惶惶不安的撒旦叛軍聽見這突如其來的呼聲，全都急轉過頭，朝寶座看

And scourg'd with many a stroak th' indignant waves.
Now had they brought the work by wondrous Art
Pontifical, a ridge of pendent Rock
Over the vext Abyss, following the track
Of Satan, to the self same place where hee [315]
First lighted from his Wing, and landed safe
From out of Chaos to the out side bare
Of this round World: with Pinns of Adamant
And Chains they made all fast, too fast they made
And durable; and now in little space [320]
The confines met of Empyrean Heav'n
And of this World, and on the left hand Hell
With long reach interpos'd; three sev'ral wayes
In sight, to each of these three places led.
And now thir way to Earth they had descri'd, [325]
To Paradise first tending, when behold
Satan in likeness of an Angel bright
Betwixt the Centaure and the Scorpion stearing
His Zenith, while the Sun in Aries rose:
Disguis'd he came, but those his Children dear [330]
Thir Parent soon discern'd, though in disguise.
Hee after Eve seduc't, unminded slunk
Into the Wood fast by, and changing shape
To observe the sequel, saw his guileful act
By Eve, though all unweeting, seconded [335]
Upon her Husband, saw thir shame that sought
Vain covertures; but when he saw descend
The Son of God to judge them terrifi'd
Hee fled, not hoping to escape, but shun
The present, fearing guiltie what his wrauth [340]
Might suddenly inflict; that past, return'd
By Night, and listening where the hapless Paire
Sate in thir sad discourse, and various plaint,
Thence gatherd his own doom, which understood
Not instant, but of future time. With joy [345]
And tidings fraught, to Hell he now return'd,
And at the brink of Chaos, neer the foot
Of this new wondrous Pontifice, unhop't
Met who to meet him came, his Ofspring dear.
Great joy was at thir meeting, and at sight [350]
Of that stupendious Bridge his joy encreas'd.
Long hee admiring stood, till Sin, his faire

^ 地獄群魔等待撒旦歸來
杜雷 版畫 1866年

地獄群魔等到了撒旦歸來，一時之間歡聲雷動，以為勝利的日子終將來臨。

去。

「是首領！」

「首領回來了，萬歲！」

「萬歲！」

歡呼聲如衝天煙火，給漆黑的地獄
帶來絢爛光芒。

「大家先別急著歡呼，靜下來聽
我宣布一個好消息，之後再一塊兒慶
祝。」

有如巨浪拍擊岩礁，擁戴聲掃除了
撒旦長途奔波的疲憊，他朝群眾揮揮
手，意氣風發地接著說：

「當日我從地獄出發，歷經萬般
險阻，飛越『混沌』和『夜』的國
度，終於發現傳說中的新樂園，那是
一個美麗如天庭的國度，上帝在其中
安置了用來替代我們的人類，想藉此
彌補天庭戰爭中巨大的損失。但可笑
的是，一顆果子就讓祂發怒，把親手
創造的摯愛物丟給『罪惡』和『死
亡』，哈！也就等同於把人類交到我
的手上啦！所以，大家快快整理行

Inchanting Daughter, thus the silence broke.

O Parent, these are thy magnific deeds,
Thy Trophies, which thou view'st as not thine own, [355]
Thou art thir Author and prime Architect:
For I no sooner in my Heart divin'd,
My Heart, which by a secret harmonie
Still moves with thine, join'd in connexion sweet,
That thou on Earth hadst prosper'd, which thy looks [360]
Now also evidence, but straight I felt
Though distant from thee Worlds between, yet felt
That I must after thee with this thy Son;
Such fatal consequence unites us three:
Hell could no longer hold us in her bounds, [365]
Nor this unvoyageable Gulf obscure
Detain from following thy illustrious track.
Thou hast atchiev'd our libertie, confin'd
Within Hell Gates till now, thou us impow'rd
To fortifie thus farr, and overlay [370]
With this portentous Bridge the dark Abyss.
Thine now is all this World, thy vertue hath won
What thy hands builded not, thy Wisdom gain'd
With odds what Warr hath lost, and fully aveng'd
Our foile in Heav'n; here thou shalt Monarch reign, [375]
There didst not; there let him still Victor sway,
As Battel hath adjudg'd, from this new World
Retiring, by his own doom alienated,
And henceforth Monarchie with thee divide
Of all things parted by th' Empyreal bounds, [380]
His Quadrature, from thy Orbicular World,
Or trie thee now more dang'rous to his Throne.

Whom thus the Prince of Darkness answerd glad.
Fair Daughter, and thou Son and Grandchild both,
High proof ye now have giv'n to be the Race [385]
Of Satan (for I glorie in the name,
Antagonist of Heav'ns Almightie King)
Amply have merited of me, of all
Th' Infernal Empire, that so neer Heav'ns dore
Triumphal with triumphal act have met, [390]
Mine with this glorious Work, and made one Realm
Hell and this World, one Realm, one Continent

^ 地獄群魔變成用腹部爬行的蛇
杜雷版畫 1866年

　　上帝深恨撒旦引誘人類犯下死亡重罪，因此懲罰他和其他部
眾化為蛇類，要他們從此以蛇的形象，世世代代受人類追打。

囊，隨我遷徙到新世界居……嘶……嘶嘶……」

撒旦話語未落，原本高亢的音調竟轉變成嘶嘶的蛇語，挺拔的身軀，也逐漸拉長蜷縮，變成一條巨大的蛇體。更可怕的是，惡魔殿裡的魔鬼們也全數化成一條條細長蜷曲的蛇類，在地上爬來爬去，數量比地中海蛇島上的蛇還要多。這是上帝降下的懲罰，要他們從此以蛇的形象，世世代代飽受人類子孫的復仇 —— 頭被人類擊碎。

接著，上帝又讓這群叛徒產生幻影，誤以為有一片樹林，樹上結滿鮮嫩欲滴的果實。於是，饑餓的群蛇互相推擠，一條條的往上堆疊，直到果實的高度，張口一咬，卻是滿嘴灰。就這樣不斷地重複，忍受饑渴之苦。

此時，「罪惡」和「死亡」已經抵達新世界，他們兵分兩路，「罪惡」打算潛到人類子孫生活的地方，在那兒散佈罪惡，污染他們的思想、

Of easie thorough-fare. Therefore while I
Descend through Darkness, on your Rode with ease
To my associate Powers, them to acquaint [395]
With these successes, and with them rejoyce,
You two this way, among these numerous Orbs
All yours, right down to Paradise descend;
There dwell and Reign in bliss, thence on the Earth
Dominion exercise and in the Aire, [400]
Chiefly on Man, sole Lord of all declar'd,
Him first make sure your thrall, and lastly kill.
My Substitutes I send ye, and Create
Plenipotent on Earth, of matchless might
Issuing from mee: on your joynt vigor now [405]
My hold of this new Kingdom all depends,
Through Sin to Death expos'd by my exploit.
If your joynt power prevailes, th' affaires of Hell
No detriment need feare, goe and be strong.

So saying he dismiss'd them, they with speed [410]
Thir course through thickest Constellations held
Spreading thir bane; the blasted Starrs lookt wan,
And Planets, Planet-strook, real Eclips
Then sufferd. Th' other way Satan went down
The Causey to Hell Gate; on either side [415]
Disparted Chaos over built exclaimd,
And with rebounding surge the barrs assaild,
That scorn'd his indignation: through the Gate,
Wide open and unguarded, Satan pass'd,
And all about found desolate; for those [420]
Appointed to sit there, had left thir charge,
Flown to the upper World; the rest were all
Farr to the inland retir'd, about the walls
Of Pandæmonium, Citie and proud seate
Of Lucifer, so by allusion calld, [425]
Of that bright Starr to Satan paragond.
There kept thir Watch the Legions, while the Grand
In Council sate, sollicitous what chance
Might intercept thir Emperour sent, so hee
Departing gave command, and they observ'd. [430]
As when the Tartar from his Russian Foe
By Astracan over the Snowie Plaines
Retires, or Bactrian Sophi from the hornes

言語和行為，使他們變成「死亡」的
食物。另一方面，「死亡」則四處逛
逛，先從花草樹木下手，再吃些鳥獸
蟲魚等食物，一邊等待母親為他帶來
人類大餐。

　　上帝在天庭看見「罪惡」和「死
亡」正於地球上蔓延，不禁搖搖頭，
嘆息說道：

　　「多可惜呀！這原本為人類所造的

Of Turkish Crescent, leaves all waste beyond
The Realm of Aladule, in his retreate [435]
To Tauris or Casbeen. So these the late
Heav'n-banisht Host, left desert utmost Hell
Many a dark League, reduc't in careful Watch
Round thir Metropolis, and now expecting
Each hour thir great adventurer from the search [440]
Of Forrein Worlds: he through the midst unmarkt,
In shew Plebeian Angel militant
Of lowest order, past; and from the dore
Of that Plutonian Hall, invisible
Ascended his high Throne, which under state [445]
Of richest texture spred, at th' upper end
Was plac't in regal lustre. Down a while
He sate, and round about him saw unseen:
At last as from a Cloud his fulgent head
And shape Starr bright appeer'd, or brighter, clad [450]
With what permissive glory since his fall
Was left him, or false glitter: All amaz'd
At that so sudden blaze the Stygian throng
Bent thir aspect, and whom they wish'd beheld,
Thir mighty Chief returnd: loud was th' acclaime: [455]
Forth rush'd in haste the great consulting Peers,
Rais'd from thir dark Divan, and with like joy
Congratulant approach'd him, who with hand
Silence, and with these words attention won.

Thrones, Dominations, Princedoms, Vertues, Powers, [460]
For in possession such, not onely of right,
I call ye and declare ye now, returnd
Successful beyond hope, to lead ye forth
Triumphant out of this infernal Pit
Abominable, accurst, the house of woe, [465]

≺　聖瑪格麗特
拉斐爾 油畫 1518年
　　從此化身為蛇類的惡魔，繼續侵擾人
間，企圖再次摧毀人類對上帝的信心。聖瑪
格麗特就是因為生前不畏惡魔的恫嚇侵擾，
堅持對上帝的信仰，死後被封為聖人，成為
照顧孕婦、產婆、護士、奶媽的守護聖徒。

∧ 聖瑪格麗特
烏偉 油畫 1620年

新世界就這麼被污染了。那罪魁禍
首還沾沾自喜地在地府大發厥詞，
以為自己得到了新樂園，其實，我默
許『罪惡』和『死亡』進入樂園，乃
是要他們去進行掃蕩，把各種不好的
都滅絕；日後，再派基督前去接管，
把『罪惡』和「死亡」及一切惡的因
子全部丟回地獄裡去，並關上地獄大
門，在地球另造一個新的、純美的世

And Dungeon of our Tyrant: Now possess,
As Lords, a spacious World, to our native Heaven
Little inferiour, by my adventure hard
With peril great atchiev'd. Long were to tell
What I have don, what sufferd, with what paine [470]
Voyag'd th' unreal, vast, unbounded deep
Of horrible confusion, over which
By Sin and Death a broad way now is pav'd
To expedite your glorious march; but I
Toild out my uncouth passage, forc't to ride [475]
Th' untractable Abysse, plung'd in the womb
Of unoriginal Night and Chaos wilde,
That jealous of thir secrets fiercely oppos'd
My journey strange, with clamorous uproare
Protesting Fate supreame; thence how I found [480]
The new created World, which fame in Heav'n
Long had foretold, a Fabrick wonderful
Of absolute perfection, therein Man
Plac't in a Paradise, by our exile
Made happie: Him by fraud I have seduc'd [485]
From his Creator, and the more to increase
Your wonder, with an Apple; he thereat
Offended, worth your laughter, hath giv'n up
Both his beloved Man and all his World,
To Sin and Death a prey, and so to us, [490]
Without our hazard, labour, or allarme,
To range in, and to dwell, and over Man
To rule, as over all he should have rul'd.
True is, mee also he hath judg'd, or rather
Mee not, but the brute Serpent in whose shape [495]
Man I deceav'd: that which to mee belongs,
Is enmity, which he will put between
Mee and Mankinde; I am to bruise his heel;
His Seed, when is not set, shall bruise my head:
A World who would not purchase with a bruise, [500]
Or much more grievous pain? Ye have th' account
Of my performance: What remains, ye Gods,
But up and enter now into full bliss.

So having said, a while he stood, expecting
Thir universal shout and high applause [505]
To fill his eare, when contrary he hears

^ 「罪惡」和「死亡」分別朝不同的方向而去
杜雷版畫 1866年

　　上帝默許罪惡和死亡侵入人間，祂要他們去
進行掃蕩，把各種不好的通通滅絕，再派基督前
去接管，另造一個新的純美世界。

界。」

　　為了重建新世界，全能者重新分派
任務給幾個地位較高的天使。

　　太陽以耀眼的光芒照射地球，分出
嚴寒和酷暑，北方有冷冽的冬季、南

On all sides, from innumerable tongues
A dismal universal hiss, the sound
Of public scorn; he wonderd, but not long
Had leasure, wondring at himself now more; [510]
His Visage drawn he felt to sharp and spare,
His Armes clung to his Ribs, his Leggs entwining
Each other, till supplanted down he fell
A monstrous Serpent on his Belly prone,
Reluctant, but in vaine: a greater power [515]
Now rul'd him, punisht in the shape he sin'd,
According to his doom: he would have spoke,
But hiss for hiss returnd with forked tongue
To forked tongue, for now were all transform'd
Alike, to Serpents all as accessories [520]
To his bold Riot: dreadful was the din
Of hissing through the Hall, thick swarming now
With complicated monsters head and taile,
Scorpion and Asp, and Amphisbæna dire,
Cerastes hornd, Hydrus, and Ellops drear, [525]
And Dipsas (not so thick swarm'd once the Soil
Bedropt with blood of Gorgon, or the Isle
Ophiusa) but still greatest hee the midst,
Now Dragon grown, larger then whom the Sun
Ingenderd in the Pythian Vale on slime, [530]
Huge Python, and his Power no less he seem'd
Above the rest still to retain; they all
Him follow'd issuing forth to th' open Field,
Where all yet left of that revolted Rout
Heav'n-fall'n, in station stood or just array, [535]
Sublime with expectation when to see
In Triumph issuing forth thir glorious Chief;
They saw, but other sight instead, a crowd
Of ugly Serpents; horror on them fell,
And horrid sympathie; for what they saw, [540]
They felt themselvs now changing; down thir arms,
Down fell both Spear and Shield, down they as fast,
And the dire hiss renew'd, and the dire form
Catcht by Contagion, like in punishment,
As in thir crime. Thus was th' applause they meant, [545]
Turn'd to exploding hiss, triumph to shame
Cast on themselves from thir own mouths. There stood
A Grove hard by, sprung up with this thir change,

方是炎熱的夏天；月亮和其他的星球，必須循著規定的軌道運行；風該怎麼吹拂，雷電該怎麼轟擊，季節也得分出春夏秋冬四季來。

環境產生了變化，生物之間也生出食物鏈的關係來，動物為了生存互相啃噬，人類也無法倖免。鳥和鳥、獸和獸、人類和鳥獸，再也無法回到先前和平共處的狀態了。

亞當看到這一幕幕動物相互獵食的血腥景象，不禁悲從中來，他喃喃自語地說道：

「為什麼我自己犯下的罪行，卻得由一代代的後世子孫來承擔？上帝既然宣判了我的死刑，就該讓我獨自承擔，帶著所有的罪惡回到塵土中去，因我本由泥土捏塑而來。只是，我的靈魂是否會跟著身體一塊兒死去呢？」

亞當懊惱的情緒感染了身旁的妻子，她看見丈夫悲哀的模樣，心疼地對丈夫說：

His will who reigns above, to aggravate
Thir penance, laden with Fruit like that [550]
Which grew in Paradise, the bait of Eve
Us'd by the Tempter: on that prospect strange
Thir earnest eyes they fix'd, imagining
For one forbidden Tree a multitude
Now ris'n, to work them furder woe or shame; [555]
Yet parcht with scalding thurst and hunger fierce,
Though to delude them sent, could not abstain,
But on they rould in heaps, and up the Trees
Climbing, sat thicker then the snakie locks
That curld Megæra: greedily they pluck'd [560]
The Frutage fair to sight, like that which grew
Neer that bituminous Lake where Sodom flam'd;
This more delusive, not the touch, but taste
Deceav'd; they fondly thinking to allay
Thir appetite with gust, instead of Fruit [565]
Chewd bitter Ashes, which th' offended taste
With spattering noise rejected: oft they assayd,
Hunger and thirst constraining, drugd as oft,
With hatefullest disrelish writh'd thir jaws
With soot and cinders fill'd; so oft they fell [570]
Into the same illusion, not as Man
Whom they triumph'd once lapst. Thus were they plagu'd
And worn with Famin, long and ceasless hiss,
Till thir lost shape, permitted, they resum'd,
Yearly enjoynd, some say, to undergo [575]
This annual humbling certain number'd days,
To dash thir pride, and joy for Man seduc't.
However some tradition they dispers'd
Among the Heathen of thir purchase got,
And Fabl'd how the Serpent, whom they calld [580]
Ophion with Eurynome, the wide-
Encroaching Eve perhaps, had first the rule
Of high Olympus, thence by Saturn driv'n
And Ops, ere yet Dictæan Jove was born.
Mean while in Paradise the hellish pair [585]
Too soon arriv'd, Sin there in power before,
Once actual, now in body, and to dwell
Habitual habitant; behind her Death
Close following pace for pace, not mounted yet
On his pale Horse: to whom Sin thus began. [590]

「別再傷心了，錯誤已經發生，現在想再多也於事無補。我們應該振作精神，想想未來該怎麼生活才對呀！」

Second of Satan sprung, all conquering Death,
What thinkst thou of our Empire now, though earnd
With travail difficult, not better farr
Then stil at Hels dark threshold to have sate watch,
Unnam'd, undreaded, and thy self half starv'd? [595]

Whom thus the Sin-born Monster answerd soon.
To mee, who with eternal Famin pine,
Alike is Hell, or Paradise, or Heaven,
There best, where most with ravin I may meet;
Which here, though plenteous, all too little seems [600]
To stuff this Maw, this vast unhide-bound Corps.

To whom th' incestuous Mother thus repli'd.
Thou therefore on these Herbs, and Fruits, and Flours
Feed first, on each Beast next, and Fish, and Fowle,
No homely morsels, and whatever thing [605]
The Sithe of Time mowes down, devour unspar'd,
Till I in Man residing through the Race,
His thoughts, his looks, words, actions all infect,
And season him thy last and sweetest prey.

This said, they both betook them several wayes, [610]
Both to destroy, or unimmortal make
All kinds, and for destruction to mature
Sooner or later; which th' Almightie seeing,
From his transcendent Seat the Saints among,
To those bright Orders utterd thus his voice. [615]

See with what heat these Dogs of Hell advance
To waste and havoc yonder World, which I
So fair and good created, and had still
Kept in that State, had not the folly of Man
Let in these wastful Furies, who impute [620]
Folly to mee, so doth the Prince of Hell
And his Adherents, that with so much ease
I suffer them to enter and possess
A place so heav'nly, and conniving seem
To gratifie my scornful Enemies, [625]
That laugh, as if transported with some fit
Of Passion, I to them had quitted all,
At random yielded up to their misrule;

∧ 亞當與夏娃
杜勒 油畫 1507年

　　看到原本美好的新世界被自己毀了，天氣出現嚴寒和酷暑，動物互相啃噬殘殺，懊悔萬分的亞當竟以嚴厲的口吻大罵夏娃，稱她為「邪惡」的毒蛇，人類也失去原先單純的美好天性，多了各種怨懟、嫉恨等情緒。

聽到夏娃溫柔的話語，亞當非但不領情，反而再次點燃心中的怒火，他瞪了妻子一眼，嚴厲地罵道：

「離我遠一點！你這條邪惡的毒蛇，妄想再用甜言蜜語來誘惑我，同樣的錯誤我不會再犯第二次了。」

「亞當⋯⋯！」

夏娃被亞當凶惡的語氣嚇壞了，她渾身顫抖、往後倒退半步，蹲在地上傷心地哭了起來。

「難道不是嗎？如果你當初肯聽我的勸，就不會被蛇利用，讓我倆失去原本的幸福生活。蛇欺騙你，你自己墮落也就罷了，又跟蛇合夥再來騙我，我怎會愚蠢的相信你夠聰敏堅貞呢？」

亞當越說越激動，竟說出這般傷人的氣話來。

聽見這番責備的話語，夏娃哭得更厲害了，斗大的淚珠一顆顆從眼眶滾下，滑過泛紅的臉頰。

「我真的不是故意的，你應該知道

And know not that I call'd and drew them thither
My Hell-hounds, to lick up the draff and filth [630]
Which mans polluting Sin with taint hath shed
On what was pure, till cramm'd and gorg'd, nigh burst
With suckt and glutted offal, at one sling
Of thy victorious Arm, well-pleasing Son,
Both Sin, and Death, and yawning Grave at last [635]
Through Chaos hurld, obstruct the mouth of Hell
For ever, and seal up his ravenous Jawes.
Then Heav'n and Earth renewd shall be made pure
To sanctitie that shall receive no staine:
Till then the Curse pronounc't on both precedes. [640]

He ended, and the Heav'nly Audience loud
Sung Halleluia, as the sound of Seas,
Through multitude that sung: Just are thy ways,
Righteous are thy Decrees on all thy Works;
Who can extenuate thee? Next, to the Son, [645]
Destin'd restorer of Mankind, by whom
New Heav'n and Earth shall to the Ages rise,
Or down from Heav'n descend. Such was thir song,
While the Creator calling forth by name
His mightie Angels gave them several charge, [650]
As sorted best with present things. The Sun
Had first his precept so to move, so shine,
As might affect the Earth with cold and heat
Scarce tollerable, and from the North to call
Decrepit Winter, from the South to bring [655]
Solstitial summers heat. To the blanc Moone
Her office they prescrib'd, to th' other five
Thir planetarie motions and aspects
In Sextile, Square, and Trine, and Opposite,
Of noxious efficacie, and when to joyne [660]
In Synod unbenigne, and taught the fixt
Thir influence malignant when to showre,
Which of them rising with the Sun, or falling,
Should prove tempestuous: To the Winds they set
Thir corners, when with bluster to confound [665]
Sea, Aire, and Shoar, the Thunder when to rowle
With terror through the dark Aereal Hall.
Some say he bid his Angels turne ascanse
The Poles of Earth twice ten degrees and more

我對你的愛有多麼地深，我甚至能夠
為你而死。我並不知道蛇是魔鬼的化
身，我只是單純的想要幫你取得更多
的知識罷了。請你、請你別再說出這
些殘忍的話語，我難過得快要不能呼
吸了。」

　　看見夏娃披頭散髮，伏在地上痛哭
的可憐模樣，亞當不由得心生憐憫，
快步走過去把她扶了起來，心疼地
說：

　　「請你原諒我，我最美麗的妻子。
我曾經那麼地深愛你，願意為你付出
一切，現在卻因為魔鬼的挑撥，而對
你口出惡言、心生怨懟。我們別再互
相埋怨了，就用愛來化解紛爭，靜靜
地等待死亡的降臨吧！」

　　夏娃揉揉紅腫的眼睛，以略帶哽咽
的聲音對亞當說：

　　「可是，我們無辜的子孫怎麼辦？
他們一生下來就需承擔我們的罪責，
不！不！我不忍心。亞當，我們不要
繁衍後代，讓罪惡與死亡就到我們這

From the Suns Axle; they with labour push'd [670]
Oblique the Centric Globe: Som say the Sun
Was bid turn Reines from th' Equinoctial Rode
Like distant breadth to Taurus with the Seav'n
Atlantick Sisters, and the Spartan Twins
Up to the Tropic Crab; thence down amaine [675]
By Leo and the Virgin and the Scales,
As deep as Capricorne, to bring in change
Of Seasons to each Clime; else had the Spring
Perpetual smil'd on Earth with vernant Flours,
Equal in Days and Nights, except to those [680]
Beyond the Polar Circles; to them Day
Had unbenighted shon, while the low Sun
To recompence his distance, in thir sight
Had rounded still th' Horizon, and not known
Or East or West, which had forbid the Snow [685]
From cold Estotiland, and South as farr
Beneath Magellan. At that tasted Fruit
The Sun, as from Thyestean Banquet, turn'd
His course intended; else how had the World
Inhabited, though sinless, more then now, [690]
Avoided pinching cold and scorching heate?
These changes in the Heav'ns, though slow, produc'd
Like change on Sea and Land, sideral blast,
Vapour, and Mist, and Exhalation hot,
Corrupt and Pestilent: Now from the North [695]
Of Norumbega, and the Samoed shoar
Bursting thir brazen Dungeon, armd with ice
And snow and haile and stormie gust and flaw,
Boreas and Cæcias and Argestes loud
And Thrascias rend the Woods and Seas upturn; [700]
With adverse blast up-turns them from the South
Notus and Afer black with thundrous Clouds
From Serraliona; thwart of these as fierce
Forth rush the Levant and the Ponent Windes
Eurus and Zephir with thir lateral noise, [705]
Sirocco, and Libecchio. Thus began
Outrage from liveless things; but Discord first
Daughter of Sin, among th' irrational,
Death introduc'd through fierce antipathie:
Beast now with Beast gan war, and Fowle with Fowle, [710]
And Fish with Fish; to graze the Herb all leaving,

裡為止好嗎？」

「傻瓜，上帝的懲罰豈容我倆改變？況且，神子在審判時說過：『女人的後代將擊碎蛇的頭。』倘若我們毀滅自我、斷絕後裔，便喪失了向敵人復仇的機會。你別再胡思亂想了，我們一塊兒回到接受上帝審判的地方去，用虔誠的心訴說滿懷的歉意，祈求天神原諒我們的罪過，並賜予我們如何應對季節變換，避開酷熱、暴風和霜雪侵襲的方法，相信只要我們真心悔過，天父一定會憐憫我們的。」

亞當說完，領著夏娃走回審判之地。

他倆淚流滿面，懊悔地俯臥在地上，連聲嘆息，訴說心中無限的歉意。

Devourd each other; nor stood much in awe
Of Man, but fled him, or with count'nance grim
Glar'd on him passing: these were from without
The growing miseries, which Adam saw [715]
Alreadie in part, though hid in gloomiest shade,
To sorrow abandond, but worse felt within,
And in a troubl'd Sea of passion tost,
Thus to disburd'n sought with sad complaint.

O miserable of happie! is this the end [720]
Of this new glorious World, and mee so late
The Glory of that Glory, who now becom
Accurst of blessed, hide me from the face
Of God, whom to behold was then my highth
Of happiness: yet well, if here would end [725]
The miserie, I deserv'd it, and would beare
My own deservings; but this will not serve;
All that I eat or drink, or shall beget,
Is propagated curse. O voice once heard
Delightfully, Encrease and multiply, [730]
Now death to hear! for what can I encrease
Or multiplie, but curses on my head?
Who of all Ages to succeed, but feeling
The evil on him brought by me, will curse
My Head, Ill fare our Ancestor impure, [735]
For this we may thank Adam; but his thanks
Shall be the execration; so besides
Mine own that bide upon me, all from mee
Shall with a fierce reflux on mee redound,
On mee as on thir natural center light [740]
Heavie, though in thir place. O fleeting joyes
Of Paradise, deare bought with lasting woes!
Did I request thee, Maker, from my Clay
To mould me Man, did I sollicite thee
From darkness to promote me, or here place [745]
In this delicious Garden? as my Will
Concurd not to my being, it were but right
And equal to reduce me to my dust,
Desirous to resigne, and render back
All I receav'd, unable to performe [750]
Thy terms too hard, by which I was to hold
The good I sought not. To the loss of that,

Sufficient penaltie, why hast thou added
The sense of endless woes? inexplicable
Thy Justice seems; yet to say truth, too late, [755]
I thus contest; then should have been refusd
Those terms whatever, when they were propos'd:
Thou didst accept them; wilt thou enjoy the good,
Then cavil the conditions? and though God
Made thee without thy leave, what if thy Son [760]
Prove disobedient, and reprov'd, retort,
Wherefore didst thou beget me? I sought it not
Wouldst thou admit for his contempt of thee
That proud excuse? yet him not thy election,
But Natural necessity begot. [765]
God made thee of choice his own, and of his own
To serve him, thy reward was of his grace,
Thy punishment then justly is at his Will.
Be it so, for I submit, his doom is fair,
That dust I am, and shall to dust returne: [770]
O welcom hour whenever! why delayes
His hand to execute what his Decree
Fixd on this day? why do I overlive,
Why am I mockt with death, and length'nd out
To deathless pain? how gladly would I meet [775]
Mortalitie my sentence, and be Earth
Insensible, how glad would lay me down
As in my Mothers lap! There I should rest
And sleep secure; his dreadful voice no more
Would Thunder in my ears, no fear of worse [780]
To mee and to my ofspring would torment me
With cruel expectation. Yet one doubt
Pursues me still, least all I cannot die,
Least that pure breath of Life, the Spirit of Man
Which God inspir'd, cannot together perish [785]
With this corporeal Clod; then in the Grave,
Or in some other dismal place who knows
But I shall die a living Death? O thought
Horrid, if true! yet why? it was but breath
Of Life that sinn'd; what dies but what had life [790]
And sin? the Bodie properly hath neither.
All of me then shall die: let this appease
The doubt, since humane reach no further knows.
For though the Lord of all be infinite,

Is his wrauth also? be it, man is not so, [795]
But mortal doom'd. How can he exercise
Wrath without end on Man whom Death must end?
Can he make deathless Death? that were to make
Strange contradiction, which to God himself
Impossible is held, as Argument [800]
Of weakness, not of Power. Will he, draw out,
For angers sake, finite to infinite
In punisht man, to satisfie his rigour
Satisfi'd never; that were to extend
His Sentence beyond dust and Natures Law, [805]
By which all Causes else according still
To the reception of thir matter act,
Not to th' extent of thir own Spheare. But say
That Death be not one stroak, as I suppos'd,
Bereaving sense, but endless miserie [810]
From this day onward, which I feel begun
Both in me, and without me, and so last
To perpetuitie; Ay me, that fear
Comes thundring back with dreadful revolution
On my defensless head; both Death and I [815]
Am found Eternal, and incorporate both,
Nor I on my part single, in mee all
Posteritie stands curst: Fair Patrimonie
That I must leave ye, Sons; O were I able
To waste it all my self, and leave ye none! [820]
So disinherited how would ye bless
Me now your curse! Ah, why should all mankind
For one mans fault thus guiltless be condemn'd,
If guiltless? But from mee what can proceed,
But all corrupt, both Mind and Will deprav'd, [825]
Not to do onely, but to will the same
With me? how can they then acquitted stand
In sight of God? Him after all Disputes
Forc't I absolve: all my evasions vain
And reasonings, though through Mazes, lead me still [830]
But to my own conviction: first and last
On mee, mee onely, as the sourse and spring
Of all corruption, all the blame lights due;
So might the wrauth. Fond wish! couldst thou support
That burden heavier then the Earth to bear [835]
Then all the World much heavier, though divided

With that bad Woman? Thus what thou desir'st,
And what thou fearst, alike destroyes all hope
Of refuge, and concludes thee miserable
Beyond all past example and future, [840]
To Satan only like both crime and doom.
O Conscience, into what Abyss of fears
And horrors hast thou driv'n me; out of which
I find no way, from deep to deeper plung'd!

Thus Adam to himself lamented loud [845]
Through the still Night, not now, as ere man fell,
Wholsom and cool, and mild, but with black Air
Accompanied, with damps and dreadful gloom,
Which to his evil Conscience represented
All things with double terror: On the ground [850]
Outstretcht he lay, on the cold ground, and oft
Curs'd his Creation, Death as oft accus'd
Of tardie execution, since denounc't
The day of his offence. Why comes not Death,
Said hee, with one thrice acceptable stroke [855]
To end me? Shall Truth fail to keep her word,
Justice Divine not hast'n to be just?
But Death comes not at call, Justice Divine
Mends not her slowest pace for prayers or cries.
O Woods, O Fountains, Hillocks, Dales and Bowrs, [860]
With other echo late I taught your Shades
To answer, and resound farr other Song.
Whom thus afflicted when sad Eve beheld,
Desolate where she sate, approaching nigh,
Soft words to his fierce passion she assay'd: [865]
But her with stern regard he thus repell'd.

Out of my sight, thou Serpent, that name best
Befits thee with him leagu'd, thy self as false
And hateful; nothing wants, but that thy shape,
Like his, and colour Serpentine may shew [870]
Thy inward fraud, to warn all Creatures from thee
Henceforth; least that too heav'nly form, pretended
To hellish falshood, snare them. But for thee
I had persisted happie, had not thy pride
And wandring vanitie, when lest was safe, [875]

Rejected my forewarning, and disdain'd
Not to be trusted, longing to be seen
Though by the Devil himself, him overweening
To over-reach, but with the Serpent meeting
Fool'd and beguil'd, by him thou, I by thee, [880]
To trust thee from my side, imagin'd wise,
Constant, mature, proof against all assaults,
And understood not all was but a shew
Rather then solid vertu, all but a Rib
Crooked by nature, bent, as now appears, [885]
More to the part sinister from me drawn,
Well if thrown out, as supernumerarie
To my just number found. O why did God,
Creator wise, that peopl'd highest Heav'n
With Spirits Masculine, create at last [890]
This noveltie on Earth, this fair defect
Of Nature, and not fill the World at once
With Men as Angels without Feminine,
Or find some other way to generate
Mankind? this mischief had not then befall'n, [895]
And more that shall befall, innumerable
Disturbances on Earth through Femal snares,
And straight conjunction with this Sex: for either
He never shall find out fit Mate, but such
As some misfortune brings him, or mistake, [900]
Or whom he wishes most shall seldom gain
Through her perversness, but shall see her gaind
By a farr worse, or if she love, withheld
By Parents, or his happiest choice too late
Shall meet, alreadie linkt and Wedlock-bound [905]
To a fell Adversarie, his hate or shame:
Which infinite calamitie shall cause
To Humane life, and houshold peace confound.

He added not, and from her turn'd, but Eve
Not so repulst, with Tears that ceas'd not flowing, [910]
And tresses all disorderd, at his feet
Fell humble, and imbracing them, besaught
His peace, and thus proceeded in her plaint.

Forsake me not thus, Adam, witness Heav'n
What love sincere, and reverence in my heart [915]

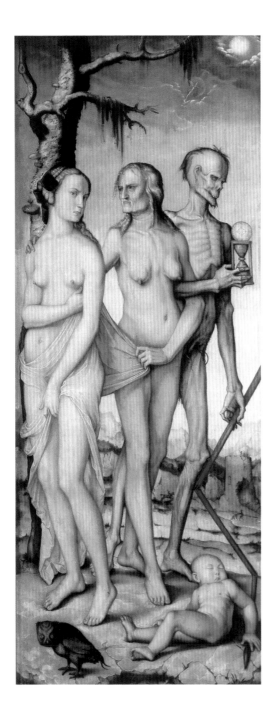

I beare thee, and unweeting have offended,
Unhappilie deceav'd; thy suppliant
I beg, and clasp thy knees; bereave me not,
Whereon I live, thy gentle looks, thy aid,
Thy counsel in this uttermost distress, [920]
My onely strength and stay: forlorn of thee,
Whither shall I betake me, where subsist?
While yet we live, scarse one short hour perhaps,
Between us two let there be peace, both joyning,
As joyn'd in injuries, one enmitie [925]
Against a Foe by doom express assign'd us,
That cruel Serpent: On me exercise not
Thy hatred for this miserie befall'n,
On me alreadie lost, mee then thy self
More miserable; both have sin'd, but thou [930]
Against God onely, I against God and thee,
And to the place of judgment will return,
There with my cries importune Heaven, that all
The sentence from thy head remov'd may light
On me, sole cause to thee of all this woe, [935]
Mee mee onely just object of his ire.

She ended weeping, and her lowlie plight,
Immovable till peace obtain'd from fault
Acknowledg'd and deplor'd, in Adam wraught
Commiseration; soon his heart relented [940]
Towards her, his life so late and sole delight,
Now at his feet submissive in distress,
Creature so faire his reconcilement seeking,
His counsel whom she had displeas'd, his aide;
As one disarm'd, his anger all he lost, [945]
And thus with peaceful words uprais'd her soon.

Unwarie, and too desirous, as before,

≪ 人類的三階段
格里恩 油畫 1539年

　　由於夏娃吃了知識果，上帝就處罰
女人必須受懷孕生子之苦，她的刑罰顯
然比男人更重一些。

So now of what thou knowst not, who desir'st
The punishment all on thy self; alas,
Beare thine own first, ill able to sustaine [950]
His full wrauth whose thou feelst as yet lest part,
And my displeasure bearst so ill. If Prayers
Could alter high Decrees, I to that place
Would speed before thee, and be louder heard,
That on my head all might be visited, [955]
Thy frailtie and infirmer Sex forgiv'n,
To me committed and by me expos'd.
But rise, let us no more contend, nor blame
Each other, blam'd enough elsewhere, but strive
In offices of Love, how we may light'n [960]
Each others burden in our share of woe;
Since this days Death denounc't, if ought I see,
Will prove no sudden, but a slow-pac't evill,
A long days dying to augment our paine,
And to our Seed (O hapless Seed!) deriv'd. [965]

To whom thus Eve, recovering heart, repli'd.
Adam, by sad experiment I know
How little weight my words with thee can finde,
Found so erroneous, thence by just event
Found so unfortunate; nevertheless, [970]
Restor'd by thee, vile as I am, to place
Of new acceptance, hopeful to regaine
Thy Love, the sole contentment of my heart
Living or dying, from thee I will not hide
What thoughts in my unquiet brest are ris'n, [975]
Tending to some relief of our extremes,
Or end, though sharp and sad, yet tolerable,
As in our evils, and of easier choice.
If care of our descent perplex us most,
Which must be born to certain woe, devourd [980]
By Death at last, and miserable it is
To be to others cause of misery,
Our own begotten, and of our Loines to bring
Into this cursed World a woful Race,
That after wretched Life must be at last [985]
Food for so foule a Monster, in thy power
It lies, yet ere Conception to prevent
The Race unblest, to being yet unbegot.

Childless thou art, Childless remaine:
So Death shall be deceav'd his glut, and with us two [990]
Be forc'd to satisfie his Rav'nous Maw.
But if thou judge it hard and difficult,
Conversing, looking, loving, to abstain
From Loves due Rites, Nuptial imbraces sweet,
And with desire to languish without hope, [995]
Before the present object languishing
With like desire, which would be miserie
And torment less then none of what we dread,
Then both our selves and Seed at once to free
From what we fear for both, let us make short, [1000]
Let us seek Death, or he not found, supply
With our own hands his Office on our selves;
Why stand we longer shivering under feares,
That shew no end but Death, and have the power,
Of many ways to die the shortest choosing, [1005]
Destruction with destruction to destroy.

She ended heer, or vehement despaire
Broke off the rest; so much of Death her thoughts
Had entertaind, as di'd her Cheeks with pale.
But Adam with such counsel nothing sway'd, [1010]
To better hopes his more attentive minde
Labouring had rais'd, and thus to Eve repli'd.

Eve, thy contempt of life and pleasure seems
To argue in thee somthing more sublime
And excellent then what thy minde contemnes; [1015]
But self-destruction therefore saught, refutes
That excellence thought in thee, and implies,
Not thy contempt, but anguish and regret
For loss of life and pleasure overlov'd.
Or if thou covet death, as utmost end [1020]
Of miserie, so thinking to evade
The penaltie pronounc't, doubt not but God
Hath wiselier arm'd his vengeful ire then so
To be forestall'd; much more I fear least Death
So snatcht will not exempt us from the paine [1025]
We are by doom to pay; rather such acts
Of contumacie will provoke the highest
To make death in us live: Then let us seek

Some safer resolution, which methinks
I have in view, calling to minde with heed [1030]
Part of our Sentence, that thy Seed shall bruise
The Serpents head; piteous amends, unless
Be meant, whom I conjecture, our grand Foe
Satan, who in the Serpent hath contriv'd
Against us this deceit: to crush his head [1035]
Would be revenge indeed; which will be lost
By death brought on our selves, or childless days
Resolv'd, as thou proposest; so our Foe
Shall scape his punishment ordain'd, and wee
Instead shall double ours upon our heads. [1040]
No more be mention'd then of violence
Against our selves, and wilful barrenness,
That cuts us off from hope, and savours onely
Rancor and pride, impatience and despite,
Reluctance against God and his just yoke [1045]
Laid on our Necks. Remember with what mild
And gracious temper he both heard and judg'd
Without wrauth or reviling; wee expected
Immediate dissolution, which we thought
Was meant by Death that day, when lo, to thee [1050]
Pains onely in Child-bearing were foretold,
And bringing forth, soon recompenc't with joy,
Fruit of thy Womb: On mee the Curse aslope
Glanc'd on the ground, with labour I must earne
My bread; what harm? Idleness had bin worse; [1055]
My labour will sustain me; and least Cold
Or Heat should injure us, his timely care
Hath unbesaught provided, and his hands
Cloath'd us unworthie, pitying while he judg'd;
How much more, if we pray him, will his ear [1060]
Be open, and his heart to pitie incline,
And teach us further by what means to shun
Th' inclement Seasons, Rain, Ice, Hail and Snow,
Which now the Skie with various Face begins
To shew us in this Mountain, while the Winds [1065]
Blow moist and keen, shattering the graceful locks
Of these fair spreading Trees; which bids us seek
Som better shroud, som better warmth to cherish
Our Limbs benumm'd, ere this diurnal Starr
Leave cold the Night, how we his gather'd beams [1070]

Reflected, may with matter sere foment,
Or by collision of two bodies grinde
The Air attrite to Fire, as late the Clouds
Justling or pusht with Winds rude in thir shock
Tine the slant Lightning, whose thwart flame driv'n down [1075]
Kindles the gummie bark of Firr or Pine,
And sends a comfortable heat from farr,
Which might supplie the Sun: such Fire to use,
And what may else be remedie or cure
To evils which our own misdeeds have wrought, [1080]
Hee will instruct us praying, and of Grace
Beseeching him, so as we need not fear
To pass commodiously this life, sustain'd
By him with many comforts, till we end
In dust, our final rest and native home. [1085]
What better can we do, then to the place
Repairing where he judg'd us, prostrate fall
Before him reverent, and there confess
Humbly our faults, and pardon beg, with tears
Watering the ground, and with our sighs the Air [1090]
Frequenting, sent from hearts contrite, in sign
Of sorrow unfeign'd, and humiliation meek.
Undoubtedly he will relent and turn
From his displeasure; in whose look serene,
When angry most he seem'd and most severe, [1095]
What else but favor, grace, and mercie shon?

So spake our Father penitent, nor Eve
Felt less remorse: they forthwith to the place
Repairing where he judg'd them prostrate fell
Before him reverent, and both confess'd [1100]
Humbly thir faults, and pardon beg'd, with tears
Watering the ground, and with thir sighs the Air
Frequenting, sent from hearts contrite, in sign
Of sorrow unfeign'd, and humiliation meek.

人類的懺悔

　　人類吃了禁果，觸犯禁令，神子基督來到伊甸園對蛇和人類進行審判，收回永生的恩澤。亞當和夏娃為乞求天父的原諒，於是回到審判之地誠心禱告，懺悔聲傳至天庭，到達上帝的耳畔，加上神子的求情，令上帝怒氣稍歇，但仍堅持將人類逐出伊甸園；於是派遣天使米迦勒前去執行驅逐任務，並告知亞當未來將會發生的事件。

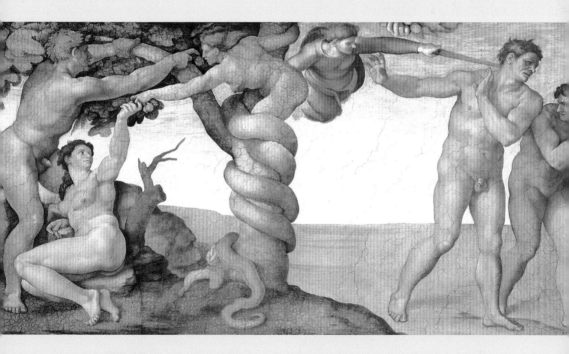

Λ **善惡樹**
米開朗基羅 西斯汀教堂壁畫 1508年

　　人類因為偷嚐禁果，和天神一樣懂得分辨善與惡，但也因此要付出慘痛的代價，上帝處罰他們必須離開伊甸園，前往其他地方耕地過活。

　　亞當和夏娃虔敬的懺悔聲藉著風往上飛升，直達天際，越過天門傳到天庭裡；神子把它們高高捧起，來到上帝的寶座前說道：

　　「啊，天父！您在人類心田播下的種子已經發芽，他們懂得自我反省，並主動地獻上悔悟的祈禱，請您聽聽他們充滿歉意的禱詞吧！日後，我將用死來替人類贖罪，現在可否先請您稍微減輕他們的罰責呢？」

　　「仁慈的兒呀！我接受你的請求，那原本也是我心中所想的。但人類觸犯了死亡重罪，為避免他們再度犯罪，前去摘食生命樹的果子，獲得永生，他們必須要離開伊甸園。這是他們自己的選擇，怪不得別人。當初，我賜給了他們永生與幸福，讓他們無憂無慮的生活；但他們卻背叛我，捨棄善、選擇惡。現在，他們終於懂得辨別善惡，卻也得付出慘痛的代價。我要在眾天使面前宣布人類的罪狀和處罰，以作為天使們言行的借鏡。」

Thus they in lowliest plight repentant stood
Praying, for from the Mercie-seat above
Prevenient Grace descending had remov'd
The stonie from thir hearts, & made new flesh
Regenerate grow instead, that sighs now breath'd [5]
Unutterable, which the Spirit of prayer
Inspir'd, and wing'd for Heav'n with speedier flight
Then loudest Oratorie: yet thir port
Not of mean suiters, nor important less
Seem'd thir Petition, then when th' ancient Pair [10]
In Fables old, less ancient yet then these,
Deucalion and chaste Pyrrha to restore
The Race of Mankind drownd, before the Shrine
Of Themis stood devout. To Heav'n thir prayers
Flew up, nor missd the way, by envious windes [15]
Blow'n vagabond or frustrate: in they passd
Dimentionless through Heav'nly dores; then clad
With incense, where the Golden Altar fum'd,
By thir great Intercessor, came in sight
Before the Fathers Throne: Them the glad Son [20]
Presenting, thus to intercede began.

See Father, what first fruits on Earth are sprung
From thy implanted Grace in Man, these Sighs
And Prayers, which in this Golden Censer, mixt
With Incense, I thy Priest before thee bring, [25]
Fruits of more pleasing savour from thy seed
Sow'n with contrition in his heart, then those
Which his own hand manuring all the Trees
Of Paradise could have produc't, ere fall'n
From innocence. Now therefore bend thine eare [30]
To supplication, heare his sighs though mute;
Unskilful with what words to pray, let mee
Interpret for him, mee his Advocate
And propitiation, all his works on mee
Good or not good ingraft, my Merit those [35]
Shall perfet, and for these my Death shall pay.
Accept me, and in mee from these receave
The smell of peace toward Mankinde, let him live
Before thee reconcil'd, at least his days
Numberd, though sad, till Death, his doom (which I [40]
To mitigate thus plead, not to reverse)

上帝語氣和緩地回答。

　　立刻，上帝身旁的侍衛天使高舉號角，吹奏出嘹亮的號聲，召集全部的天使們前來。那高亢響亮的聲音，劃過天庭的每一處角落——生長著不凋花的綠蔭下、泉水池畔等地方；聽見號聲的天使莫不放下手邊工作，急急奔向寶座的方向。很快地，所有的天使都來了。於是上帝開口宣布：

　　「諸位天使，人類已經能夠同我們一樣分辨善與惡，但這是由偷嚐禁果得來的，為防止他們再去偷吃生命樹的果實而獲得永生，我決定把人類逐出伊甸園，而這項任務，就交由米迦勒來執行。」

　　說到這裡，上帝轉頭

◁ 聖米迦勒
克里維立 畫板 1476年
　　聖米迦勒經常被描繪成英姿煥發的屠龍勇士。

To better life shall yeeld him, where with mee
All my redeemd may dwell in joy and bliss,
Made one with me as I with thee am one.

To whom the Father, without Cloud, serene. [45]
All thy request for Man, accepted Son,
Obtain, all thy request was my Decree:
But longer in that Paradise to dwell,
The Law I gave to Nature him forbids:
Those pure immortal Elements that know [50]
No gross, no unharmoneous mixture foule,
Eject him tainted now, and purge him off
As a distemper, gross to aire as gross,
And mortal food, as may dispose him best
For dissolution wrought by Sin, that first [55]
Distemperd all things, and of incorrupt
Corrupted. I at first with two fair gifts
Created him endowd, with Happiness
And Immortalitie: that fondly lost,
This other serv'd but to eternize woe; [60]
Till I provided Death; so Death becomes
His final remedie, and after Life
Tri'd in sharp tribulation, and ref'ind
By Faith and faithful works, to second Life,
Wak't in the renovation of the just, [65]
Resignes him up with Heav'n and Earth renewd.
But let us call to Synod all the Blest
Through Heav'ns wide bounds; from them I will not hide
My judgments, how with Mankind I proceed,
As how with peccant Angels late they saw; [70]
And in thir state, though firm, stood more confirmd.

He ended, and the Son gave signal high
To the bright Minister that watchd, hee blew
His Trumpet, heard in Oreb since perhaps
When God descended, and perhaps once more [75]
To sound at general Doom. Th' Angelic blast
Filld all the Regions: from thir blissful Bowrs
Of Amarantin Shade, Fountain or Spring,
By the waters of Life, where ere they sate
In fellowships of joy: the Sons of Light [80]
Hasted, resorting to the Summons high,

對米迦勒說道：

「米迦勒，你立即率領一隊掌管火
燄的天使前去伊甸園，守衛樂園免遭
魔鬼再度入侵；另外，在以溫和的方
式驅逐人類之前，得先向他們預示未
來將會發生的事情。最後，記得要在
伊甸園的東邊，安設守衛天使和四面
轉動發出火燄的劍，把守通往生命樹
的每條道路。[1]」

「是的，全能的天父。我現在就出
發。」米迦勒恭敬地回答，並立刻動
身前往地球。

此時，伊甸園裡的亞當和夏娃正做
完晨間禱告，恐懼的心因誠心祈禱而
生出一股新的希望來，亞當微笑地對
妻子說：

「既然上帝要讓我們的子孫去擊碎

註1：出自《舊約‧創世紀》：「耶和華神說：『那
人已經與我們相似，能知道善惡。現在恐
怕他伸手又摘生命樹的果子吃，就永遠活
著。』耶和華神便打發他出伊甸園去，耕種
他所自出之土。於是把他趕出去了。又在伊
甸園的東邊安設基路伯，和四面轉動發火燄
的劍，要把守生命樹的道路。」

And took thir Seats; till from his Throne supream
Th' Almighty thus pronouncd his sovran Will.

O Sons, like one of us Man is become
To know both Good and Evil, since his taste [85]
Of that defended Fruit; but let him boast
His knowledge of Good lost, and Evil got,
Happier, had suffic'd him to have known
Good by it self, and Evil not at all.
He sorrows now, repents, and prayes contrite, [90]
My motions in him, longer then they move,
His heart I know, how variable and vain
Self-left. Least therefore his now bolder hand
Reach also of the Tree of Life, and eat,
And live for ever, dream at least to live [95]
For ever, to remove him I decree,
And send him from the Garden forth to Till
The Ground whence he was taken, fitter soile.

Michael, this my behest have thou in charge,
Take to thee from among the Cherubim [100]
Thy choice of flaming Warriors, least the Fiend
Or in behalf of Man, or to invade
Vacant possession som new trouble raise:
Hast thee, and from the Paradise of God
Without remorse drive out the sinful Pair, [105]
From hallowd ground th' unholie, and denounce
To them and to thir Progenie from thence
Perpetual banishment. Yet least they faint
At the sad Sentence rigorously urg'd,
For I behold them softn'd and with tears [110]
Bewailing thir excess, all terror hide.
If patiently thy bidding they obey,
Dismiss them not disconsolate; reveale
To Adam what shall come in future dayes,
As I shall thee enlighten, intermix [115]
My Cov'nant in the womans seed renewd;
So send them forth, though sorrowing, yet in peace:
And on the East side of the Garden place,
Where entrance up from Eden easiest climbes,
Cherubic watch, and of a Sword the flame [120]
Wide waving, all approach farr off to fright,

蛇的頭，表示暫時我們並不會面臨死亡的威脅，所以收起恐懼的心吧！我相信只要我們誠心的祈禱，必能平息上帝的怒意，獲得祂仁慈的寬恕。」

「是呀！時候不早了，我們得快點開始工作。從今以後，我不會再離開你的身旁，只要能夠住在這裡，與你一塊兒生活，我便感到心滿意足了。」夏娃寬心地回答。

但是，命運已經揭開它殘酷的面紗。米迦勒帶領大隊的天使已經降臨地球，並且接掌了樂園。

遠遠地，亞當看見一個光輝的身影朝向他們走來，於是對夏娃說：

「你先避開一會兒吧！上帝派天使來了，恐怕又有新的變故。」

話才剛剛說完，米迦勒便已來到面前，身上穿著燦亮的軍裝，腰間佩帶利劍，手持長槍，渾身散發出王者的氣慨。

「亞當，上帝已經聽見你們的禱告，祂決定延長你們的壽命，使你

And guard all passage to the Tree of Life:
Least Paradise a receptacle prove
To Spirits foule, and all my Trees thir prey,
With whose stol'n Fruit Man once more to delude. [125]

He ceas'd; and th' Archangelic Power prepar'd
For swift descent, with him the Cohort bright
Of watchful Cherubim; four faces each
Had, like a double Janus, all thir shape
Spangl'd with eyes more numerous then those [130]
Of Argus, and more wakeful then to drouze,
Charm'd with Arcadian Pipe, the Pastoral Reed
Of Hermes, or his opiate Rod. Mean while
To resalute the World with sacred Light
Leucothea wak'd, and with fresh dews imbalmd [135]
The Earth, when Adam and first Matron Eve
Had ended now thir Orisons, and found,
Strength added from above, new hope to spring
Out of despaire, joy, but with fear yet linkt;
Which thus to Eve his welcome words renewd. [140]

Eve, easily may Faith admit, that all
The good which we enjoy, from Heav'n descends;
But that from us ought should ascend to Heav'n
So prevalent as to concerne the mind
Of God high-blest, or to incline his will, [145]
Hard to belief may seem; yet this will Prayer,
Or one short sigh of humane breath, up-borne
Ev'n to the Seat of God. For since I saught
By Prayer th' offended Deitie to appease,
Kneel'd and before him humbl'd all my heart, [150]
Methought I saw him placable and mild,
Bending his eare; perswasion in me grew
That I was heard with favour; peace returnd
Home to my brest, and to my memorie
His promise, that thy Seed shall bruise our Foe; [155]
Which then not minded in dismay, yet now
Assures me that the bitterness of death
Is past, and we shall live. Whence Haile to thee,
Eve rightly call'd, Mother of all Mankind,
Mother of all things living, since by thee [160]
Man is to live, and all things live for Man.

們有懺悔的機會，以此彌補犯下的罪
行。但伊甸園不能讓你們再繼續住
下去了，你們必須馬上離開，前往其
他的地方耕地過活。」米迦勒以嚴肅
的語氣向亞當傳達上帝的旨意，一邊
把摘下的頭盔夾在腋下，發出閃閃星
光。

　　亞當聽見這話，悲痛地說不出話
來，他雙腳發抖愣在那兒。

♡ 米迦勒帶領大隊天使降臨伊甸園
杜雷 版畫 1866年

　　上帝派米迦勒率領火燄天使前往伊甸園，準
備驅逐亞當和夏娃，避免他們又去吃生命樹的果
實，重新取得長生不老的能力。

To whom thus Eve with sad demeanour meek.
Ill worthie I such title should belong
To me transgressour, who for thee ordaind
A help, became thy snare; to mee reproach [165]
Rather belongs, distrust and all dispraise:
But infinite in pardon was my Judge,
That I who first brought Death on all, am grac't
The sourse of life; next favourable thou,
Who highly thus to entitle me voutsaf'st, [170]
Farr other name deserving. But the Field
To labour calls us now with sweat impos'd,
Though after sleepless Night; for see the Morn,
All unconcern'd with our unrest, begins
Her rosie progress smiling; let us forth, [175]
I never from thy side henceforth to stray,
Wherere our days work lies, though now enjoind
Laborious, till day droop; while here we dwell,
What can be toilsom in these pleasant Walkes?
Here let us live, though in fall'n state, content. [180]

So spake, so wish'd much-humbl'd Eve, but Fate
Subscrib'd not; Nature first gave Signs, imprest
On Bird, Beast, Aire, Aire suddenly eclips'd
After short blush of Morn; nigh in her sight
The Bird of Jove, stoopt from his aerie tour, [185]
Two Birds of gayest plume before him drove:
Down from a Hill the Beast that reigns in Woods,
First hunter then, pursu'd a gentle brace,
Goodliest of all the Forrest, Hart and Hinde;
Direct to th' Eastern Gate was bent thir flight. [190]
Adam observ'd, and with his Eye the chase
Pursuing, not unmov'd to Eve thus spake.

O Eve, some furder change awaits us nigh,
Which Heav'n by these mute signs in Nature shews
Forerunners of his purpose, or to warn [195]
Us haply too secure of our discharge
From penaltie, because from death releast
Some days; how long, and what till then our life,
Who knows, or more then this, that we are dust,
And thither must return and be no more. [200]
Why else this double object in our sight

伊甸園的故事
貝利公爵時禱書 1410年

　　亞當和夏娃原本知識未開，在伊甸園無憂無慮地生活著。兩人吃下知識果之後，開始羞於赤身裸體，趕忙以無花果葉遮避身體，卻也因為背棄上帝的諄諄告誡，被迫離開美好的樂園。

　　夏娃躲在近處，聽到這個噩耗不禁悲從中來，傷心地出聲叫道：

　　「我們一定得離開嗎？花園裡的花朵將由誰來照顧？每一株新生的花兒都有我的祝福，我細心地呵護它們，為它們命名，可是現在，它們卻得在太陽的曝曬下乾枯萎縮了；我們不能再回到舒適芳香的居所，得到污濁潮溼的異地到處流浪，這種生活比死亡更加悲慘呀！」

Of flight pursu'd in th' Air and ore the ground
One way the self-same hour? why in the East
Darkness ere Dayes mid-course, and Morning light
More orient in yon Western Cloud that draws [205]
O're the blew Firmament a radiant white,
And slow descends, with somthing heav'nly fraught.

He err'd not, for by this the heav'nly Bands
Down from a Skie of Jasper lighted now
In Paradise, and on a Hill made alt, [210]
A glorious Apparition, had not doubt
And carnal fear that day dimm'd Adams eye.
Not that more glorious, when the Angels met
Jacob in Mahanaim, where he saw
The field Pavilion'd with his Guardians bright; [215]
Nor that which on the flaming Mount appeerd
In Dothan, cover'd with a Camp of Fire,
Against the Syrian King, who to surprize
One man, Assassin-like had levied Warr,
Warr unproclam'd. The Princely Hierarch [220]
In thir bright stand, there left his Powers to seise
Possession of the Garden; hee alone,
To find where Adam shelterd, took his way,
Not unperceav'd of Adam, who to Eve,
While the great Visitant approachd, thus spake. [225]

Eve, now expect great tidings, which perhaps
Of us will soon determin, or impose
New Laws to be observ'd; for I descrie
From yonder blazing Cloud that veils the Hill
One of the heav'nly Host, and by his Gate [230]
None of the meanest, some great Potentate
Or of the Thrones above, such Majestie
Invests him coming? yet not terrible,
That I should fear, nor sociably mild,
As Raphael, that I should much confide, [235]
But solemn and sublime, whom not to offend,
With reverence I must meet, and thou retire.
He ended; and th' Arch-Angel soon drew nigh,
Not in his shape Celestial, but as Man
Clad to meet Man; over his lucid Armes [240]
A militarie Vest of purple flowd

米迦勒發現夏娃躲在樹叢後方，便溫和地安慰她說：

「你別這麼想，樂園本來就不是為你所造的，況且你並不孤單，只要跟在亞當身邊，到任何地方都是美好的居所。」

亞當回過神來，沮喪地對米迦勒說：

「離開這裡的話，我便再無機會見著上帝的容顏了，雖然有萬分的心痛與不捨，但我仍會遵從祂的命令，退出這個快樂的居所。」

「亞當，上帝是無所不在的，並不僅僅存在於樂園中；天地萬物皆由祂所造，因此，祂便存在於陸面、海洋和天空所有的生物之中。就算你遷移到平地，祂也無時無刻不在你身邊。你應當堅定信仰，隨時記取上帝的恩澤。我來這兒是要向你預示人類未來的事情，現在，請跟著我到山上去吧！」

這兒是伊甸園裡最高的一座山，從

Livelier then Meliboean, or the graine
Of Sarra, worn by Kings and Hero's old
In time of Truce; Iris had dipt the wooff;
His starrie Helme unbuckl'd shew'd him prime [245]
In Manhood where Youth ended; by his side
As in a glistering Zodiac hung the Sword,
Satans dire dread, and in his hand the Spear.
Adam bowd low, hee Kingly from his State
Inclin'd not, but his coming thus declar'd. [250]

Adam, Heav'ns high behest no Preface needs:
Sufficient that thy Prayers are heard, and Death,
Then due by sentence when thou didst transgress,
Defeated of his seisure many dayes
Giv'n thee of Grace, wherein thou may'st repent, [255]
And one bad act with many deeds well done
Mayst cover: well may then thy Lord appeas'd
Redeem thee quite from Deaths rapacious claime;
But longer in this Paradise to dwell
Permits not; to remove thee I am come, [260]
And send thee from the Garden forth to till
The ground whence thou wast tak'n, fitter Soile.

He added not, for Adam at the newes
Heart-strook with chilling gripe of sorrow stood,
That all his senses bound; Eve, who unseen [265]
Yet all had heard, with audible lament
Discover'd soon the place of her retire.

O unexpected stroke, worse then of Death!
Must I thus leave thee Paradise? thus leave
Thee Native Soile, these happie Walks and Shades, [270]
Fit haunt of Gods? where I had hope to spend,
Quiet though sad, the respit of that day
That must be mortal to us both. O flours,
That never will in other Climate grow,
My early visitation, and my last [275]
At Eev'n, which I bred up with tender hand
From the first op'ning bud, and gave ye Names,
Who now shall reare ye to the Sun, or ranke
Your Tribes, and water from th' ambrosial Fount?
Thee lastly nuptial Bowre, by mee adornd [280]

峰頂可以望見非常遙遠的地方，但米
迦勒為了讓亞當看得更加清楚，還幫
他揭去了因吃下禁果而長出的眼中薄
膜，再拿珍貴的明目草、茴香和生命
泉水幫他洗滌雙眼，然後對亞當說，

　　「你睜開眼睛看看，你犯下的原罪
為後代帶來什麼樣的後果吧！」

　　亞當睜開雙眼，看見一大片土地，
這邊是汗流浹背的農人彎腰割下金黃
色的稻穗，紮成一綑一綑堆疊起來，
並隨意撿取一些當做祭品；另一邊則
是牧人在草地上放牧，並精心挑選了
初生的羔羊，用來宰殺祭祀。兩者中
間有一座祭壇，農人和牧人分別來到
這裡，在祭壇供上祭品。上帝降下火
燄，把犧牲燃燒殆盡，表示接受了牧
人的祭祀；農人不若牧人誠心，所以
上帝不接受他的祭品。農人見牧人獨
自得到上帝的垂青，一怒之下拿石頭
把他給砸死了[2]。

　　亞當深感訝異，悲痛地詢問米迦
勒：

With what to sight or smell was sweet; from thee
How shall I part, and whither wander down
Into a lower World, to this obscure
And wilde, how shall we breath in other Aire
Less pure, accustomd to immortal Fruits? [285]

Whom thus the Angel interrupted milde.
Lament not Eve, but patiently resigne
What justly thou hast lost; nor set thy heart,
Thus over-fond, on that which is not thine;
Thy going is not lonely, with thee goes [290]
Thy Husband, him to follow thou art bound;
Where he abides, think there thy native soile.

Adam by this from the cold sudden damp
Recovering, and his scatterd spirits returnd,
To Michael thus his humble words addressd. [295]

Celestial, whether among the Thrones, or nam'd
Of them the Highest, for such of shape may seem
Prince above Princes, gently hast thou tould
Thy message, which might else in telling wound,
And in performing end us; what besides [300]
Of sorrow and dejection and despair
Our frailtie can sustain, thy tidings bring,
Departure from this happy place, our sweet
Recess, and onely consolation left
Familiar to our eyes, all places else [305]

註2：出自《舊約‧創世紀》該隱殺亞伯
　　的事：「夏娃就懷孕了，生了該
　　隱，……又生了該隱的兄弟亞伯。亞
　　伯是牧羊的，該隱是種地的。有一
　　日，該隱拿地裡的出產為供物獻給耶
　　和華；亞伯也將他羊群中頭生的和羊
　　的脂油獻上。耶和華看中了亞伯和
　　他的供物，只是不看中該隱和他的
　　供物。該隱就大大地發怒，變了臉
　　色。……該隱與他兄弟亞伯說話，二
　　人正在田間，該隱起來打他兄弟亞
　　伯，把他殺了。」

「上帝不是接受了牧人的獻祭嗎？為什麼還讓他遭受如此可怕的災難？」

米迦勒搖搖頭，同情地回答：

「那兩人都是你的兒子，耕種田地的是哥哥該隱，放牧羊群的則是弟弟亞伯，哥哥嫉妒弟弟的祭品獨為上帝所接受，於是狠心地殺了他，這血腥的行為必得報復，而那信仰堅貞的則

▽ **該隱殺死亞伯**
雷尼 油畫 1598年

　　該隱和亞伯是亞當和夏娃的兒子。該隱因為殘殺弟弟，被上帝趕出家門，再也沒有見過父母的面。他的子孫更是縱欲享樂，辜負了上帝的恩賜。

Inhospitable appeer and desolate,
Nor knowing us nor known: and if by prayer
Incessant I could hope to change the will
Of him who all things can, I would not cease
To wearie him with my assiduous cries: [310]
But prayer against his absolute Decree
No more availes then breath against the winde,
Blown stifling back on him that breaths it forth:
Therefore to his great bidding I submit.
This most afflicts me, that departing hence, [315]
As from his face I shall be hid, deprivd
His blessed count'nance; here I could frequent,
With worship, place by place where he voutsaf'd
Presence Divine, and to my Sons relate;
On this Mount he appeerd, under this Tree [320]
Stood visible, among these Pines his voice
I heard, here with him at this Fountain talk'd:
So many grateful Altars I would reare
Of grassie Terfe, and pile up every Stone
Of lustre from the brook, in memorie, [325]
Or monument to Ages, and thereon
Offer sweet smelling Gumms and Fruits and Flours:
In yonder nether World where shall I seek
His bright appearances, or foot step-trace?
For though I fled him angrie, yet recall'd [330]
To life prolongd and promisd Race, I now
Gladly behold though but his utmost skirts
Of glory, and farr off his steps adore.

To whom thus Michael with regard benigne.
Adam, thou know'st Heav'n his, and all the Earth. [335]
Not this Rock onely; his Omnipresence fills
Land, Sea, and Aire, and every kinde that lives,
Fomented by his virtual power and warmd:
All th' Earth he gave thee to possess and rule,
No despicable gift; surmise not then [340]
His presence to these narrow bounds confin'd
Of Paradise or Eden: this had been
Perhaps thy Capital Seate, from whence had spred
All generations, and had hither come
From all the ends of th' Earth, to celebrate [345]
And reverence thee thir great Progenitor.

會回歸塵土。」

「唉！這就是死亡嗎？多麼殘忍恐怖，以這樣的方式回歸塵土，想起來便叫人忍不住發抖哩！」亞當難過極了，忍不住嘆了一口氣。

「這只不過是死亡的其中一種形式，除了剛才你所看見的被重擊死亡，還有被火燒死、被水淹死、餓死、飽死、因疾病而死，更有許多奇奇怪怪的死亡方式；人在死亡後，更得進入淒涼陰森的墓穴。而這些，都是因為夏娃觸犯禁令所造成的。」

米迦勒說完，伸手一揮，立即出現一幅悲慘的畫面。那是一間像是醫院的屋子，裡頭躺著許多症狀不同的病患，有的面色蒼白、有的肢體不全、有的咳嗽不止、有的渾身痙攣……痛苦的呻吟聲不斷從人群中傳來，刺痛亞當的耳膜。

「看見這麼悲慘的景象，誰還敢繁衍後代？難道就因為犯下一次錯誤，便得遭受如此嚴厲的處罰？造物主為

But this præeminence thou hast lost, brought down
To dwell on eeven ground now with thy Sons:
Yet doubt not but in Vallie and in Plaine
God is as here, and will be found alike [350]
Present, and of his presence many a signe
Still following thee, still compassing thee round
With goodness and paternal Love, his Face
Express, and of his steps the track Divine.
Which that thou mayst beleeve, and be confirmd [355]
Ere thou from hence depart, know I am sent
To shew thee what shall come in future dayes
To thee and to thy Ofspring; good with bad
Expect to hear, supernal Grace contending
With sinfulness of Men; thereby to learn [360]
True patience, and to temper joy with fear
And pious sorrow, equally enur'd
By moderation either state to beare,
Prosperous or adverse: so shalt thou lead
Safest thy life, and best prepar'd endure [365]
Thy mortal passage when it comes. Ascend
This Hill; let Eve (for I have drencht her eyes)
Here sleep below while thou to foresight wak'st,
As once thou slepst, while Shee to life was formd.

To whom thus Adam gratefully repli'd. [370]
Ascend, I follow thee, safe Guide, the path
Thou lead'st me, and to the hand of Heav'n submit,
However chast'ning, to the evil turne
My obvious breast, arming to overcom
By suffering, and earne rest from labour won, [375]
If so I may attain. So both ascend
In the Visions of God: It was a Hill
Of Paradise the highest, from whose top
The Hemisphere of Earth in cleerest Ken
Stretcht out to amplest reach of prospect lay. [380]
Not higher that Hill nor wider looking round,
Whereon for different cause the Tempter set
Our second Adam in the Wilderness,
To shew him all Earths Kingdomes and thir Glory.
His Eye might there command wherever stood [385]
City of old or modern Fame, the Seat
Of mightiest Empire, from the destind Walls

何不憐憫與祂形像類似的人類，讓他們稍微免除這些痛苦呢？」亞當淚流滿面，傷心地悲嘆。

「正因為人類是依照造物主的形像塑造的，更應該警惕自身，努力維護造物主的姿容。但夏娃卻背叛上帝，觸犯禁令，使得人類必須以殘缺、淒慘的外貌，用來宣告已被上帝捨棄的事實。」米迦勒語重心長地說道。

「我無法反駁你的說法，我也必須服從這個事實。但是有沒有比較和緩的死亡方式，讓人類平靜地回歸塵土呢？」亞當問道。

「有的，只要人類能夠謹守住『適度』的原則，吃東西時不要暴飲暴食，生命自會依循大自然的法則，像樹上的果實，熟透了，便自然掉落。人類年老的時候，體力會逐漸衰弱，頭髮變白、感官慢慢遲鈍，生命的香膏緩緩焚盡，終至死亡。生命長短自有它的定數，所以不要過份的愛憎，要順其自然地生活。現在讓我們看看

Of Cambalu, seat of Cathaian Can
And Samarchand by Oxus, Temirs Throne,
To Paquin of Sinæan Kings, and thence [390]
To Agra and Lahor of great Mogul
Down to the golden Chersonese, or where
The Persian in Ecbatan sate, or since
In Hispahan, or where the Russian Ksar
In Mosco, or the Sultan in Bizance, [395]
Turchestan-born; nor could his eye not ken
Th' Empire of Negus to his utmost Port
Ercoco and the less Maritim Kings
Mombaza, and Quiloa, and Melind,
And Sofala thought Ophir, to the Realme [400]
Of Congo, and Angola fardest South;
Or thence from Niger Flood to Atlas Mount
The Kingdoms of Almansor, Fez and Sus,
Marocco and Algiers, and Tremisen;
On Europe thence, and where Rome was to sway [405]
The World: in Spirit perhaps he also saw
Rich Mexico the seat of Motezume,
And Cusco in Peru, the richer seat
Of Atabalipa, and yet unspoil'd
Guiana, whose great Citie Geryons Sons [410]
Call El Dorado: but to nobler sights
Michael from Adams eyes the Filme remov'd
Which that false Fruit that promis'd clearer sight
Had bred; then purg'd with Euphrasie and Rue
The visual Nerve, for he had much to see; [415]
And from the Well of Life three drops instill'd.
So deep the power of these Ingredients pierc'd,
Eevn to the inmost seat of mental sight,
That Adam now enforc't to close his eyes,
Sunk down and all his Spirits became intranst: [420]
But him the gentle Angel by the hand
Soon rais'd, and his attention thus recall'd.

Adam, now ope thine eyes, and first behold
Th' effects which thy original crime hath wrought
In some to spring from thee, who never touch'd [425]
Th' excepted Tree, nor with the Snake conspir'd,
Nor sinn'd thy sin, yet from that sin derive
Corruption to bring forth more violent deeds.

另一番景象吧！」米迦勒回答。

　　亞當望向前方，看見一片廣闊的平原，上面有各種顏色的帳棚；帳棚旁邊的草地上，有許多牲畜在低頭吃草。遠遠地，傳來一陣陣悠揚的樂音，有人在帳棚裡撥動琴弦，彈奏出宛如天籟一般的旋律。草原的另外一邊，有人把燒紅的青銅和生鐵溶合，流動的金屬液被注入模子裡，造出了一批工具；接著，人們使用這些工具鑄造了許多的物品[3]。

　　臨近平原的高山斜坡上，住著一群信仰上帝、觀察天文的人，他們來到平原上，看見裝扮華麗、容貌嬌豔的女子從帳棚裡走出來，隨著優美的琴音輕歌曼舞，心中愛的情弦隨即被撥開來，與她們墜入情網；當夜晚來

註3：此處內容出自《舊約·創世紀》，拉麥是該隱的後代子孫，「拉麥娶了兩個妻，一個名叫亞大，一個名叫洗拉。亞大生雅八，雅八就是住帳棚、牧養牲畜之人的祖師。雅八的兄弟名叫猶八，他是一切彈琴吹簫之人的祖師。洗拉又生了土八該隱，他是打造各樣銅鐵利器的。」

His eyes he op'nd, and beheld a field,
Part arable and tilth, whereon were Sheaves [430]
New reapt, the other part sheep-walks and foulds;
Ith' midst an Altar as the Land-mark stood
Rustic, of grassie sord; thither anon
A sweatie Reaper from his Tillage brought
First Fruits, the green Eare, and the yellow Sheaf, [435]
Uncull'd, as came to hand; a Shepherd next
More meek came with the Firstlings of his Flock
Choicest and best; then sacrificing, laid
The Inwards and thir Fat, with Incense strew'd,
On the cleft Wood, and all due Rites perform'd. [440]
His Offring soon propitious Fire from Heav'n
Consum'd with nimble glance, and grateful steame;
The others not, for his was not sincere;
Whereat hee inlie rag'd, and as they talk'd,
Smote him into the Midriff with a stone [445]
That beat out life; he fell, and deadly pale
Groand out his Soul with gushing bloud effus'd.
Much at that sight was Adam in his heart
Dismai'd, and thus in haste to th' Angel cri'd.

O Teacher, some great mischief hath befall'n [450]
To that meek man, who well had sacrif'c'd;
Is Pietie thus and pure Devotion paid?

T' whom Michael thus, hee also mov'd, repli'd.
These two are Brethren, Adam, and to come
Out of thy loyns; th' unjust the just hath slain, [455]
For envie that his Brothers Offering found
From Heav'n acceptance; but the bloodie Fact
Will be aveng'd, and th' others Faith approv'd
Loose no reward, though here thou see him die,
Rowling in dust and gore. To which our Sire. [460]

Alas, both for the deed and for the cause!
But have I now seen Death? Is this the way
I must return to native dust? O sight
Of terrour, foul and ugly to behold,
Horrid to think, how horrible to feel! [465]

To whom thus Michael. Death thou hast seen

臨，一對對相擁的戀人舉行了盛大的
婚禮，新人在搖曳的火光中深情款款
地相互凝視[4]。

　　美麗的花環、悠揚的歌聲，婚禮的
歡樂景象感動了亞當的心。

　　「這景象真是美好、和平、幸福，
較之先前充滿恨意與死亡的兩幕好太
多了。」

　　「什麼是好的呢？不要只借助眼
睛來判斷好壞，像剛剛你所見到的帳
棚，充滿著歡樂的景象，但住在裡面
的卻是殘殺弟弟的該隱的後代。他們
雖然擁有上帝的恩賜，卻無一絲感恩
的心；由他們所生下的美麗如女神的
女人們，更是縱欲享樂，喪失美好的
婦德。」米迦勒接著說：

　　「這些女子媚惑了男人，使他們拋
棄一切美好的德性，不顧尊嚴地拜倒

註4：此處說的是亞當的小兒子塞特後裔的事，出自
　　　《舊約・創世紀》：「亞當活到一百三十歲，
　　　生了一個兒子，形像樣式和自己相似，就給他
　　　起名叫塞特。」據說，塞特住在山上。

In his first shape on man; but many shapes
Of Death, and many are the wayes that lead
To his grim Cave, all dismal; yet to sense
More terrible at th' entrance then within. [470]
Some, as thou saw'st, by violent stroke shall die,
By Fire, Flood, Famin, by Intemperance more
In Meats and Drinks, which on the Earth shall bring
Diseases dire, of which a monstrous crew
Before thee shall appear; that thou mayst know [475]
What miserie th' inabstinence of Eve
Shall bring on men. Immediately a place
Before his eyes appeard, sad, noysom, dark,
A Lazar-house it seemd, wherein were laid
Numbers of all diseas'd, all maladies [480]
Of gastly Spasm, or racking torture, qualmes
Of heart-sick Agonie, all feavorous kinds,
Convulsions, Epilepsies, fierce Catarrhs,
Intestin Stone and Ulcer, Colic pangs,
Dæmoniac Phrenzie, moaping Melancholie [485]
And Moon-struck madness, pining Atrophie
Marasmus and wide-wasting Pestilence,
Dropsies, and Asthma's, and Joint-racking Rheums.
Dire was the tossing, deep the groans, despair
Tended the sick busiest from Couch to Couch; [490]
And over them triumphant Death his Dart
Shook, but delaid to strike, though oft invokt
With vows, as thir chief good, and final hope.
Sight so deform what heart of Rock could long
Drie-ey'd behold? Adam could not, but wept, [495]
Though not of Woman born; compassion quell'd
His best of Man, and gave him up to tears
A space, till firmer thoughts restrain'd excess,
And scarce recovering words his plaint renew'd.

O miserable Mankind, to what fall [500]
Degraded, to what wretched state reserv'd!
Better end heer unborn. Why is life giv'n
To be thus wrested from us? rather why
Obtruded on us thus? who if we knew
What we receive, would either not accept [505]
Life offer'd, or soon beg to lay it down,
Glad to be so dismist in peace. Can thus

在她們腳邊，從此沉溺於淫逸。」

「唉呀！女人為男人帶來了災禍。」亞當惋惜地說。

「其實只要男人不那麼閒散疏懶，能夠善用天賦的本領與智慧，就能不辜負上帝的恩賜，保住自己的地位。我們繼續往下看。」米迦勒回答。

接著出現的是鄉村與都市的景象。體格壯碩的兵士們眼露凶光，殺氣騰騰地在高大的城門、塔樓周遭巡視；戒備森嚴的營區裡，士兵們有的在揮舞兵器、有的在操練兵陣、有的在練習騎射，做好隨時出征的準備。

荒野上，一座遭受到血腥攻擊的城鎮，血流成河；凶狠的軍隊奪去了所有的牲畜和財物，極目所見，只剩下斷垣殘壁和遍地的屍體。

另一邊，爆發戰事的大都市砲聲隆隆，被侵襲的一方死守城門，從樓頂投射槍箭；發動侵略的一方則出動雲梯，發射大砲加以攻擊。傳令兵四處奔走，召集將領前來開會，議堂上言

Th' Image of God in man created once
So goodly and erect, though faultie since,
To such unsightly sufferings be debas't [510]
Under inhuman pains? Why should not Man,
Retaining still Divine similitude
In part, from such deformities be free,
And for his Makers Image sake exempt?

Thir Makers Image, answerd Michael, then [515]
Forsook them, when themselves they villifi'd
To serve ungovern'd appetite, and took
His Image whom they serv'd, a brutish vice,
Inductive mainly to the sin of Eve.
Therefore so abject is thir punishment, [520]
Disfiguring not Gods likeness, but thir own,
Or if his likeness, by themselves defac't
While they pervert pure Natures healthful rules
To loathsom sickness, worthily, since they
Gods Image did not reverence in themselves. [525]

I yield it just, said Adam, and submit.
But is there yet no other way, besides
These painful passages, how we may come
To Death, and mix with our connatural dust?

There is, said Michael, if thou well observe [530]
The rule of not too much, by temperance taught
In what thou eatst and drinkst, seeking from thence
Due nourishment, not gluttonous delight,
Till many years over thy head return:
So maist thou live, till like ripe Fruit thou drop [535]
Into thy Mothers lap, or be with ease
Gatherd, not harshly pluckt, for death mature:
This is old age; but then thou must outlive
Thy youth, thy strength, thy beauty, which will change
To witherd weak and gray; thy Senses then [540]
Obtuse, all taste of pleasure must forgoe,
To what thou hast, and for the Aire of youth
Hopeful and cheerful, in thy blood will reigne
A melancholly damp of cold and dry
To weigh thy spirits down, and last consume [545]
The Balme of Life. To whom our Ancestor.

語紛擾，各個黨派激烈地爭辯。

　　這遍地烽火、暴力和血腥的畫面讓亞當痛苦極了，他流下淚來，哽咽地說道：

　　「這些體格健壯的人都成了「死亡」的信徒嗎？他們殘暴凶狠，毫無人性，比弒弟的該隱更加冷血無情。這個被「罪惡」所統領的世界，還找得出正義之士嗎？」

　　「上帝的兒子們和人的女子生下這些體格壯碩、英武有名的人，他們是不良的品種、善與惡的結晶；他們擅長戰鬥，以武力來奪取他人的城池和牲畜，殺人無數，並以此為樂趣，給人類帶來了無窮的災難。5

　　殺戮為這些孔武有力的人帶來顯赫的名聲，滿懷正義公理的人卻無人知曉。以諾 ── 你的第七代孫子；謹守

註5：出自《舊約·創世紀》：「當人在世上多起來，又生女兒的時候，神的兒子們看見人的女子美貌，就隨意挑選，娶來為妻。……後來神的兒子們和人的女子們交合生子，那就是上古英武有名的人。」

Henceforth I flie not Death, nor would prolong
Life much, bent rather how I may be quit
Fairest and easiest of this combrous charge,
Which I must keep till my appointed day [550]
Of rendring up, and patiently attend
My dissolution. Michael repli'd,

Nor love thy Life, nor hate; but what thou livst
Live well, how long or short permit to Heav'n:
And now prepare thee for another sight. [555]

He lookd and saw a spacious Plaine, whereon
Were Tents of various hue; by some were herds
Of Cattel grazing: others, whence the sound
Of Instruments that made melodious chime
Was heard, of Harp and Organ; and who moovd [560]
Thir stops and chords was seen: his volant touch
Instinct through all proportions low and high
Fled and pursu'd transverse the resonant fugue.
In other part stood one who at the Forge
Labouring, two massie clods of Iron and Brass [565]
Had melted (whether found where casual fire
Had wasted woods on Mountain or in Vale,
Down to the veins of Earth, thence gliding hot
To som Caves mouth, or whether washt by stream
From underground) the liquid Ore he dreind [570]
Into fit moulds prepar'd; from which he formd
First his own Tooles; then, what might else be wrought
Fusil or grav'n in mettle. After these,
But on the hether side a different sort
From the high neighbouring Hills, which was thir Seat, [575]
Down to the Plain descended: by thir guise
Just men they seemd, and all thir study bent
To worship God aright, and know his works
Not hid, nor those things last which might preserve
Freedom and Peace to men: they on the Plain [580]
Long had not walkt, when from the Tents behold
A Beavie of fair Women, richly gay
In Gems and wanton dress; to the Harp they sung
Soft amorous Ditties, and in dance came on:
The Men though grave, ey'd them, and let thir eyes [585]
Rove without rein, till in the amorous Net

上帝的教誨，四處宣揚真理，曾經預示人類將面臨上帝的審判，因此遭受眾人的憎恨，陷身危險的境地。

由於以諾雖身處混濁的世間，卻能夠堅守正直公義，終於得到上帝的恩澤，被接到美麗的天國享受幸福與永生[6]。

這個景象在提醒你，要虛心接受懲罰、嚴守善念。接下來的畫面，要讓你看看善與惡之人給自己的未來帶來什麼樣的後果。」

戰爭的火光消失，隨之而來的景象仍是罪惡的；男男女女不論結婚與否，皆縱情酒食、相擁跳舞，日夜狂歡作樂，耽溺於淫慾享受。

挪亞是亞當的小兒子塞特的後代子孫，他正直公義、為人虔誠，穿梭

註6：出自《新約‧猶大書》：「亞當的七世孫以諾曾預言這些人說：『看哪，主帶著他的千萬聖者降臨，要在眾人身上行審判，證實那一切不敬虔的人所妄行一切不敬虔的事，又證實不敬虔之罪人所說頂撞他的剛愎話。』這些人是私下議論，常發怨言的，隨從自己的情慾而行，口中說誇大的話，為得便宜諂媚人。」

Fast caught, they lik'd, and each his liking chose;
And now of love they treat till th'Eevning Star
Loves Harbinger appeerd; then all in heat
They light the Nuptial Torch, and bid invoke [590]
Hymen, then first to marriage Rites invok't;
With Feast and Musick all the Tents resound.
Such happy interview and fair event
Of love and youth not lost, Songs, Garlands, Flours,
And charming Symphonies attach'd the heart [595]
Of Adam, soon enclin'd to admit delight,
The bent of Nature; which he thus express'd.

True opener of mine eyes, prime Angel blest,
Much better seems this Vision, and more hope
Of peaceful dayes portends, then those two past; [600]
Those were of hate and death, or pain much worse,
Here Nature seems fulfilld in all her ends.

To whom thus Michael. Judg not what is best
By pleasure, though to Nature seeming meet,
Created, as thou art, to nobler end [605]
Holie and pure, conformitie divine.
Those Tents thou sawst so pleasant, were the Tents
Of wickedness, wherein shall dwell his Race
Who slew his Brother; studious they appere
Of Arts that polish Life, Inventers rare, [610]
Unmindful of thir Maker, though his Spirit
Taught them, but they his gifts acknowledg'd none.
Yet they a beauteous ofspring shall beget;
For that fair femal Troop thou sawst, that seemd
Of Goddesses, so blithe, so smooth, so gay, [615]
Yet empty of all good wherein consists
Womans domestic honour and chief praise;
Bred onely and completed to the taste
Of lustful appetence, to sing, to dance,
To dress, and troule the Tongue, and roule the Eye. [620]
To these that sober Race of Men, whose lives
Religious titl'd them the Sons of God,
Shall yield up all thir vertue, all thir fame
Ignobly, to the traines and to the smiles
Of these fair Atheists, and now swim in joy, [625]
(Erelong to swim at large) and laugh; for which

在縱慾的人群之間，諄諄告誡眾人應悔改向善，但終告失敗。於是他登上高山、砍伐巨木，造了一艘大船；船的內部分成上、中、下三層，並儲存了各種動物所需的食糧。跟著，他到處捕捉地球上的生物，牲畜、鳥類和昆蟲等，成雙成對地被帶到船艙裡。最後，當挪亞和妻子與三個兒子閃、含、雅弗跟兒媳們，一塊走進大船之後，船門便被關上了[7]。

此時，狂風驟起、烏雲密佈，天上降下滂沱大雨；猛烈的雨勢帶來洪水，淹沒了大地上所有的高山、島

註7：出自《舊約‧創世紀》：「神就對挪亞說：『凡有血氣的人，他的盡頭已經來到我面前，因為地上滿了他們的強暴，我要把他們和地一併毀滅。你要用歌斐木造一隻方舟，分一間一間地造，裡外抹上松香。方舟的造法乃是這樣：要長三百肘，寬五十肘，高三十肘。方舟上邊要留透光處，高一肘。方舟的門要開在旁邊。方舟要分上、中、下三層。……你和你的全家都要進入方舟，因為在這世代中，我見你在我面前是義人。凡潔淨的畜類，你要帶七公七母；不潔淨的畜類，你要帶一公一母；空中的飛鳥也要帶七公七母，可以留種，活在全地上；因為再過七天，我要降雨在地上四十晝夜，把我所造的各種活物都從地上除滅。』挪亞就遵著耶和華所吩咐的行了。」

The world erelong a world of tears must weepe.

To whom thus Adam of short joy bereft.
O pittie and shame, that they who to live well
Enterd so faire, should turn aside to tread [630]
Paths indirect, or in the mid way faint!
But still I see the tenor of Mans woe
Holds on the same, from Woman to begin.

From Mans effeminate slackness it begins,
Said th' Angel, who should better hold his place [635]
By wisdome, and superiour gifts receav'd.
But now prepare thee for another Scene.

He lookd and saw wide Territorie spred
Before him, Towns, and rural works between,
Cities of Men with lofty Gates and Towrs, [640]
Concours in Arms, fierce Faces threatning Warr,
Giants of mightie Bone, and bould emprise;
Part wield thir Arms, part courb the foaming Steed,
Single or in Array of Battel rang'd
Both Horse and Foot, nor idely mustring stood; [645]
One way a Band select from forage drives
A herd of Beeves, faire Oxen and faire Kine
From a fat Meddow ground; or fleecy Flock,
Ewes and thir bleating Lambs over the Plaine,
Thir Bootie; scarce with Life the Shepherds flye, [650]
But call in aide, which makes a bloody Fray;
With cruel Tournament the Squadrons joine;
Where Cattle pastur'd late, now scatterd lies
With Carcasses and Arms th'ensanguind Field
Deserted: Others to a Citie strong [655]
Lay Seige, encampt; by Batterie, Scale, and Mine,
Assaulting; others from the Wall defend
With Dart and Jav'lin, Stones and sulfurous Fire;
On each hand slaughter and gigantic deeds.
In other part the scepter'd Haralds call [660]
To Council in the Citie Gates: anon
Grey-headed men and grave, with Warriours mixt,
Assemble, and Harangues are heard, but soon
In factious opposition, till at last
Of middle Age one rising, eminent [665]

嶼、湖泊和生活在陸地的各種生物，包括人類[8]。

亞當雙腳發軟，難過得幾乎昏厥，米迦勒連忙扶住他，只聽見亞當喃喃自語：

註8：出自《舊約‧創世紀》：「洪水氾濫在地上四十天，水往上長，把方舟從地上漂起。……水勢在地上極其浩大，天下的高山都淹沒了。水勢比山高過十五肘，山嶺都淹沒了。凡在地上有血肉的動物，就是飛鳥、牲畜、走獸和爬在地上的昆蟲，以及所有的人都死了；凡在旱地上、鼻孔有氣息的生靈都死了；凡地上各類的活物，連人帶牲畜、昆蟲，以及空中的飛鳥，都從地上除滅了，只留下挪亞和那些與他同在方舟裡的。」

In wise deport, spake much of Right and Wrong,
Of Justice, of Religion, Truth and Peace,
And Judgment from above: him old and young
Exploded, and had seiz'd with violent hands,
Had not a Cloud descending snatch'd him thence [670]
Unseen amid the throng: so violence
Proceeded, and Oppression, and Sword-Law
Through all the Plain, and refuge none was found.
Adam was all in tears, and to his guide
Lamenting turnd full sad; O what are these, [675]
Deaths Ministers, not Men, who thus deal Death
Inhumanly to men, and multiply
Ten thousandfould the sin of him who slew
His Brother; for of whom such massacher
Make they but of thir Brethren, men of men? [680]
But who was that Just Man, whom had not Heav'n
Rescu'd, had in his Righteousness bin lost?

To whom thus Michael. These are the product
Of those ill mated Marriages thou saw'st:
Where good with bad were matcht, who of themselves [685]
Abhor to joyn; and by imprudence mixt,
Produce prodigious Births of bodie or mind.
Such were these Giants, men of high renown;
For in those dayes Might onely shall be admir'd,
And Valour and Heroic Vertu call'd; [690]
To overcome in Battle, and subdue
Nations, and bring home spoils with infinite
Man-slaughter, shall be held the highest pitch
Of human Glorie, and for Glorie done
Of triumph, to be styl'd great Conquerours, [695]
Patrons of Mankind, Gods, and Sons of Gods,
Destroyers rightlier call'd and Plagues of men.
Thus Fame shall be atchiev'd, renown on Earth,
And what most merits fame in silence hid.

◁ 挪亞依上帝的指示建造方舟
杜雷 版畫 1866年

挪亞為人正直虔誠，上帝要毀滅世界之前，先指示他建造一艘大船，將陸地上的生物成雙成對地帶入船中避難。

「都怪我！誰叫我意志不堅、觸犯禁令，喚來『罪惡』和『死亡』，讓地球滿怖血腥、暴力和慾望，使得後代子孫必須以集體的毀滅來洗滌罪惡。」

米迦勒安慰亞當，並要他繼續看下去。只見挪亞所建造的大船，正漂流在水面上，隨著洪水載浮載沉。經過四十個晝夜，浪濤止息，洶湧的洪水緩緩消退了；陽光照在平靜的水面，反射出白晃晃的亮光，眩人眼目。亞拉臘山現出水面，大船便停在山頂上9。

But hee the seventh from thee, whom thou beheldst [700]
The onely righteous in a World perverse,
And therefore hated, therefore so beset
With Foes for daring single to be just,
And utter odious Truth, that God would come
To judge them with his Saints: Him the most High [705]
Rapt in a balmie Cloud with winged Steeds
Did, as thou sawst, receave, to walk with God
High in Salvation and the Climes of bliss,
Exempt from Death; to shew thee what reward
Awaits the good, the rest what punishment? [710]
Which now direct thine eyes and soon behold.

He look'd, and saw the face of things quite chang'd;
The brazen Throat of Warr had ceast to roar,
All now was turn'd to jollitie and game,
To luxurie and riot, feast and dance, [715]
Marrying or prostituting, as befell,
Rape or Adulterie, where passing faire
Allurd them; thence from Cups to civil Broiles.
At length a Reverend Sire among them came,
And of thir doings great dislike declar'd, [720]
And testifi'd against thir wayes; hee oft
Frequented thir Assemblies, whereso met,
Triumphs or Festivals, and to them preachd

>> 挪亞建造方舟
巴薩諾 油畫 1670年
　　挪亞遵從上帝旨意，建造一艘大方舟，引領各種牲畜、鳥類和昆蟲上船避禍。

^ 陸地上所有的一切都被大洪水所淹沒
杜雷 版畫 1866年

上帝引來大洪水，陸地上的各種生物盡數淹沒，也包括人類在內。

挪亞打開大船的窗戶，放出一隻烏鴉，烏鴉在外面飛來飛去，很快地又飛了回來；挪亞又放出一隻鴿子，但到處都是水，鴿子找不到落腳處，於是飛回船上。過了七天，挪亞再度放出鴿子，牠在外面飛了一整天，到了晚上，牠從外面飛回來，嘴裡銜著新鮮的橄欖葉子，為挪亞帶來「地上的

註9：亞拉臘山位於現在的亞美尼亞。

Conversion and Repentance, as to Souls
In prison under Judgments imminent: [725]
But all in vain: which when he saw, he ceas'd
Contending, and remov'd his Tents farr off;
Then from the Mountain hewing Timber tall,
Began to build a Vessel of huge bulk,
Measur'd by Cubit, length, and breadth, and highth, [730]
Smeard round with Pitch, and in the side a dore
Contriv'd, and of provisions laid in large
For Man and Beast: when loe a wonder strange!
Of every Beast, and Bird, and Insect small
Came sevens, and pairs, and enterd in, as taught [735]
Thir order; last the Sire, and his three Sons
With thir four Wives; and God made fast the dore.
Meanwhile the Southwind rose, and with black wings
Wide hovering, all the Clouds together drove
From under Heav'n; the Hills to their supplie [740]
Vapour, and Exhalation dusk and moist,
Sent up amain; and now the thick'nd Skie
Like a dark Ceeling stood; down rush'd the Rain
Impetuous, and continu'd till the Earth
No more was seen; the floating Vessel swum [745]
Uplifted; and secure with beaked prow
Rode tilting o're the Waves, all dwellings else
Flood overwhelmd, and them with all thir pomp
Deep under water rould; Sea cover'd Sea,
Sea without shoar; and in thir Palaces [750]
Where luxurie late reign'd, Sea-monsters whelp'd
And stabl'd; of Mankind, so numerous late,
All left, in one small bottom swum imbark't.
How didst thou grieve then, Adam, to behold
The end of all thy Ofspring, end so sad, [755]
Depopulation; thee another Floud,
Of tears and sorrow a Floud thee also drown'd,
And sunk thee as thy Sons; till gently reard
By th' Angel, on thy feet thou stoodst at last,
Though comfortless, as when a Father mourns [760]
His Children, all in view destroyd at once;
And scarce to th' Angel utterdst thus thy plaint.

O Visions ill foreseen! better had I
Liv'd ignorant of future, so had borne

水乾了」的訊息[10]。

於是挪亞領著一家人走出船艙，他
們高舉雙手、淚光閃爍地感謝上天的
恩德；此時，天上有雲朵飄過，雲中
的彩虹將天空潑灑得絢麗繽紛，這是
和平的記號，表示上帝願意重新賜福
予人類[11]。

註10：出自《舊約‧創世紀》：「過了四十天，挪
　　　亞開了方舟的窗戶，放出一隻烏鴉去。那烏
　　　鴉飛來飛去，直到地上的水都乾了。他又放
　　　出一隻鴿子去，要看看水從地上退了沒有。
　　　但遍地上都是水，鴿子找不著落腳之地，就
　　　回到方舟挪亞那裡，挪亞伸手把鴿子接進方
　　　舟來。他又等了七天，再把鴿子從方舟放出
　　　去。到了晚上，鴿子回到他那裡，嘴裡叼著
　　　一個新擰下來的橄欖葉子，挪亞就知道地上
　　　的水退了。」

註11：出自《舊約‧創世紀》：「神說：『我與你
　　　們並你們這裡的各樣活物所立的永約是有記
　　　號的。我把虹放在雲彩中，這就可作我與地
　　　立約的記號了。我使雲彩蓋地的時候，必有
　　　虹現在雲彩中，我便記念我與你們和各樣有
　　　血肉的活物所立的約，水就再不氾濫毀壞一
　　　切有血肉的物了。虹必現在雲彩中，我看
　　　見，就要記念我與地上各樣有血肉的活物所
　　　立的永約。』」

My part of evil onely, each dayes lot [765]
Anough to bear; those now, that were dispenst
The burd'n of many Ages, on me light
At once, by my foreknowledge gaining Birth
Abortive, to torment me ere thir being,
With thought that they must be. Let no man seek [770]
Henceforth to be foretold what shall befall
Him or his Childern, evil he may be sure,
Which neither his foreknowing can prevent,
And hee the future evil shall no less
In apprehension then in substance feel [775]
Grievous to bear: but that care now is past,
Man is not whom to warne: those few escapt
Famin and anguish will at last consume
Wandring that watrie Desert: I had hope
When violence was ceas't, and Warr on Earth, [780]
All would have then gon well, peace would have crownd
With length of happy dayes the race of man;
But I was farr deceav'd; for now I see
Peace to corrupt no less then Warr to waste.
How comes it thus? unfould, Celestial Guide, [785]
And whether here the Race of man will end.
To whom thus Michael. Those whom last thou sawst
In triumph and luxurious wealth, are they
First seen in acts of prowess eminent
And great exploits, but of true vertu void; [790]
Who having spilt much blood, and don much waste
Subduing Nations, and achievd thereby
Fame in the World, high titles, and rich prey,
Shall change thir course to pleasure, ease, and sloth,
Surfet, and lust, till wantonness and pride [795]
Raise out of friendship hostil deeds in Peace.
The conquerd also, and enslav'd by Warr
Shall with thir freedom lost all vertu loose
And fear of God, from whom thir pietie feign'd
In sharp contest of Battel found no aide [800]
Against invaders; therefore cool'd in zeale
Thenceforth shall practice how to live secure,
Worldlie or dissolute, on what thir Lords
Shall leave them to enjoy; for th' Earth shall bear
More then anough, that temperance may be tri'd: [805]
So all shall turn degenerate, all deprav'd,

鴿子飛回方舟
米雷 油畫 1851年

　　挪亞放出鴿子，鴿子從外面銜回一根新鮮的
橄欖枝葉，挪亞這才確信地上的洪水退了，於是
領著家人走出船艙，開創他們的新生活。

Justice and Temperance, Truth and Faith forgot;
One Man except, the onely Son of light
In a dark Age, against example good,
Against allurement, custom, and a World [810]
Offended; fearless of reproach and scorn,
Or violence, hee of wicked wayes
Shall them admonish, and before them set
The paths of righteousness, how much more safe,
And full of peace, denouncing wrauth to come [815]
On thir impenitence; and shall returne
Of them derided, but of God observd
The one just Man alive; by his command
Shall build a wondrous Ark, as thou beheldst,
To save himself and houshold from amidst [820]
A World devote to universal rack.
No sooner hee with them of Man and Beast
Select for life shall in the Ark be lodg'd,
And shelterd round, but all the Cataracts
Of Heav'n set open on the Earth shall powre [825]

Raine day and night, all fountains of the Deep
Broke up, shall heave the Ocean to usurp
Beyond all bounds, till inundation rise
Above the highest Hills: then shall this Mount
Of Paradise by might of Waves be moovd [830]
Out of his place, pushd by the horned floud,
With all his verdure spoil'd, and Trees adrift
Down the great River to the op'ning Gulf,
And there take root an Iland salt and bare,
The haunt of Seales and Orcs, and Sea-mews clang. [835]
To teach thee that God attributes to place
No sanctitie, if none be thither brought
By Men who there frequent, or therein dwell.
And now what further shall ensue, behold.

He lookd, and saw the Ark hull on the floud, [840]
Which now abated, for the Clouds were fled,
Drivn by a keen North- winde, that blowing drie
Wrinkl'd the face of Deluge, as decai'd;
And the cleer Sun on his wide watrie Glass
Gaz'd hot, and of the fresh Wave largely drew, [845]
As after thirst, which made thir flowing shrink
From standing lake to tripping ebbe, that stole
With soft foot towards the deep, who now had stopt
His Sluces, as the Heav'n his windows shut.
The Ark no more now flotes, but seems on ground [850]
Fast on the top of som high mountain fixt.
And now the tops of Hills as Rocks appeer;
With clamor thence the rapid Currents drive
Towards the retreating Sea thir furious tyde.
Forthwith from out the Arke a Raven flies, [855]
And after him, the surer messenger,
A Dove sent forth once and agen to spie
Green Tree or ground whereon his foot may light;
The second time returning, in his Bill
An Olive leafe he brings, pacific signe: [860]
Anon drie ground appeers, and from his Arke
The ancient Sire descends with all his Train;
Then with uplifted hands, and eyes devout,
Grateful to Heav'n, over his head beholds
A dewie Cloud, and in the Cloud a Bow [865]
Conspicuous with three listed colours gay,

Betok'ning peace from God, and Cov'nant new.
Whereat the heart of Adam erst so sad
Greatly rejoyc'd, and thus his joy broke forth.

O thou that future things canst represent [870]
As present, Heav'nly instructer, I revive
At this last sight, assur'd that Man shall live
With all the Creatures, and thir seed preserve.
Farr less I now lament for one whole World
Of wicked Sons destroyd, then I rejoyce [875]
For one Man found so perfet and so just,
That God voutsafes to raise another World
From him, and all his anger to forget.
But say, what mean those coloured streaks in Heavn,
Distended as the Brow of God appeas'd, [880]
Or serve they as a flourie verge to binde
The fluid skirts of that same watrie Cloud,
Least it again dissolve and showr the Earth?

To whom th' Archangel. Dextrously thou aim'st;
So willingly doth God remit his Ire, [885]
Though late repenting him of Man deprav'd,

Griev'd at his heart, when looking down he saw
The whole Earth fill'd with violence, and all flesh
Corrupting each thir way; yet those remoov'd,
Such grace shall one just Man find in his sight, [890]
That he relents, not to blot out mankind,
And makes a Covenant never to destroy
The Earth again by flood, nor let the Sea
Surpass his bounds, nor Rain to drown the World
With Man therein or Beast; but when he brings [895]
Over the Earth a Cloud, will therein set
His triple-colour'd Bow, whereon to look
And call to mind his Cov'nant: Day and Night,
Seed time and Harvest, Heat and hoary Frost
Shall hold thir course, till fire purge all things new, [900]
Both Heav'n and Earth, wherein the just shall dwell.

▽ 挪亞方舟
米開朗基羅 西斯汀教堂壁畫 1508年
　　人類的表現實在太讓上帝失望了，因此
他降下大水，集體毀滅的方式來洗滌罪惡。

Chapter 12 > 逐出伊甸園

　　天使米迦勒接受上帝的任命，前往地球執行驅逐人類的任務。他先預示亞當大洪水毀滅人類的事件；接著，再告訴他亞伯拉罕的事跡；最後，傳達了神子將為人類降生、死亡、復活和升天的過程。知曉人類未來的命運之後，米迦勒領著亞當和夏娃離開伊甸園，剩下守衛天使和不斷揮舞的火劍，把守著生命樹的道路。

▽ 巴別塔
老布勒爾哲 油畫 1563年

　　人類妄想要搭建通天巨塔，上帝讓他們說出各種不同的語言，使得他們因為無法溝通而中斷築塔的工作。

米迦勒讓亞當看完世界的毀滅與新世界的誕生後，暫時停下來歇口氣，然後又繼續對亞當說：

「挪亞一家在上帝的庇佑下，迅速繁殖生衍，成為人類的第二個源頭；他們敬畏天神，堅守正義與公理，辛勤耕作農田、飼養牲畜，因此能有豐碩的穀物與肥碩的牛羊群。他們從中挑選最好的羔羊、小牛，並以親自釀造的葡萄酒，做為祭祀上帝的祭品。挪亞的三個兒子各有其後裔，他們分散各地，在地上分為邦國，各國和平相處，就這樣過了一段寧靜的歲月。

「後來，一個名叫寧錄的野心份子出現了。他發動戰爭，以暴力來降服那些反對他的人，並自稱為首領，剝奪了上帝賜予人類天生的自由。他善於狩獵，四處追逐獵物，完全不把上帝放在眼裡，在上帝面前是個叛逆的獵人[1]。

「此時的人們，做出一件讓上帝不悅的事情。他們從伊甸出發，往西邊

As one who in his journey bates at Noone,
Though bent on speed, so heer the Archangel paus'd
Betwixt the world destroy'd and world restor'd,
If Adam aught perhaps might interpose;
Then with transition sweet new Speech resumes. [5]

Thus thou hast seen one World begin and end;
And Man as from a second stock proceed.
Much thou hast yet to see, but I perceave
Thy mortal sight to faile; objects divine
Must needs impaire and wearie human sense: [10]
Henceforth what is to com I will relate,
Thou therefore give due audience, and attend.
This second sours of Men, while yet but few;
And while the dread of judgement past remains
Fresh in thir mindes, fearing the Deitie, [15]
With some regard to what is just and right
Shall lead thir lives and multiplie apace,
Labouring the soile, and reaping plenteous crop,
Corn wine and oyle; and from the herd or flock,
Oft sacrificing Bullock, Lamb, or Kid, [20]
With large Wine-offerings pour'd, and sacred Feast,
Shal spend thir dayes in joy unblam'd, and dwell
Long time in peace by Families and Tribes
Under paternal rule; till one shall rise
Of proud ambitious heart, who not content [25]
With fair equalitie, fraternal state,
Will arrogate Dominion undeserv'd
Over his brethren, and quite dispossess
Concord and law of Nature from the Earth,
Hunting (and Men not Beasts shall be his game) [30]
With Warr and hostile snare such as refuse
Subjection to his Empire tyrannous:
A mightie Hunter thence he shall be styl'd
Before the Lord, as in despite of Heav'n,
Or from Heav'n claming second Sovrantie; [35]

註1：寧錄為含的兒子古實所生，關於他的事跡見《舊約‧創世紀》：「古實又生寧錄，他為世上英雄之首。他在耶和華面前是個英勇的獵戶。」

擴展，來到一片遼闊的平原，上頭有河流經過，是一處肥沃的土地；於是他們便在這裡建築都城，並妄想搭一座通天高塔，用來集中所有部落，傳揚自己的聲名。

「上帝希望全世界都有人類居住，對於人類擅自築塔的事並不贊成，於是祂讓負責建塔的人說出各種不同的語言，使他們無法溝通，並因此感到憤怒、沮喪和爭吵，紛紛擾擾的情緒讓他們停下手中的工作，通天塔終究沒有完成[2]。」

亞當搖搖頭，生氣地罵道：「這些人並沒有權力奪取他人的自由，而且，他們竟然蔑視上帝，還妄想登上天庭，真是太愚蠢了！」

「自從你犯下錯誤，就給後代子孫帶來了原罪，人類內在自我約束的理性已被蒙蔽，真正的自由因而無法獨自留存；因此，狂妄者輕視上帝，並

註2：關於通天高塔的內容，請參照本書第三卷，註4。

And from Rebellion shall derive his name,
Though of Rebellion others he accuse.
Hee with a crew, whom like Ambition joyns
With him or under him to tyrannize,
Marching from Eden towards the West, shall finde [40]
The Plain, wherein a black bituminous gurge
Boiles out from under ground, the mouth of Hell;
Of Brick, and of that stuff they cast to build
A Citie and Towre, whose top may reach to Heav'n;
And get themselves a name, least far disperst [45]
In foraign Lands thir memorie be lost,
Regardless whether good or evil fame.
But God who oft descends to visit men
Unseen, and through thir habitations walks
To mark thir doings, them beholding soon, [50]
Comes down to see thir Citie, ere the Tower
Obstruct Heav'n Towrs, and in derision sets
Upon thir Tongues a various Spirit to rase
Quite out thir Native Language, and instead
To sow a jangling noise of words unknown: [55]
Forthwith a hideous gabble rises loud
Among the Builders; each to other calls
Not understood, till hoarse, and all in rage,
As mockt they storm; great laughter was in Heav'n
And looking down, to see the hubbub strange [60]
And hear the din; thus was the building left
Ridiculous, and the work Confusion nam'd.

Whereto thus Adam fatherly displeas'd.
O execrable Son so to aspire
Above his Brethren, to himself assuming [65]
Authoritie usurpt, from God not giv'n:
He gave us onely over Beast, Fish, Fowl
Dominion absolute; that right we hold
By his donation; but Man over men
He made not Lord; such title to himself [70]
Reserving, human left from human free.
But this Usurper his encroachment proud
Stayes not on Man; to God his Tower intends
Siege and defiance: Wretched man! what food
Will he convey up thither to sustain [75]
Himself and his rash Armie, where thin Aire

施用武力把同胞踩在腳底下，如奴隸
一般地驅使。

「上帝摒棄了這群不敬之徒，讓他
們邁向自我毀滅之路；祂另外揀選了
一個雖生活在充滿暴力與偽神的環境
中，卻明智忠誠的人，那便是閃的後
裔亞伯拉罕[3]。

「上帝要亞伯拉罕離開故鄉，到迦
南[4]去建立新的居所；於是亞伯拉罕帶
領親人遷移到上帝賜福之地，並在那
兒繁衍子孫[5]。

「亞伯拉罕生了兩個兒子，大的
叫以撒，小的叫以實瑪利；以撒的兒
子雅各有十二個兒子，從他們繁衍出
去，由迦南往外發展，到達尼羅河岸
的埃及。這十二人即為猶太人十二支
派的祖先，當中有個名叫約瑟的，憑
著上帝的賜福登上高位，被埃及的法
老派去治理埃及全地[6]。」

說到這，米迦勒稍微停頓了一下，
然後繼續描述：

「後來，約瑟的父親和兄弟們遷居

Above the Clouds will pine his entrails gross,
And famish him of Breath, if not of Bread?

To whom thus Michael. Justly thou abhorr'st
That Son, who on the quiet state of men [80]
Such trouble brought, affecting to subdue
Rational Libertie; yet know withall,
Since thy original lapse, true Libertie
Is lost, which alwayes with right Reason dwells
Twinn'd, and from her hath no dividual being: [85]
Reason in man obscur'd, or not obeyd,
Immediately inordinate desires
And upstart Passions catch the Government
From Reason, and to servitude reduce
Man till then free. Therefore since hee permits [90]

註3：亞伯拉罕原名亞伯蘭，遵照上帝的指
　　示改名為亞伯拉罕，是挪亞的兒子閃
　　的後裔。
註4：迦南地約為今日的巴勒斯坦地區。
註5：亞伯拉罕遷居的事跡見《舊約·創世
　　紀》：「耶和華對亞伯蘭說：『你要
　　離開本地、本族、父家，往我所要指
　　示你的地去。我必叫你成為大國。我
　　必賜福給你，叫你的名為大，你也要
　　叫別人得福。為你祝福的，我必賜福
　　與他；那咒詛你的，我必咒詛他。地
　　上的萬族都要因你得福。』亞伯蘭就
　　照著耶和華的吩咐去了。」
註6：約瑟為雅各疼愛的兒子，聰敏機靈，
　　被兄弟們賣給米甸的商人；他被米甸
　　人帶到埃及，轉賣給法老的內臣。後
　　來憑著聰明才智，被法老重用。其事
　　跡見《舊約·創世紀》：「法老又對
　　約瑟說：『我派你治理埃及全地。』
　　法老就摘下手上打印的戒指，戴在約
　　瑟的手上，給他穿上細麻衣，把金鏈
　　戴在他的頸項上。又叫約瑟坐他的副
　　車，喝道的在前呼叫說：『跪下！』
　　這樣，法老派他治理埃及全地。」

到埃及來，在此繁衍後裔，以色列人的數量越來越多，埃及人備感威脅，於是開始排斥外來族群。埃及法老把以色列人當成奴隸役使，並下令殺掉他們新生的男嬰；這其中，有一對兄弟——亞倫與摩西，受到上帝的召喚，要他們把以色列人帶回迦南去[7]。

「摩西前去面見埃及法老，請求他讓

註7：摩西是以色列人的孩子，被埃及公主扶養長大，他的事跡見《舊約．出埃及記》：「有一個利未家的人，娶了一個利未女子為妻。那女人懷孕，生一個兒子，見他俊美，就藏了他三個月。後來不能再藏，就取了一個蒲草箱，抹上石漆和石油，將孩子放在裡頭，把箱子擱在河邊的蘆荻中。孩子的姐姐遠遠站著，要知道他究竟怎麼樣。法老的女兒來到河邊洗澡，她的使女們在河邊行走。她看見箱子在蘆荻中，就打發一個婢女拿來。她打開箱子，看見那孩子。……孩子漸長，婦人把他帶到法老的女兒那裡，就作了她的兒子。她給孩子起名叫摩西，意思說：『因我把他從水裡拉出來』。」

❯ 亞伯拉罕西遷
莫納爾 油畫1880年

上帝要亞伯拉罕離開故鄉，帶著家人和羊群到迦南去建立新的居所。

˄ 埃及十災（由左至右分別為蠅災、蛙災、畜疫之災）

以色列人和平地離開埃及，但法老堅決反對，不但加重猶太人的工作量，更拒絕承認有上帝的存在。於是，上天降下各種可怕的災難──尼羅河水變紅、數百萬隻青蛙四處亂跳、大量蒼蠅藉食物傳播疾病、所有的牛隻突然暴斃、身體長瘡、冰雹打壞農作物、雷電燒掉食糧的種子、蝗蟲吃光所有植物、沙風暴遮住陽光三日、以及埃及人的長子都死了[8]。

「埃及法老在痛失長子之後，不得不讓步，同意以色列人離開。

「摩西領著數以萬計的以色列人，和牛群、羊隻、駱駝，並各種從埃及人那兒奪來的金器、銀器和衣裳等，

Within himself unworthie Powers to reign
Over free Reason, God in Judgement just
Subjects him from without to violent Lords;
Who oft as undeservedly enthrall
His outward freedom: Tyrannie must be, [95]
Though to the Tyrant thereby no excuse.
Yet somtimes Nations will decline so low
From vertue, which is reason, that no wrong,
But Justice, and some fatal curse annext
Deprives them of thir outward libertie, [100]
Thir inward lost: Witness th' irreverent Son
Of him who built the Ark, who for the shame
Don to his Father, heard this heavie curse,
Servant of Servants, on his vitious Race.
Thus will this latter, as the former World, [105]
Still tend from bad to worse, till God at last
Wearied with their iniquities, withdraw
His presence from among them, and avert
His holy Eyes; resolving from thenceforth
To leave them to thir own polluted wayes; [110]
And one peculiar Nation to select
From all the rest, of whom to be invok'd,
A Nation from one faithful man to spring:
Him on this side Euphrates yet residing,

註8：上帝在埃及降下十項災難的事跡出自
　　　《舊約‧出埃及記》，請參照本書第
　　　一卷註5。

用磚軛負載，這不同於神像巨石的重量，讓他們歡欣鼓舞，浩浩蕩蕩地從埃及離開。

「當他們走到紅海邊的時候，突然聽見一陣雷聲，原來，埃及法老背棄了承諾，親自率領軍隊前來追殺以色列人，並誓言將他們碎屍萬段，死在埃及大軍的車輪底下。以色列人聽見的雷聲，其實就是戰車在黃沙上奔騰的聲音。

「上帝顯現奇蹟，用蔽天的雲和衝天火柱阻撓埃及軍隊前進；另一邊，風吹紅海，海水往兩邊分開，形成高聳的牆垣，中間現出乾地，以色列人攜老扶幼，加快腳步走在海中乾地，極欲擺脫後方的埃及追兵。待所有的以色列人穿越紅海，上帝又使海水復原，淹沒了埃及人的車輛、馬匹和所有士兵。

「逃離了埃及人的魔

Bred up in Idol-worship; O that men [115]
(Canst thou believe?) should be so stupid grown,
While yet the Patriark liv'd, who scap'd the Flood,
As to forsake the living God, and fall
To worship thir own work in Wood and Stone
For Gods! yet him God the most High voutsafes [120]
To call by Vision from his Fathers house,
His kindred and false Gods, into a Land
Which he will shew him, and from him will raise
A mightie Nation, and upon him showre
His benediction so, that in his Seed [125]
All Nations shall be blest; he straight obeys
Not knowing to what Land, yet firm believes:
I see him, but thou canst not, with what Faith
He leaves his Gods, his Friends, and native Soile
Ur of Chaldæa, passing now the Ford [130]
To Haran, after a cumbrous Train
Of Herds and Flocks, and numerous servitude;
Not wandring poor, but trusting all his wealth
With God, who call'd him, in a land unknown.
Canaan he now attains, I see his Tents [135]

▼ 埃及人的長子之死
亞瑪泰德瑪 油畫 1872年

　　當第十災降臨，埃及人長子通通暴斃，痛失愛子的法老不得不讓步，無條件答應以色列人離開，不必再當埃及人的奴隸了。

分開紅海
盧伊尼 油畫 1515年

失去奴隸的埃及人很快就後悔了，於是法老王派兵追趕以色列人，上帝再顯奇蹟，將紅海的海水硬生生分開，待以色列人通過之後，又使海水復原，淹沒了埃及人的追兵。

掌，摩西繼續領著族人前進，他們來到迦南曠野，在那兒紮營；從西奈山上傳來雷轟、閃電和密雲，上帝在火中降於山上，遍山震動，召喚摩西前去。

「摩西在西奈山上待了四十晝夜，帶回兩塊刻有上帝律令的法版；但當他走進以色列人的營地，卻看見他們縱慾狂歡、言行放蕩，還鑄造了一隻

Pitcht about Sechem, and the neighbouring Plaine
Of Moreh; there by promise he receaves
Gift to his Progenie of all that Land;
From Hamath Northward to the Desert South
(Things by thir names I call, though yet unnam'd)
From Hermon East to the great Western Sea,
Mount Hermon, yonder Sea, each place behold
In prospect, as I point them; on the shoare
Mount Carmel; here the double-founted stream
Jordan, true limit Eastward; but his Sons
Shall dwell to Senir, that long ridge of Hills.
This ponder, that all Nations of the Earth
Shall in his Seed be blessed; by that Seed
Is meant thy great deliverer, who shall bruise
The Serpents head; whereof to thee anon
Plainlier shall be reveald. This Patriarch blest,
Whom faithful Abraham due time shall call,
A Son, and of his Son a Grand-childe leaves,
Like him in faith, in wisdom, and renown;
The Grandchilde with twelve Sons increast, departs
From Canaan, to a land hereafter call'd
Egypt, divided by the River Nile;
See where it flows, disgorging at seaven mouthes
Into the Sea: to sojourn in that Land
He comes invited by a yonger Son
In time of dearth, a Son whose worthy deeds
Raise him to be the second in that Realme
Of Pharao: there he dies, and leaves his Race
Growing into a Nation, and now grown
Suspected to a sequent King, who seeks
To stop thir overgrowth, as inmate guests
Too numerous; whence of guests he makes them slaves
Inhospitably, and kills thir infant Males:
Till by two brethren (those two brethren call
Moses and Aaron) sent from God to claime
His people from enthralment, they return
With glory and spoile back to thir promis'd Land.
But first the lawless Tyrant, who denies
To know thir God, or message to regard,
Must be compelld by Signes and Judgements dire;
To blood unshed the Rivers must be turnd,
Frogs, Lice and Flies must all his Palace fill

金牛犢，向它頂禮膜拜，並稱它為領
以色列人出埃及的神。

「摩西大為震怒，召來支持他的利
未部落，一舉殲滅叛亂者。然後，他
再次登上西奈山頂，高舉法版，面容
嚴肅地向山下的以色列人宣告上帝十
項戒律[9]；他並預言日後將產生一位

With loath'd intrusion, and fill all the land;
His Cattel must of Rot and Murren die,
Botches and blaines must all his flesh imboss, [180]
And all his people; Thunder mixt with Haile,
Haile mixt with fire must rend th' Egyptian Skie
And wheel on th' Earth, devouring where it rouls;
What it devours not, Herb, or Fruit, or Graine,
A darksom Cloud of Locusts swarming down [185]
Must eat, and on the ground leave nothing green:
Darkness must overshadow all his bounds,
Palpable darkness, and blot out three dayes;

註9：上帝的十項戒律為：(一)除了耶和華
　　以外，不可以信仰其他的神。(二)不
　　可以雕刻、崇拜偶像。(三)不可以
　　妄稱耶和華的名。(四)第七日為安息
　　日，不可以工作。(五)不可以不孝敬
　　父母。(六)不可以殺人。(七)不可以
　　姦淫。(八)不可以偷盜。(九)不可以
　　作假見證陷害人。(十)不可以貪戀別
　　人的財物。

▽ 渡過紅海
布魯齊諾 壁畫 1540 年

　　畫中摩西安慰著驚魂未定的猶太人。埃及士
兵在海水回捲的一瞬間被巨浪吞沒了。摩西頭上
的角由兩束金光勾勒，給整個壁畫帶來一絲隨意
和幽默感。

偉大的人，有一個極其輝煌的時代，好
讓各個時代的先知們都能夠讚頌他[10]。

「頒布完十誡，摩西要眾人遵照
上帝的旨意建造聖所，他們用帳幕搭
起一個可移動的殿堂，裡頭有一個皂
莢木做成的櫃子，用來放上帝的法版
和聖物。聖櫃的上方放黃金造的施恩
座，座位兩旁各安置一個金色的基路

Last with one midnight stroke all the first-born
Of Egypt must lie dead. Thus with ten wounds [190]
The River-dragon tam'd at length submits
To let his sojourners depart, and oft
Humbles his stubborn heart, but still as Ice
More hard'nd after thaw, till in his rage
Pursuing whom he late dismissd, the Sea [195]
Swallows him with his Host, but them lets pass
As on drie land between two christal walls,
Aw'd by the rod of Moses so to stand
Divided, till his rescu'd gain thir shoar:
Such wondrous power God to his Saint will lend, [200]
Though present in his Angel, who shall goe
Before them in a Cloud, and Pillar of Fire,
By day a Cloud, by night a Pillar of Fire,
To guide them in thir journey, and remove
Behinde them, while th' obdurat King pursues: [205]
All night he will pursue, but his approach
Darkness defends between till morning Watch;
Then through the Firey Pillar and the Cloud
God looking forth will trouble all his Host
And craze thir Chariot wheels: when by command [210]
Moses once more his potent Rod extends
Over the Sea; the Sea his Rod obeys;
On thir imbattelld ranks the Waves return,
And overwhelm thir Warr: the Race elect
Safe towards Canaan from the shoar advance [215]
Through the wilde Desert, not the readiest way,
Least entring on the Canaanite allarmd
Warr terrifie them inexpert, and feare
Return them back to Egypt, choosing rather
Inglorious life with servitude; for life [220]

註10：偉大的人，指神子基督。

≪ **摩西於西奈山頂頒布上帝的十項戒律**
杜雷 版畫 1866年

　　摩西看到以色列人縱欲狂歡，還膜拜
金牛，不禁大為震怒。他登上西奈山頂，
高舉法版，宣告上帝的十項戒律。

∧ **摩西高舉十誡**
林布蘭 油畫 1659年

　　摩西登上西奈山頂，高舉上帝賜予的法版，
宣告十項戒律，並預言日後將產生一位偉大的
人，開創一個極其輝煌的時代。

伯天使；然後要把黃金做的七盞燈點
燃，發出耀眼的光芒，代表上帝的聖
火永不熄滅。帳幕的上空，白天有雲
彩跟隨，夜間雲中有火，就這樣一路
引領以色列人到上帝應許亞伯拉罕和
其子孫的土地[11]。

To noble and ignoble is more sweet
Untraind in Armes, where rashness leads not on.
This also shall they gain by thir delay
In the wide Wilderness, there they shall found
Thir government, and thir great Senate choose [225]
Through the twelve Tribes, to rule by Laws ordaind:
God from the Mount of Sinai, whose gray top
Shall tremble, he descending, will himself
In Thunder Lightning and loud Trumpets sound
Ordaine them Lawes; part such as appertaine [230]
To civil Justice, part religious Rites
Of sacrifice, informing them, by types
And shadowes, of that destind Seed to bruise
The Serpent, by what meanes he shall achieve
Mankinds deliverance. But the voice of God [235]
To mortal eare is dreadful; they beseech
That Moses might report to them his will,
And terror cease; he grants what they besaught
Instructed that to God is no access
Without Mediator, whose high Office now [240]
Moses in figure beares, to introduce
One greater, of whose day he shall foretell,
And all the Prophets in thir Age the times
Of great Messiah shall sing. Thus Laws and Rites
Establisht, such delight hath God in Men [245]
Obedient to his will, that he voutsafes
Among them to set up his Tabernacle,
The holy One with mortal Men to dwell:
By his prescript a Sanctuary is fram'd
Of Cedar, overlaid with Gold, therein [250]
An Ark, and in the Ark his Testimony,
The Records of his Cov'nant, over these
A Mercie-seat of Gold between the wings
Of two bright Cherubim, before him burn
Seaven Lamps as in a Zodiac representing [255]
The Heav'nly fires; over the Tent a Cloud
Shall rest by Day, a fiery gleame by Night,
Save when they journie, and at length they come,

註11：上帝應許亞伯拉罕和其子孫的土地，
　　　指迦南。

「偉大的先知摩西臨死之前把約法傳給約書亞，讓他繼承自己，繼續引導以色列人。約書亞帶領群眾渡過約旦河，為了取回迦南地發動許多戰爭；在決定性的一場戰爭中，上帝幫助約書亞，讓太陽停駐在基遍上空，月亮停在亞雅崙谷，使白晝延長了十二個小時。以色列人藉此加足火力，持續發動攻擊，終於取得勝利，奪回迦南之地[12]。」

聽到這裡，亞當開口詢問：「聽了您描述亞伯拉罕及其子孫蒙主恩賜的事情，我感到安心多了；我不明白的是，上帝對人類頒布了那麼多的法律，表示祂認為人間仍充滿了無窮的罪惡，但祂又何以要同人類在一塊兒呢？」

「自從你犯下錯誤，『罪惡』便主宰了人類。藉由法律，人類可發覺自身的墮落，但人類是無法靠法律來除去『罪惡』的；必須經由內心真誠的信仰，才能找回公理與正義。

Conducted by his Angel to the Land
Promisd to Abraham and his Seed: the rest [260]
Were long to tell, how many Battels fought,
How many Kings destroyd, and Kingdoms won,
Or how the Sun shall in mid Heav'n stand still
A day entire, and Nights due course adjourne,
Mans voice commanding, Sun in Gibeon stand, [265]
And thou Moon in the vale of Aialon,
Till Israel overcome; so call the third
From Abraham, Son of Isaac, and from him
His whole descent, who thus shall Canaan win.

Here Adam interpos'd. O sent from Heav'n, [270]
Enlightner of my darkness, gracious things
Thou hast reveald, those chiefly which concerne
Just Abraham and his Seed: now first I finde
Mine eyes true op'ning, and my heart much eas'd,
Erwhile perplext with thoughts what would becom [275]
Of mee and all Mankind; but now I see
His day, in whom all Nations shall be blest,
Favour unmerited by me, who sought
Forbidd'n knowledge by forbidd'n means.
This yet I apprehend not, why to those [280]
Among whom God will deigne to dwell on Earth
So many and so various Laws are giv'n;
So many Laws argue so many sins
Among them; how can God with such reside?

To whom thus Michael. Doubt not but that sin [285]
Will reign among them, as of thee begot;
And therefore was Law given them to evince
Thir natural pravitie, by stirring up
Sin against Law to fight; that when they see

註12：約書亞的事跡見《舊約‧約書亞記》：「當耶和華將亞摩利人交付以色列人的日子，約書亞就禱告耶和華，在以色列人眼前說：『日頭啊，你要停在基遍；月亮啊，你要止在亞雅崙谷。』於是日頭停留，月亮止住，直等國民向敵人報仇。」

「以色列人回到迦南之地後，安居樂業、建設國家，過了一段日子，罪惡又潛入眾人的心中，使他們不願聽從上帝的訓誡。於是，上帝發怒，讓他們被俘虜到巴比倫，做了七十年的奴隸。但在這之前，出過幾位知名的人物，比方說 —— 大衛王，救世祖即出自他的王統，他在位將近四十年，統治大部分的以色列人領土。

「神賜給大衛的兒子所羅門極大的智慧、聰明和廣大的心，如同海沙不可測量。他雖為上帝建造華麗的聖殿，卻觸犯上帝的律例，崇拜偶像、戀愛異族嬪妃等，加上百姓所犯的種種罪惡，終於觸怒神威，使以色列人流放異鄉[13]。

「後來，以色列人從巴比倫離開回到故鄉，第二年，並在耶路撒冷重建聖殿，但『罪惡』卻始終跟著他們。終於，在生活逐漸邁向安定富裕之時，貪婪又再度出現，人們互相爭執，紛紛擾擾，連聖殿都玷污了。

Law can discover sin, but not remove, [290]
Save by those shadowie expiations weak,
The bloud of Bulls and Goats, they may conclude
Some bloud more precious must be paid for Man,
Just for unjust, that in such righteousness
To them by Faith imputed, they may finde [295]
Justification towards God, and peace
Of Conscience, which the Law by Ceremonies
Cannot appease, nor Man the moral part
Perform, and not performing cannot live.
So Law appears imperfet, and but giv'n [300]
With purpose to resign them in full time
Up to a better Cov'nant, disciplin'd
From shadowie Types to Truth, from Flesh to Spirit,
From imposition of strict Laws, to free
Acceptance of large Grace, from servil fear [305]
To filial, works of Law to works of Faith.
And therefore shall not Moses, though of God
Highly belov'd, being but the Minister
Of Law, his people into Canaan lead;
But Joshua whom the Gentiles Jesus call, [310]
His Name and Office bearing, who shall quell
The adversarie Serpent, and bring back
Through the worlds wilderness long wanderd man
Safe to eternal Paradise of rest.
Meanwhile they in thir earthly Canaan plac't [315]
Long time shall dwell and prosper, but when sins
National interrupt thir public peace,
Provoking God to raise them enemies:
From whom as oft he saves them penitent
By Judges first, then under Kings; of whom [320]
The second, both for pietie renownd
And puissant deeds, a promise shall receive
Irrevocable, that his Regal Throne

註13：所羅門王的事跡出自《舊約·列王記上》：「以色列人出埃及地後四百八十年，所羅門作以色列王第四年西弗月，就是二月，開工建造耶和華的殿。」其餘內容，請參照本書第一卷註10。

^ 告知受胎
簡提列斯基 油畫 1610年

　　天使指著天上，告知馬利亞將孕育上帝之子，羞怯的馬利亞搖著手，簡直不敢相信會有這樣的事情。

國家的統治權，最後終於落入異族之手。

　　「在猶太王國滅亡的歲月裡，以色列人等待的救世主耶穌，在原猶太地方的伯利恆誕生了。當時，天空異常地出現一顆星星，引領遠方的聖人前來伏拜；他們帶著黃金、乳香和沒藥等禮物，在天使悠揚的聖歌聲中，獻給剛出生的彌賽亞 —— 耶穌。

For ever shall endure; the like shall sing
All Prophecie, That of the Royal Stock [325]
Of David (so I name this King) shall rise
A Son, the Womans Seed to thee foretold,
Foretold to Abraham, as in whom shall trust
All Nations, and to Kings foretold, of Kings
The last, for of his Reign shall be no end. [330]
But first a long succession must ensue,
And his next Son for Wealth and Wisdom fam'd,
The clouded Ark of God till then in Tents
Wandring, shall in a glorious Temple enshrine.
Such follow him, as shall be registerd [335]
Part good, part bad, of bad the longer scrowle,
Whose foul Idolatries, and other faults
Heapt to the popular summe, will so incense
God, as to leave them, and expose thir Land,
Thir Citie, his Temple, and his holy Ark [340]
With all his sacred things, a scorn and prey
To that proud Citie, whose high Walls thou saw'st
Left in confusion, Babylon thence call'd.
There in captivitie he lets them dwell
The space of seventie years, then brings them back, [345]
Remembring mercie, and his Cov'nant sworn
To David, stablisht as the dayes of Heav'n.
Returnd from Babylon by leave of Kings
Thir Lords, whom God dispos'd, the house of God
They first re-edifie, and for a while [350]
In mean estate live moderate, till grown
In wealth and multitude, factious they grow;
But first among the Priests dissension springs,
Men who attend the Altar, and should most
Endeavour Peace: thir strife pollution brings [355]
Upon the Temple it self: at last they seise
The Scepter, and regard not Davids Sons,
Then loose it to a stranger, that the true
Anointed King Messiah might be born
Barr'd of his right; yet at his Birth a Starr [360]
Unseen before in Heav'n proclaims him com,
And guides the Eastern Sages, who enquire
His place, to offer Incense, Myrrh, and Gold;
His place of birth a solemn Angel tells
To simple Shepherds, keeping watch by night; [365]

「馬利亞以處女之身分生子，因為上帝揀選她作為耶穌的母親，日後，耶穌將登上天庭寶座，繼承天父的王位[14]。」

米迦勒說到這裡，見亞當似乎有話要說，便停了下來。

「太好了！我終於明白上帝所說的：『女人的子孫將擊碎蛇的頭』的真正意涵了。上帝與人類的女子結合，生下神與人的孩子，他將帶領

They gladly thither haste, and by a Quire
Of squadrond Angels hear his Carol sung.
A Virgin is his Mother, but his Sire
The Power of the most High; he shall ascend
The Throne hereditarie, and bound his Reign [370]
With earths wide bounds, his glory with the Heav'ns.

He ceas'd, discerning Adam with such joy
Surcharg'd, as had like grief bin dew'd in tears,
Without the vent of words, which these he breathd.

O Prophet of glad tidings, finisher [375]
Of utmost hope! now clear I understand
What oft my steddiest thoughts have searcht in vain,
Why our great expectation should be call'd
The seed of Woman: Virgin Mother, Haile,
High in the love of Heav'n, yet from my Loynes [380]

▽ 三王來朝
波提切利 油畫 1482年

　　耶穌基督由處女馬利亞所生，遠方的聖人代著黃金、乳香和沒藥前來朝拜。

註14：彌賽亞，即救世主耶穌，其誕生的事跡見《新約‧馬太福音》：「耶穌基督降生的事記在下面：他母親馬利亞已經許配了約瑟，還沒有迎娶，馬利亞就從聖靈懷了孕。他丈夫約瑟是個義人，不願意明明地羞辱她，想要暗暗地把她休了。正思念這事的時候，有主的使者向他夢中顯現，說：『大衛的子孫約瑟，不要怕，只管娶過你的妻子馬利亞來，因她所懷的孕是從聖靈來的。她將要生一個兒子，你要給他起名叫耶穌，因他要將自己的百姓從罪惡裡救出來。』……當希律王的時候，耶穌生在猶太的伯利恆。有幾個博士從東方來到耶路撒冷，說：『那生下來作猶太人之王的在哪裡？我們在東方看見他的星，特來拜他。』……他們看見那星，就大大地歡喜。進了房子，看見小孩子和他母親馬利亞，就俯伏拜那小孩子，揭開寶盒，拿黃金、乳香、沒藥為禮物獻給他。」

人類擊碎蛇的頭，蛇也會咬他們的腳後跟。我想知道，這場戰鬥何時開始呢？」亞當充滿驚喜，熱切地問著。

「救世主誕生在人間，主要的目的並非消滅撒旦，撒旦原本是天庭的天使，雖然已被擊敗沉淪地獄，卻仍具有強大的力量。所以，這並不是一次兩次就可以解決的戰爭。

「耶穌將以自己的生命，換來人類的自我覺醒，他們將誠心地服從上帝，遵守上帝的律法，用信仰的力量，把遍地的『罪惡』與『死亡』逐出人間，即擊碎蛇 —— 魔鬼的頭。

「神的兒子 —— 救世主耶穌基督，被鞭打、羞辱且釘死在十字架上，人類從他的犧牲中獲得救贖，尋回愛與堅貞的信仰；但別擔心，耶穌失去的僅止是肉身而已，三天後的早晨，他將再度復活，差遣門徒在世間向萬民宣揚真理，並教導人們，藉由施洗來洗淨身上的罪惡[15]。

「人類將明白，只要有虔誠的信

Thou shalt proceed, and from thy Womb the Son
Of God most High; So God with man unites.
Needs must the Serpent now his capital bruise
Expect with mortal paine: say where and when
Thir fight, what stroke shall bruise the Victors heel [385].

To whom thus Michael. Dream not of thir fight,
As of a Duel, or the local wounds
Of head or heel: not therefore joynes the Son
Manhood to God-head, with more strength to foil
Thy enemie; nor so is overcome [390]
Satan, whose fall from Heav'n, a deadlier bruise,
Disabl'd not to give thee thy deaths wound:
Which hee, who comes thy Saviour, shall recure,
Not by destroying Satan, but his works
In thee and in thy Seed: nor can this be, [395]
But by fulfilling that which thou didst want,
Obedience to the Law of God, impos'd
On penaltie of death, and suffering death,
The penaltie to thy transgression due,
And due to theirs which out of thine will grow: [400]
So onely can high Justice rest appaid.
The Law of God exact he shall fulfill
Both by obedience and by love, though love
Alone fulfill the Law; thy punishment

註15：耶穌犧牲的事跡見《新約・馬太福音》：「巡撫的兵就把耶穌帶進衙門，叫全營的兵都聚集在他那裡。他們給他脫了衣服，穿上一件朱紅色袍子；用荊棘編作冠冕，戴在他頭上；拿一根葦子放在他右手裡，跪在他面前，戲弄他說：『恭喜，猶太人的王啊！』又吐唾沫在他臉上，拿葦子打他的頭。……他們既將他釘在十字架上，就拈鬮分他的衣服，又坐在那裡看守他。在他頭以上安一個牌子，寫著他的罪狀，說：『這是猶太人的王耶穌。』當時，有兩個強盜和他同釘十字架，一個在右邊，一個在左邊。」

◁ 米迦勒預告耶穌的釘刑
布雷克 水彩畫 1808年

　　米迦勒告知亞當，救世主耶穌將被鞭
打、羞辱且釘死在十字架上，人類從他的犧
牲中得到救贖，尋回愛與堅貞的力量。

He shall endure by coming in the Flesh [405]
To a reproachful life and cursed death,
Proclaiming Life to all who shall believe
In his redemption, and that his obedience
Imputed becomes theirs by Faith, his merits
To save them, not thir own, though legal works. [410]
For this he shall live hated, be blasphem'd,
Seis'd on by force, judg'd, and to death condemnd
A shameful and accurst, naild to the Cross
By his own Nation, slaine for bringing Life;
But to the Cross he nailes thy Enemies, [415]
The Law that is against thee, and the sins
Of all mankinde, with him there crucifi'd,
Never to hurt them more who rightly trust
In this his satisfaction; so he dies,
But soon revives, Death over him no power [420]
Shall long usurp; ere the third dawning light
Returne, the Starres of Morn shall see him rise
Out of his grave, fresh as the dawning light,
Thy ransom paid, which Man from death redeems,
His death for Man, as many as offerd Life [425]
Neglect not, and the benefit imbrace
By Faith not void of workes: this God-like act
Annuls thy doom, the death thou shouldst have dy'd,
In sin for ever lost from life; this act
Shall bruise the head of Satan, crush his strength [430]
Defeating Sin and Death, his two maine armes,
And fix farr deeper in his head thir stings
Then temporal death shall bruise the Victors heel,
Or theirs whom he redeems, a death like sleep,
A gentle wafting to immortal Life. [435]
Nor after resurrection shall he stay
Longer on Earth then certaine times to appeer
To his Disciples, Men who in his Life
Still follow'd him; to them shall leave in charge

仰，就能在付出死亡的代價之後，如
在睡夢中一般輕輕飄起，飛往永恆的
生命。

　　「到了那一天，撒旦與他的部眾將
驚愕地逃離，而耶穌則帶著勝利的笑
容回到天庭，坐在天父右手邊的寶座
同享榮光；天上人間，所有的人一塊
兒生活在伊甸園般的幸福園地。」

　　「當救世主回到天上，少數的跟隨
者有能力引導人們邁向真理嗎？」亞

當問道。

「是的，他們會有足夠的能力。因為天上將會降下聖靈附在他們身上，使他們生出愛的力量；藉由愛，上帝的律令被牢牢嵌入心底，指引他們真理的道路。撒旦的邪惡誘惑不了他們，死亡也無法叫他們感到害怕，人類的心靈因此得到慰藉。

「聖靈先是傾注在耶穌的門徒身上，經由他們四處宣導，尋得受洗的信徒，聖靈藉著受洗的過程，注入到他們心中。最後，他們要面對死亡，在經過死亡的過程之後，肉身化做塵土，靈魂則飛升到天上永享幸福。而那些耽溺於邪惡誘惑的則會沉淪，並受到嚴厲的懲罰。

「當救世主再度降臨，善人將被彰顯，惡人則受罪罰；黑暗世界隨著撒旦一塊滅亡，新的世界滿結歡樂的果實與永恆的幸福。」米迦勒微笑地回答。

「我明白了，順從上帝是最好的選

To teach all nations what of him they learn'd [440]
And his Salvation, them who shall beleeve
Baptizing in the profluent streame, the signe
Of washing them from guilt of sin to Life
Pure, and in mind prepar'd, if so befall,
For death, like that which the redeemer dy'd. [445]
All Nations they shall teach; for from that day
Not onely to the Sons of Abrahams Loines
Salvation shall be Preacht, but to the Sons
Of Abrahams Faith wherever through the world;
So in his seed all Nations shall be blest. [450]
Then to the Heav'n of Heav'ns he shall ascend
With victory, triumphing through the aire
Over his foes and thine; there shall surprise
The Serpent, Prince of aire, and drag in Chaines
Through all his Realme, and there confounded leave; [455]
Then enter into glory, and resume
His Seat at Gods right hand, exalted high
Above all names in Heav'n; and thence shall come,
When this worlds dissolution shall be ripe,
With glory and power to judge both quick and dead [460]
To judge th' unfaithful dead, but to reward
His faithful, and receave them into bliss,
Whether in Heav'n or Earth, for then the Earth
Shall all be Paradise, far happier place
Then this of Eden, and far happier daies. [465]

So spake th' Archangel Michael, then paus'd,
As at the Worlds great period; and our Sire
Replete with joy and wonder thus repli'd.

O goodness infinite, goodness immense!
That all this good of evil shall produce, [470]
And evil turn to good; more wonderful
Then that which by creation first brought forth
Light out of darkness! full of doubt I stand,
Whether I should repent me now of sin
By mee done and occasiond, or rejoyce [475]
Much more, that much more good thereof shall spring,
To God more glory, more good will to Men
From God, and over wrauth grace shall abound.
But say, if our deliverer up to Heav'n

擇，我將追求豐富的知識，並敬畏天神。人如果在最小的事上不義，在大事上也不義，因此我們要不斷地行善，以善來制惡；對虔誠的信仰者來說，死亡將是通向永生的門檻。這就是救世主所要教導給我們的訊息。」亞當這樣說著。

「你明瞭了這些，便是到達智慧的

△ **逐出伊甸園**
布雷克　水彩畫 1808年
　　米迦勒率領著掌管火燄的天使前來接管伊甸園，告知亞當和夏娃該是他們離開的時候了。

Must reascend, what will betide the few [480]
His faithful, left among th' unfaithful herd,
The enemies of truth; who then shall guide
His people, who defend? will they not deale
Wors with his followers then with him they dealt?

Be sure they will, said th' Angel; but from Heav'n [485]
Hee to his own a Comforter will send,
The promise of the Father, who shall dwell
His Spirit within them, and the Law of Faith
Working through love, upon thir hearts shall write,
To guide them in all truth, and also arme [490]
With spiritual Armour, able to resist
Satans assaults, and quench his fierie darts,
What Man can do against them, not affraid,
Though to the death, against such cruelties
With inward consolations recompenc't, [495]
And oft supported so as shall amaze
Thir proudest persecuters: for the Spirit
Powrd first on his Apostles, whom he sends
To evangelize the Nations, then on all
Baptiz'd, shall them with wondrous gifts endue [500]
To speak all Tongues, and do all Miracles,
As did thir Lord before them. Thus they win
Great numbers of each Nation to receave
With joy the tidings brought from Heav'n: at length
Thir Ministry perform'd, and race well run, [505]
Thir doctrine and thir story written left,
They die; but in thir room, as they forewarne,
Wolves shall succeed for teachers, grievous Wolves,
Who all the sacred mysteries of Heav'n
To thir own vile advantages shall turne [510]
Of lucre and ambition, and the truth
With superstitions and traditions taint,
Left onely in those written Records pure,
Though not but by the Spirit understood.
Then shall they seek to avail themselves of names, [515]
Places and titles, and with these to joine
Secular power, though feigning still to act
By spiritual, to themselves appropriating
The Spirit of God, promisd alike and giv'n
To all Beleevers; and from that pretense, [520]

≪ **逐出伊甸園**
瑪薩奇歐 溼壁畫 1428年

米迦勒持劍守住伊甸園，命亞當和夏娃立刻離開，隨即封鎖的伊甸園的大門。亞當和夏娃掩面痛哭，卻也只能擦乾眼淚，往茫茫世界踏出未知的旅程。

Spiritual Lawes by carnal power shall force
On every conscience; Laws which none shall finde
Left them inrould, or what the Spirit within
Shall on the heart engrave. What will they then
But force the Spirit of Grace it self, and binde [525]
His consort Libertie; what, but unbuild
His living Temples, built by Faith to stand,
Thir own Faith not anothers: for on Earth
Who against Faith and Conscience can be heard
Infallible? yet many will presume: [530]
Whence heavie persecution shall arise
On all who in the worship persevere
Of Spirit and Truth; the rest, farr greater part,
Well deem in outward Rites and specious formes
Religion satisfi'd; Truth shall retire [535]
Bestuck with slandrous darts, and works of Faith
Rarely be found: so shall the World goe on,
To good malignant, to bad men benigne,
Under her own waight groaning till the day
Appeer of respiration to the just, [540]
And vengeance to the wicked, at return
Of him so lately promiss'd to thy aid
The Womans seed, obscurely then foretold,
Now amplier known thy Saviour and thy Lord,
Last in the Clouds from Heav'n to be reveald [545]
In glory of the Father, to dissolve
Satan with his perverted World, then raise
From the conflagrant mass, purg'd and refin'd,
New Heav'ns, new Earth, Ages of endless date
Founded in righteousness and peace and love [550]
To bring forth fruits Joy and eternal Bliss.

He ended; and thus Adam last reply'd.
How soon hath thy prediction, Seer blest,

頂點，別再繼續朝上探索了。你已知道眾星球的名字、識得天上諸神和奧妙的知識；有關上帝的創造，天上、空中、地面、海洋等一切事物；享受財富、統治國家……。這些知識本身不具重要性，重要的是虔誠的信仰、

美好的德行、學習忍耐與節制、加上
愛，這些才是重要的東西，有了它
們，你就能永不失足，得到永生。

　　「現在，該是我們離開的時候
了。」

　　米迦勒說完，隨即領著亞當下山，
回到夏娃身邊。

　　「你們回來啦！」夏娃從睡夢中

Measur'd this transient World, the Race of time,
Till time stand fixt: beyond is all abyss, [555]
Eternitie, whose end no eye can reach.
Greatly instructed I shall hence depart.
Greatly in peace of thought, and have my fill
Of knowledge, what this Vessel can containe;
Beyond which was my folly to aspire. [560]
Henceforth I learne, that to obey is best,
And love with feare the onely God, to walk
As in his presence, ever to observe
His providence, and on him sole depend,
Merciful over all his works, with good [565]
Still overcoming evil, and by small
Accomplishing great things, by things deemd weak
Subverting worldly strong, and worldly wise
By simply meek; that suffering for Truths sake
Is fortitude to highest victorie, [570]
And to the faithful Death the Gate of Life;
Taught this by his example whom I now
Acknowledge my Redeemer ever blest.

To whom thus also th' Angel last repli'd:
This having learnt, thou hast attained the summe [575]
Of wisdom; hope no higher, though all the Starrs
Thou knewst by name, and all th' ethereal Powers,
All secrets of the deep, all Natures works,
Or works of God in Heav'n, Aire, Earth, or Sea,
And all the riches of this World enjoydst, [580]
And all the rule, one Empire; onely add
Deeds to thy knowledge answerable, add Faith,
Add vertue, Patience, Temperance, add Love,
By name to come call'd Charitie, the soul
Of all the rest: then wilt thou not be loath [585]
To leave this Paradise, but shalt possess
A Paradise within thee, happier farr.
Let us descend now therefore from this top
Of Speculation; for the hour precise
Exacts our parting hence; and see the Guards, [590]

≪ 逐出樂園
西薩里 油彩畫

醒來，神情愉悅地對亞當說：「上帝
曾經來到我的夢境，向我預示好的未
來。所以我心甘情願地跟隨你，因為
有你的地方，才是幸福的所在。就讓
我們離開這兒，讓後代子孫經由信仰
與救贖，再重新得回幸福美麗的園地
吧！」

　　「走吧！」米迦勒帶著人類的始
祖 ── 亞當和夏娃，步履匆忙地走向
伊甸園東邊大門；在他們背後，掌管
火燄的天使已進駐伊甸園，把守著通
往生命樹的每條道路。他們一邁出東
門，大門立即封鎖，上頭有張可怕的
面孔，守衛天使和四面轉動發出火燄

By mee encampt on yonder Hill, expect
Thir motion, at whose Front a flaming Sword,
In signal of remove, waves fiercely round;
We may no longer stay: go, waken Eve;
Her also I with gentle Dreams have calm'd [595]
Portending good, and all her spirits compos'd
To meek submission: thou at season fit
Let her with thee partake what thou hast heard,
Chiefly what may concern her Faith to know,
The great deliverance by her Seed to come [600]
(For by the Womans Seed) on all Mankind.
That ye may live, which will be many dayes,
Both in one Faith unanimous though sad,
With cause for evils past, yet much more cheer'd
With meditation on the happie end. [605]

He ended, and they both descend the Hill;
Descended, Adam to the Bowre where Eve
Lay sleeping ran before, but found her wak't;
And thus with words not sad she him receav'd.

Whence thou returnst, and whither wentst, I know; [610]
For God is also in sleep, and Dreams advise,
Which he hath sent propitious, some great good
Presaging, since with sorrow and hearts distress
Wearied I fell asleep: but now lead on;
In mee is no delay; with thee to goe, [615]

◁ 消失的伊甸園
希土克 1897年

　　原本和藹可親，對人
類呵護有加的天使，如今
卻板起面孔，鐵面無私地
要求亞當和夏娃離開，曾
經美好和樂的伊甸園，從
此消失不再。人類只能靠
自己的力量去披荊斬棘，
開創屬於自己的家園。

　　人類的命運已經決定，亞當和夏娃知道從此要靠自己胼手胝足，為生活奮鬥，然而回顧曾經居住過的美麗樂園，想到原本無憂無慮的生活，也不禁留下懊悔和不捨的淚水來。

　　　　　　　　　　　　　　　　　　　　　　　Is

here; without thee here to stay,
Is to go hence unwilling; thou to mee
Art all things under Heav'n, all places thou,
Who for my wilful crime art banisht hence.
This further consolation yet secure [620]
I carry hence; though all by mee is lost,
Such favour I unworthie am voutsaft,
By mee the Promis'd Seed shall all restore.

So spake our Mother Eve, and Adam heard
Well pleas'd, but answer'd not; for now too nigh [625]
Th' Archangel stood, and from the other Hill
To thir fixt Station, all in bright array
The Cherubim descended; on the ground
Gliding meteorous, as Ev'ning Mist
Ris'n from a River o're the marish glides, [630]
And gathers ground fast at the Labourers heel
Homeward returning. High in Front advanc't,
The brandisht Sword of God before them blaz'd
Fierce as a Comet; which with torrid heat,
And vapour as the Libyan Air adust, [635]
Began to parch that temperate Clime; whereat
In either hand the hastning Angel caught
Our lingring Parents, and to th' Eastern Gate
Led them direct, and down the Cliff as fast
To the subjected Plaine; then disappear'd. [640]
They looking back, all th' Eastern side beheld
Of Paradise, so late thir happie seat,
Wav'd over by that flaming Brand, the Gate
With dreadful Faces throng'd and fierie Armes:
Som natural tears they drop'd, but wip'd them soon; [645]
The World was all before them, where to choose
Thir place of rest, and Providence thir guide:
They hand in hand with wandring steps and slow,
Through Eden took thir solitarie way.

的劍也不斷揮舞著，發出閃亮的光芒。

　　米迦勒完成任務，消失了。

　　亞當和夏娃轉頭回顧兩人居住過的美麗樂園，不由地流下淚來。然後，他們抹乾眼淚，手牽著手，往茫茫世界踏出孤寂的旅程。

國家圖書館出版品預行編目資料

失樂園 / 米爾頓原著；劉怡君改寫
二版.；臺中市：好讀，2020.12
面： 公分，──（新視界 ； 11）

ISBN 978-986-178-530-1（平裝）

873.51   109017692

好讀出版

新視界11

失樂園【新裝珍藏版】

線上讀者回函：
請掃描QRCODE

原著／米爾頓
改寫／劉怡君
圖片解說／陳彬彬
總編輯／鄧茵茵
文字編輯／莊銘桓
美術編輯／陳麗蕙
行銷企劃／劉恩綺
發行所／好讀出版有限公司
台中市407西屯區工業30路1號
台中市407西屯區大有街13號（編輯部）
TEL:04-23157795 FAX:04-23144188   http://howdo.morningstar.com.tw
（如對本書編輯或內容有意見，請來電或上網告訴我們）
法律顧問／陳思成律師

總經銷／知己圖書股份有限公司
106台北市大安區辛亥路一段30號9樓
TEL：02-2367204423672047 FAX：02-23635741
407台中市西屯區工業30路1號1樓
TEL：04-23595819 FAX：04-23595493
E-mail：service@morningstar.com.tw
網路書店：http://www.morningstar.com.tw
讀者專線：04-23595819 # 230
郵政劃撥：15060393（知己圖書股份有限公司）
印刷／上好印刷股份有限公司
如有破損或裝訂錯誤，請寄回知己圖書更換

初版／西元 2010 年 8 月 15 日
二版／西元 2020 年 12 月 1 日
定價：369 元

Published by How-Do Publishing Co., Ltd.
2020 Printed in Taiwan
All rights reserved.
ISBN 978-986-178-530-1